MR. WOLF'S CLASS

ARON NELS STEINKE

graphix

AN IMPRINT OF

■ SCHOLASTIC

For Don and Alona

Library of Congress Control Number: 2017945601

ISBN 978-1-338-04769-1 (hardcover)
ISBN 978-1-338-04768-4 (paperback)

10 9 8 7 6 5 20 21 22

Printed in China 62
First edition, July 2018

Edited by Cassandra Pelham Fulton
Book design by Phil Falco
Creative Director: David Saylor

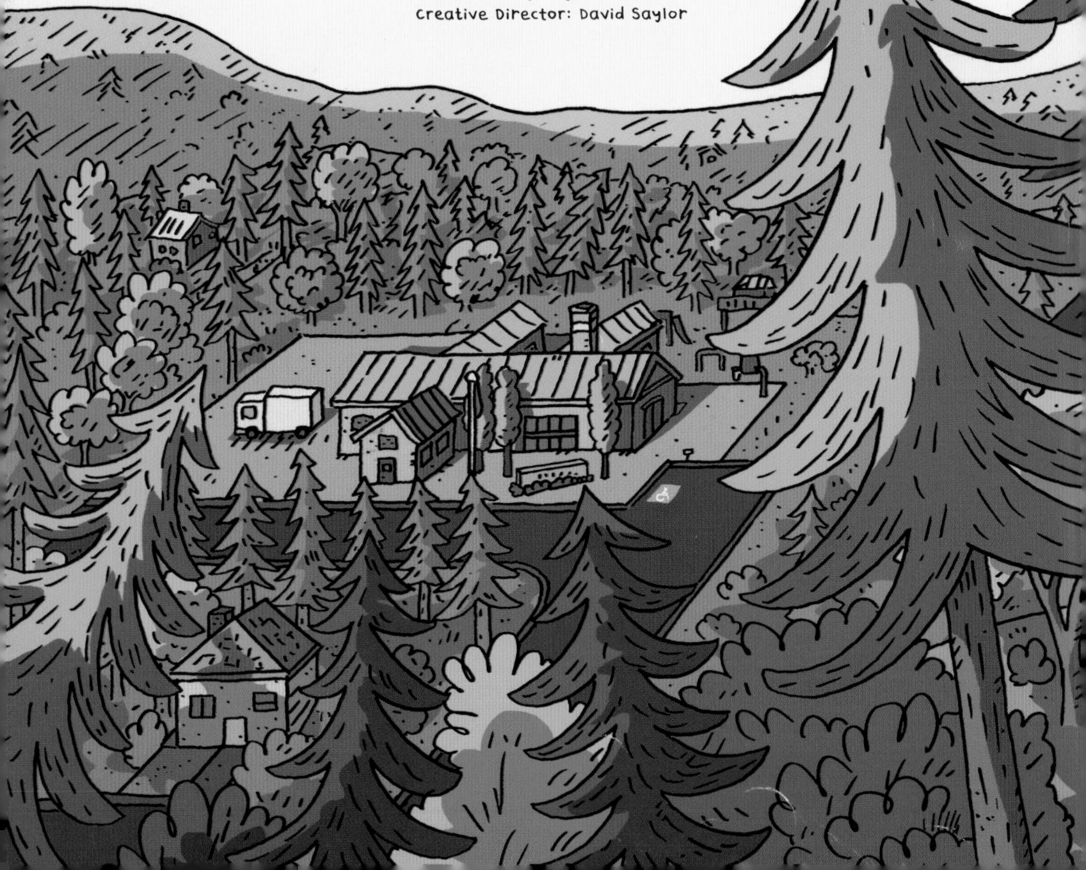

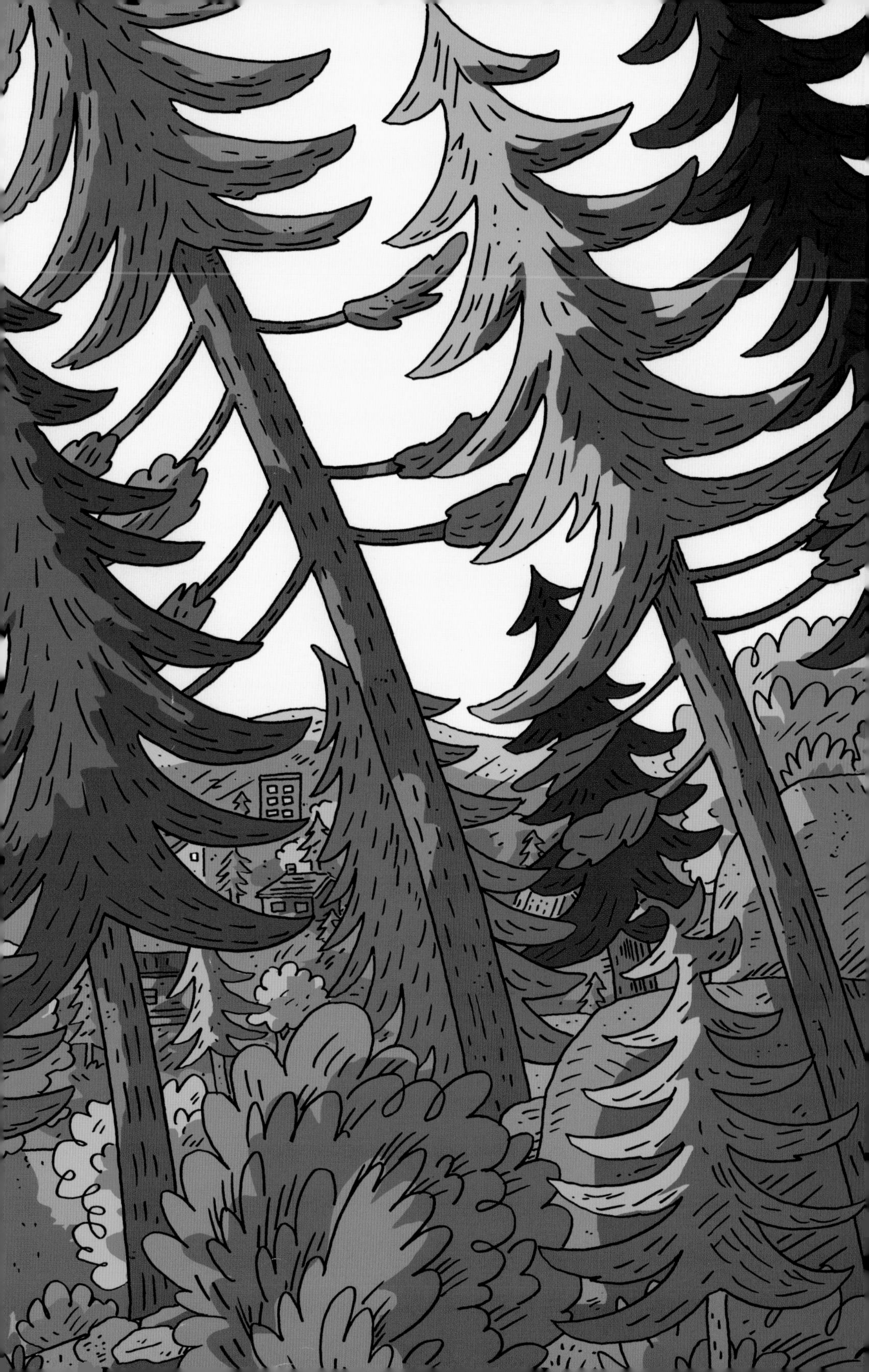

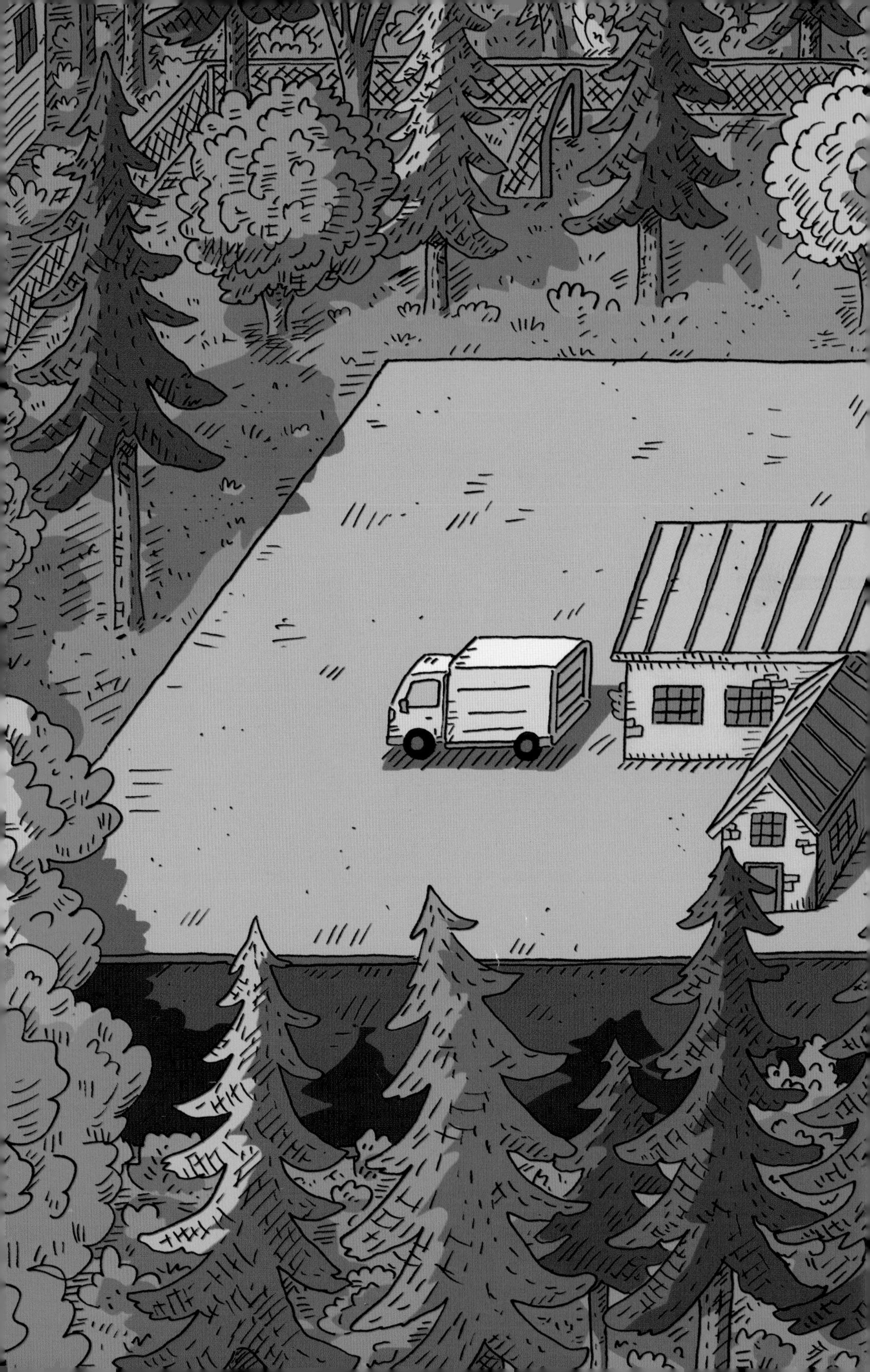

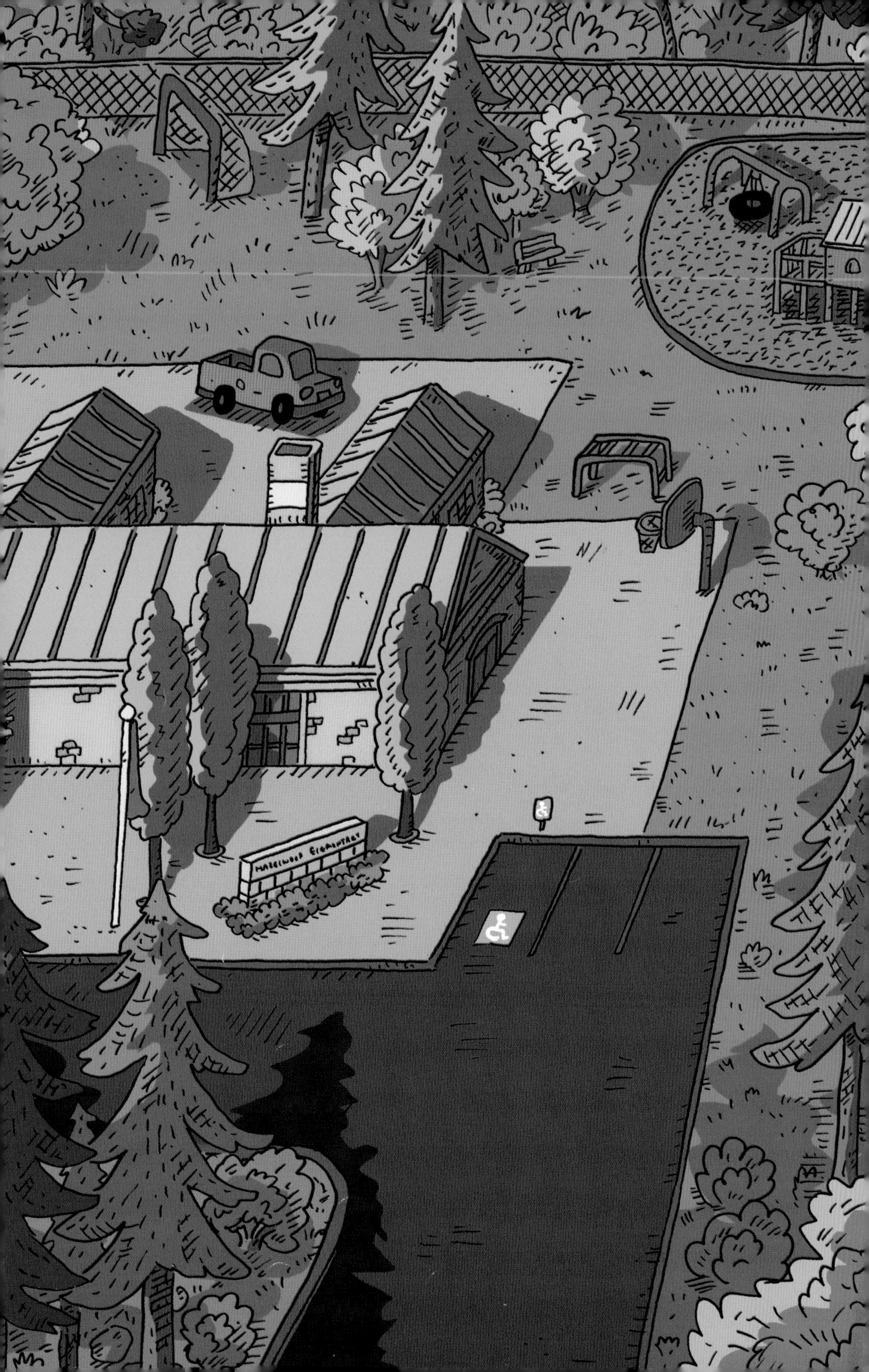
HAZELWOOD ELEMENTARY

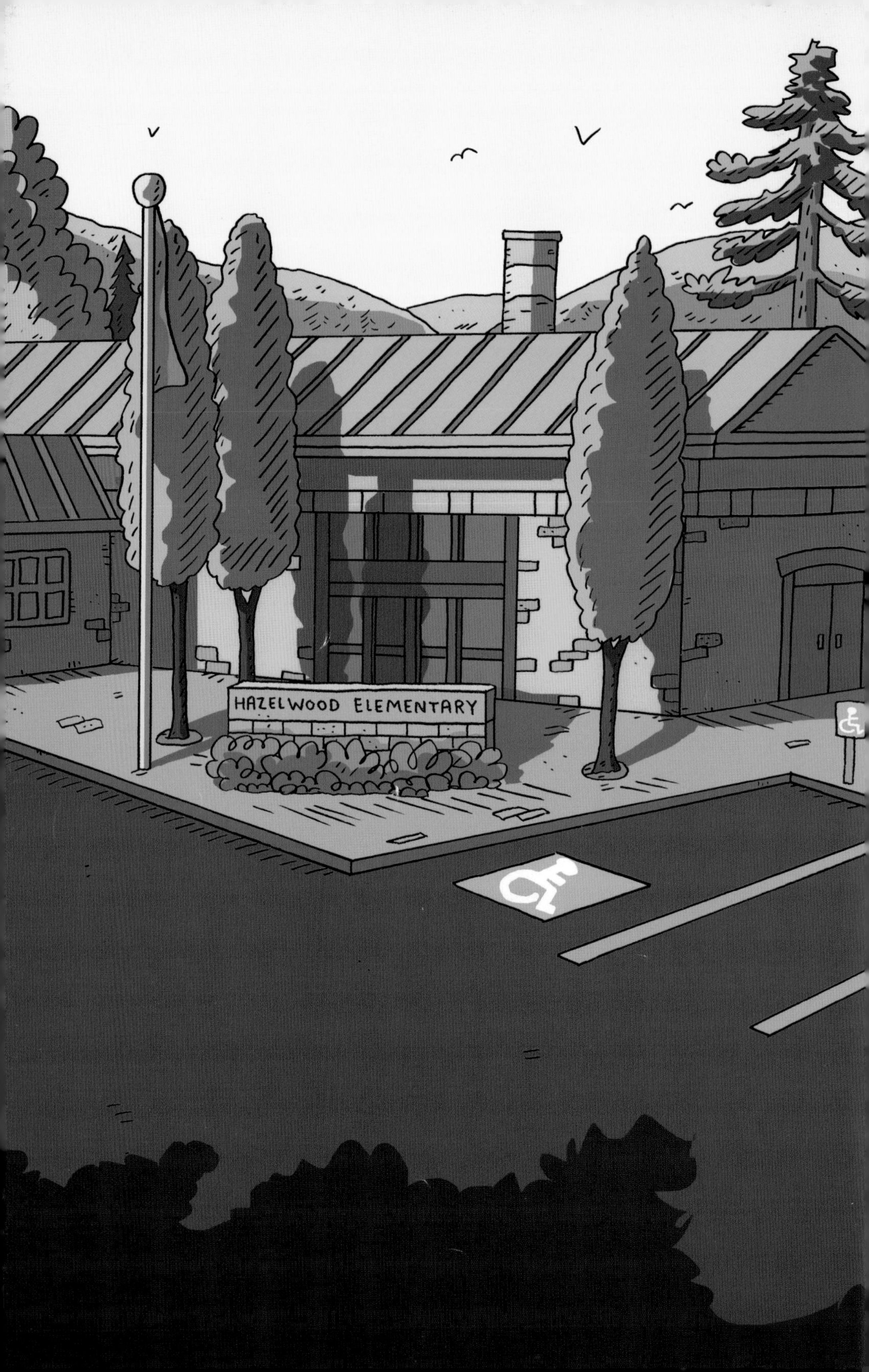
HAZELWOOD ELEMENTARY

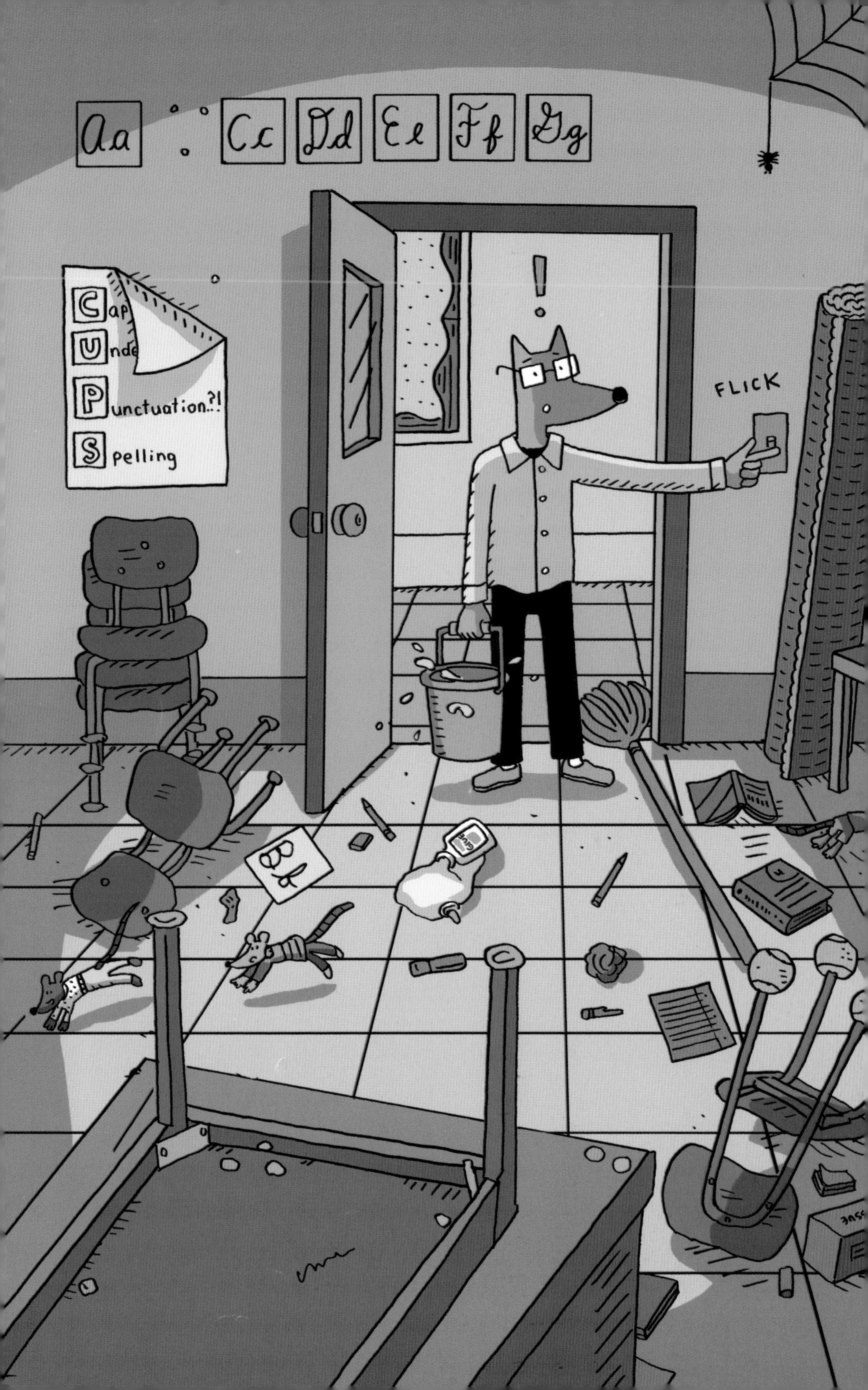
Aa
Cc
Dd
Ee
Ff
Gg
Cap
Unde
Punctuation?!
Spelling
!
FLICK
GLUE

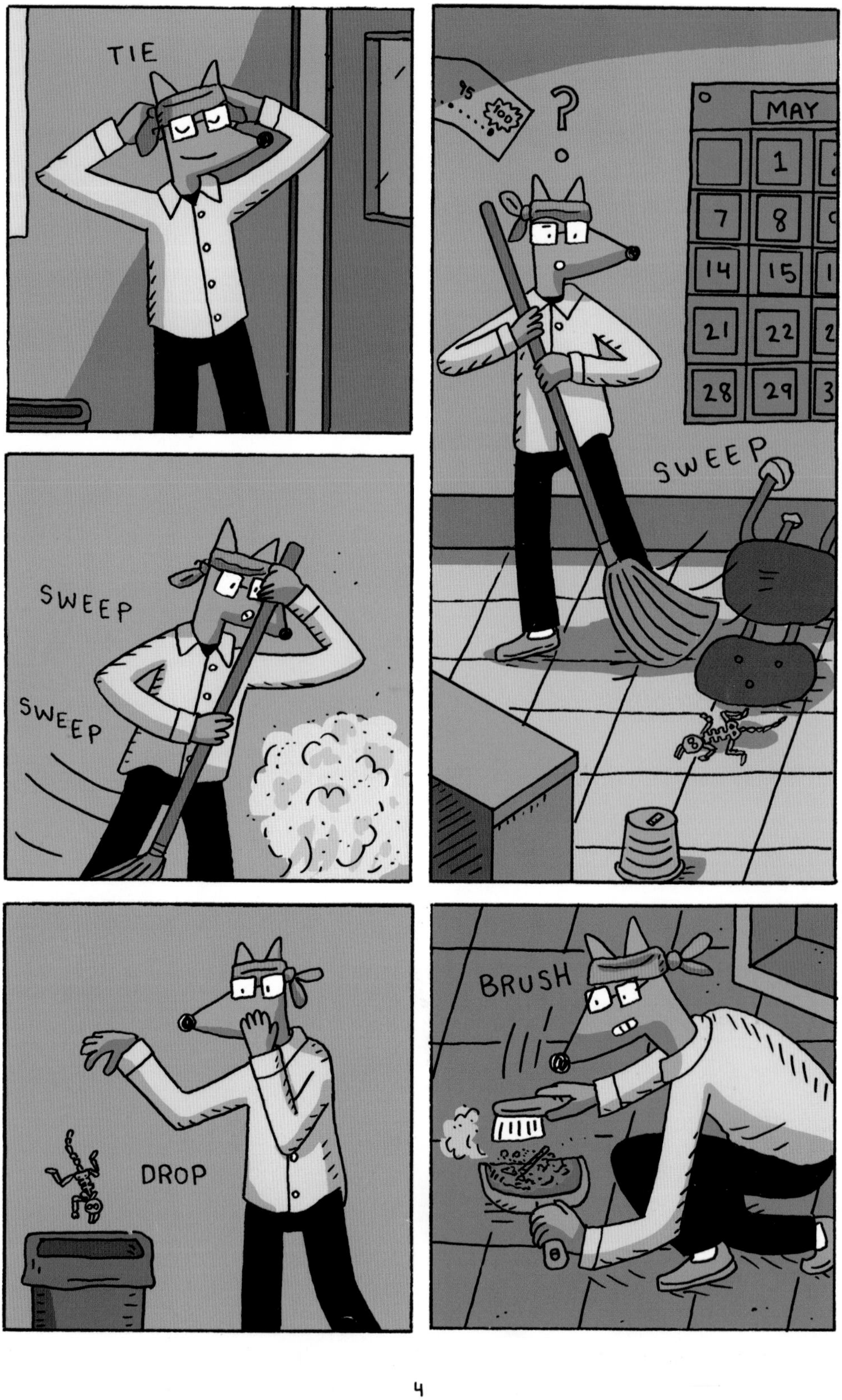
TIE
?
MAY
SWEEP
SWEEP
SWEEP
DROP
BRUSH

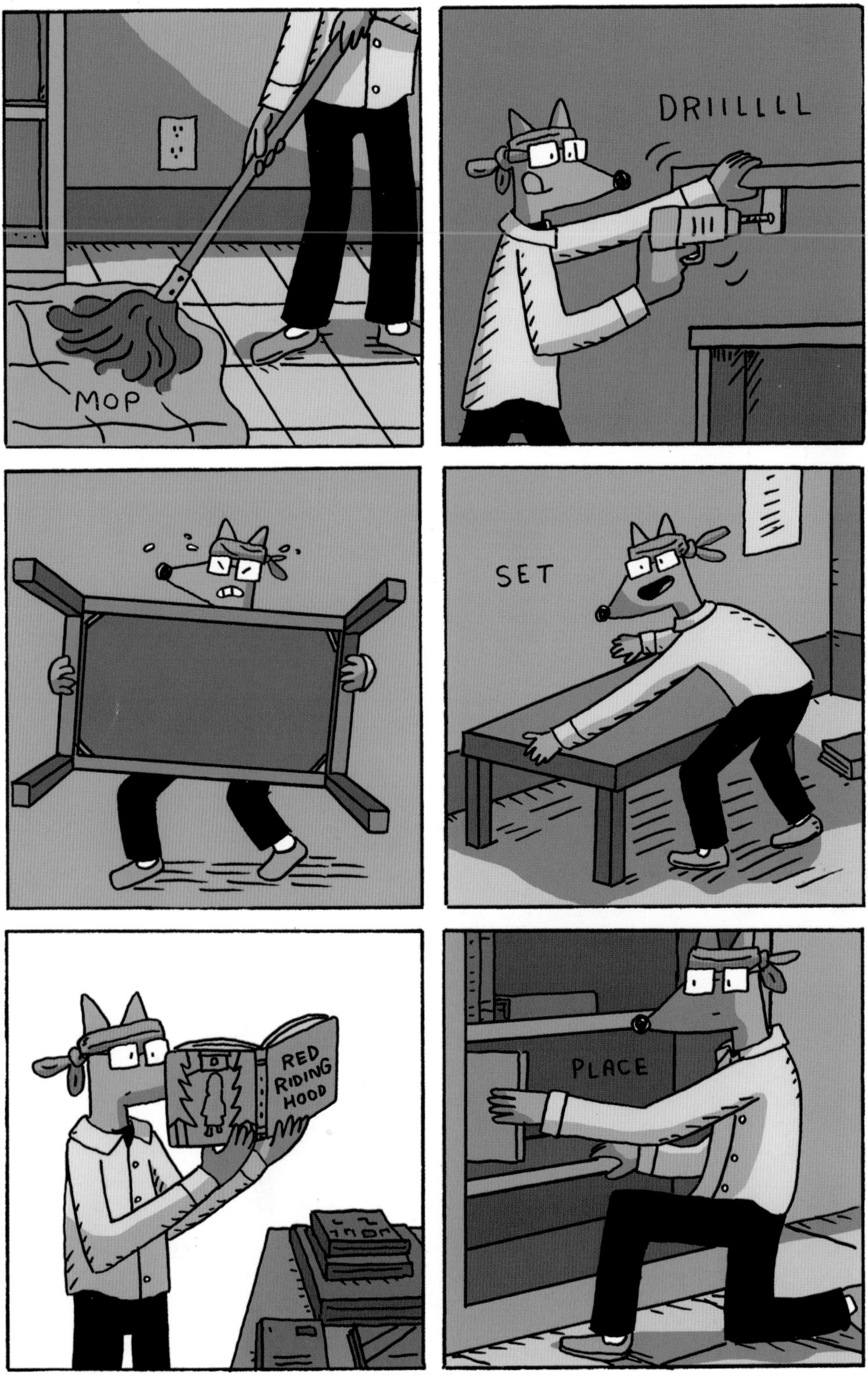
MOP
DRIILLLL
SET
RED RIDING HOOD
PLACE

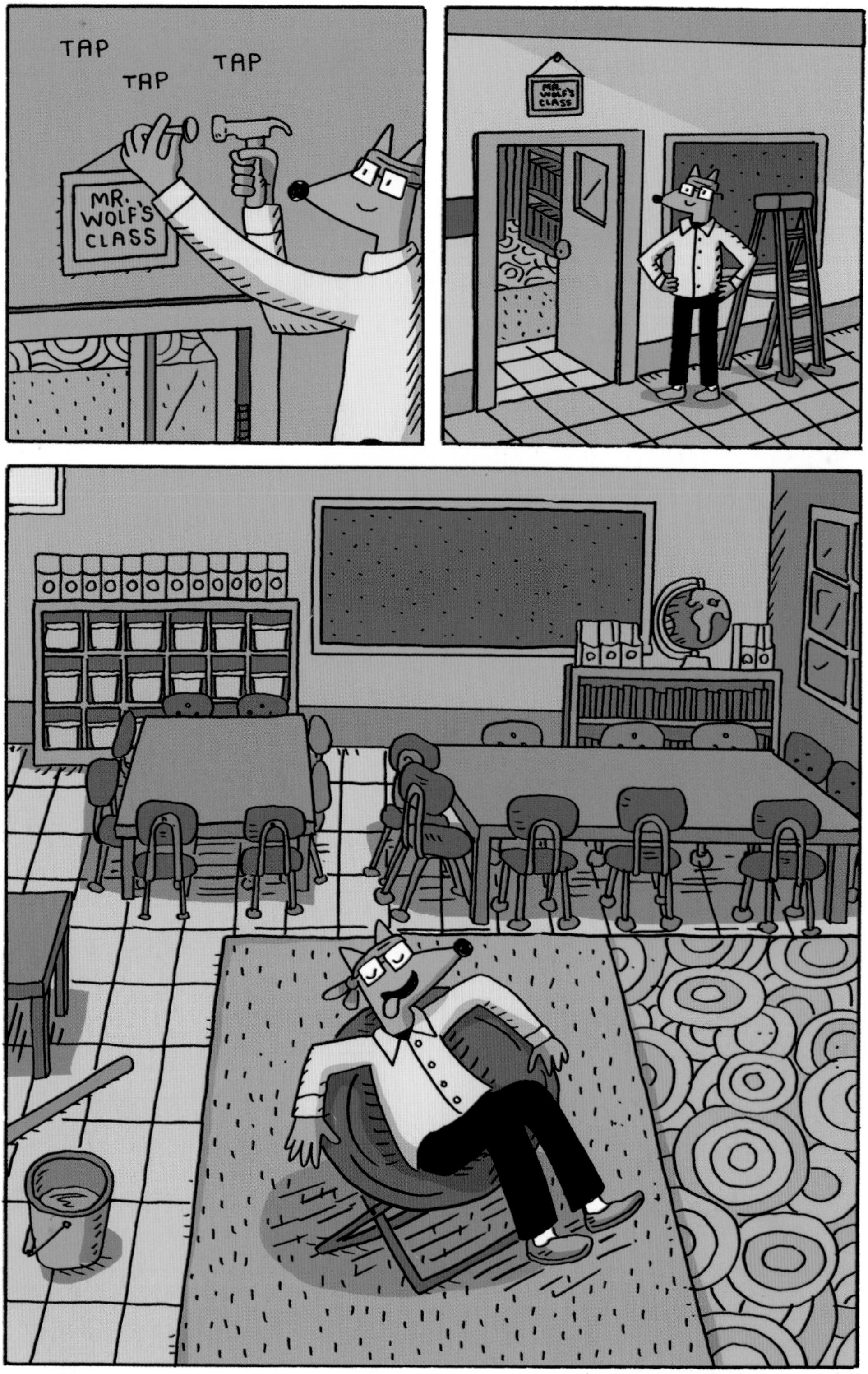
TAP
TAP
TAP
MR. WOLF'S CLASS
MR. WOLF'S CLASS

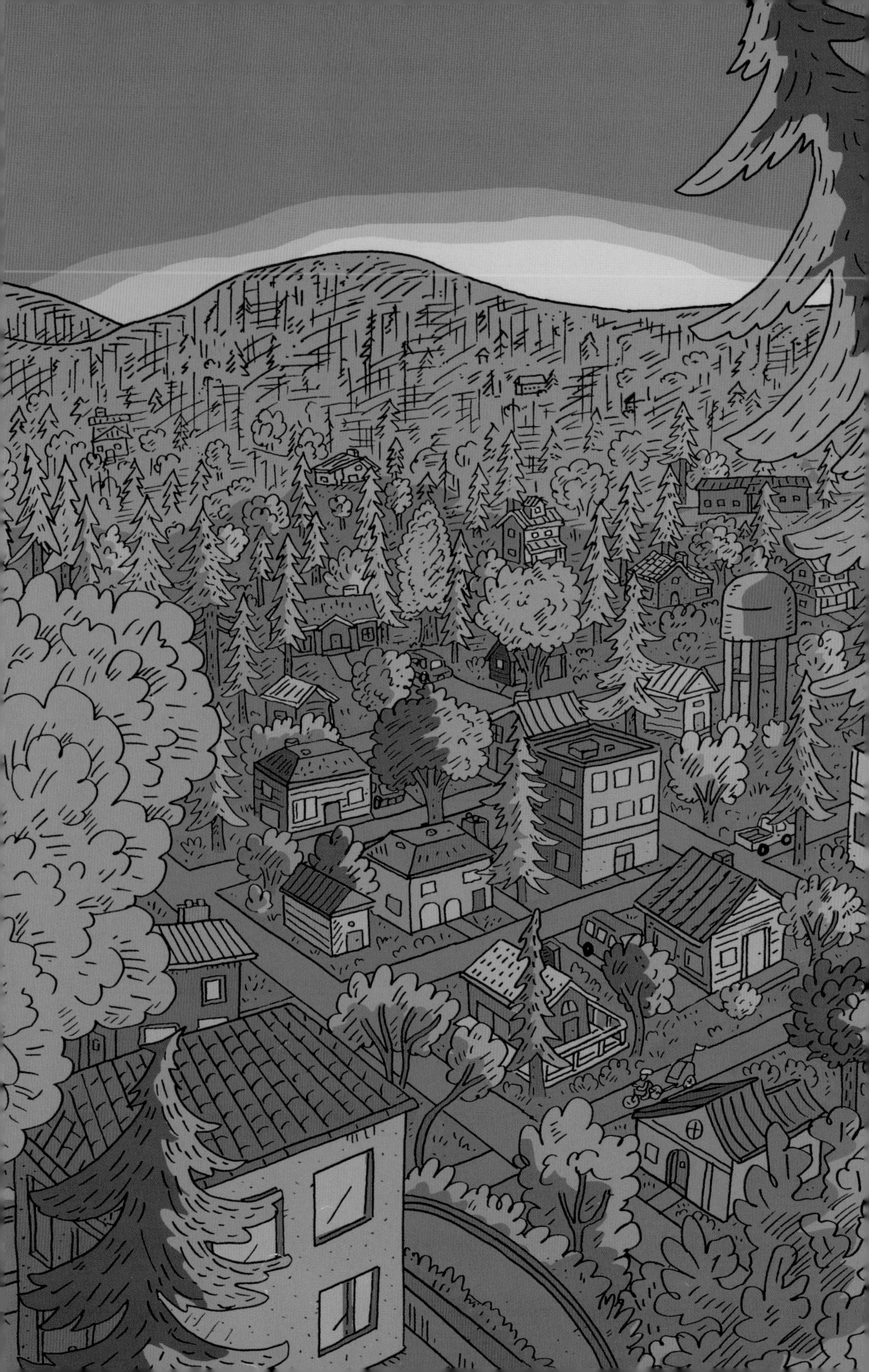

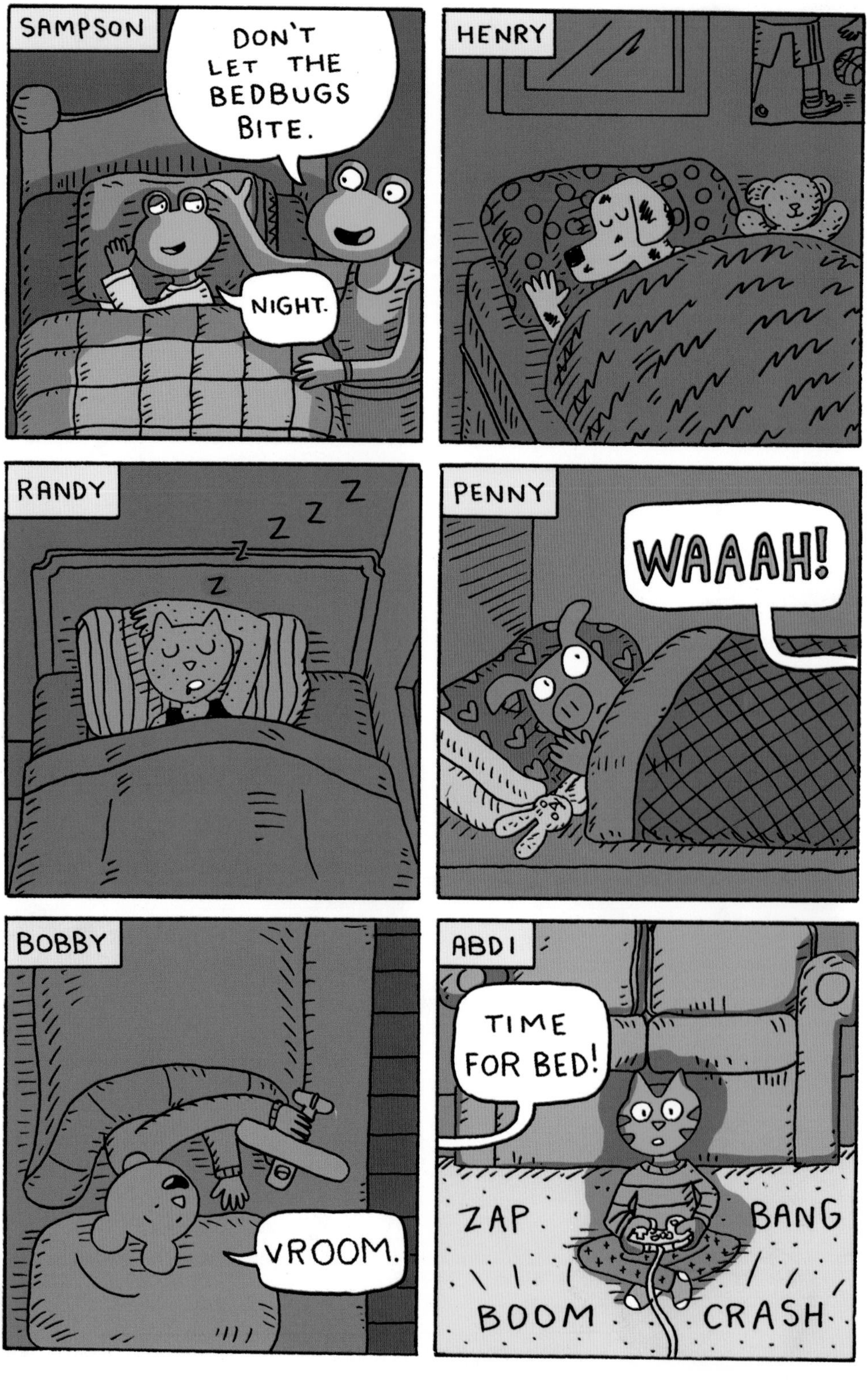
SAMPSON
DON'T LET THE BEDBUGS BITE.
NIGHT.
HENRY
RANDY
Z Z Z Z Z
PENNY
WAAAH!
BOBBY
VROOM.
ABDI
TIME FOR BED!
ZAP
BANG
BOOM
CRASH

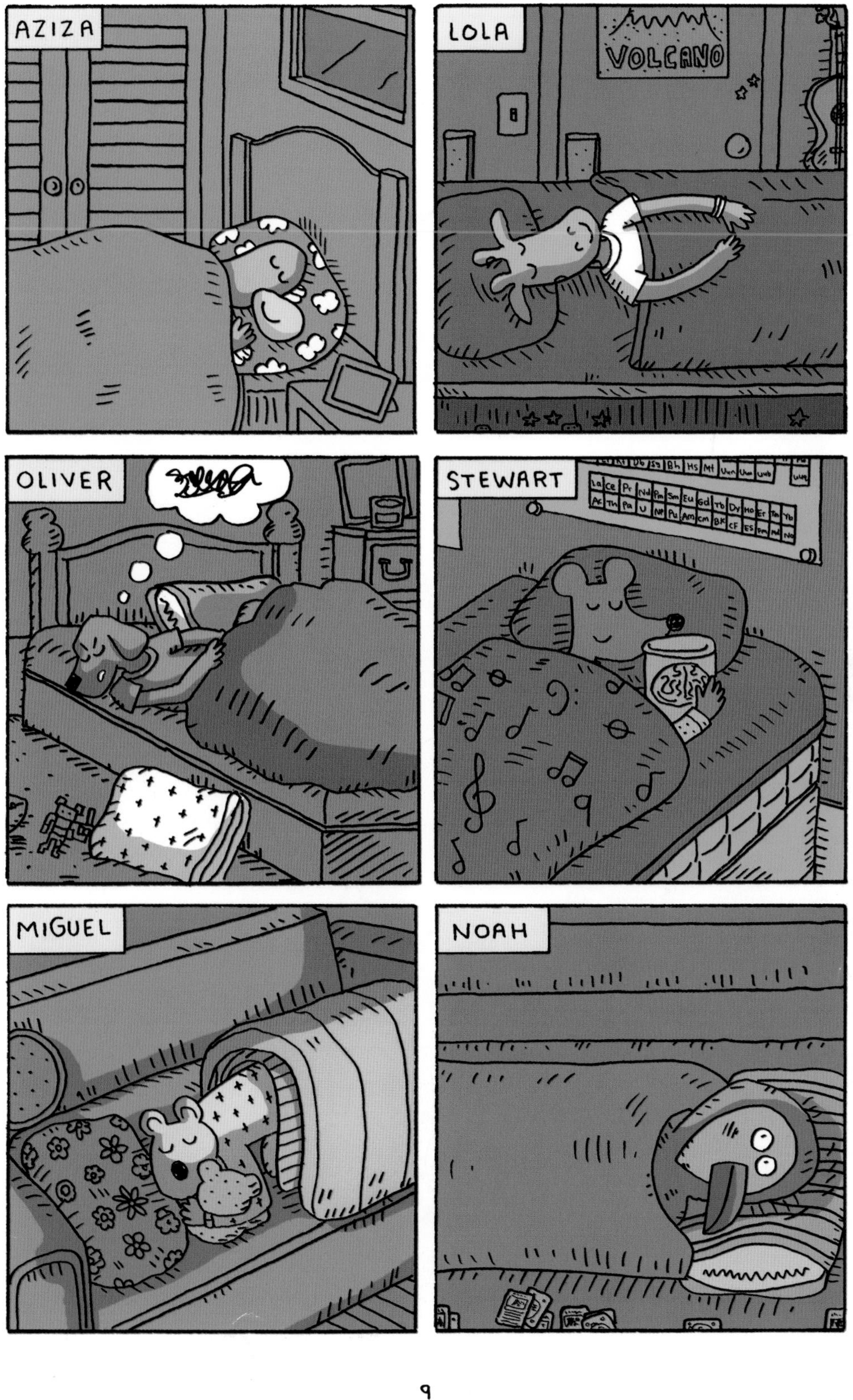
AZIZA
LOLA
VOLCANO
OLIVER
STEWART
MIGUEL
NOAH

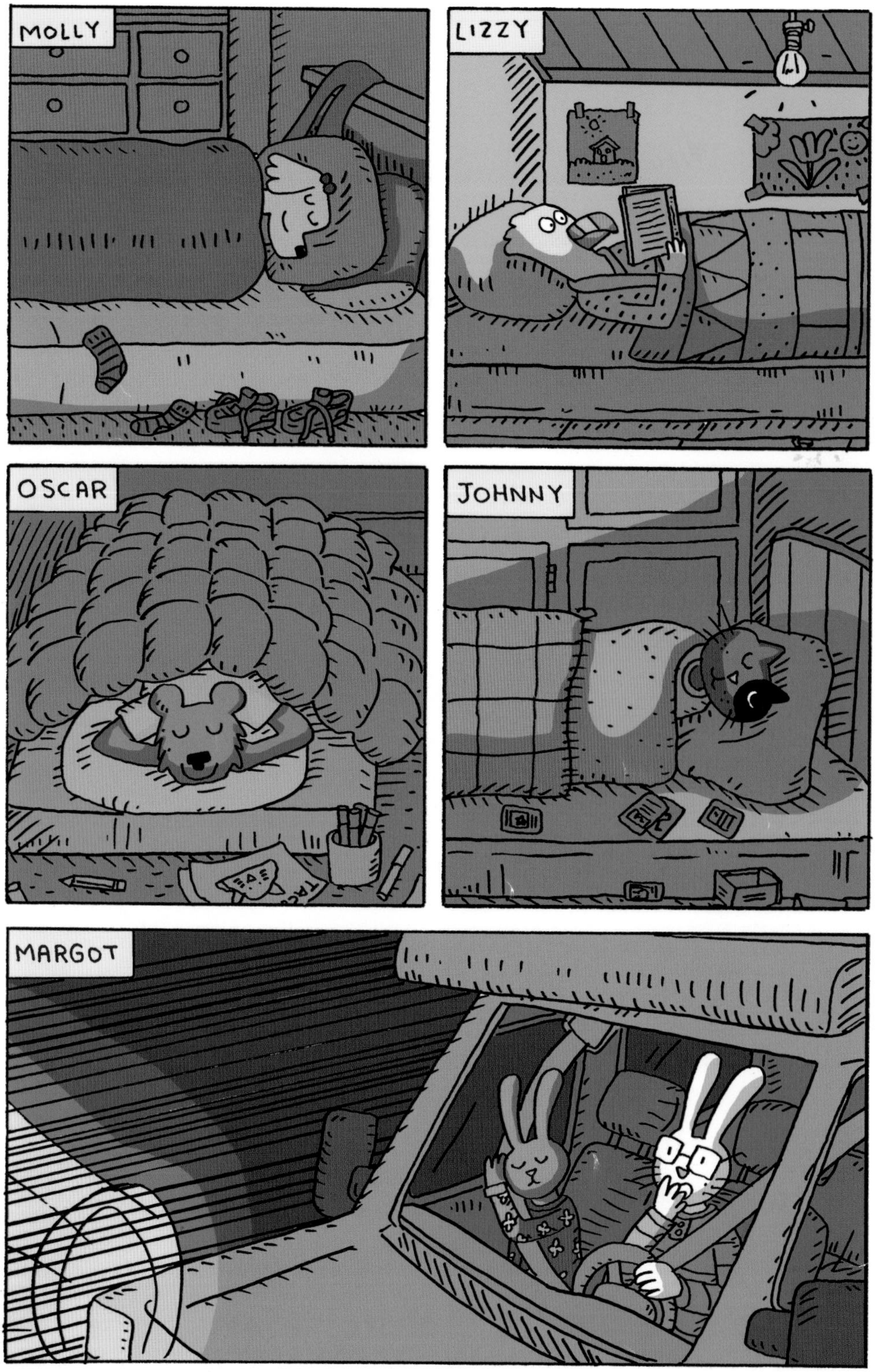
MOLLY
LIZZY
OSCAR
JOHNNY
MARGOT

CHAPTER ONE
Wake Up

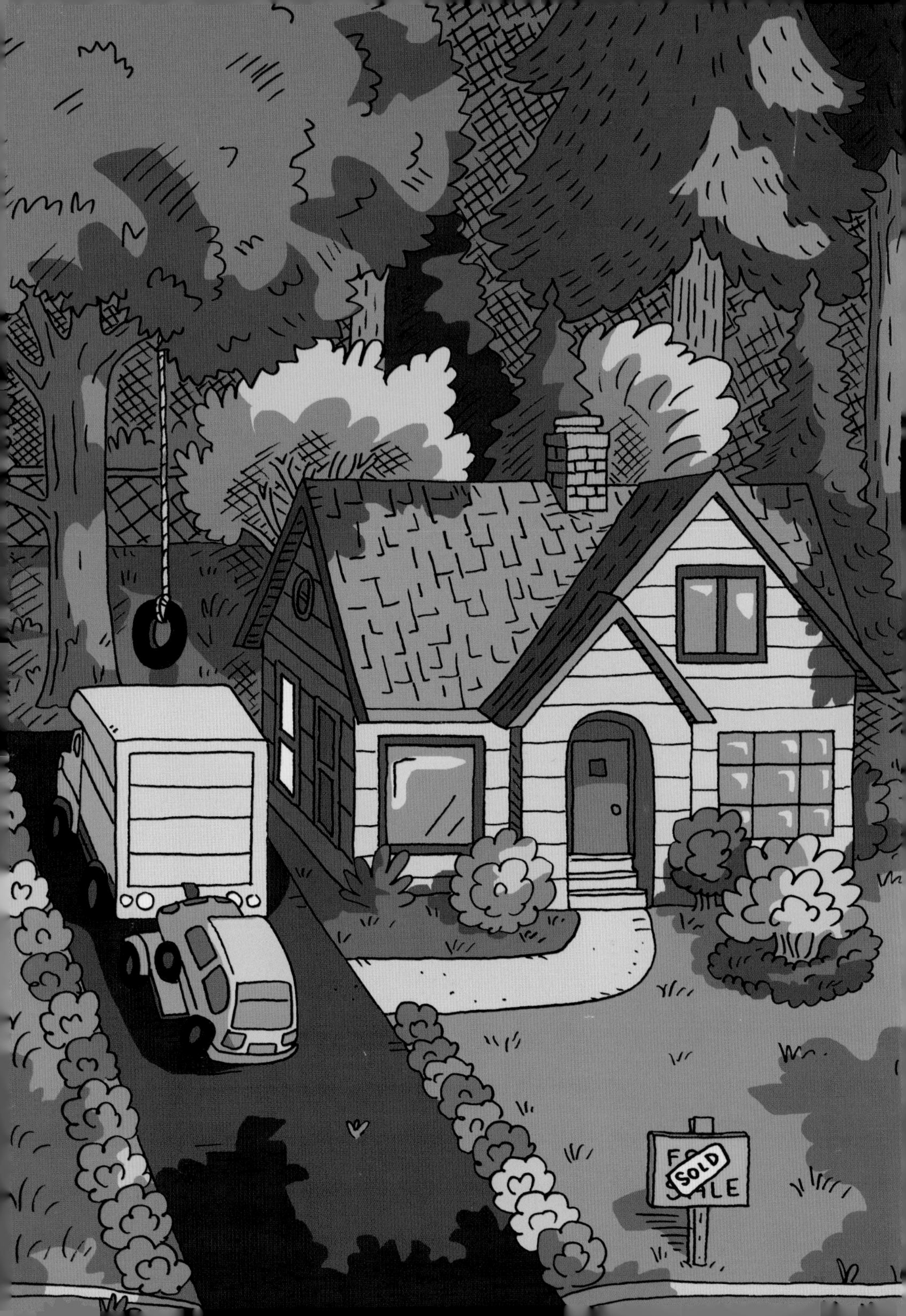
SOLD

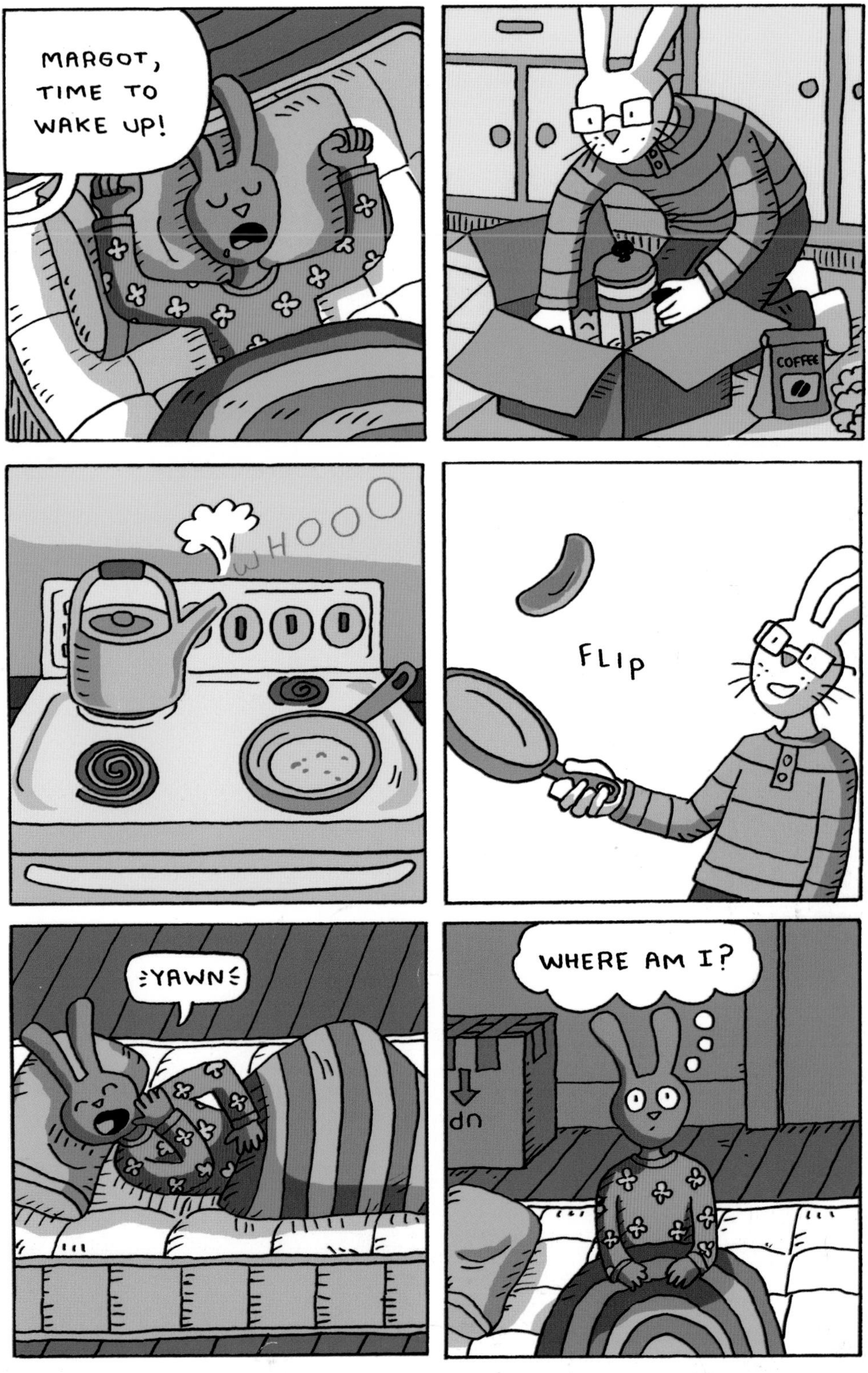
MARGOT, TIME TO WAKE UP!
COFFEE
WHOOOO
FLIP
YAWN
WHERE AM I?
dn

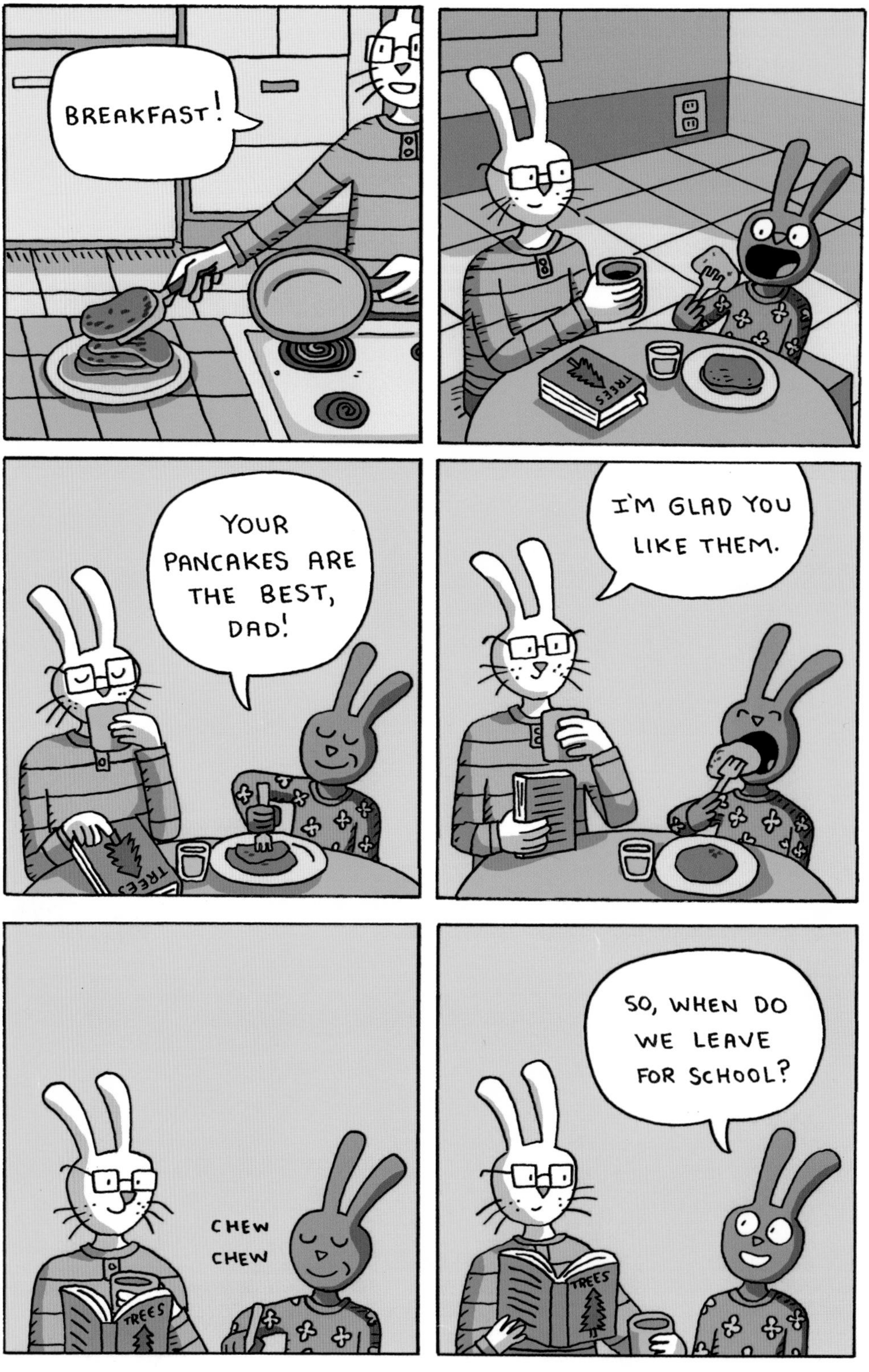
BREAKFAST!
TREES
YOUR PANCAKES ARE THE BEST, DAD!
TREES
I'M GLAD YOU LIKE THEM.
CHEW CHEW
TREES
SO, WHEN DO WE LEAVE FOR SCHOOL?
TREES

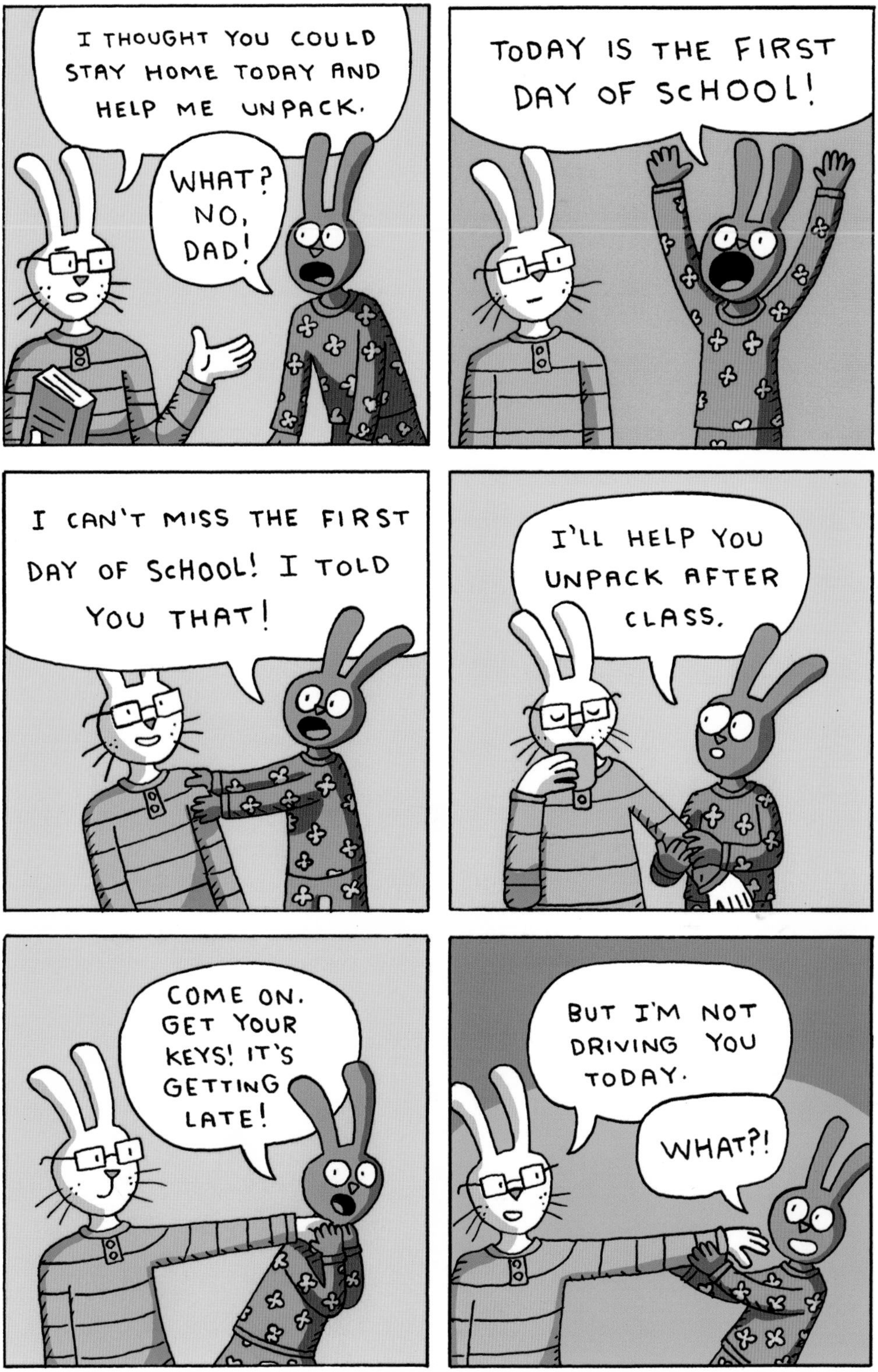
I THOUGHT YOU COULD STAY HOME TODAY AND HELP ME UNPACK.
WHAT? NO, DAD!
TODAY IS THE FIRST DAY OF SCHOOL!
I CAN'T MISS THE FIRST DAY OF SCHOOL! I TOLD YOU THAT!
I'LL HELP YOU UNPACK AFTER CLASS.
COME ON. GET YOUR KEYS! IT'S GETTING LATE!
BUT I'M NOT DRIVING YOU TODAY.
WHAT?!

THERE'S A BUS THAT COMES RIGHT BY THE HOUSE.

REALLY?! A YELLOW SCHOOL BUS?! I'VE ALWAYS WANTED TO RIDE ONE.

DO YOU NEED TO GO TO THE BATHROOM FIRST?

NO, I ALREADY WENT.

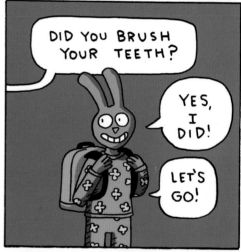

DID YOU BRUSH YOUR TEETH?

YES, I DID!

LET'S GO!

BUT AREN'T YOU GOING TO CHANGE OUT OF YOUR PAJAMAS FIRST?

ACK!

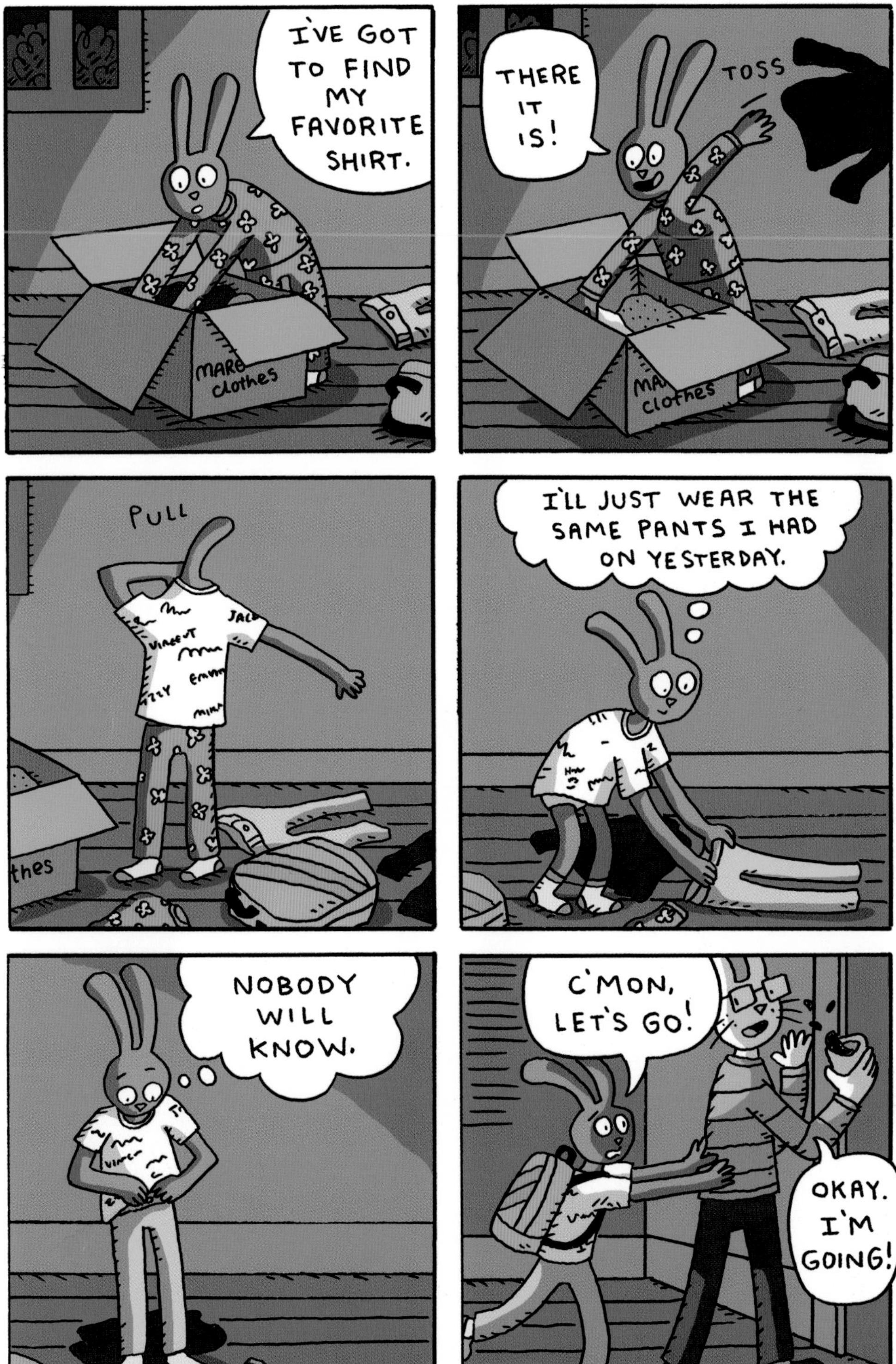
I'VE GOT TO FIND MY FAVORITE SHIRT.
MARC clothes
THERE IT IS!
TOSS
MARC clothes
PULL
I'LL JUST WEAR THE SAME PANTS I HAD ON YESTERDAY.
NOBODY WILL KNOW.
C'MON, LET'S GO!
OKAY. I'M GOING!

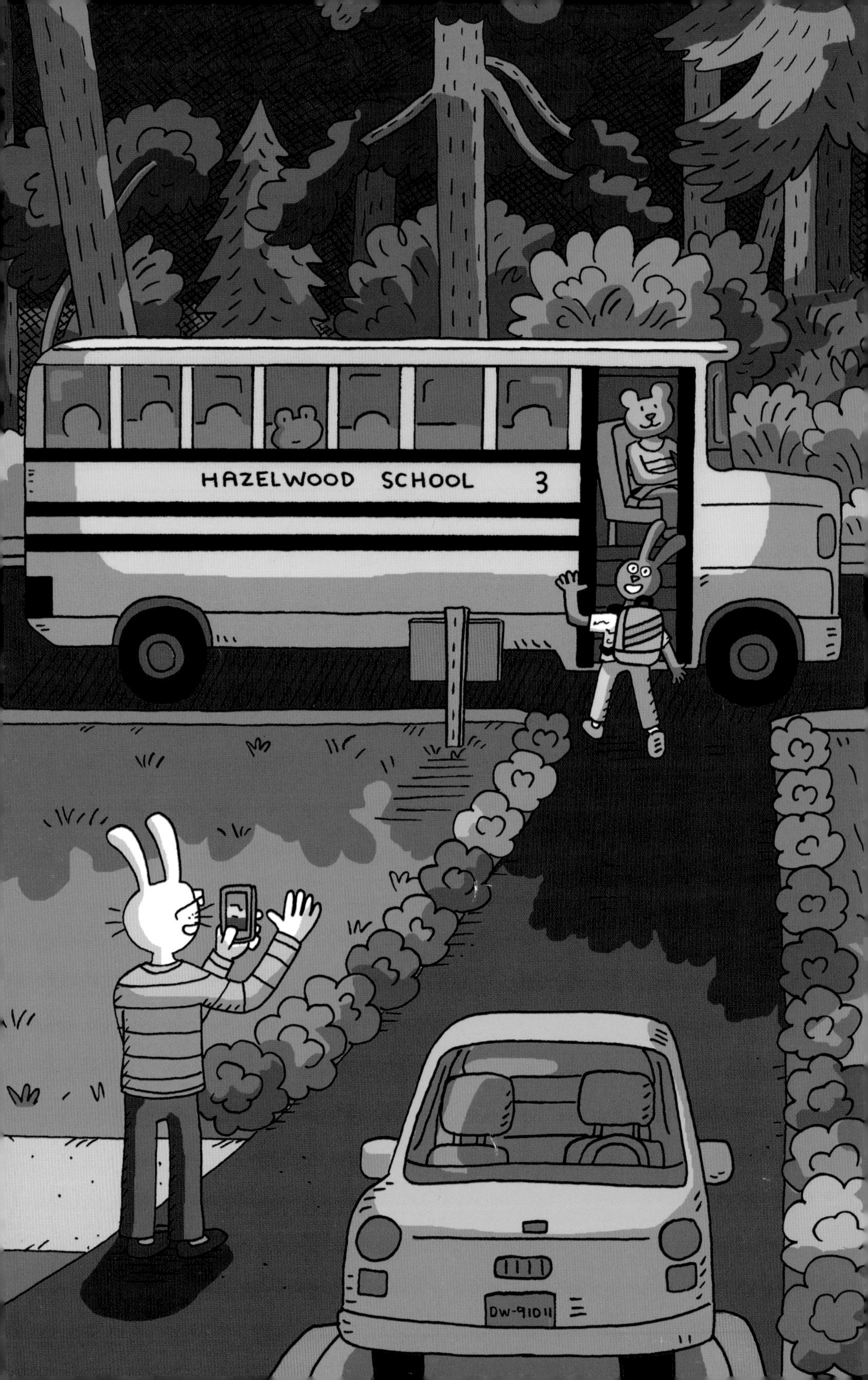
HAZELWOOD SCHOOL 3
DW-91011

CHAPTER TWO
Hold It!

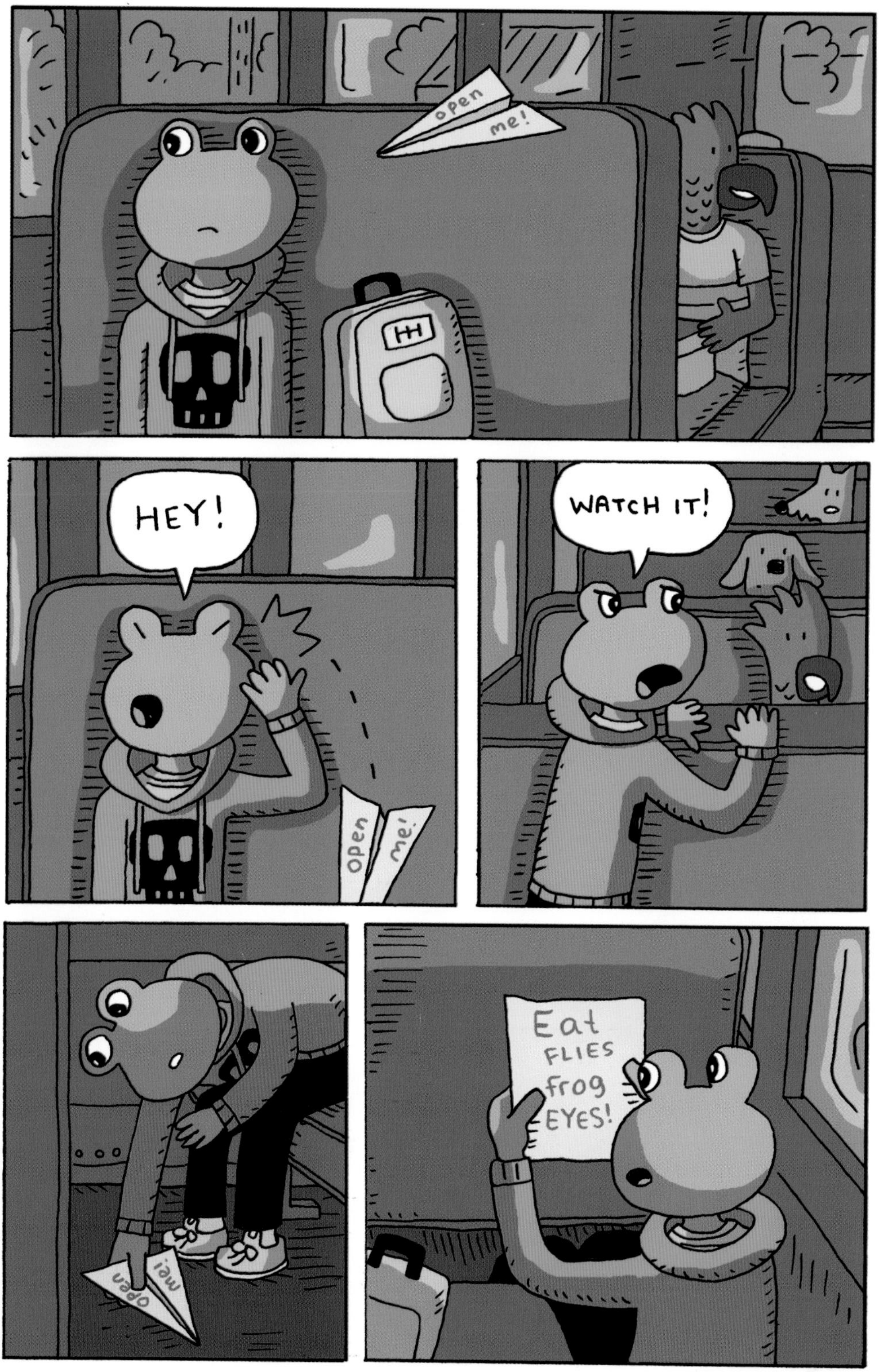
open
me!
HEY!
open
me!
WATCH IT!
open
me!
Eat
FLIES
frog
EYES!

CRUMPLE

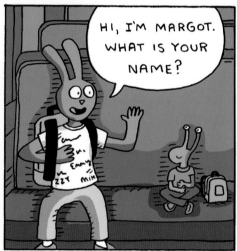

HI, I'M MARGOT. WHAT IS YOUR NAME?

OH NO!

GURGLE

I NEED TO GO TO THE BATHROOM.

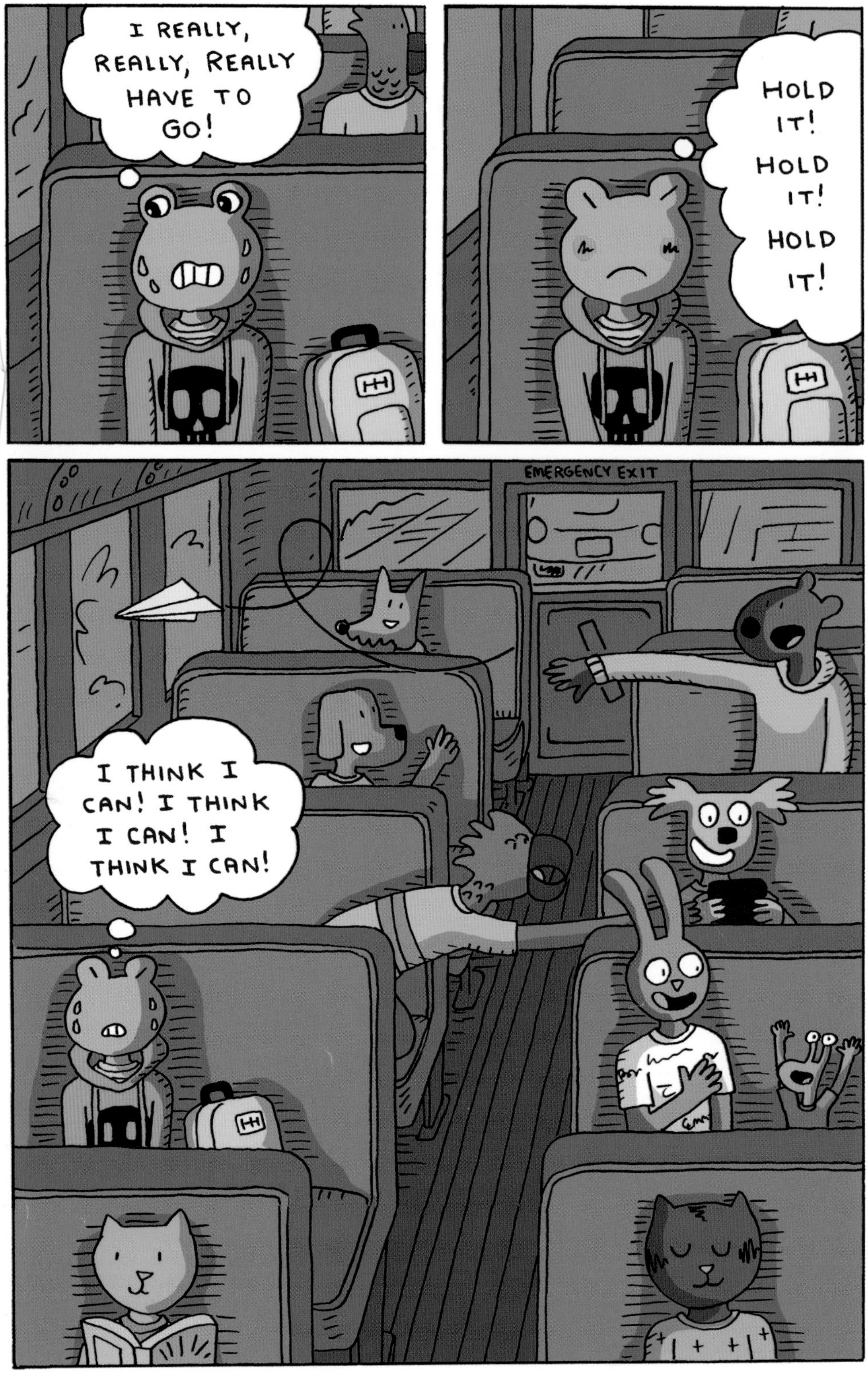
I REALLY, REALLY, REALLY HAVE TO GO!
HOLD IT! HOLD IT! HOLD IT!
EMERGENCY EXIT
I THINK I CAN! I THINK I CAN! I THINK I CAN!

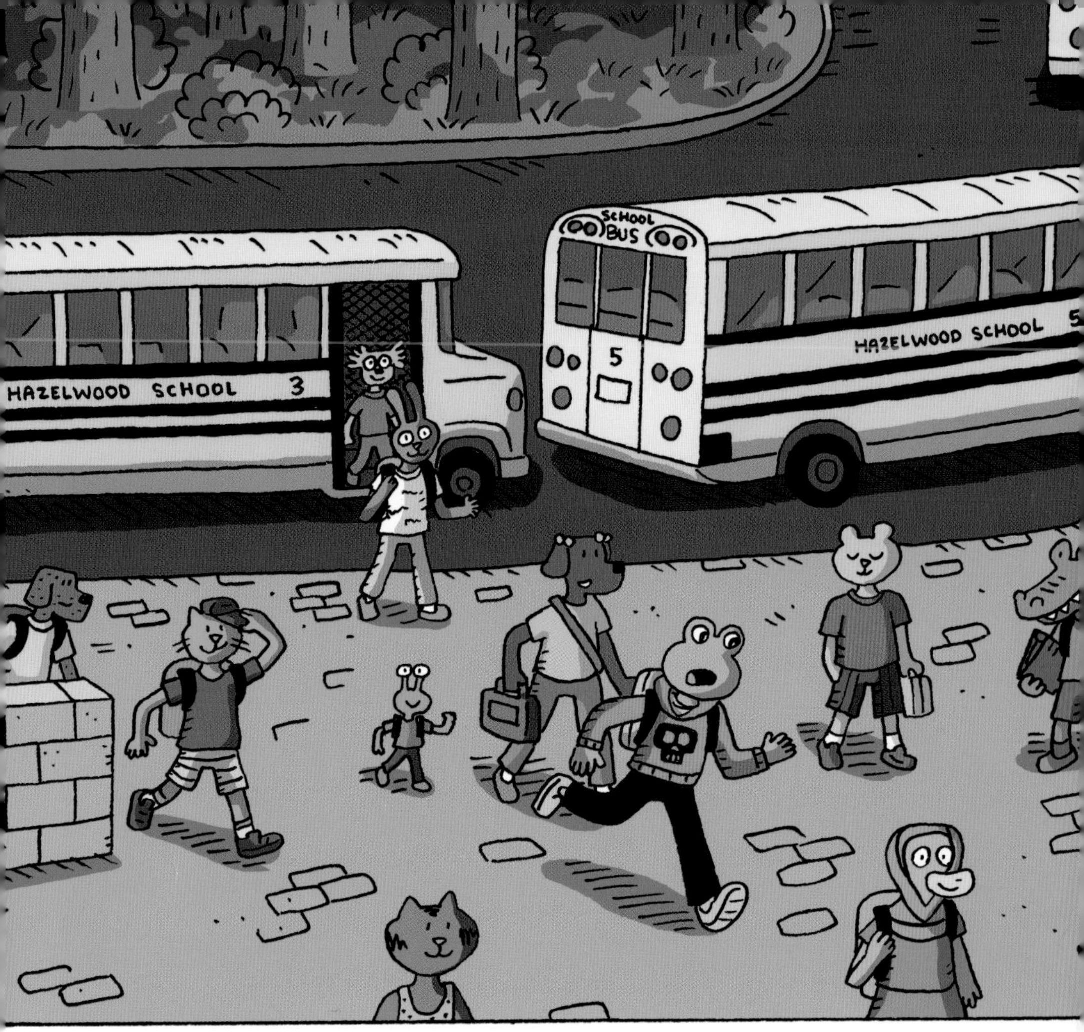
SCHOOL BUS
HAZELWOOD SCHOOL 3
5
HAZELWOOD SCHOOL 5

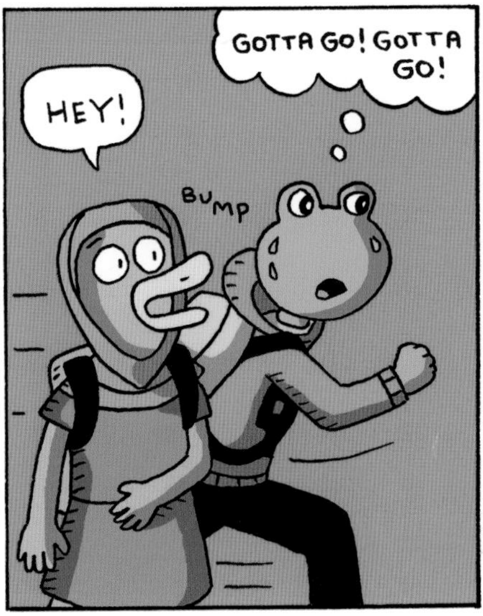
HEY!
GOTTA GO! GOTTA GO!
BUMP

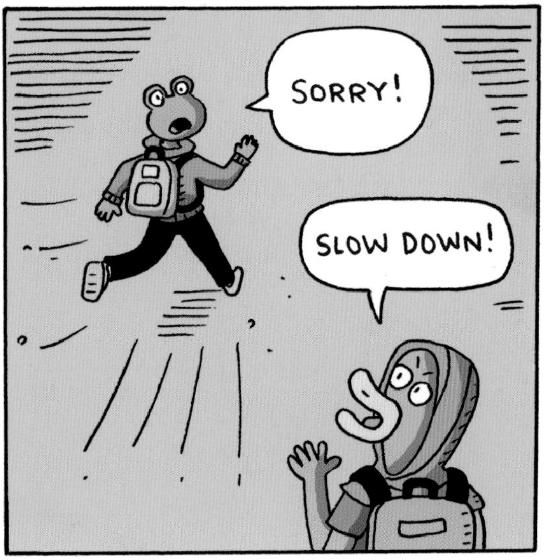
SORRY!
SLOW DOWN!

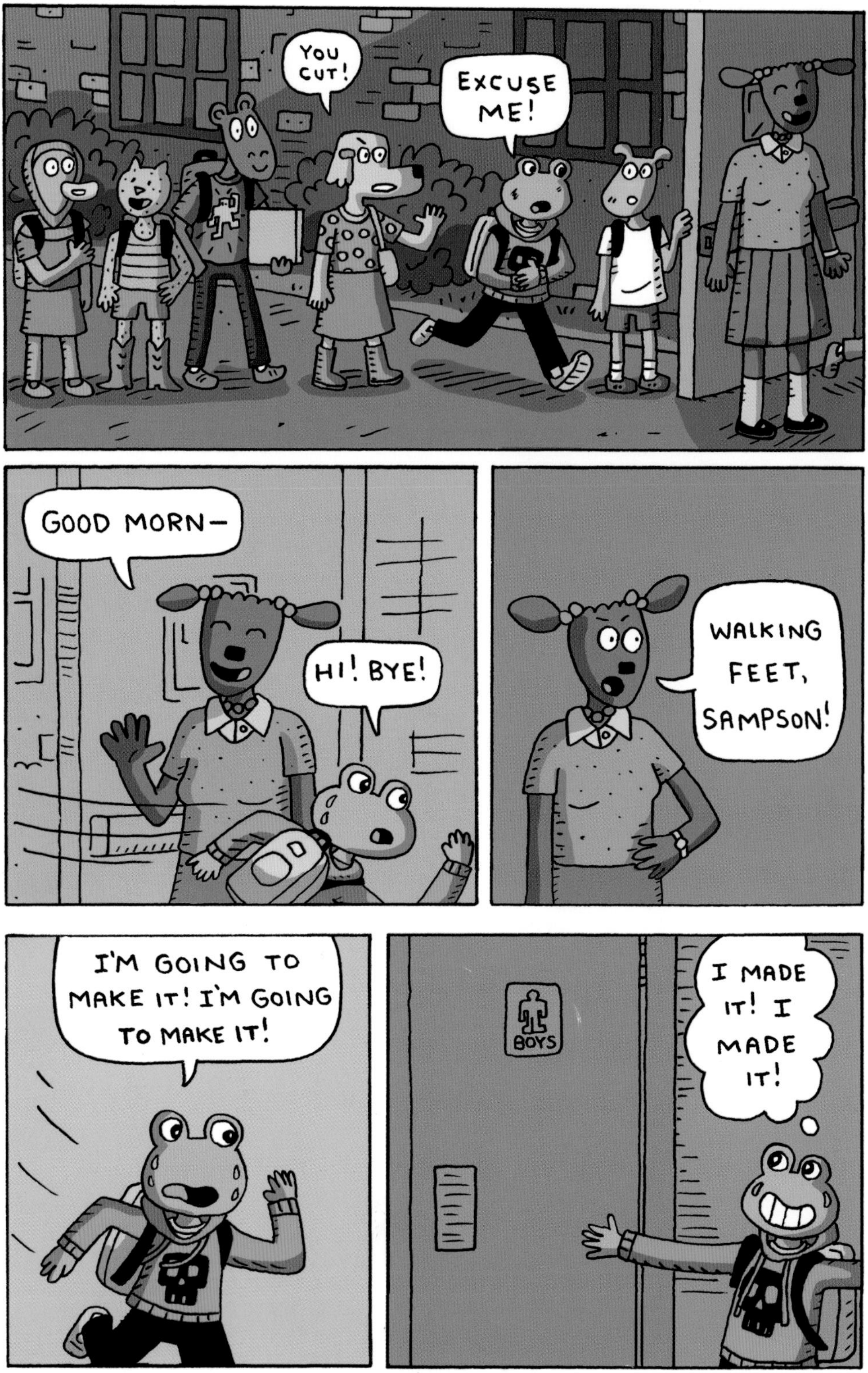
YOU CUT!
EXCUSE ME!
GOOD MORN—
HI! BYE!
WALKING FEET, SAMPSON!
I'M GOING TO MAKE IT! I'M GOING TO MAKE IT!
BOYS
I MADE IT! I MADE IT!

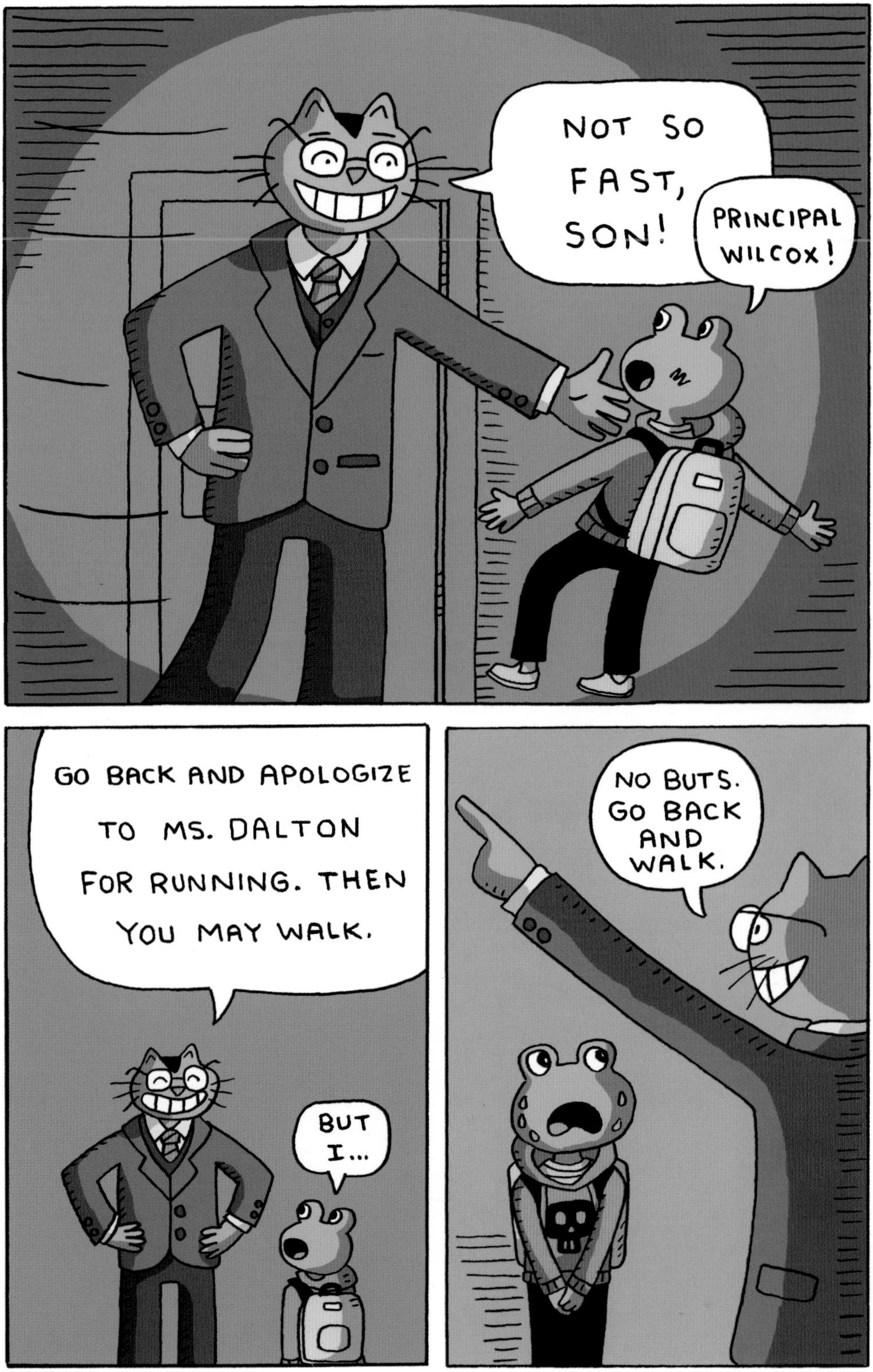
NOT SO FAST, SON!
PRINCIPAL WILCOX!
GO BACK AND APOLOGIZE TO MS. DALTON FOR RUNNING. THEN YOU MAY WALK.
BUT I...
NO BUTS. GO BACK AND WALK.

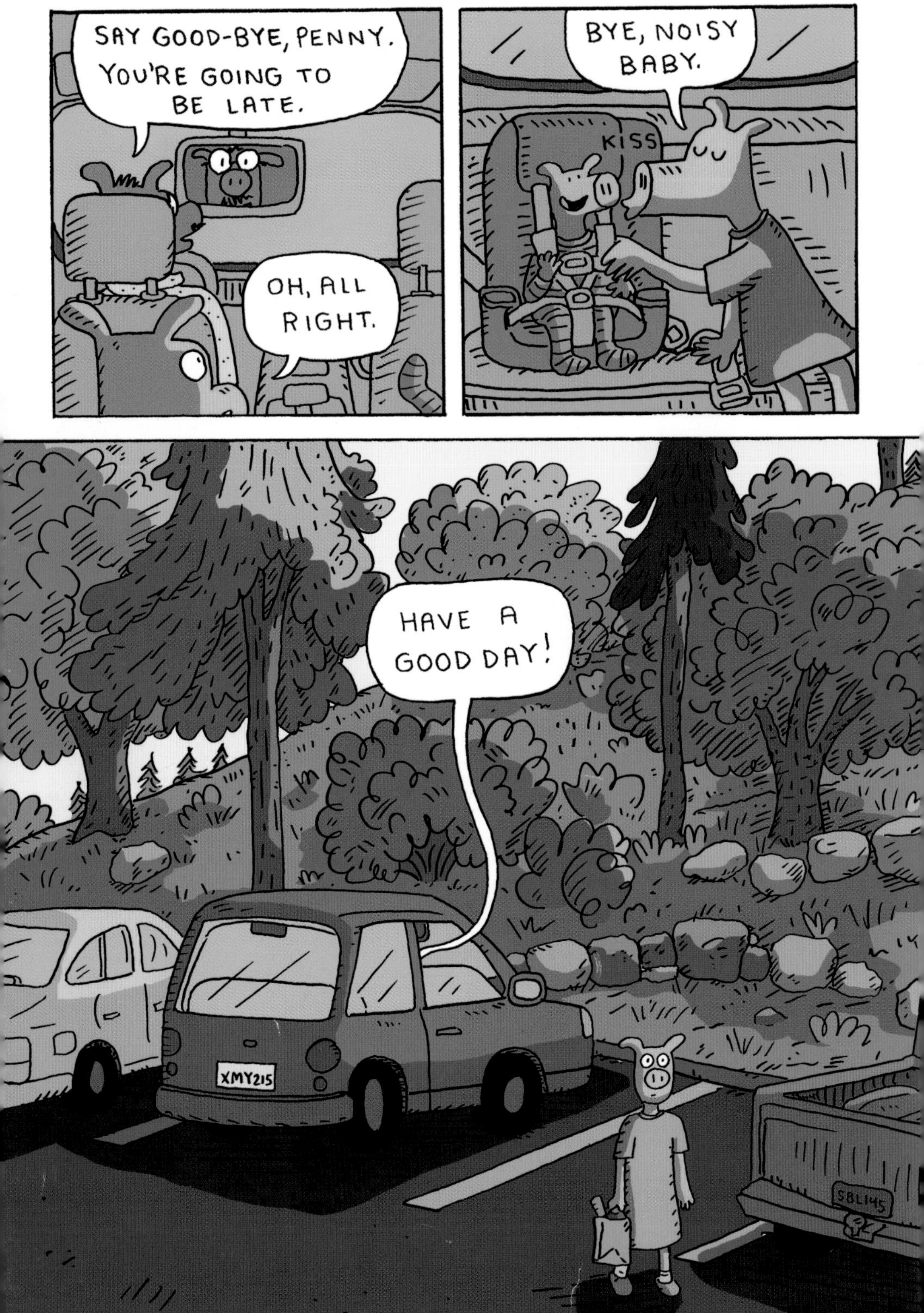
SAY GOOD-BYE, PENNY. YOU'RE GOING TO BE LATE.
OH, ALL RIGHT.
BYE, NOISY BABY.
KISS
HAVE A GOOD DAY!
XMY215
SBL145

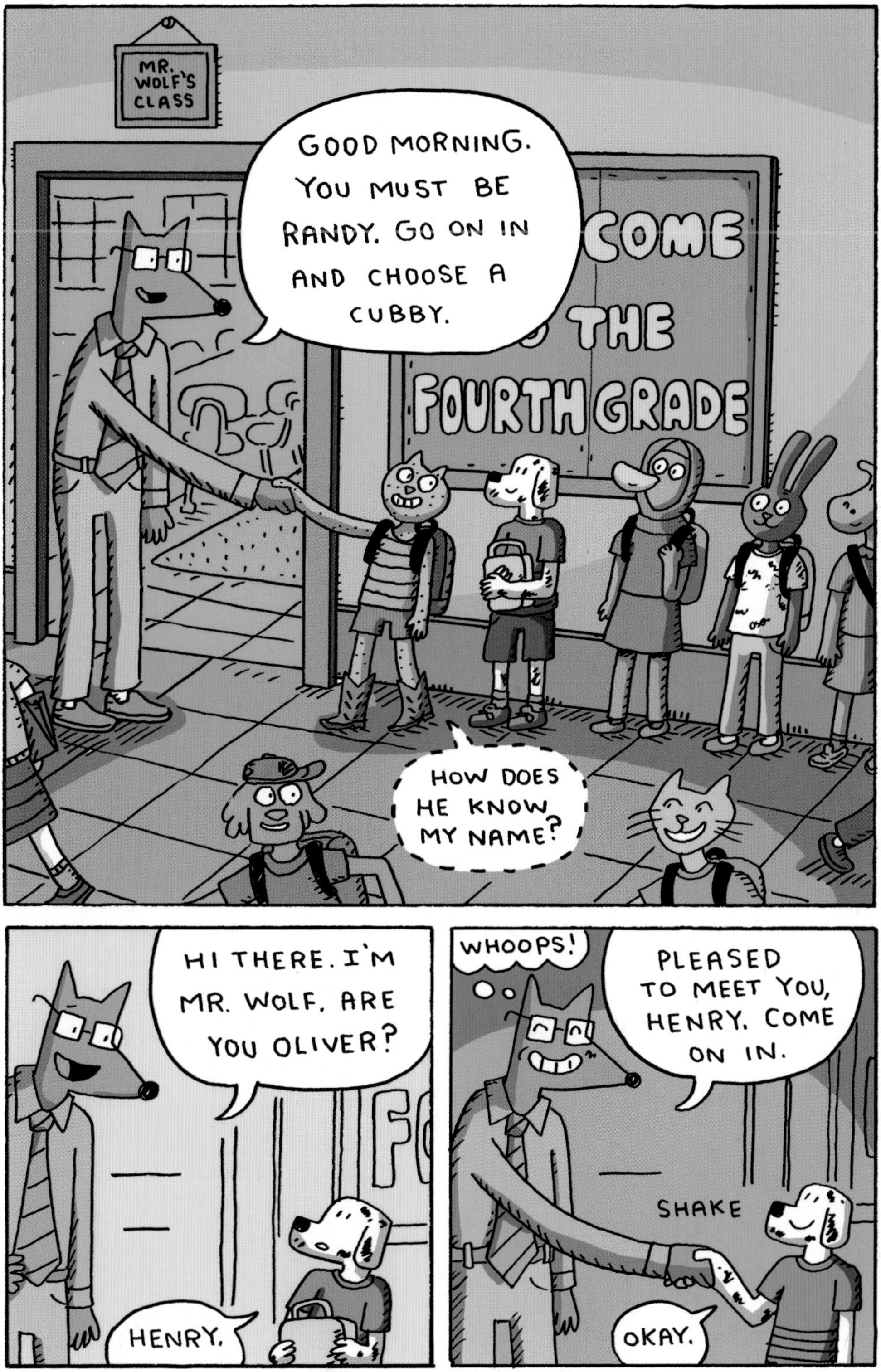
MR. WOLF'S CLASS
GOOD MORNING. YOU MUST BE RANDY. GO ON IN AND CHOOSE A CUBBY.
COME THE FOURTH GRADE
HOW DOES HE KNOW MY NAME?
HI THERE. I'M MR. WOLF. ARE YOU OLIVER?
HENRY.
WHOOPS!
PLEASED TO MEET YOU, HENRY. COME ON IN.
SHAKE
OKAY.

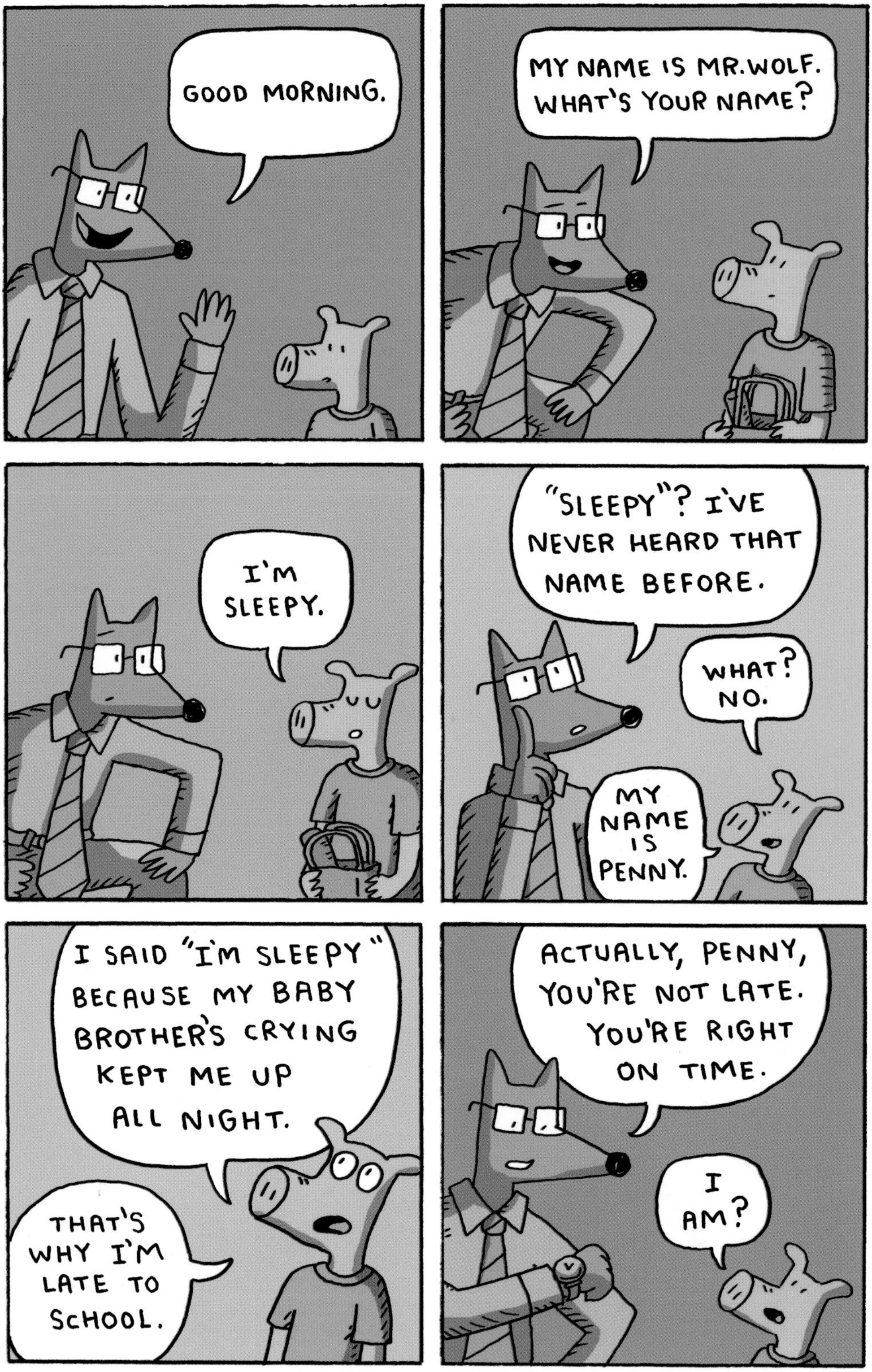
GOOD MORNING.
MY NAME IS MR. WOLF. WHAT'S YOUR NAME?
I'M SLEEPY.
"SLEEPY"? I'VE NEVER HEARD THAT NAME BEFORE.
WHAT? NO.
MY NAME IS PENNY.
I SAID "I'M SLEEPY" BECAUSE MY BABY BROTHER'S CRYING KEPT ME UP ALL NIGHT.
THAT'S WHY I'M LATE TO SCHOOL.
ACTUALLY, PENNY, YOU'RE NOT LATE. YOU'RE RIGHT ON TIME.
I AM?

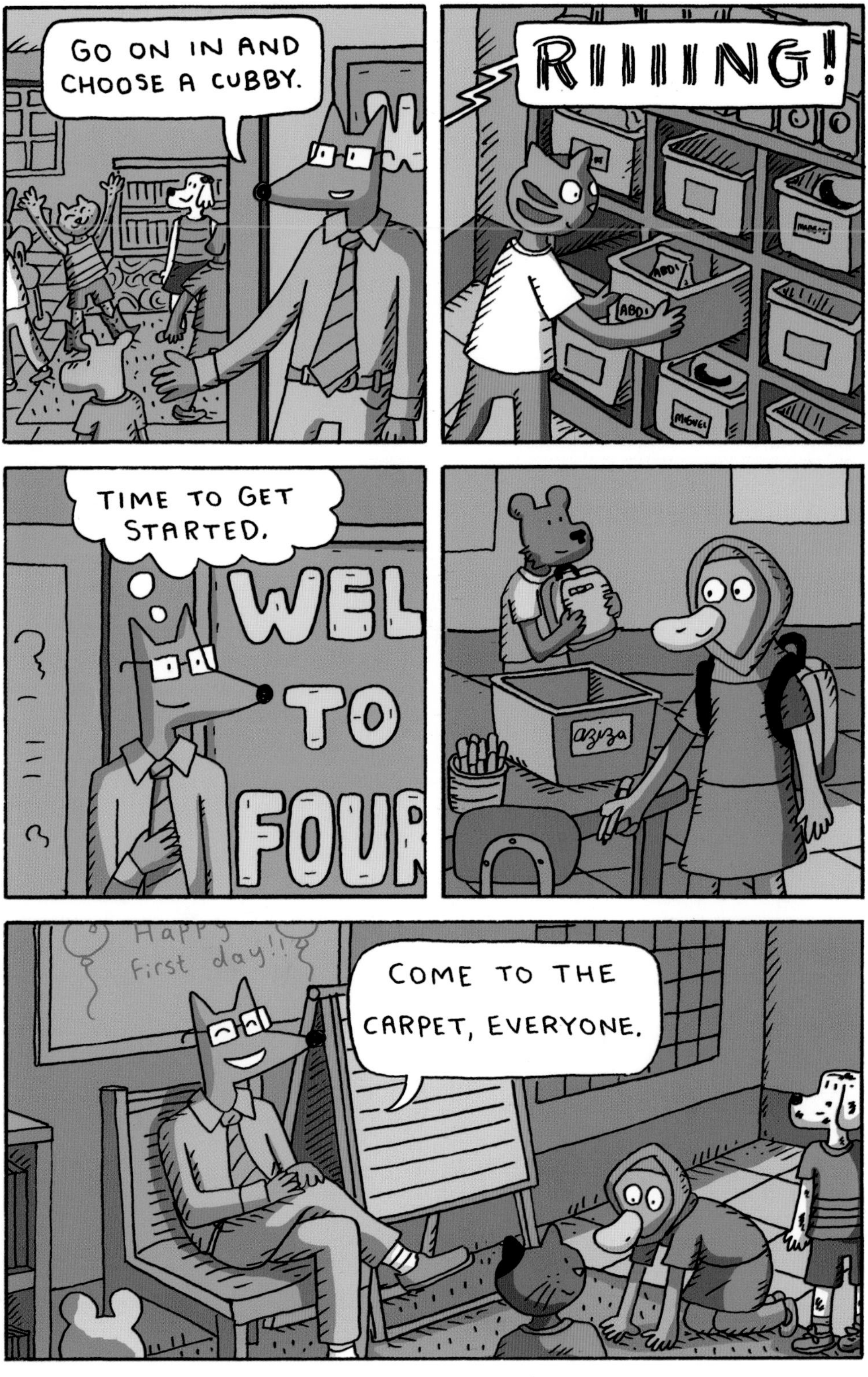
GO ON IN AND CHOOSE A CUBBY.
RIIIING!
ABDI
MIGUEL
TIME TO GET STARTED.
WEL TO FOUR
aziza
Happy First day!!
COME TO THE CARPET, EVERYONE.

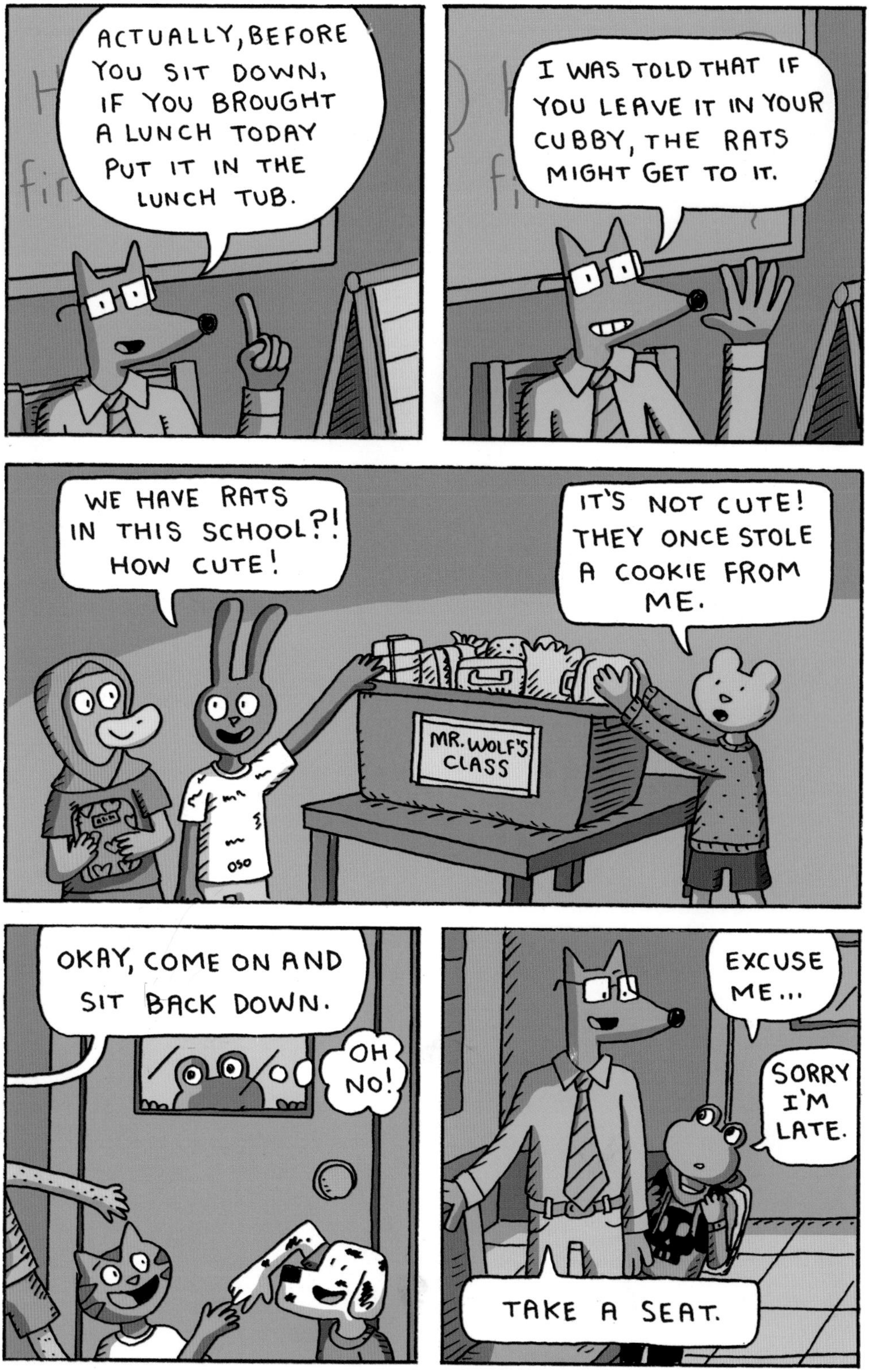
ACTUALLY, BEFORE YOU SIT DOWN, IF YOU BROUGHT A LUNCH TODAY PUT IT IN THE LUNCH TUB.
I WAS TOLD THAT IF YOU LEAVE IT IN YOUR CUBBY, THE RATS MIGHT GET TO IT.
WE HAVE RATS IN THIS SCHOOL?! HOW CUTE!
IT'S NOT CUTE! THEY ONCE STOLE A COOKIE FROM ME.
MR. WOLF'S CLASS
OSO
OKAY, COME ON AND SIT BACK DOWN.
OH NO!
EXCUSE ME...
SORRY I'M LATE.
TAKE A SEAT.

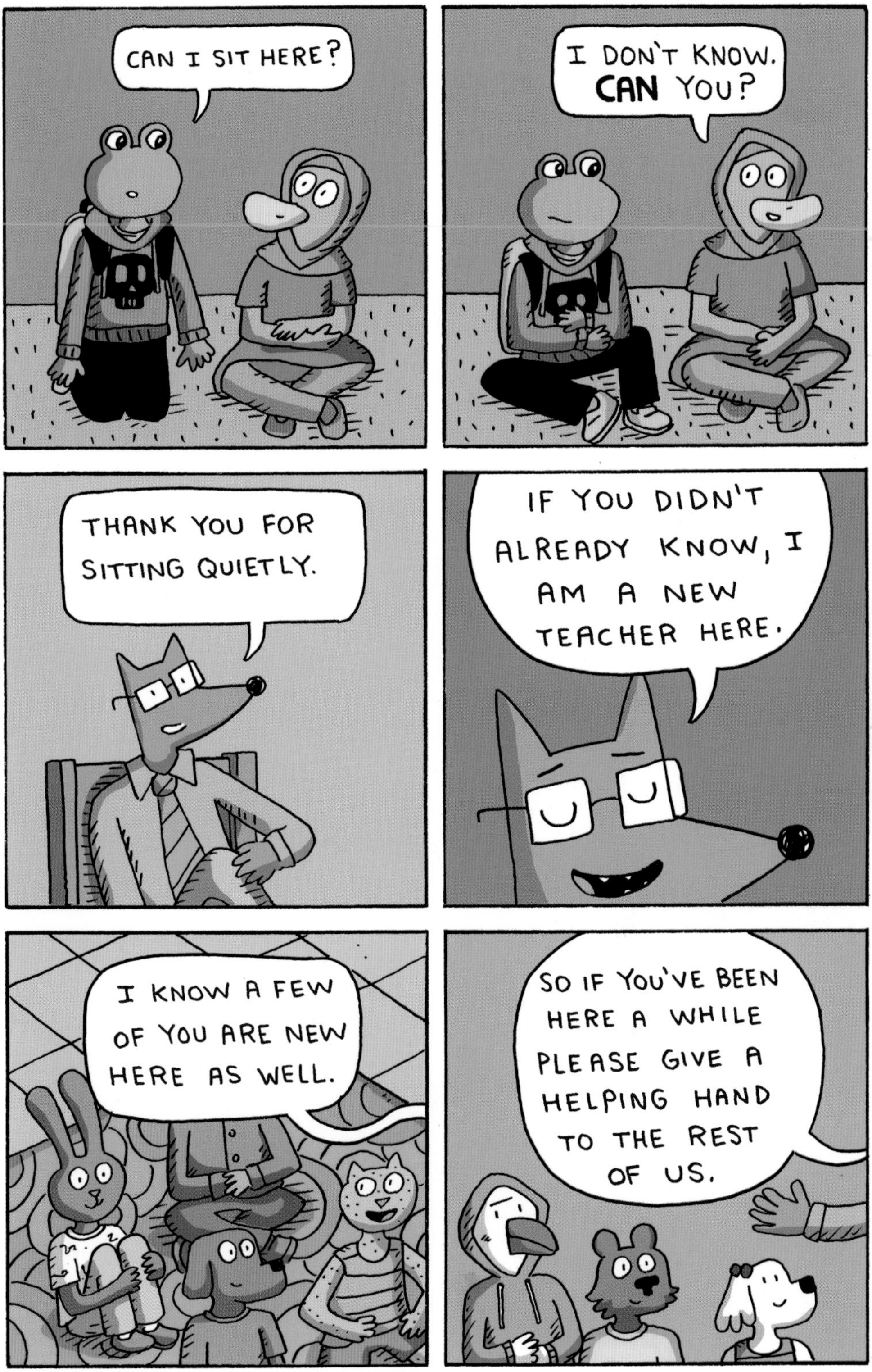
CAN I SIT HERE?
I DON'T KNOW. **CAN** YOU?
THANK YOU FOR SITTING QUIETLY.
IF YOU DIDN'T ALREADY KNOW, I AM A NEW TEACHER HERE.
I KNOW A FEW OF YOU ARE NEW HERE AS WELL.
SO IF YOU'VE BEEN HERE A WHILE PLEASE GIVE A HELPING HAND TO THE REST OF US.

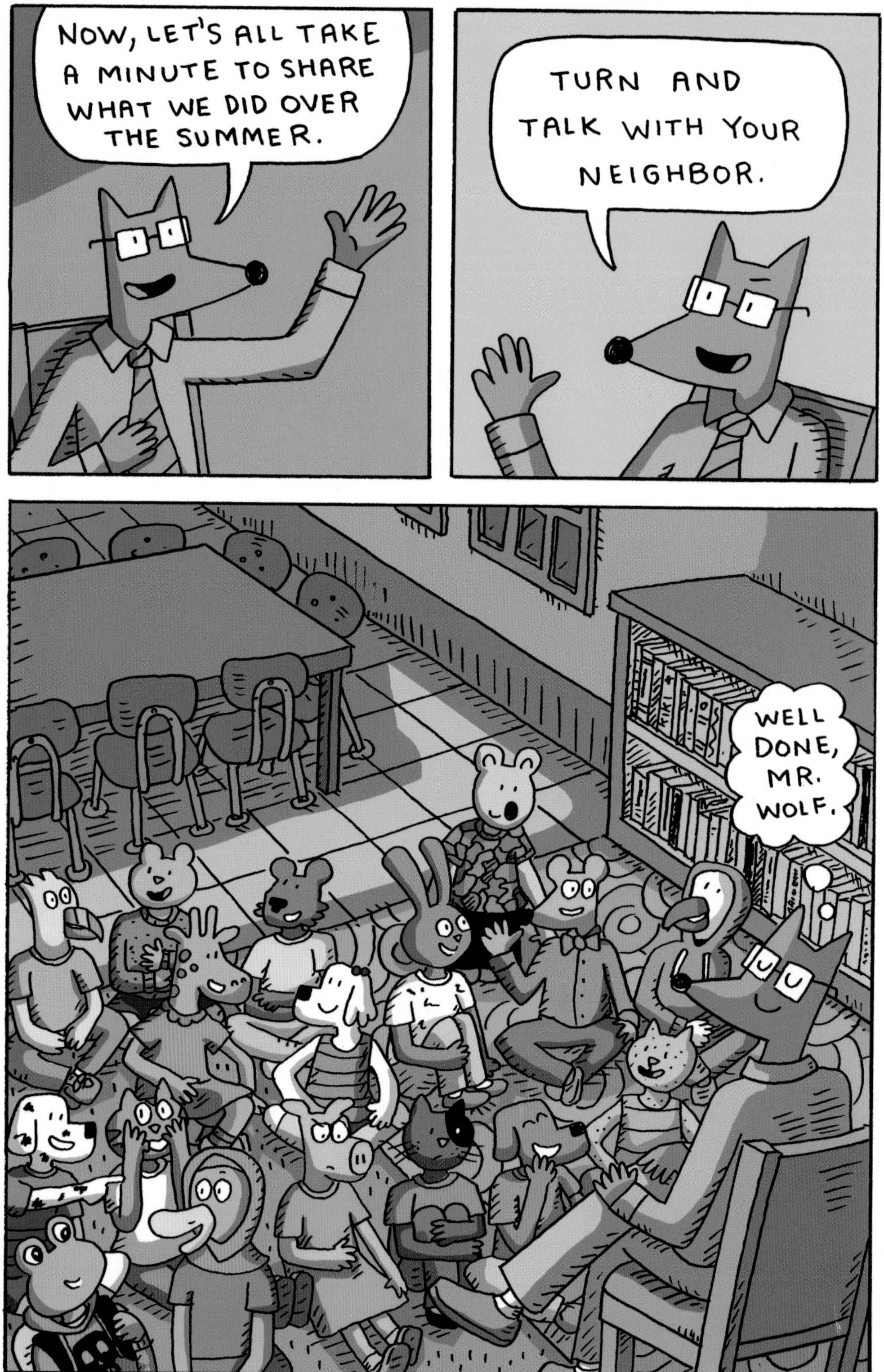
NOW, LET'S ALL TAKE A MINUTE TO SHARE WHAT WE DID OVER THE SUMMER.
TURN AND TALK WITH YOUR NEIGHBOR.
WELL DONE, MR. WOLF.

CHAPTER THREE
Palindromes

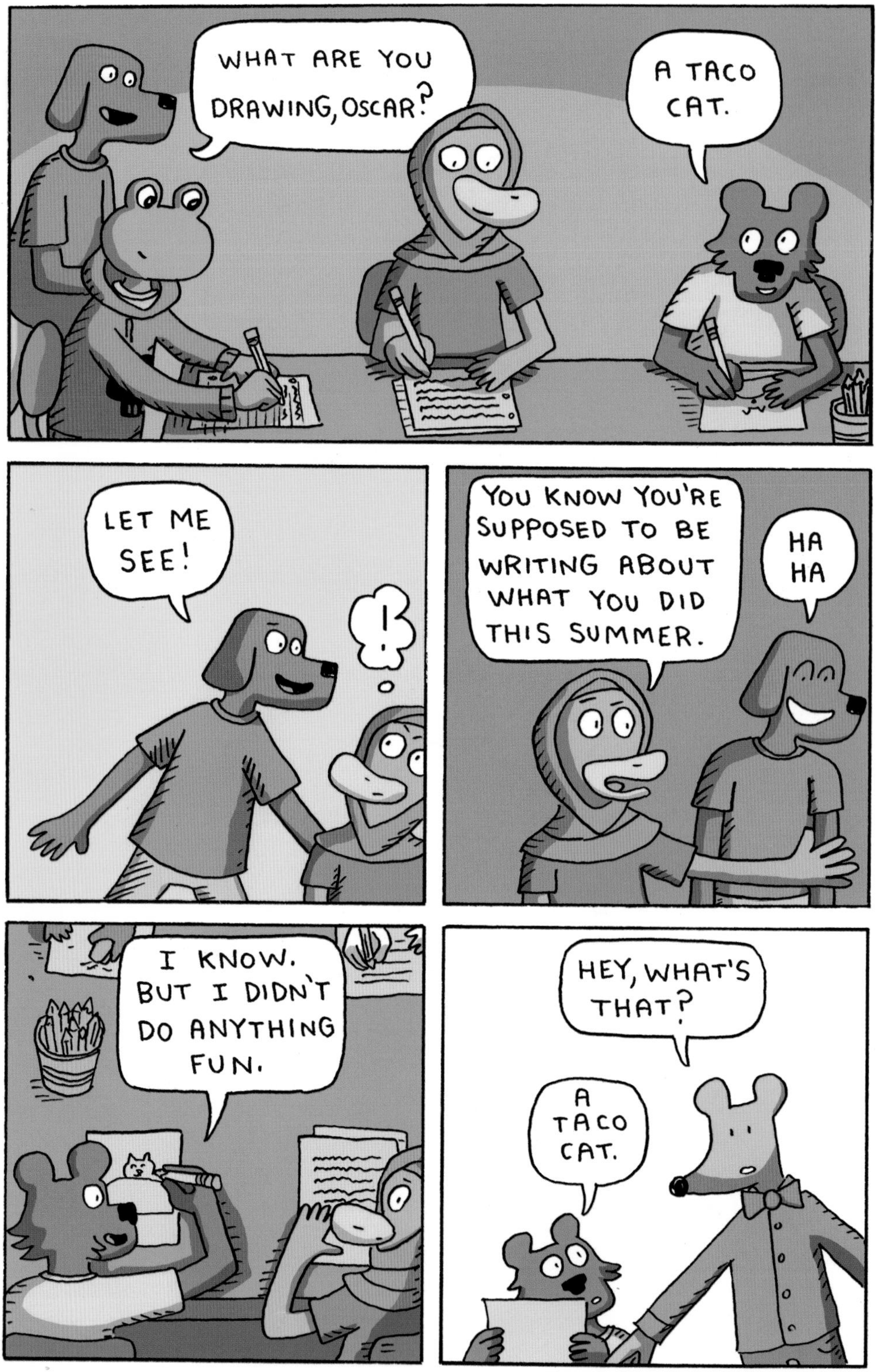
WHAT ARE YOU DRAWING, OSCAR?
A TACO CAT.
LET ME SEE!
!
YOU KNOW YOU'RE SUPPOSED TO BE WRITING ABOUT WHAT YOU DID THIS SUMMER.
HA HA
I KNOW. BUT I DIDN'T DO ANYTHING FUN.
HEY, WHAT'S THAT?
A TACO CAT.

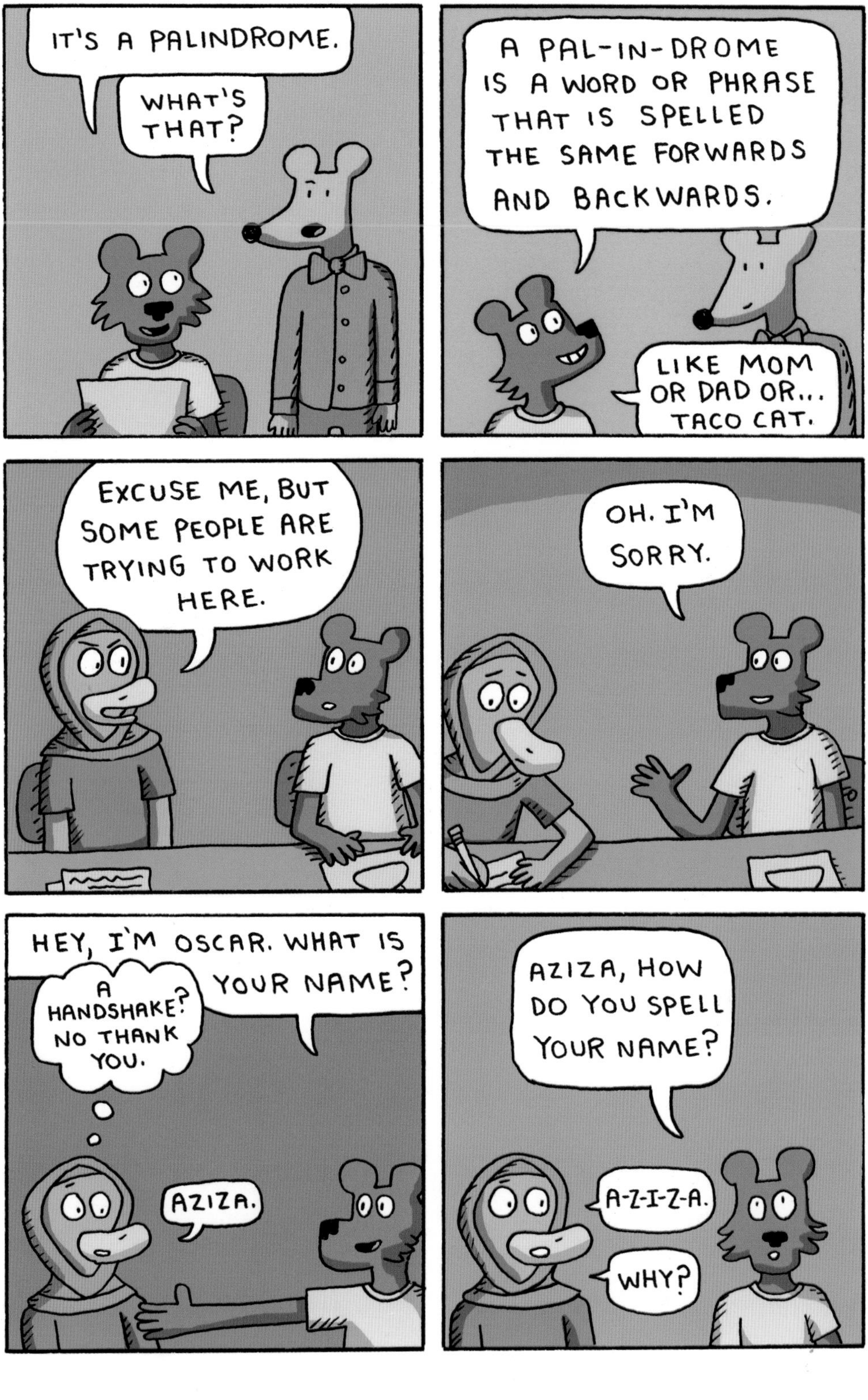
IT'S A PALINDROME.
WHAT'S THAT?
A PAL-IN-DROME IS A WORD OR PHRASE THAT IS SPELLED THE SAME FORWARDS AND BACKWARDS.
LIKE MOM OR DAD OR... TACO CAT.
EXCUSE ME, BUT SOME PEOPLE ARE TRYING TO WORK HERE.
OH. I'M SORRY.
HEY, I'M OSCAR. WHAT IS YOUR NAME?
A HANDSHAKE? NO THANK YOU.
AZIZA.
AZIZA, HOW DO YOU SPELL YOUR NAME?
A-Z-I-Z-A.
WHY?

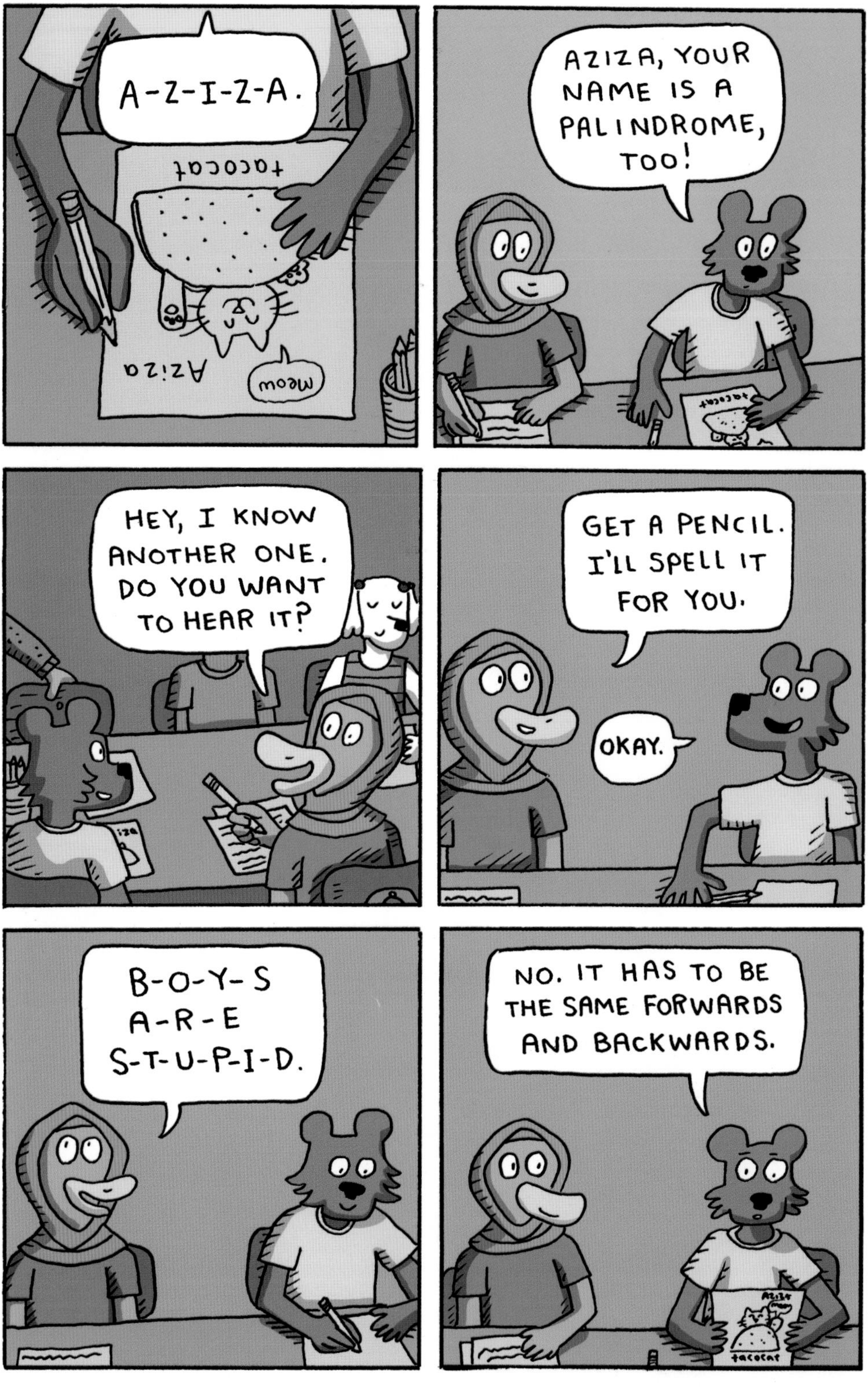
A-Z-I-Z-A.
tacocat
meow
Aziza
AZIZA, YOUR NAME IS A PALINDROME, TOO!
HEY, I KNOW ANOTHER ONE. DO YOU WANT TO HEAR IT?
GET A PENCIL. I'LL SPELL IT FOR YOU.
OKAY.
B-O-Y-S A-R-E S-T-U-P-I-D.
NO. IT HAS TO BE THE SAME FORWARDS AND BACKWARDS.

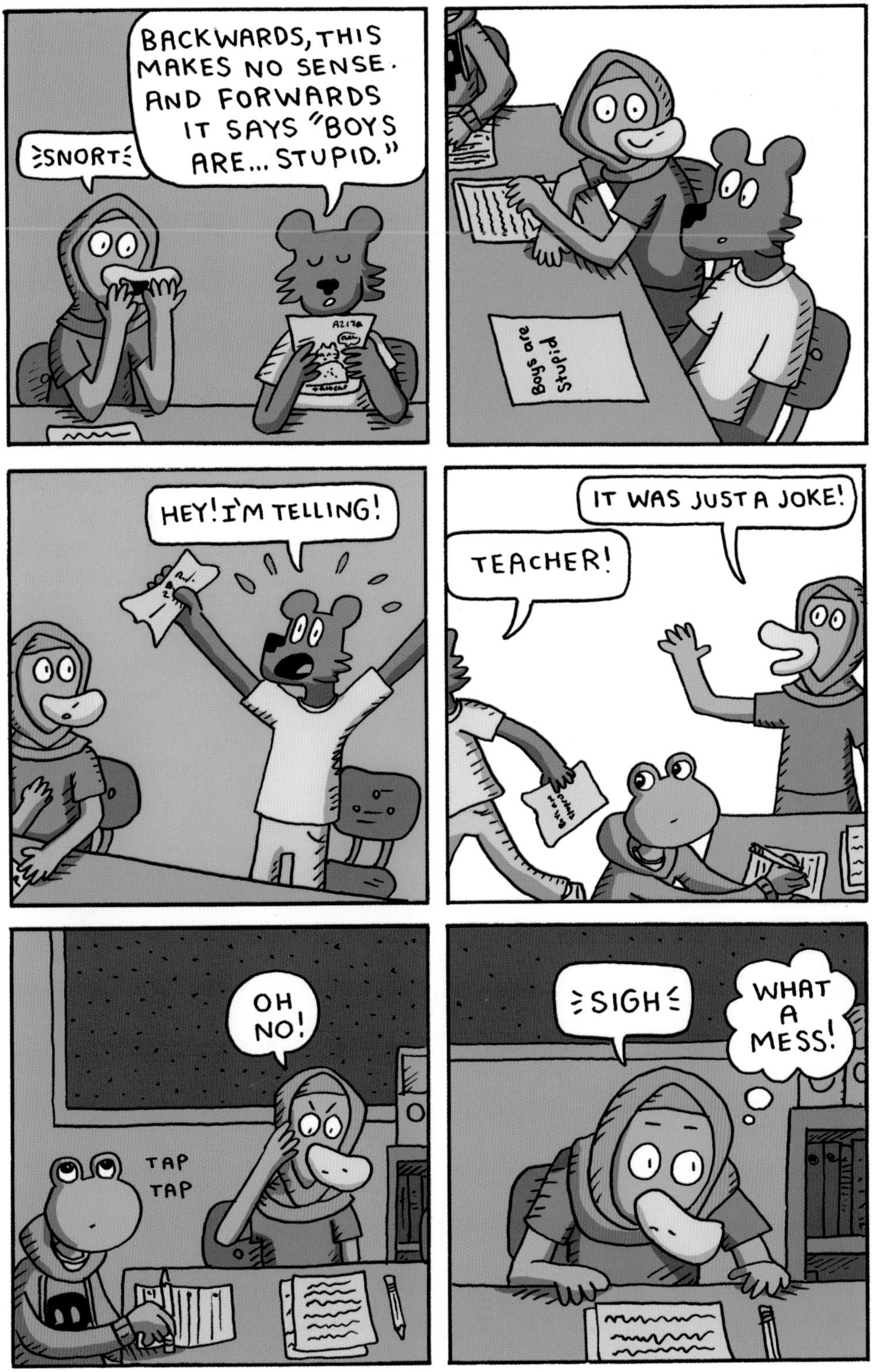
SNORT
BACKWARDS, THIS MAKES NO SENSE. AND FORWARDS IT SAYS "BOYS ARE... STUPID."
Boys are Stupid
HEY! I'M TELLING!
IT WAS JUST A JOKE!
TEACHER!
OH NO!
TAP TAP
SIGH
WHAT A MESS!

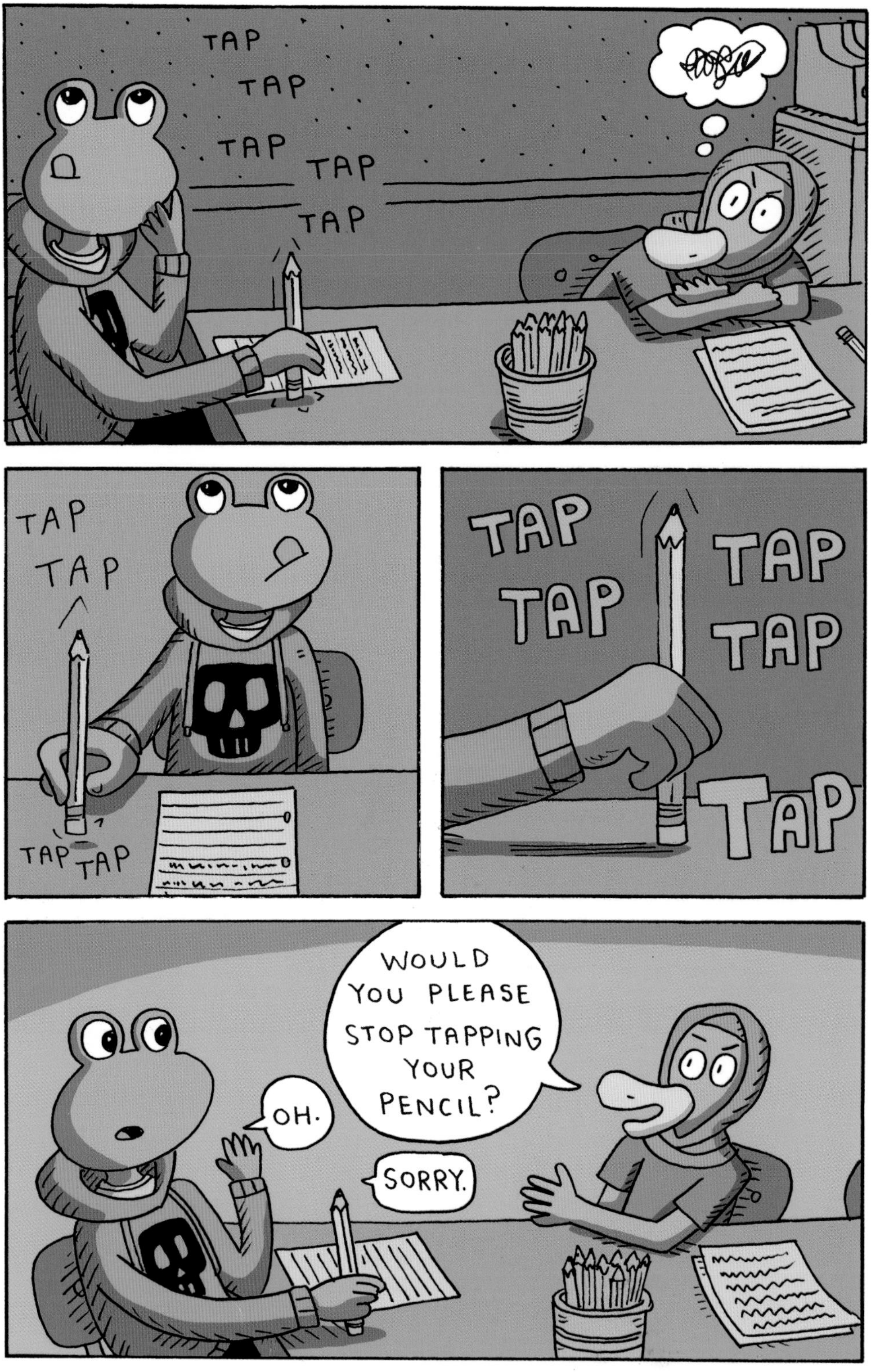
TAP
TAP
TAP
TAP
TAP
TAP
TAP
TAP TAP
TAP
TAP
TAP
TAP
TAP
WOULD YOU PLEASE STOP TAPPING YOUR PENCIL?
OH.
SORRY.

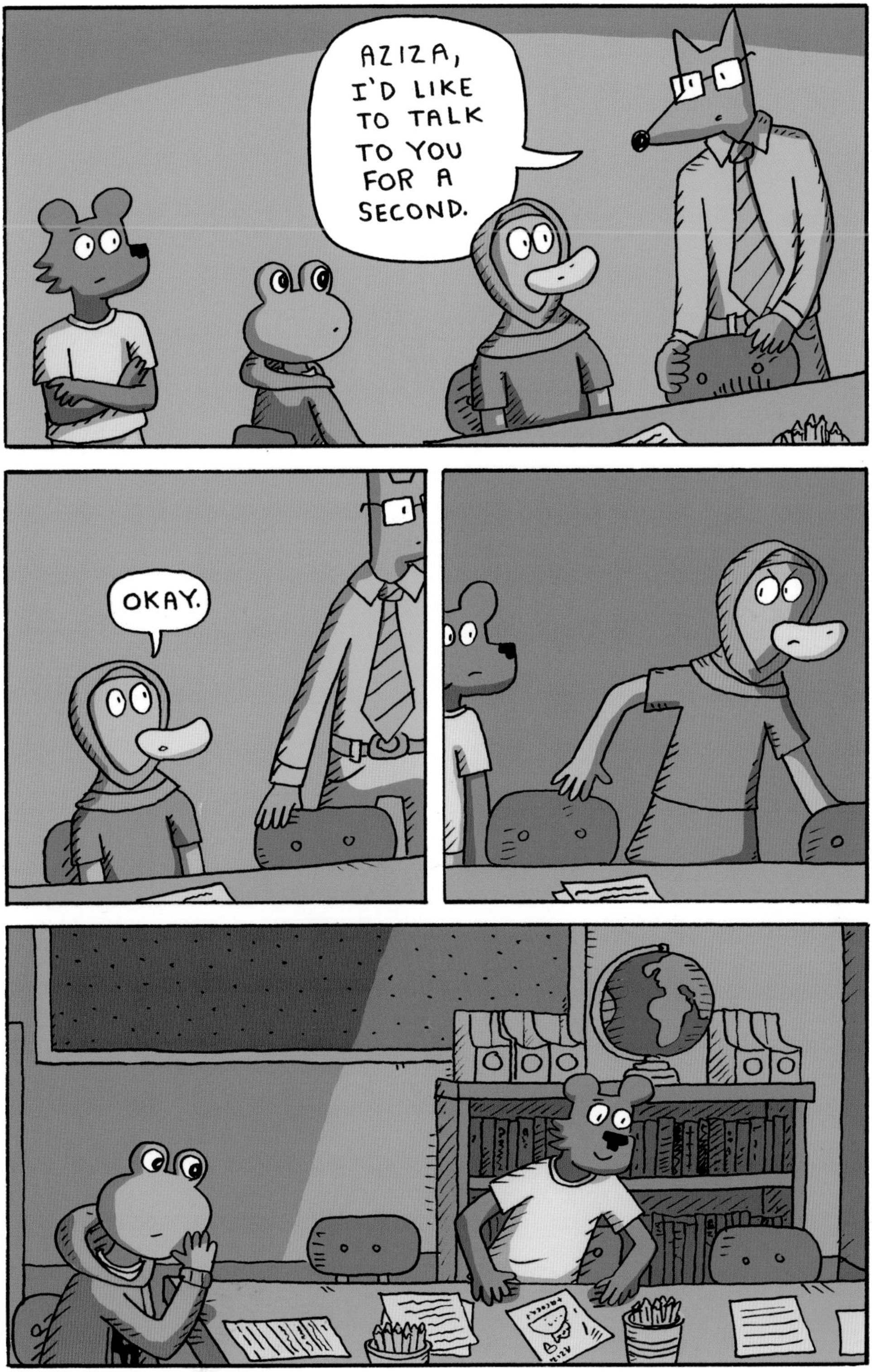
AZIZA, I'D LIKE TO TALK TO YOU FOR A SECOND.
OKAY.

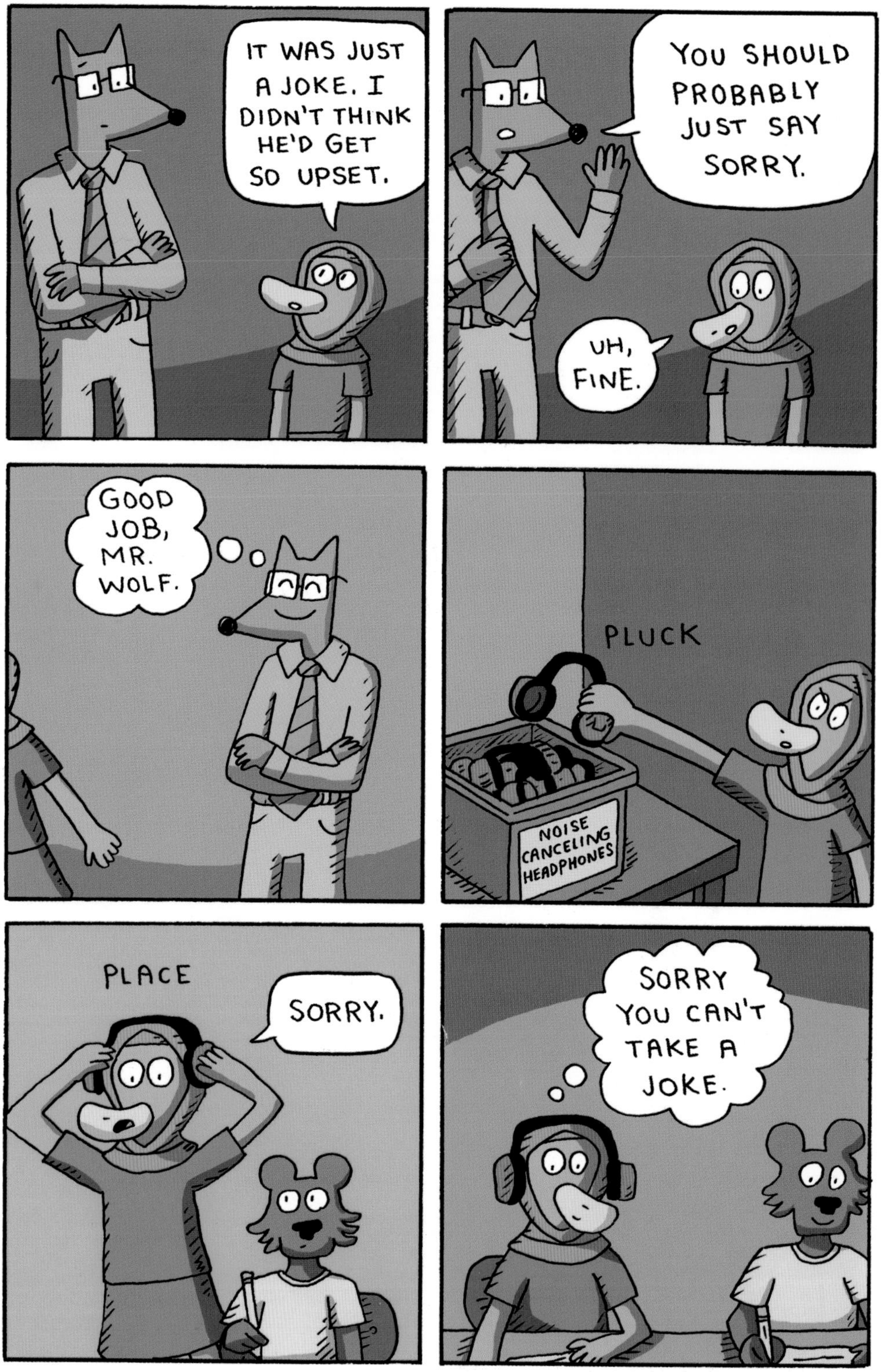
IT WAS JUST A JOKE. I DIDN'T THINK HE'D GET SO UPSET.
YOU SHOULD PROBABLY JUST SAY SORRY.
UH, FINE.
GOOD JOB, MR. WOLF.
PLUCK
NOISE CANCELING HEADPHONES
PLACE
SORRY.
SORRY YOU CAN'T TAKE A JOKE.

CHAPTER FOUR

Peace and Quiet

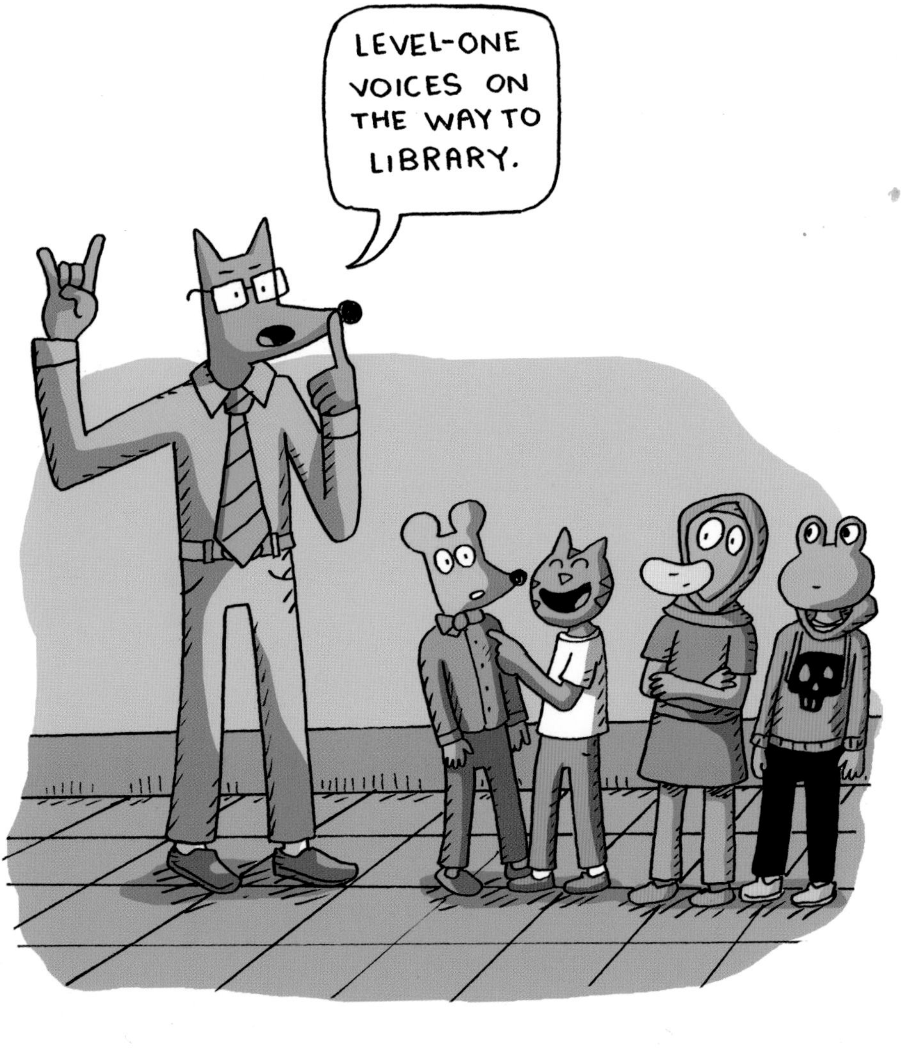

LEVEL-ONE VOICES ON THE WAY TO LIBRARY.

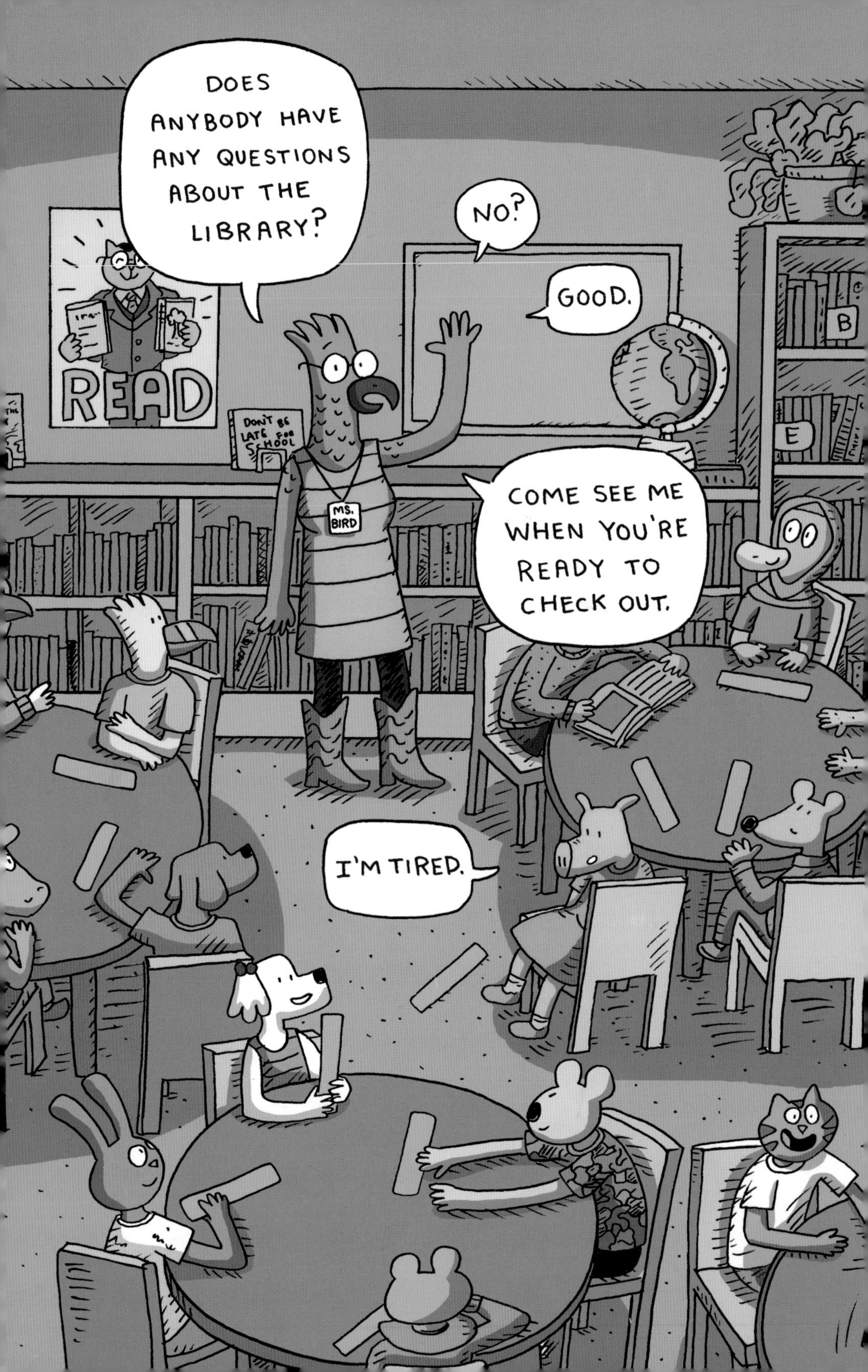
DOES ANYBODY HAVE ANY QUESTIONS ABOUT THE LIBRARY?
NO?
GOOD.
COME SEE ME WHEN YOU'RE READY TO CHECK OUT.
I'M TIRED.
READ
DON'T BE LATE FOR SCHOOL
MS. BIRD

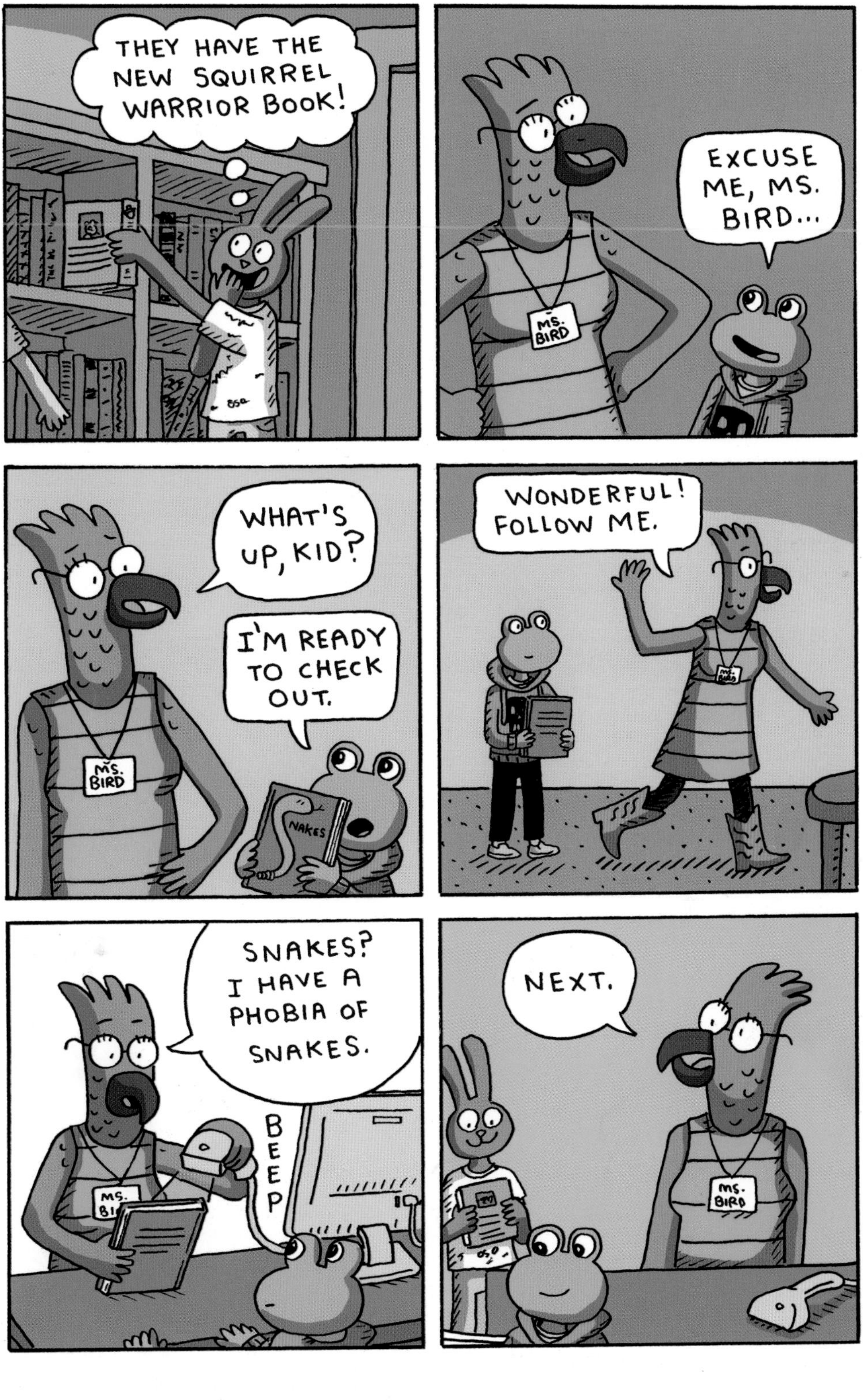
THEY HAVE THE NEW SQUIRREL WARRIOR BOOK!
EXCUSE ME, MS. BIRD...
MS. BIRD
WHAT'S UP, KID?
I'M READY TO CHECK OUT.
MS. BIRD
WONDERFUL! FOLLOW ME.
SNAKES? I HAVE A PHOBIA OF SNAKES.
BEEP
NEXT.
MS. BIRD

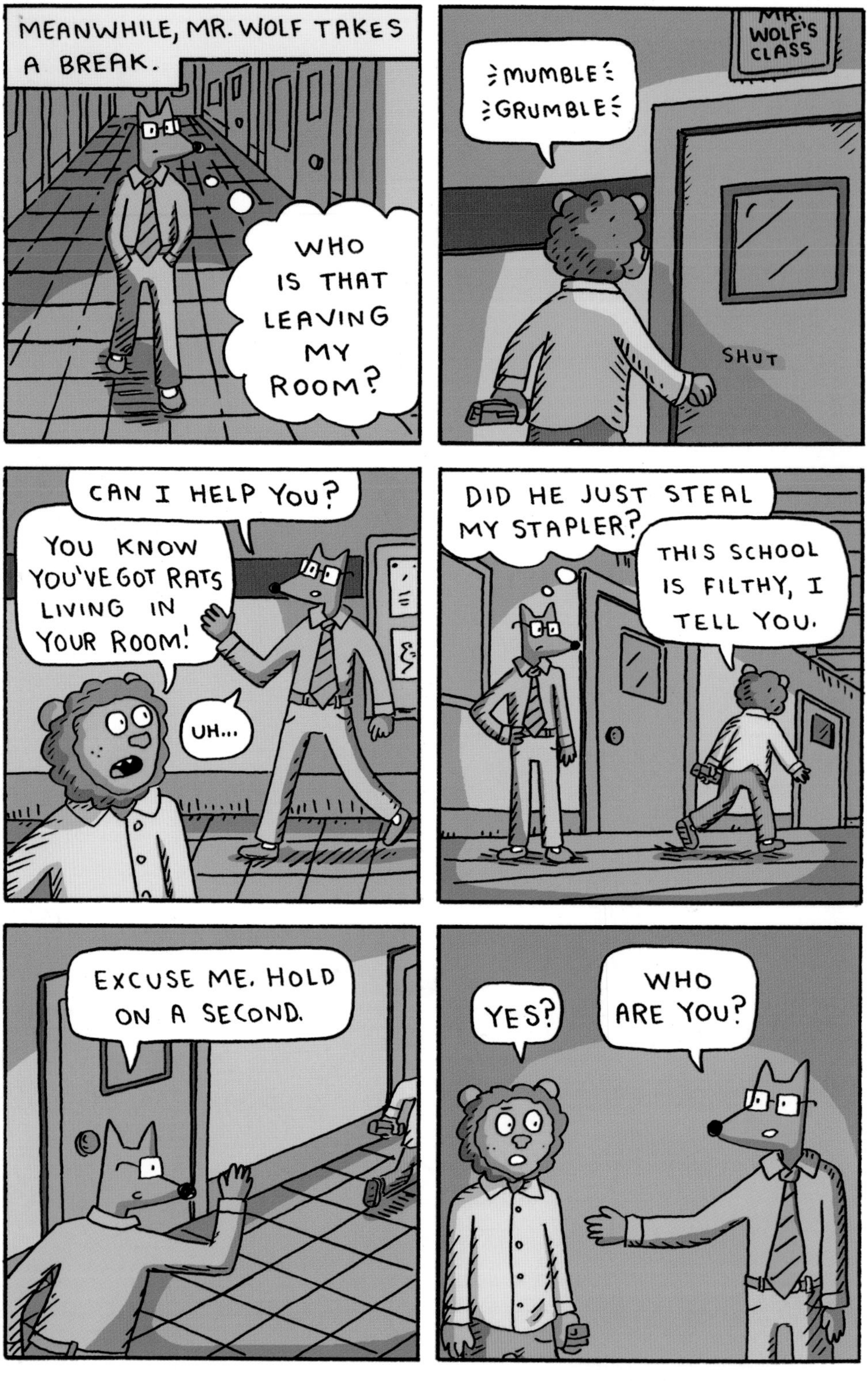
MEANWHILE, MR. WOLF TAKES A BREAK.
WHO IS THAT LEAVING MY ROOM?
MR. WOLF'S CLASS
MUMBLE GRUMBLE
SHUT
CAN I HELP YOU?
YOU KNOW YOU'VE GOT RATS LIVING IN YOUR ROOM!
UH...
DID HE JUST STEAL MY STAPLER?
THIS SCHOOL IS FILTHY, I TELL YOU.
EXCUSE ME. HOLD ON A SECOND.
YES?
WHO ARE YOU?

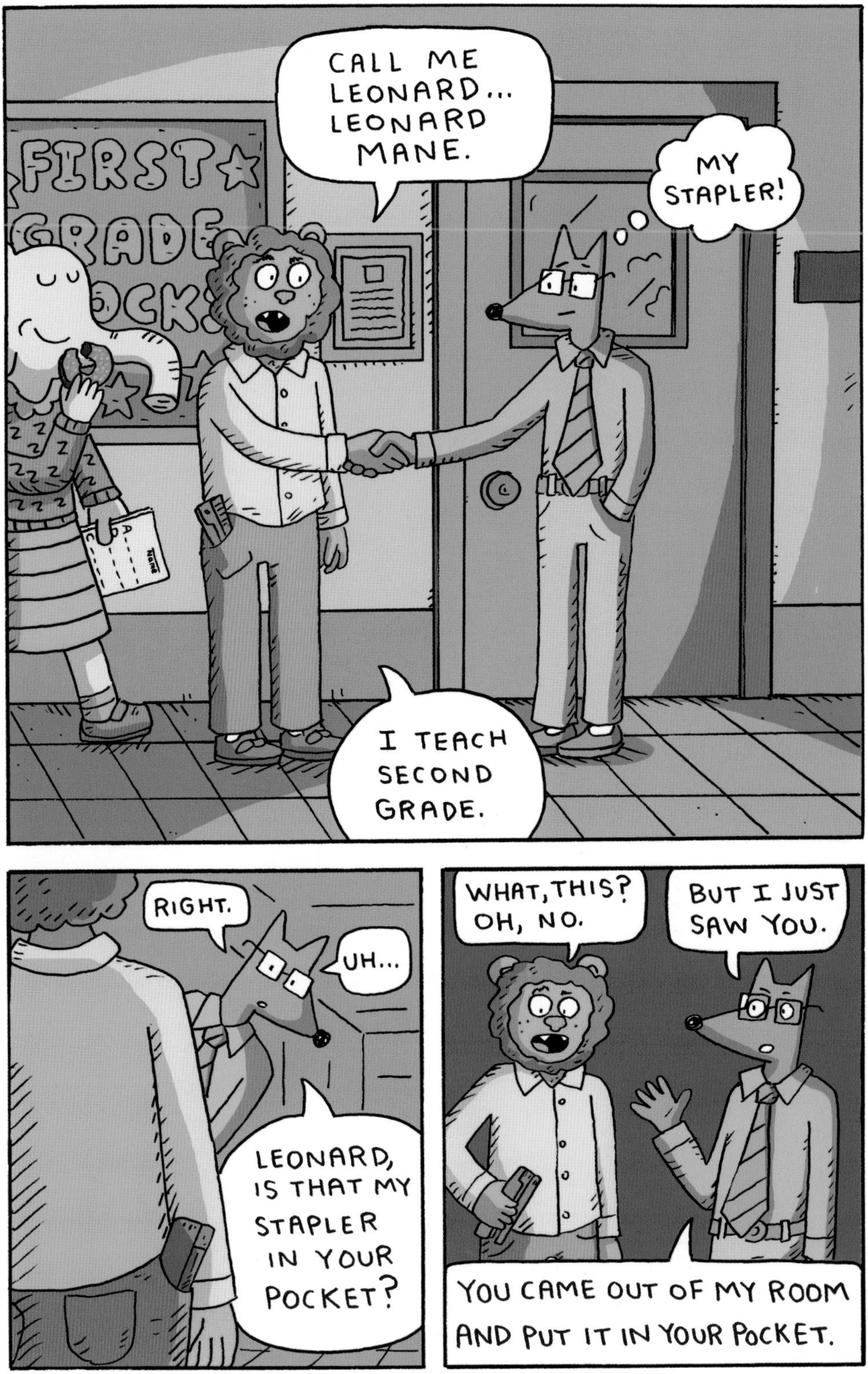
CALL ME LEONARD... LEONARD MANE.
MY STAPLER!
I TEACH SECOND GRADE.
RIGHT.
UH...
LEONARD, IS THAT MY STAPLER IN YOUR POCKET?
WHAT, THIS? OH, NO.
BUT I JUST SAW YOU.
YOU CAME OUT OF MY ROOM AND PUT IT IN YOUR POCKET.

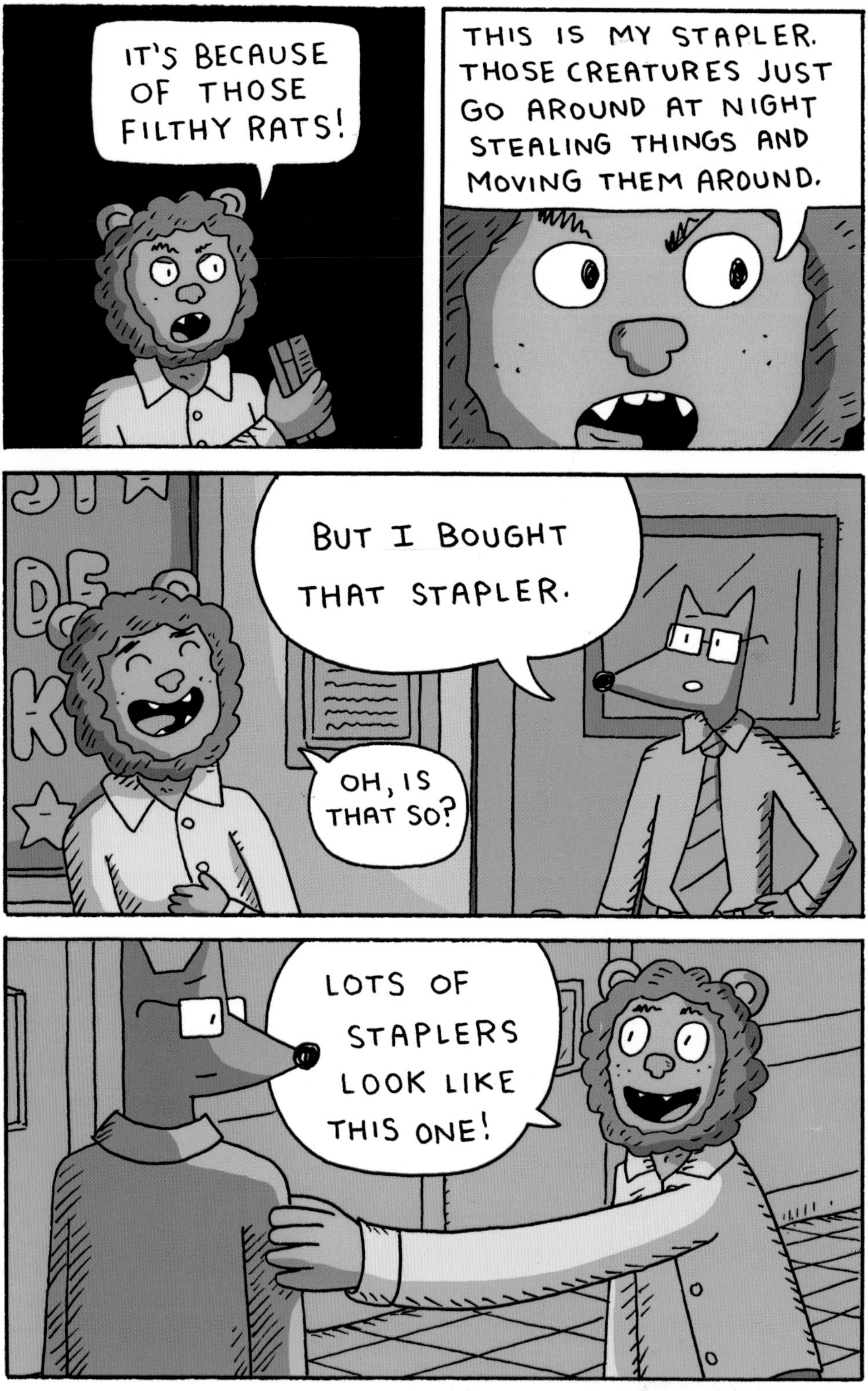
IT'S BECAUSE OF THOSE FILTHY RATS!
THIS IS MY STAPLER. THOSE CREATURES JUST GO AROUND AT NIGHT STEALING THINGS AND MOVING THEM AROUND.
BUT I BOUGHT THAT STAPLER.
OH, IS THAT SO?
LOTS OF STAPLERS LOOK LIKE THIS ONE!

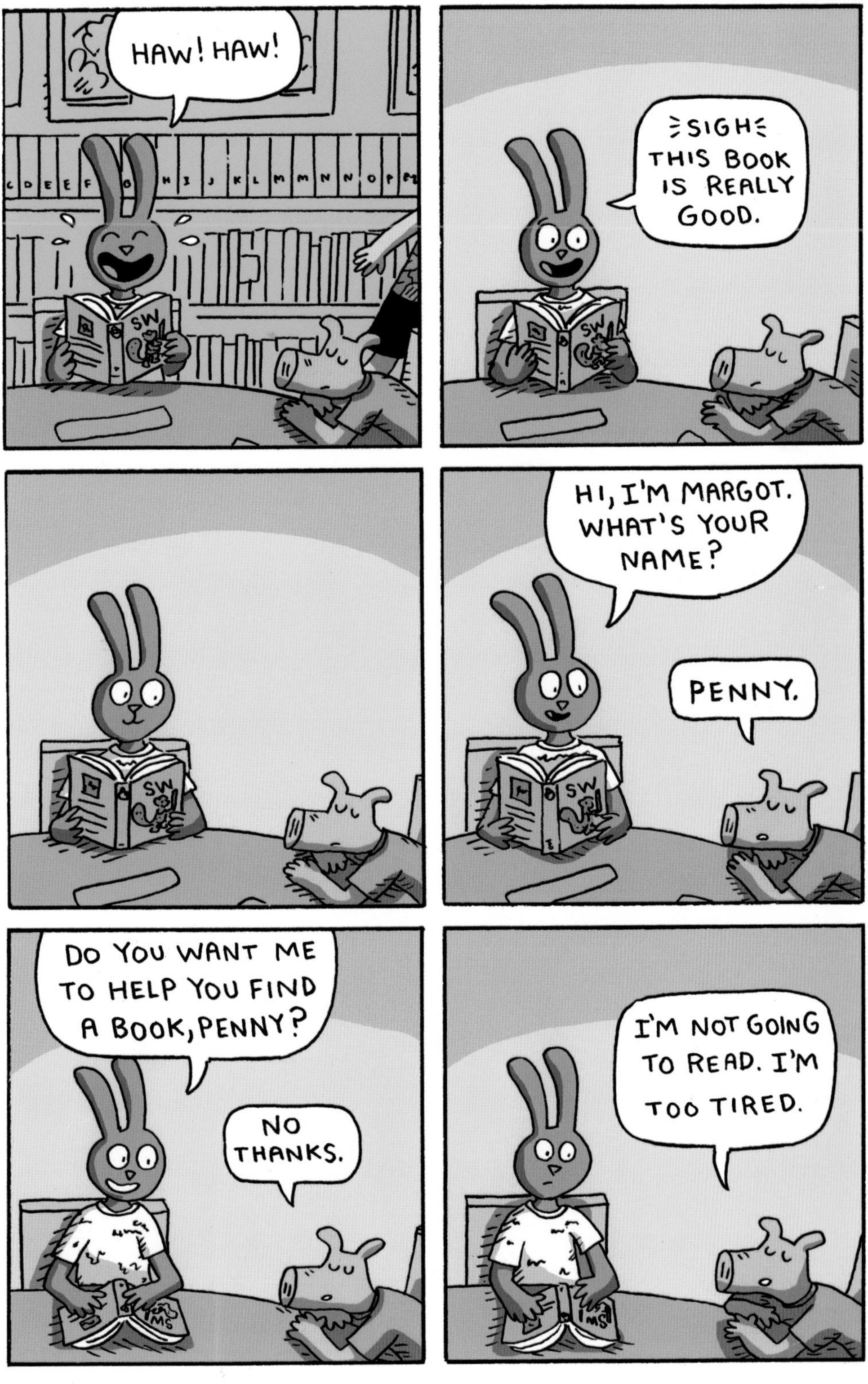
HAW! HAW!
SIGH THIS BOOK IS REALLY GOOD.
HI, I'M MARGOT. WHAT'S YOUR NAME?
PENNY.
DO YOU WANT ME TO HELP YOU FIND A BOOK, PENNY?
NO THANKS.
I'M NOT GOING TO READ. I'M TOO TIRED.

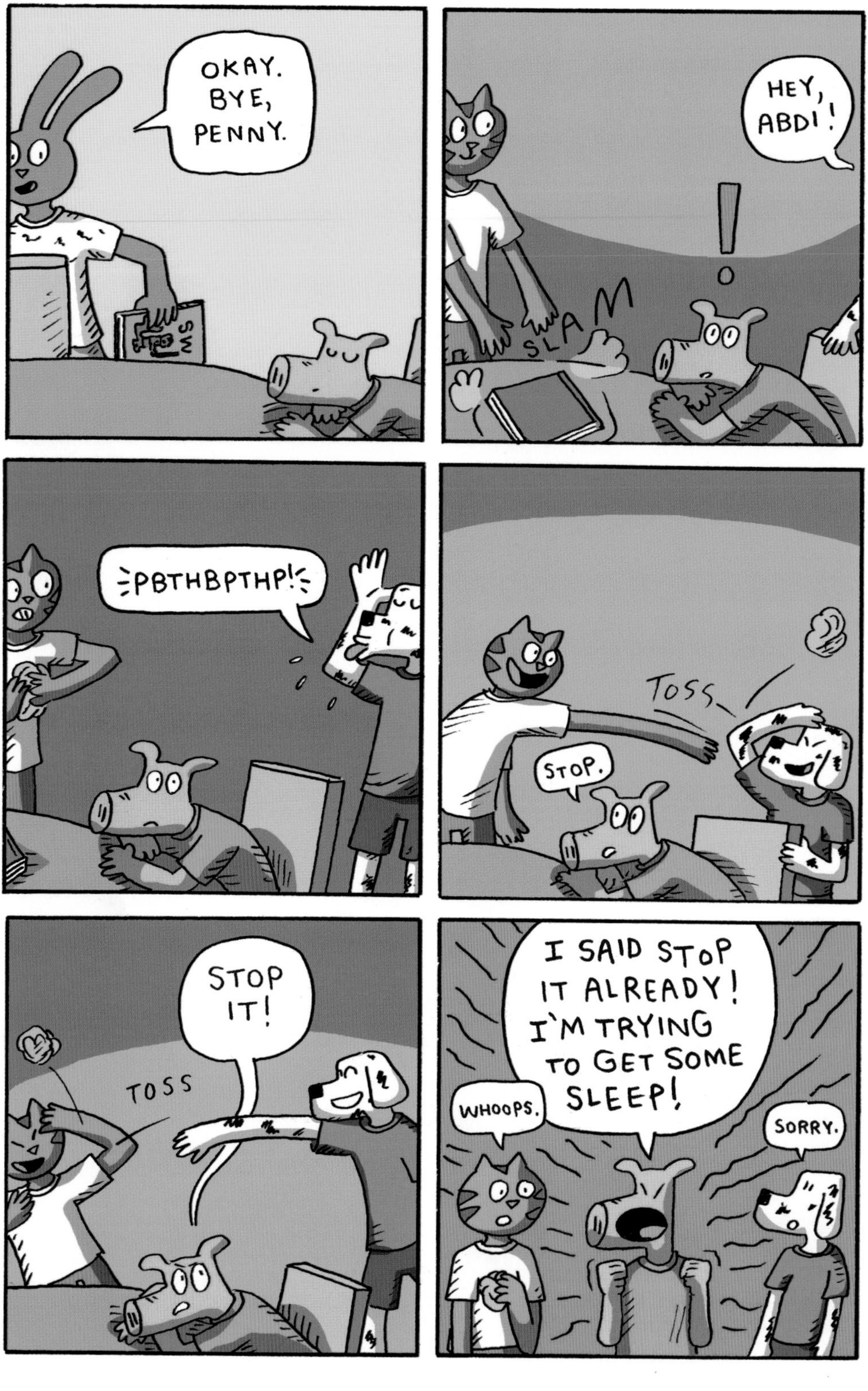
OKAY. BYE, PENNY.
HEY, ABDI!
!
SLAM
PBTHBPTHP!
TOSS
STOP.
STOP IT!
TOSS
I SAID STOP IT ALREADY! I'M TRYING TO GET SOME SLEEP!
WHOOPS.
SORRY.

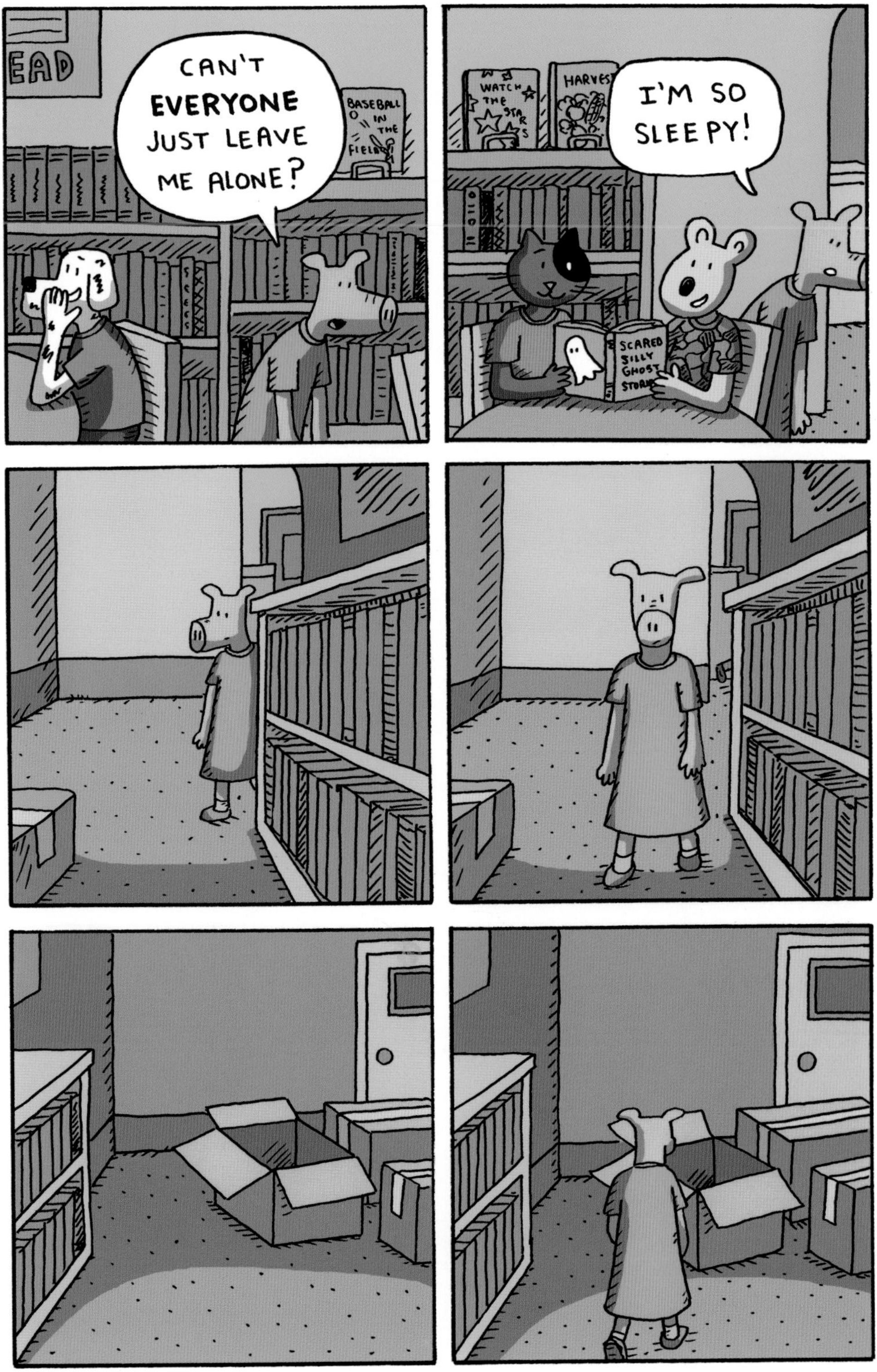
EAD
CAN'T **EVERYONE** JUST LEAVE ME ALONE?
BASEBALL IN THE FIELD
WATCH THE STARS
HARVEST
I'M SO SLEEPY!
SCARED SILLY GHOST STORIES

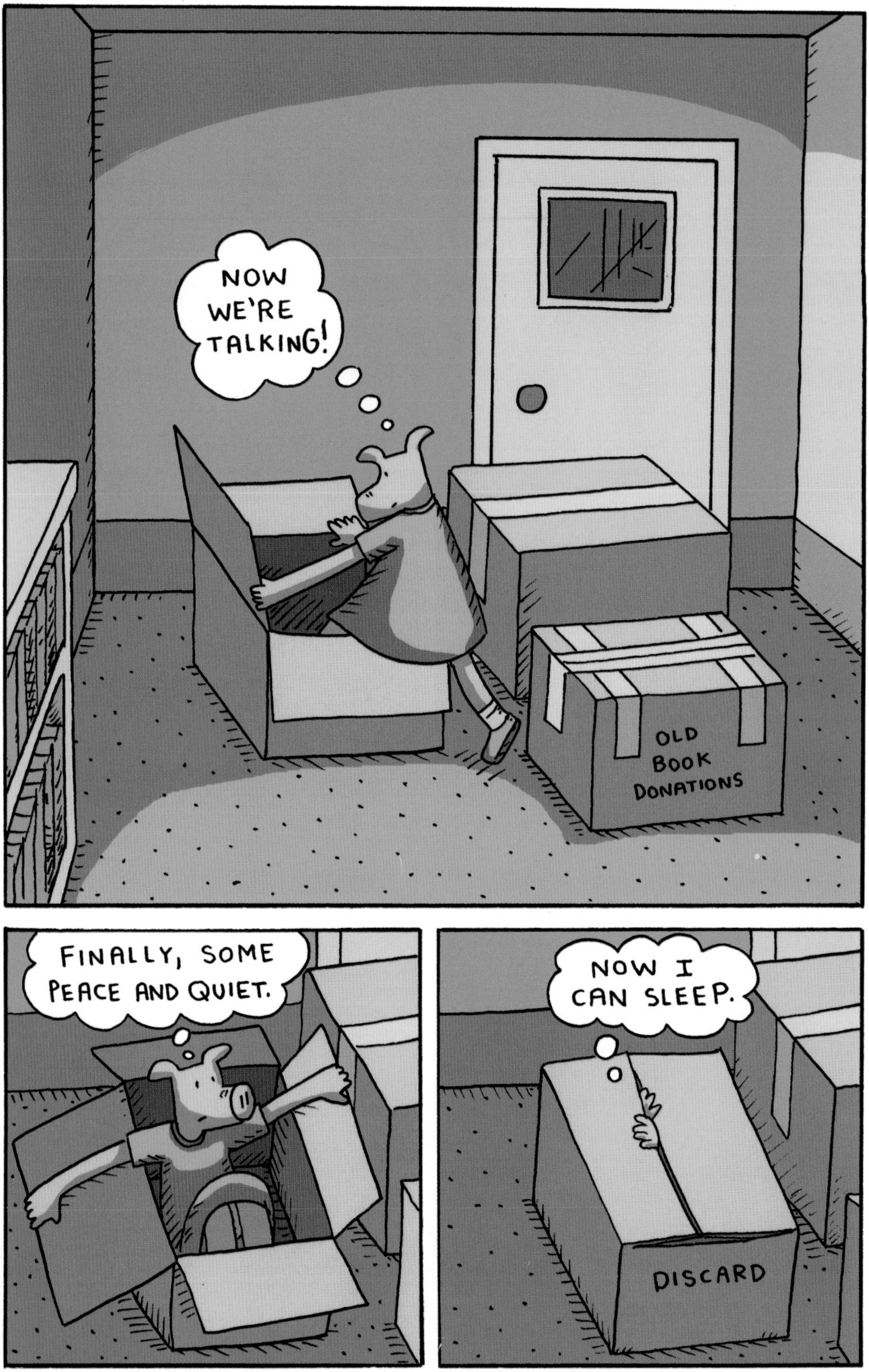
NOW WE'RE TALKING!
OLD BOOK DONATIONS
FINALLY, SOME PEACE AND QUIET.
NOW I CAN SLEEP.
DISCARD

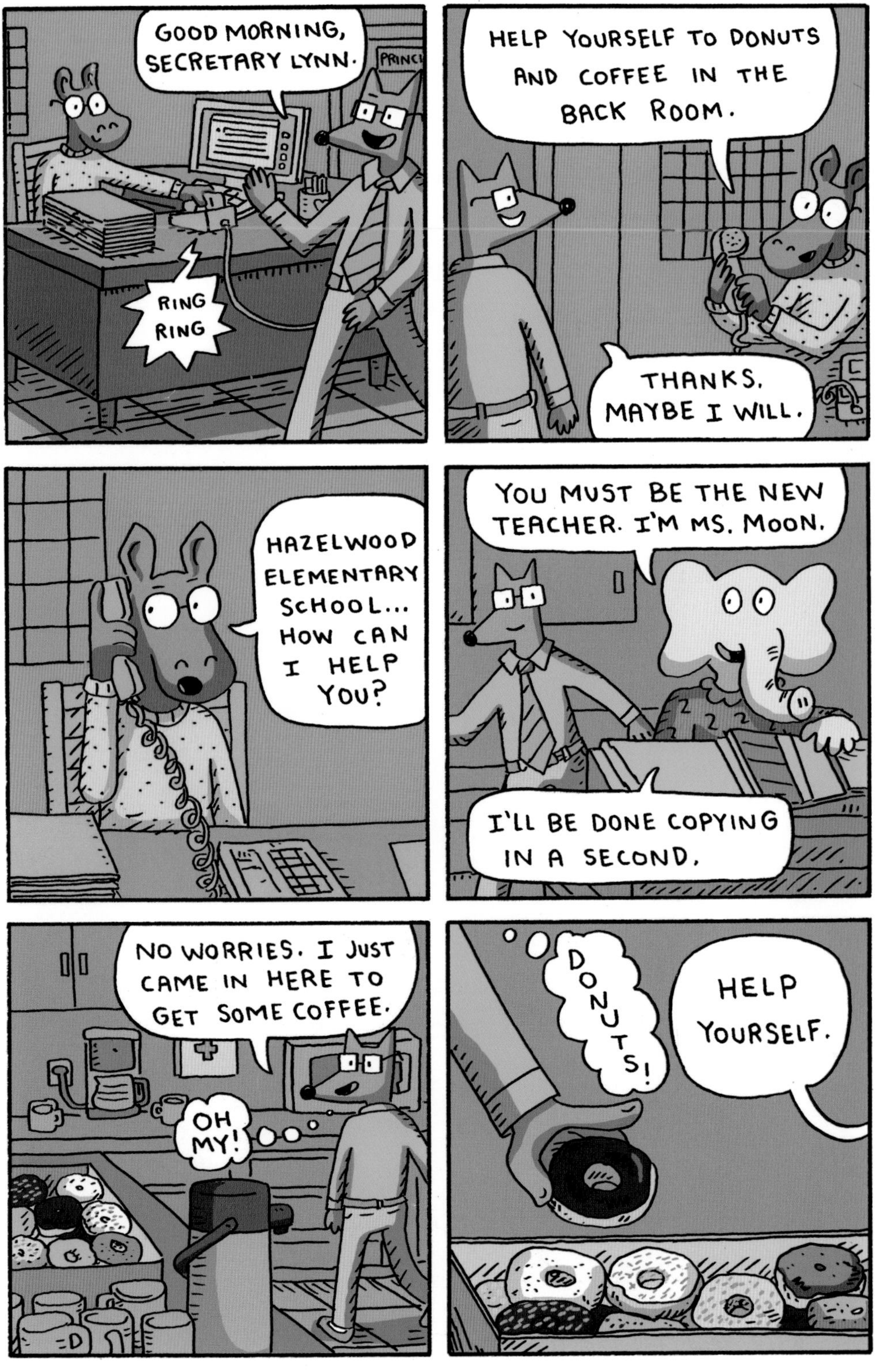
GOOD MORNING, SECRETARY LYNN.
PRINC
RING RING
HELP YOURSELF TO DONUTS AND COFFEE IN THE BACK ROOM.
THANKS. MAYBE I WILL.
HAZELWOOD ELEMENTARY SCHOOL... HOW CAN I HELP YOU?
YOU MUST BE THE NEW TEACHER. I'M MS. MOON.
I'LL BE DONE COPYING IN A SECOND.
NO WORRIES. I JUST CAME IN HERE TO GET SOME COFFEE.
OH MY!
DONUTS!
HELP YOURSELF.

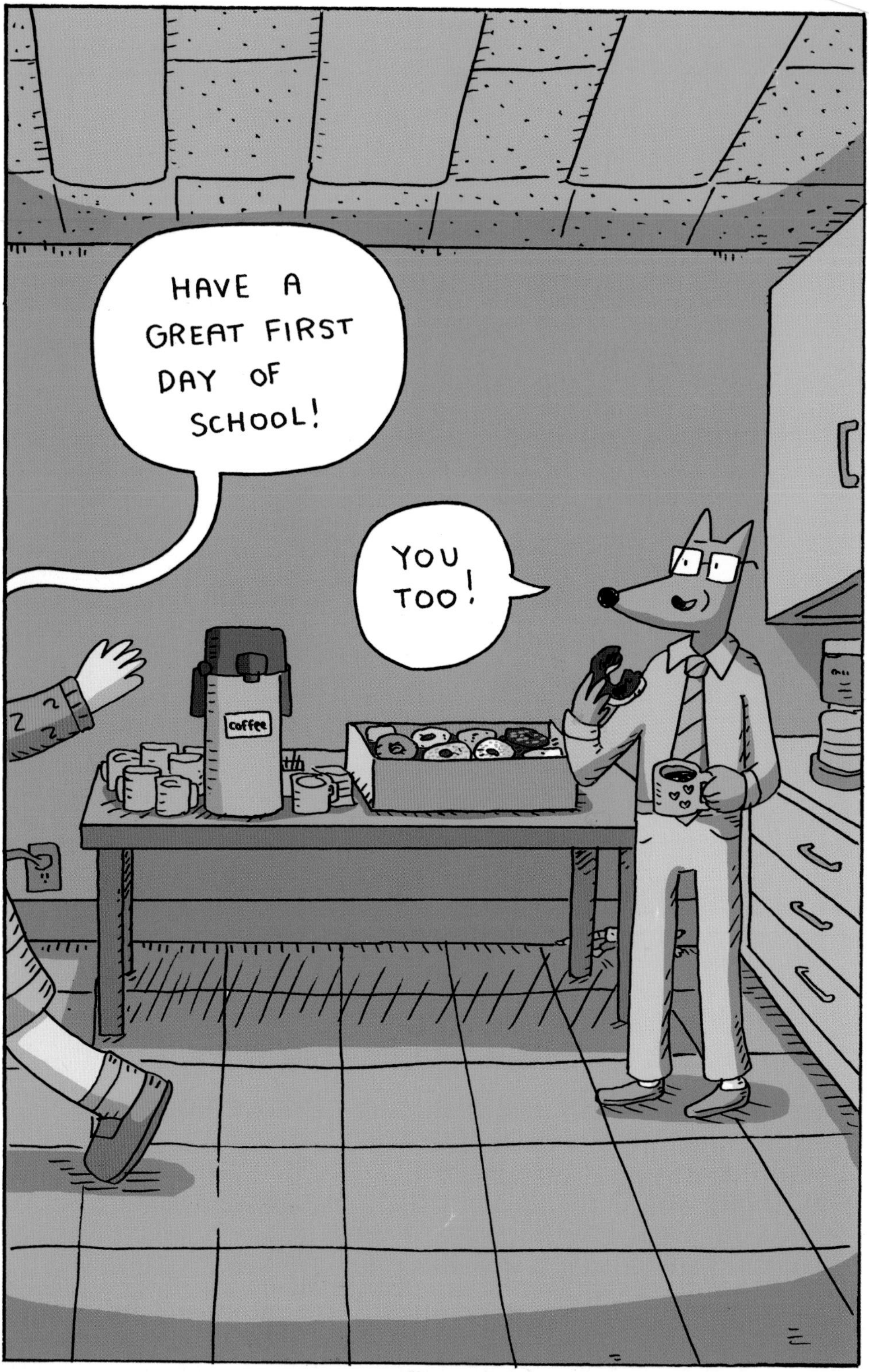
HAVE A GREAT FIRST DAY OF SCHOOL!
YOU TOO!
coffee

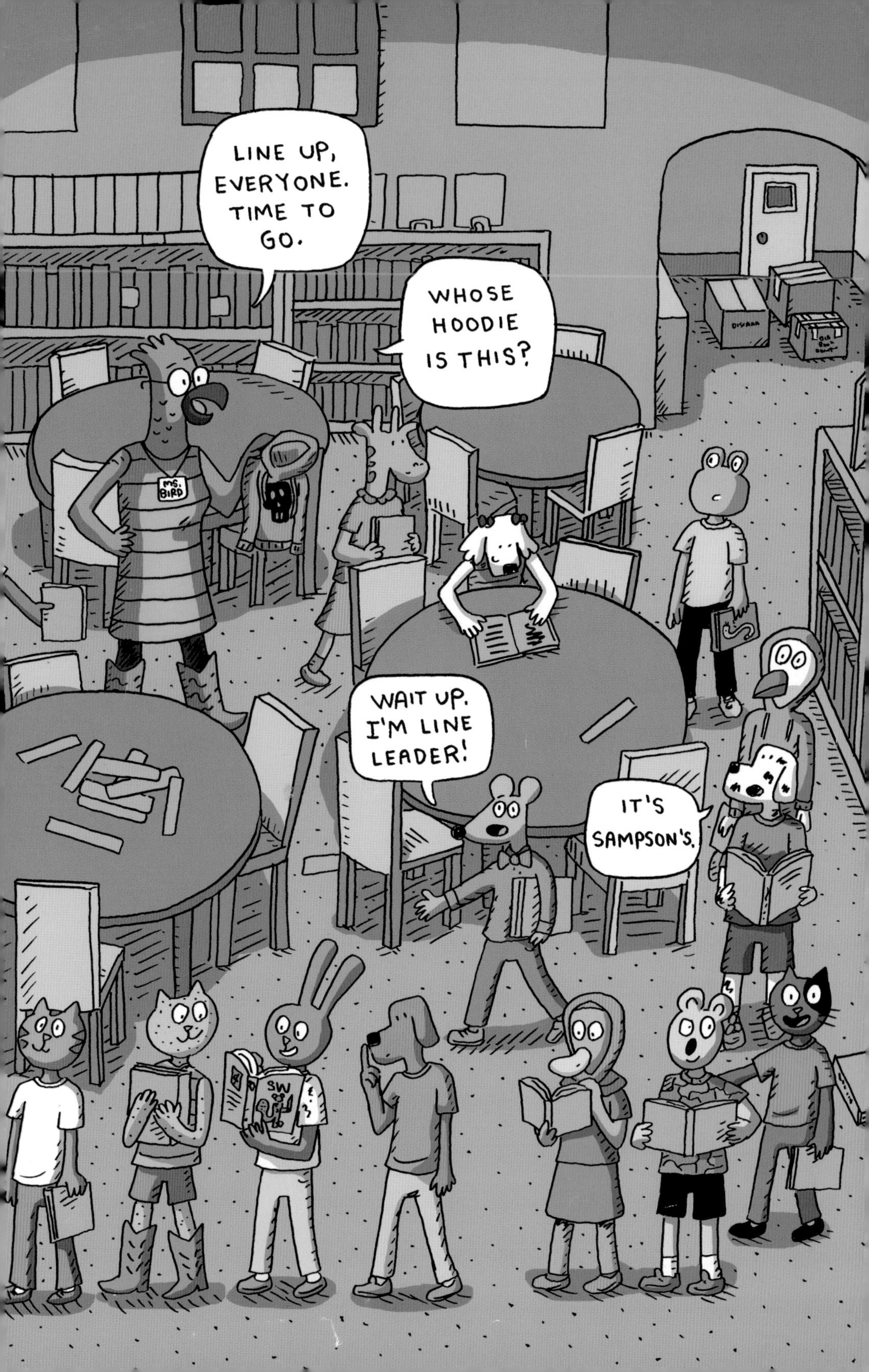
LINE UP, EVERYONE. TIME TO GO.
WHOSE HOODIE IS THIS?
WAIT UP. I'M LINE LEADER!
IT'S SAMPSON'S.

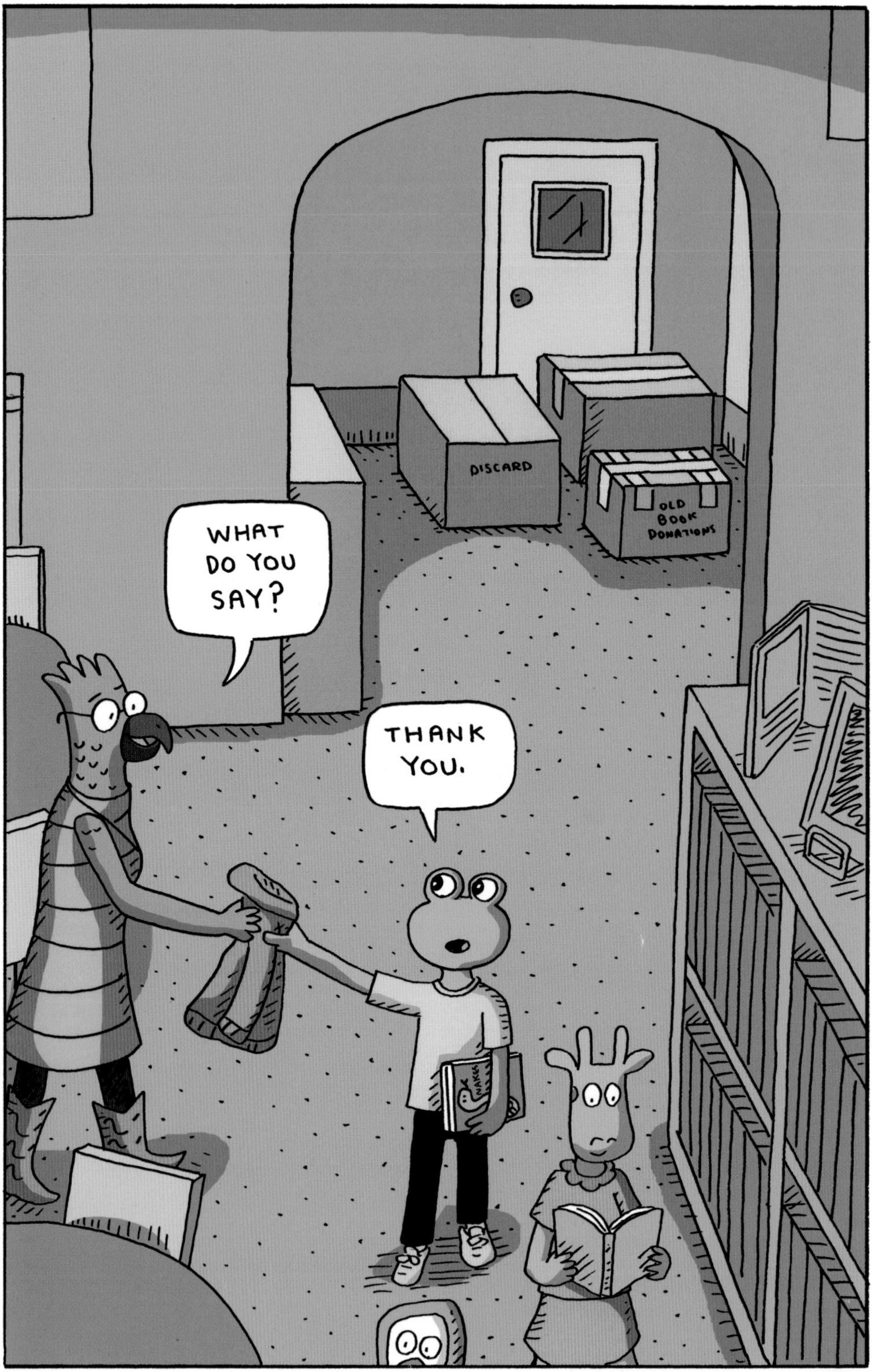
DISCARD
OLD BOOK DONATIONS
WHAT DO YOU SAY?
THANK YOU.

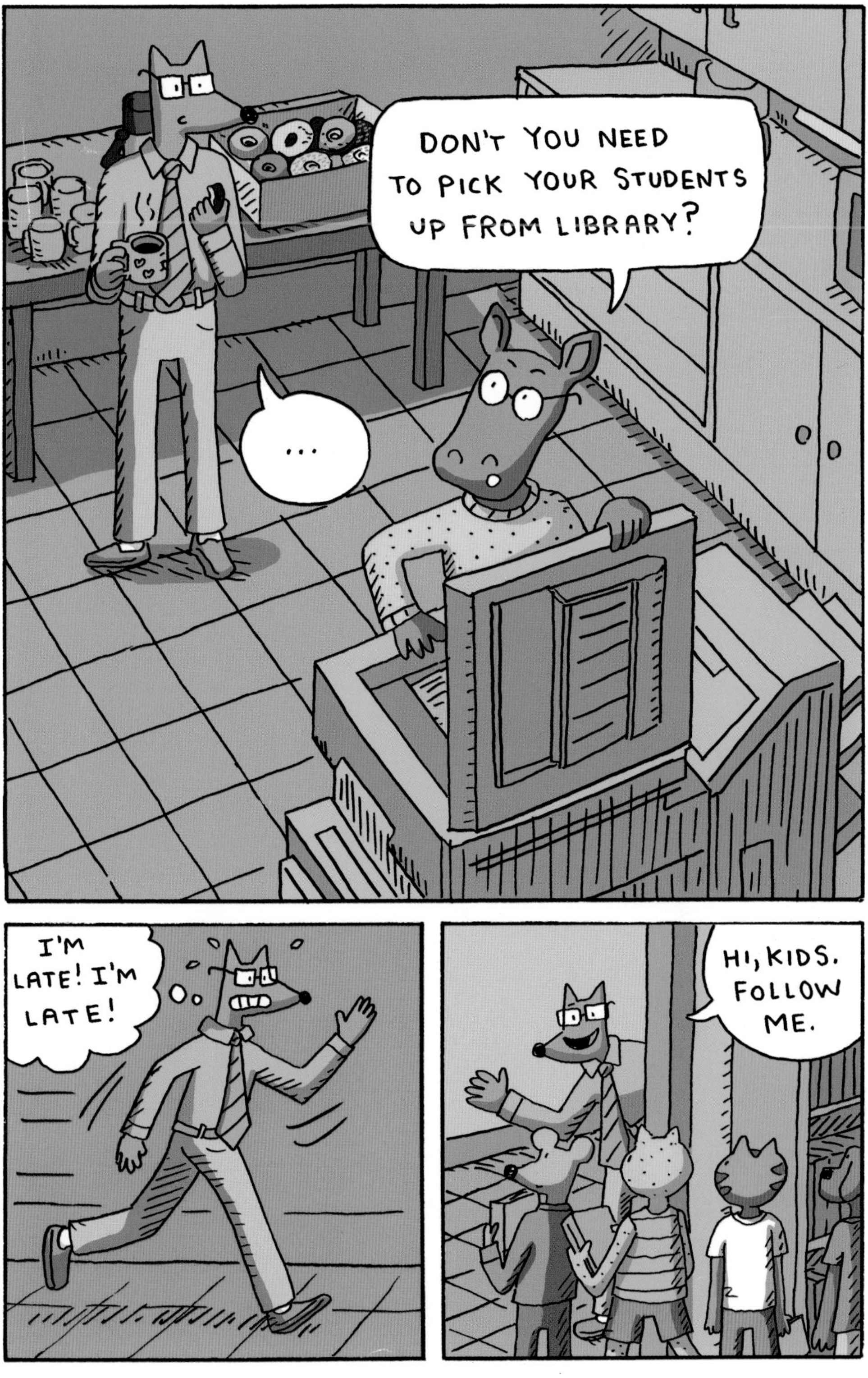
DON'T YOU NEED TO PICK YOUR STUDENTS UP FROM LIBRARY?
...
I'M LATE! I'M LATE!
HI, KIDS. FOLLOW ME.

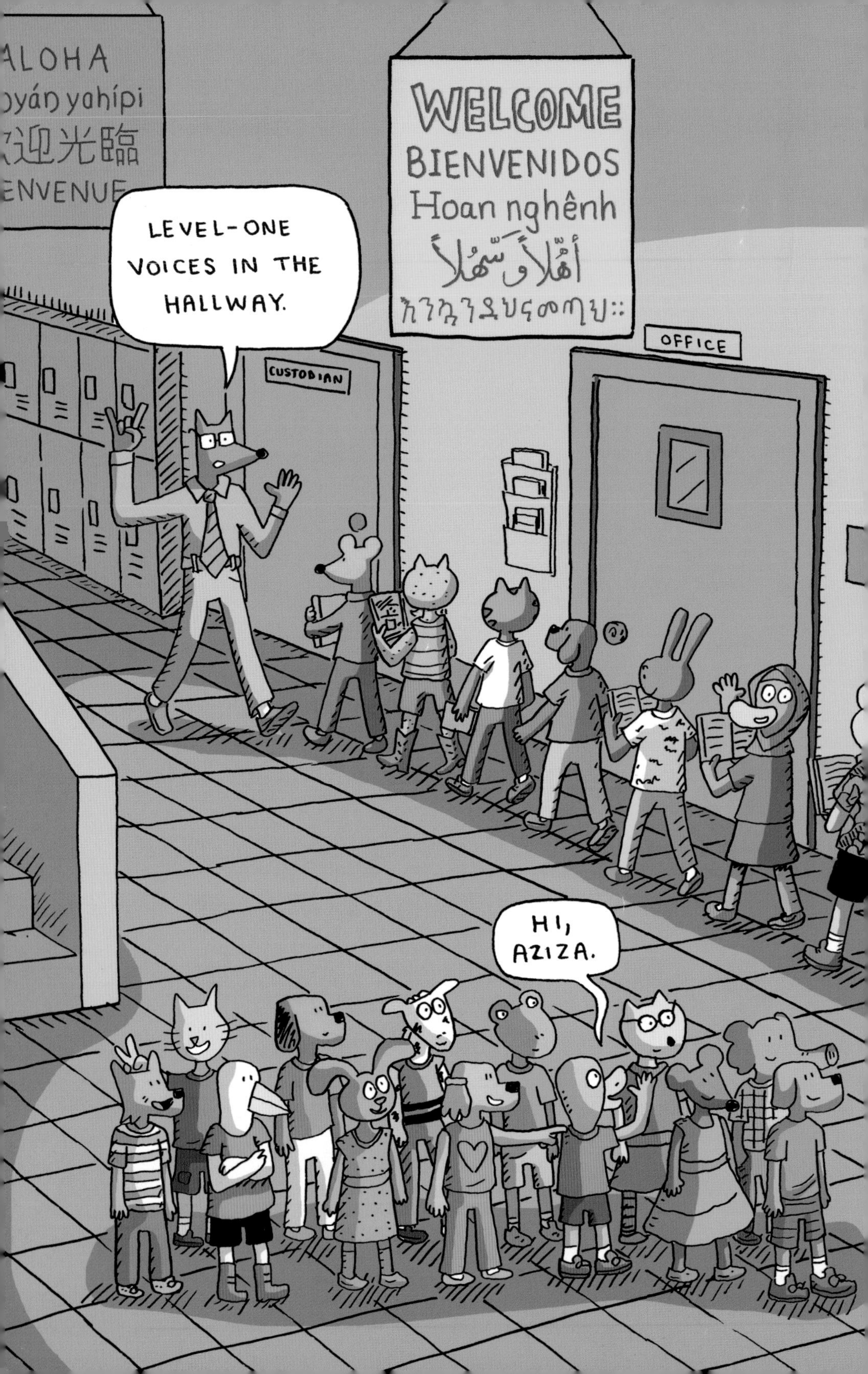
ALOHA
oyán yahípi
歡迎光臨
ENVENUE
WELCOME
BIENVENIDOS
Hoan nghênh
أهلاً وسهلاً
እንኳን ደህና መጣህ።
LEVEL-ONE VOICES IN THE HALLWAY.
CUSTODIAN
OFFICE
HI, AZIZA.

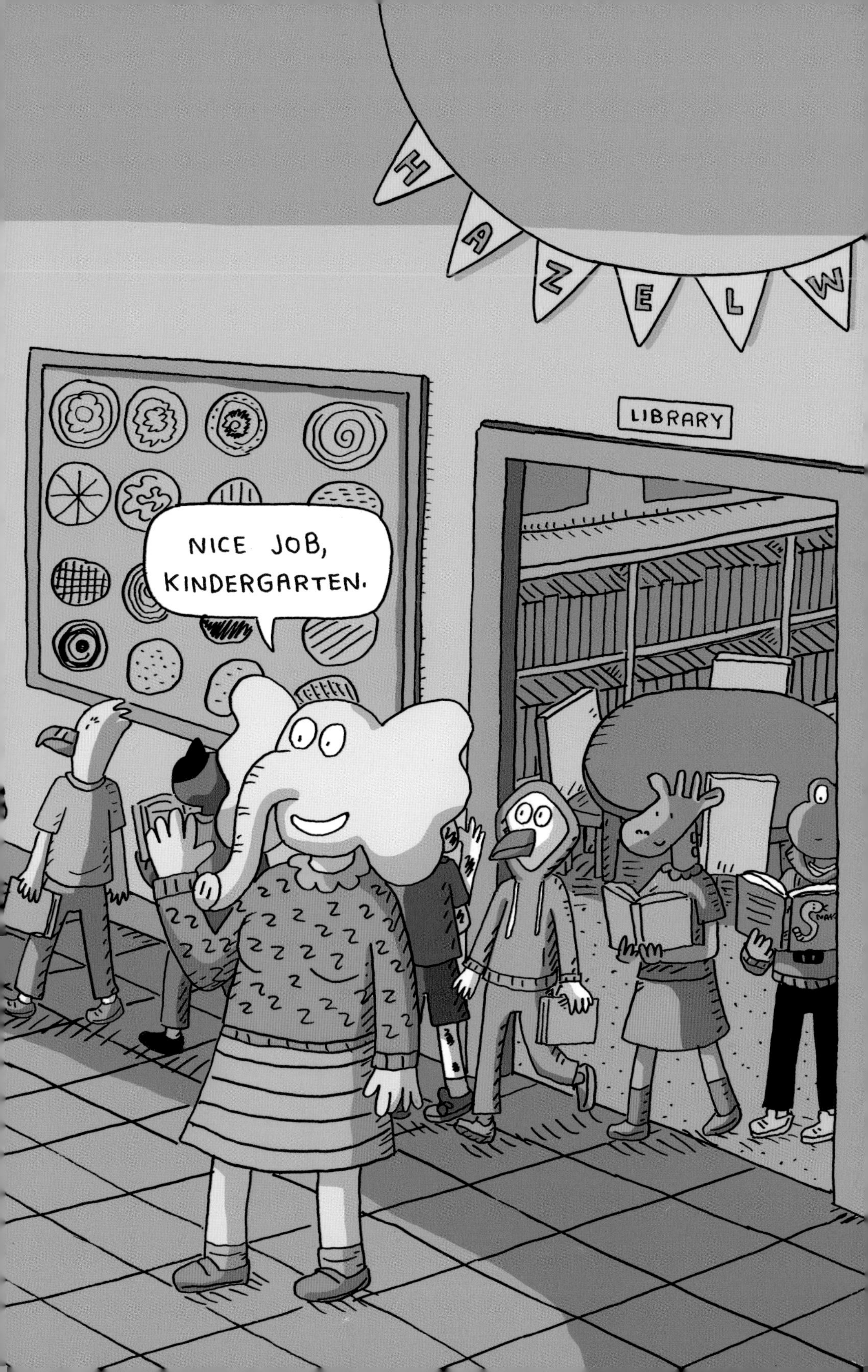
HAZELW
LIBRARY
NICE JOB, KINDERGARTEN.

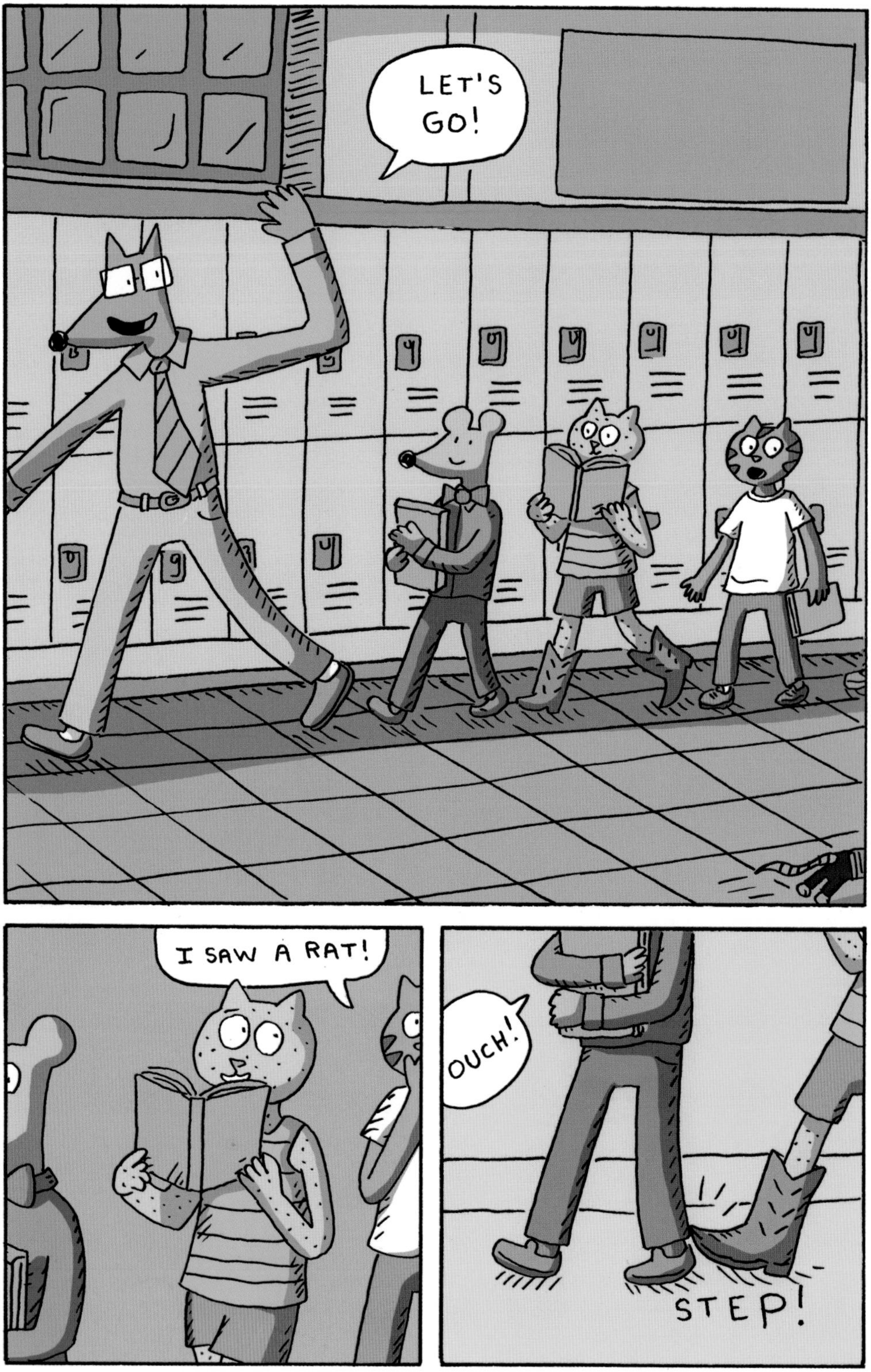
LET'S GO!
I SAW A RAT!
OUCH!
STEP!

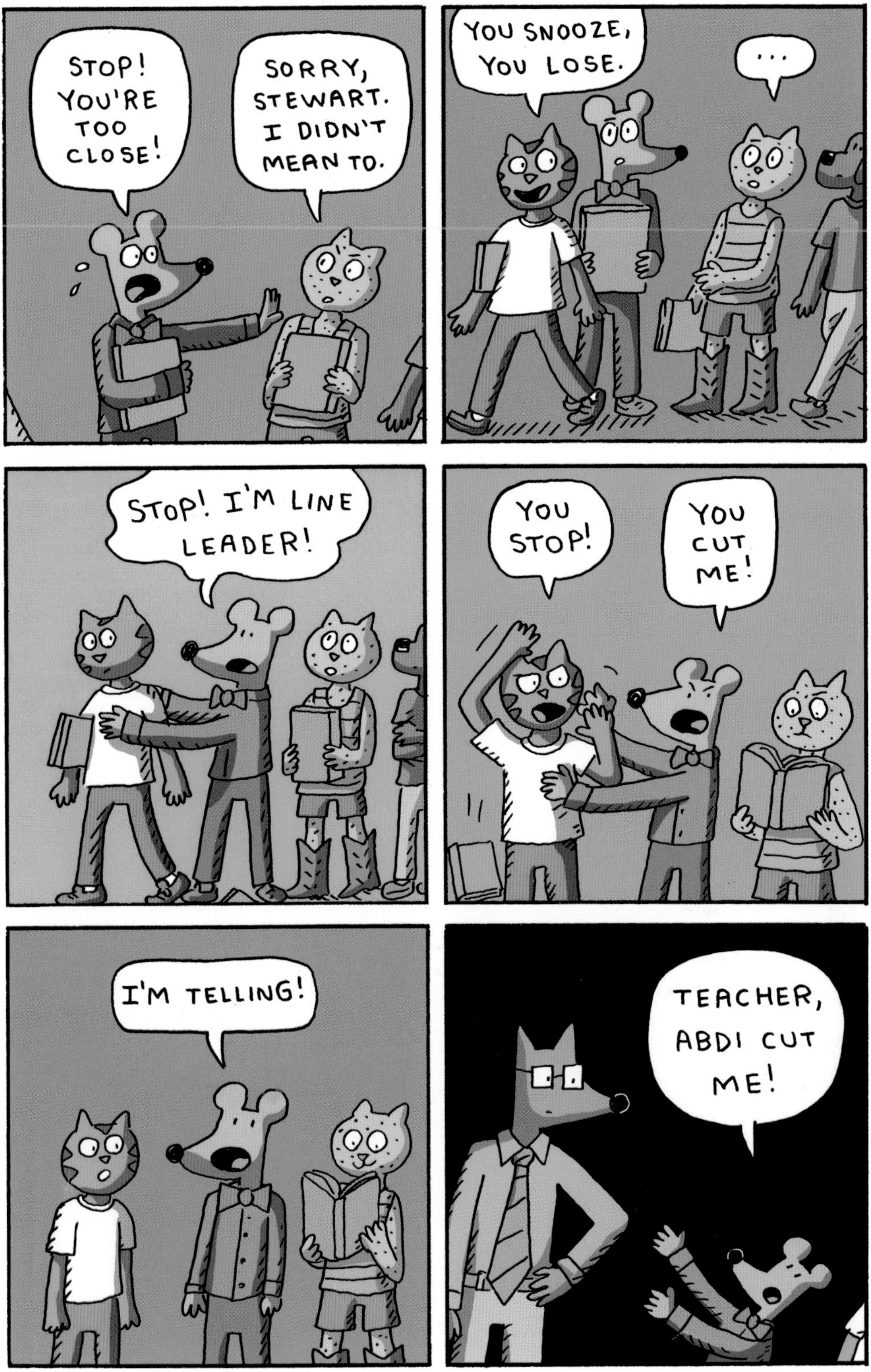
STOP! YOU'RE TOO CLOSE!
SORRY, STEWART. I DIDN'T MEAN TO.
YOU SNOOZE, YOU LOSE.
...
STOP! I'M LINE LEADER!
YOU STOP!
YOU CUT ME!
I'M TELLING!
TEACHER, ABDI CUT ME!

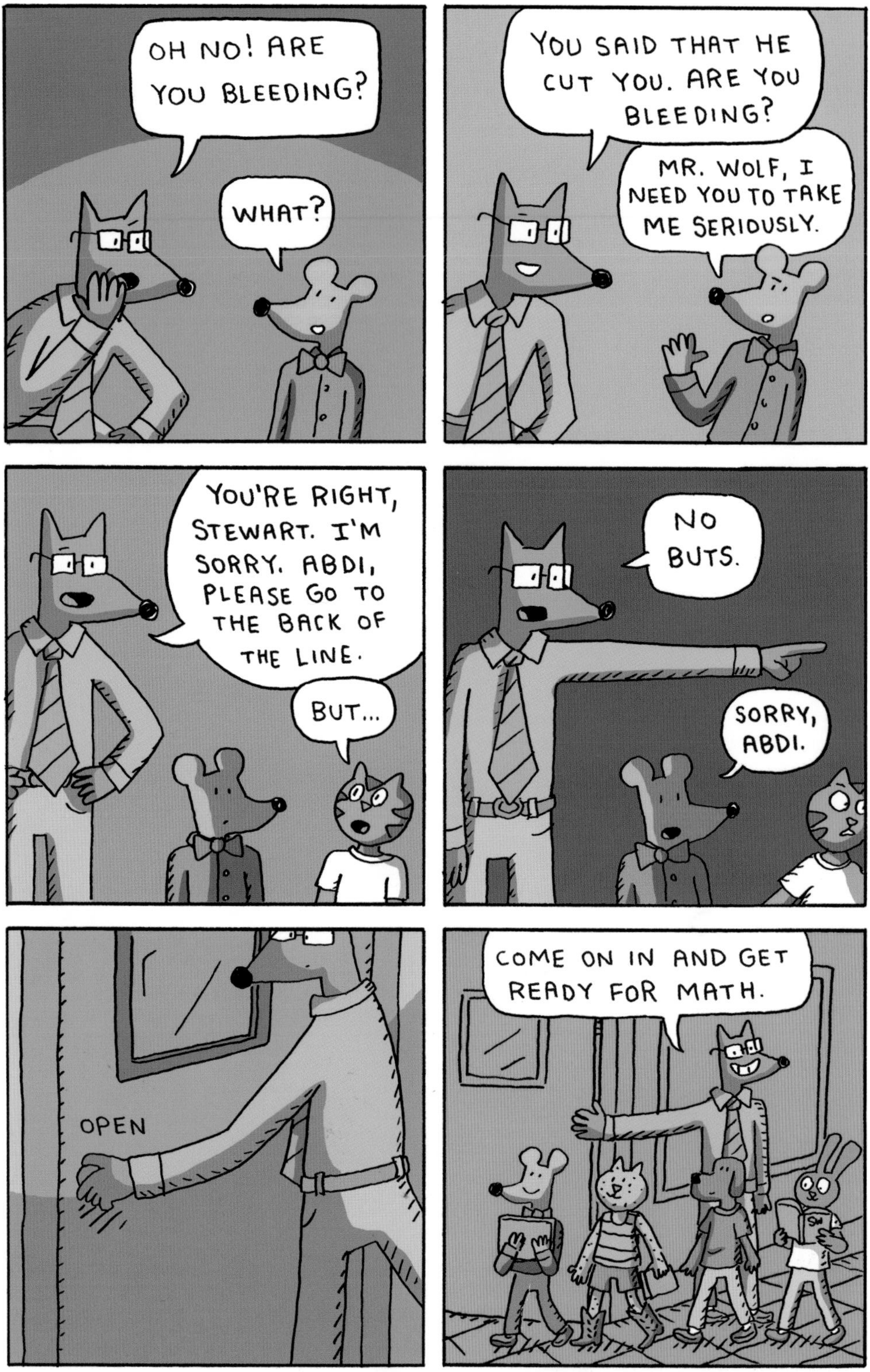
OH NO! ARE YOU BLEEDING?
WHAT?
YOU SAID THAT HE CUT YOU. ARE YOU BLEEDING?
MR. WOLF, I NEED YOU TO TAKE ME SERIOUSLY.
YOU'RE RIGHT, STEWART. I'M SORRY. ABDI, PLEASE GO TO THE BACK OF THE LINE.
BUT...
NO BUTS.
SORRY, ABDI.
OPEN
COME ON IN AND GET READY FOR MATH.

CHAPTER FIVE

Survey Says

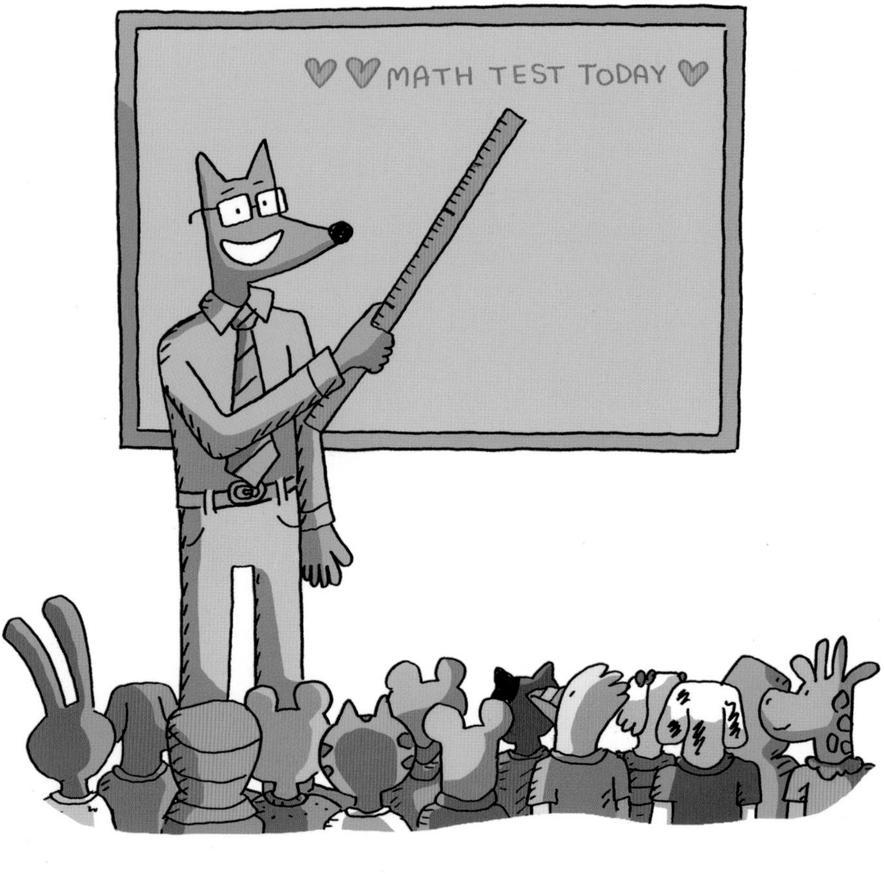
MATH TEST TODAY

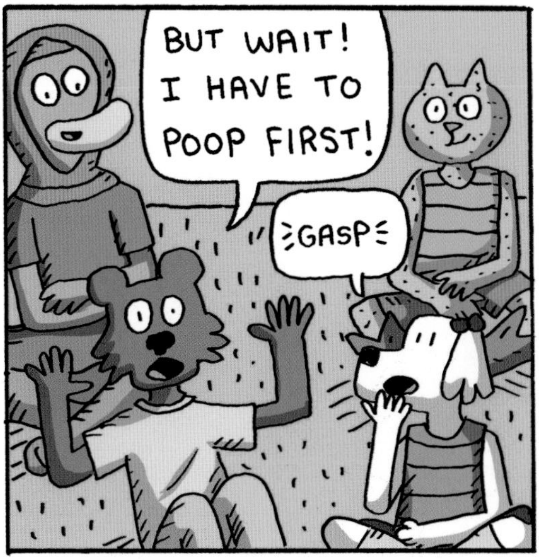
BUT WAIT! I HAVE TO POOP FIRST!
GASP

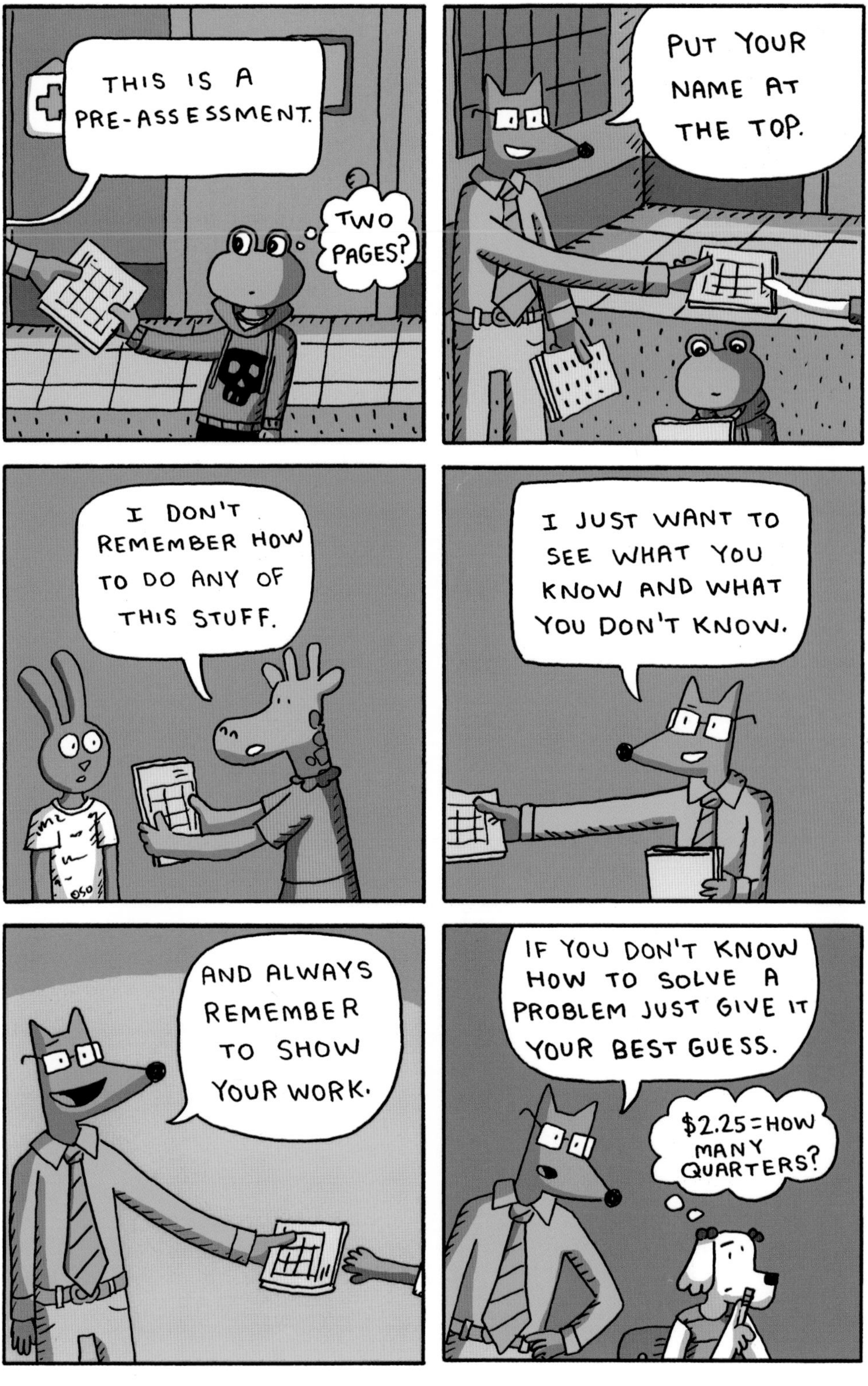
THIS IS A PRE-ASSESSMENT.
TWO PAGES?
PUT YOUR NAME AT THE TOP.
I DON'T REMEMBER HOW TO DO ANY OF THIS STUFF.
I JUST WANT TO SEE WHAT YOU KNOW AND WHAT YOU DON'T KNOW.
AND ALWAYS REMEMBER TO SHOW YOUR WORK.
IF YOU DON'T KNOW HOW TO SOLVE A PROBLEM JUST GIVE IT YOUR BEST GUESS.
$2.25=HOW MANY QUARTERS?

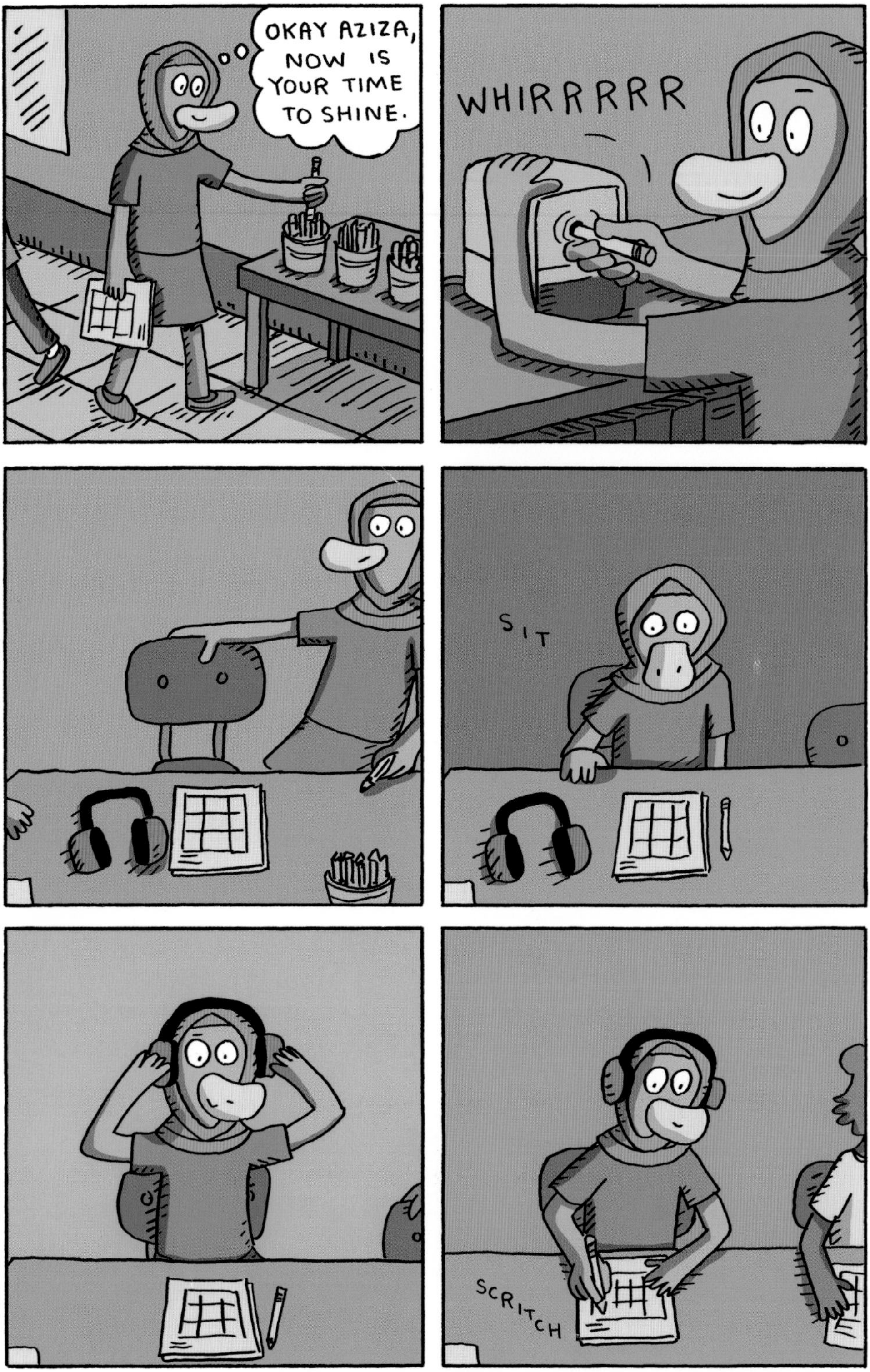
OKAY AZIZA, NOW IS YOUR TIME TO SHINE.
WHIRRRRR
SIT
SCRITCH

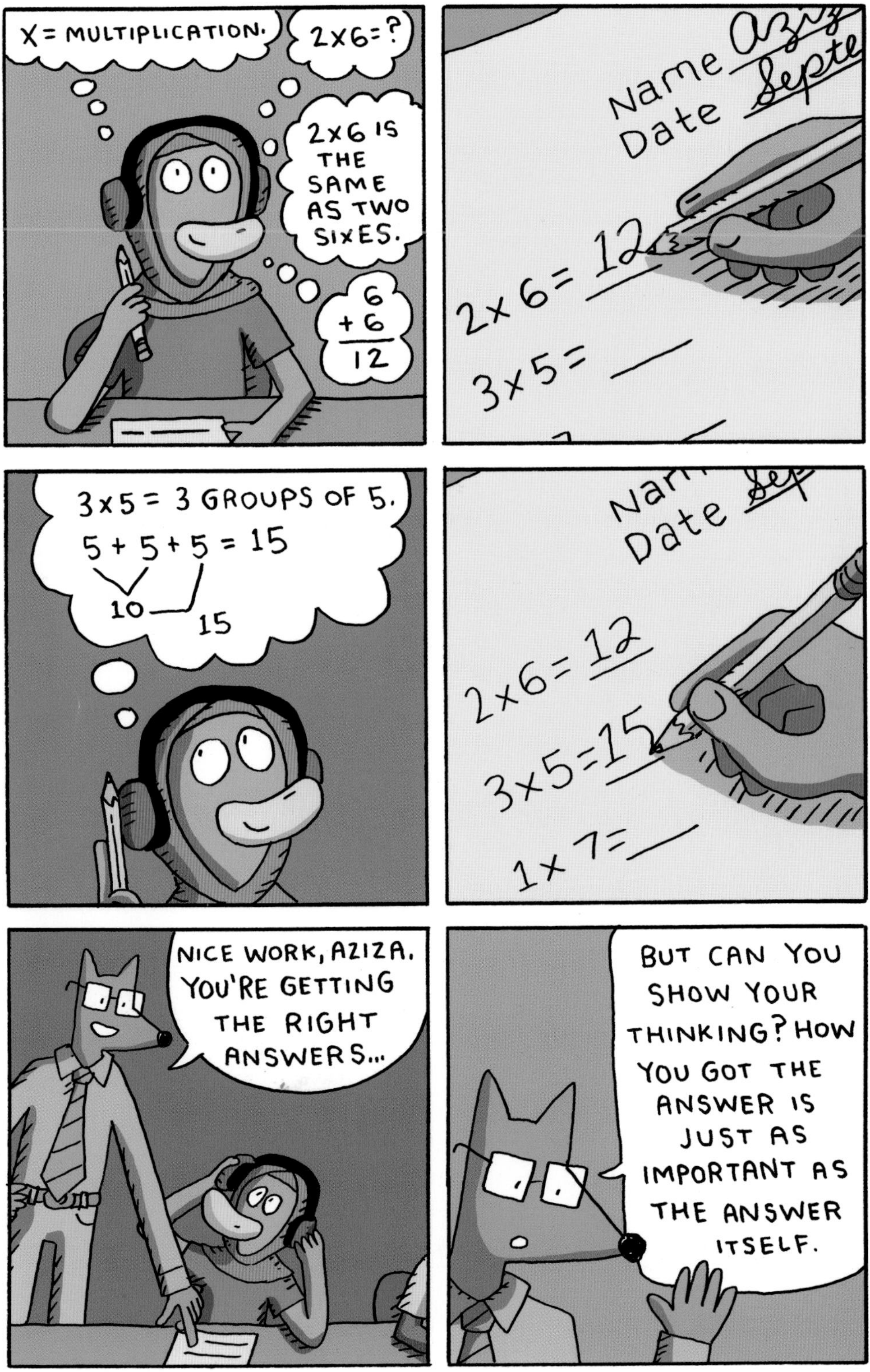
X = MULTIPLICATION.
2X6=?
2X6 IS THE SAME AS TWO SIXES.
6
+6
12
Name Aziz
Date Septe
2x6= 12
3x5=
3x5 = 3 GROUPS OF 5.
5 + 5 + 5 = 15
10
15
Date Sep
2x6= 12
3x5=15
1x7=
NICE WORK, AZIZA. YOU'RE GETTING THE RIGHT ANSWERS...
BUT CAN YOU SHOW YOUR THINKING? HOW YOU GOT THE ANSWER IS JUST AS IMPORTANT AS THE ANSWER ITSELF.

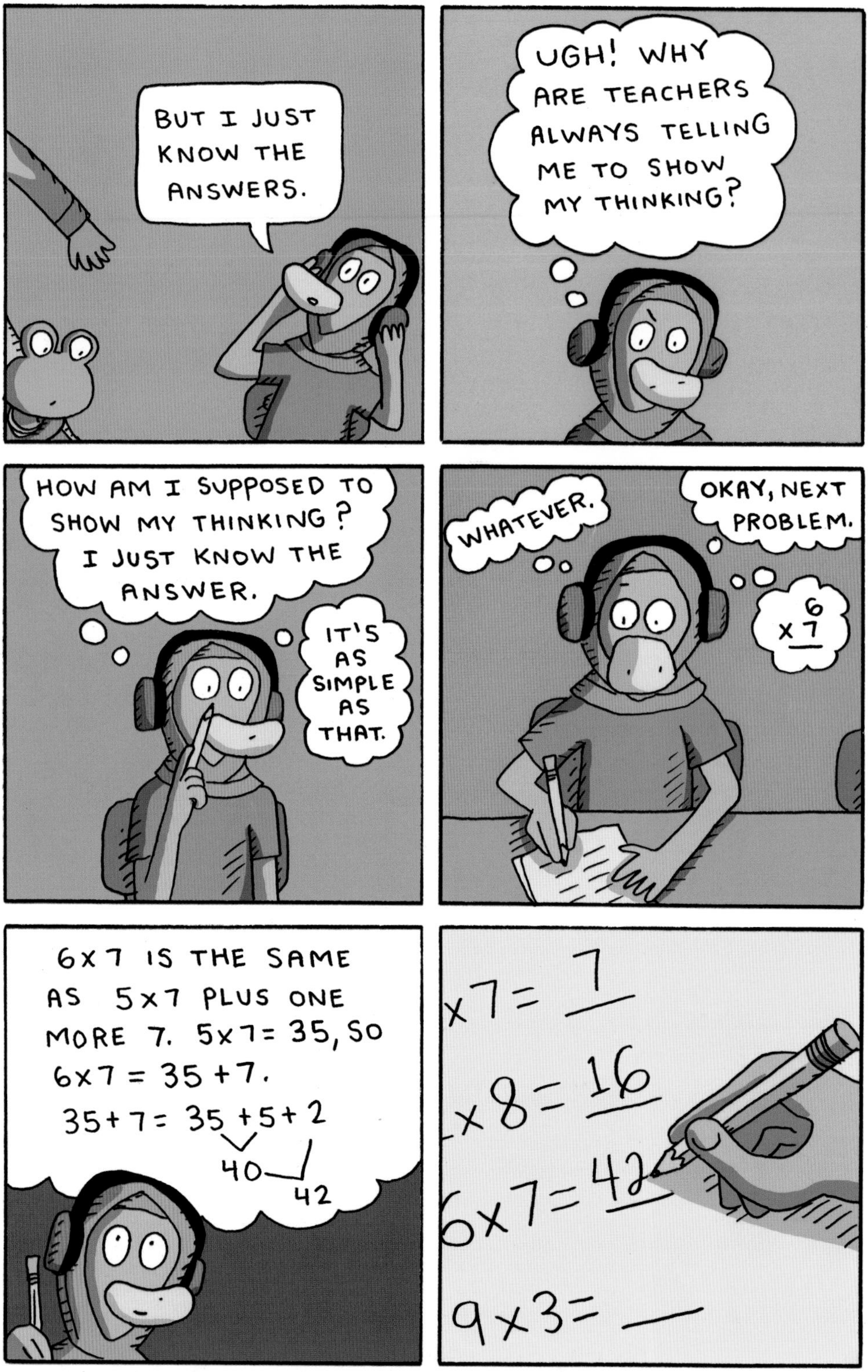
BUT I JUST KNOW THE ANSWERS.
UGH! WHY ARE TEACHERS ALWAYS TELLING ME TO SHOW MY THINKING?
HOW AM I SUPPOSED TO SHOW MY THINKING? I JUST KNOW THE ANSWER.
IT'S AS SIMPLE AS THAT.
WHATEVER.
OKAY, NEXT PROBLEM.
6
x 7
6x7 IS THE SAME AS 5x7 PLUS ONE MORE 7. 5x7 = 35, SO 6x7 = 35 + 7.
35+7 = 35 +5+ 2
40
42
x7= 7
x8= 16
6x7= 42
9x3=

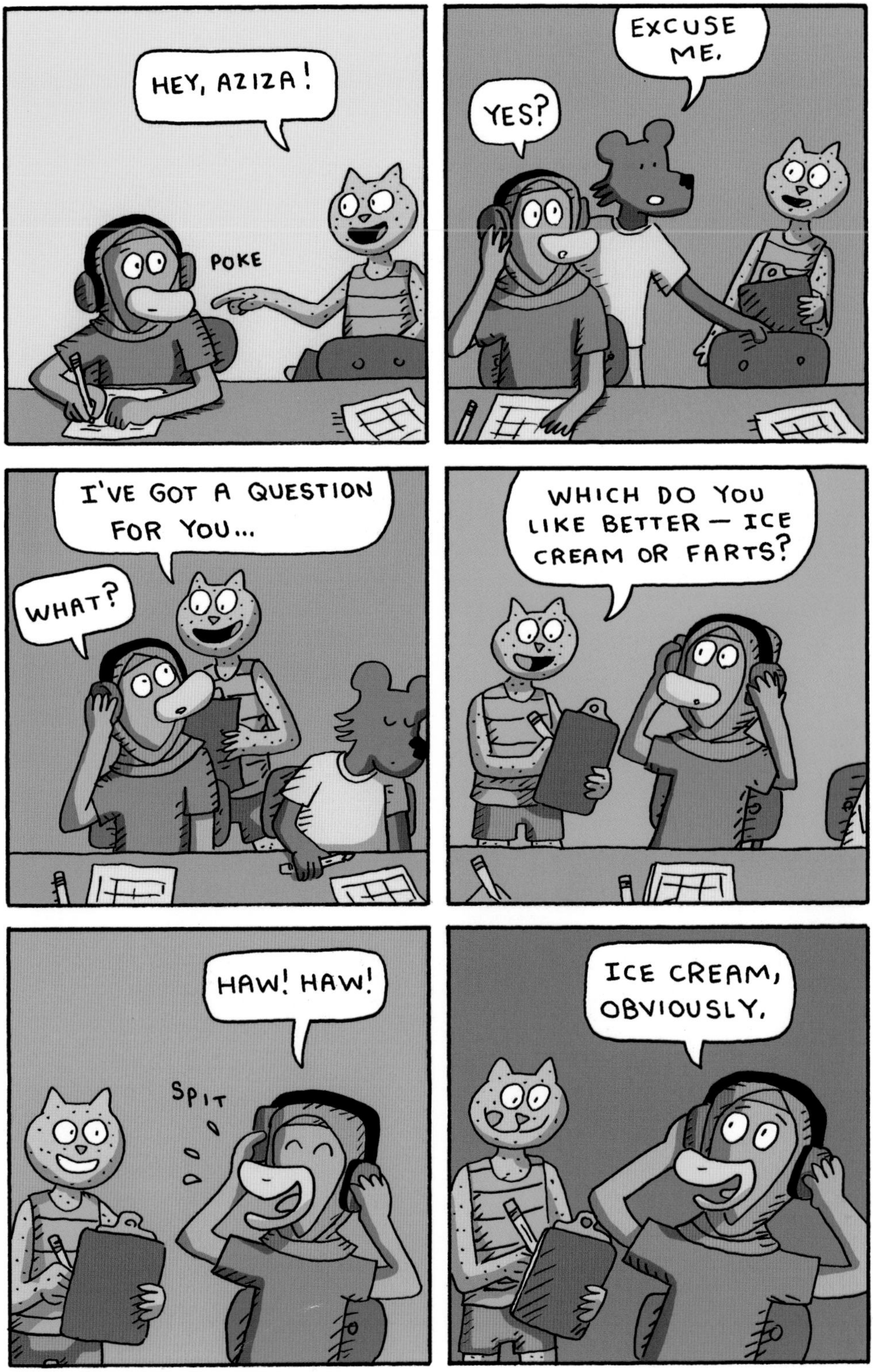
HEY, AZIZA!
POKE
EXCUSE ME.
YES?
I'VE GOT A QUESTION FOR YOU...
WHAT?
WHICH DO YOU LIKE BETTER — ICE CREAM OR FARTS?
HAW! HAW!
SPIT
ICE CREAM, OBVIOUSLY.

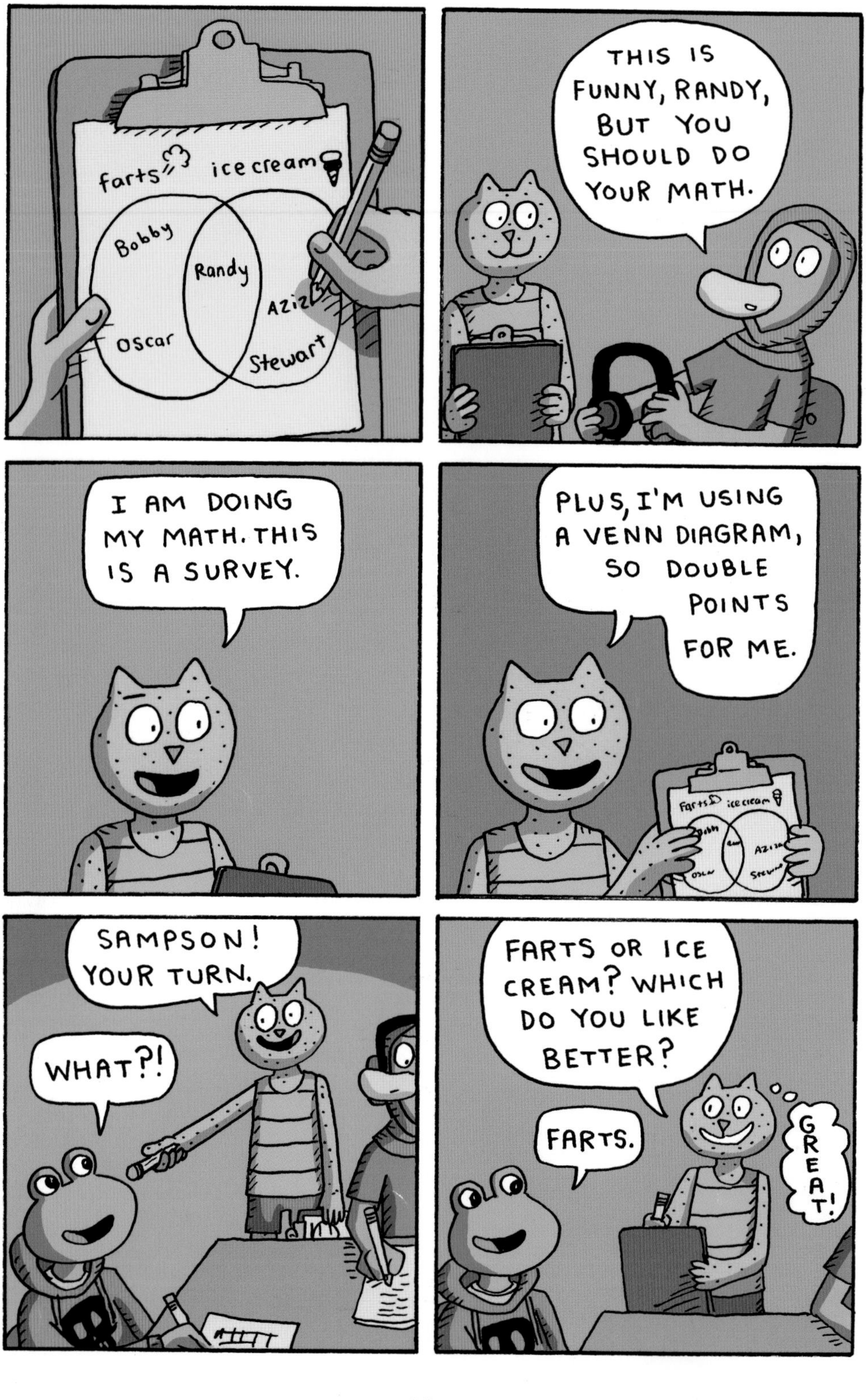
farts
ice cream
Bobby
Randy
Aziz
Oscar
Stewart
THIS IS FUNNY, RANDY, BUT YOU SHOULD DO YOUR MATH.
I AM DOING MY MATH. THIS IS A SURVEY.
PLUS, I'M USING A VENN DIAGRAM, SO DOUBLE POINTS FOR ME.
SAMPSON! YOUR TURN.
WHAT?!
FARTS OR ICE CREAM? WHICH DO YOU LIKE BETTER?
FARTS.
GREAT!

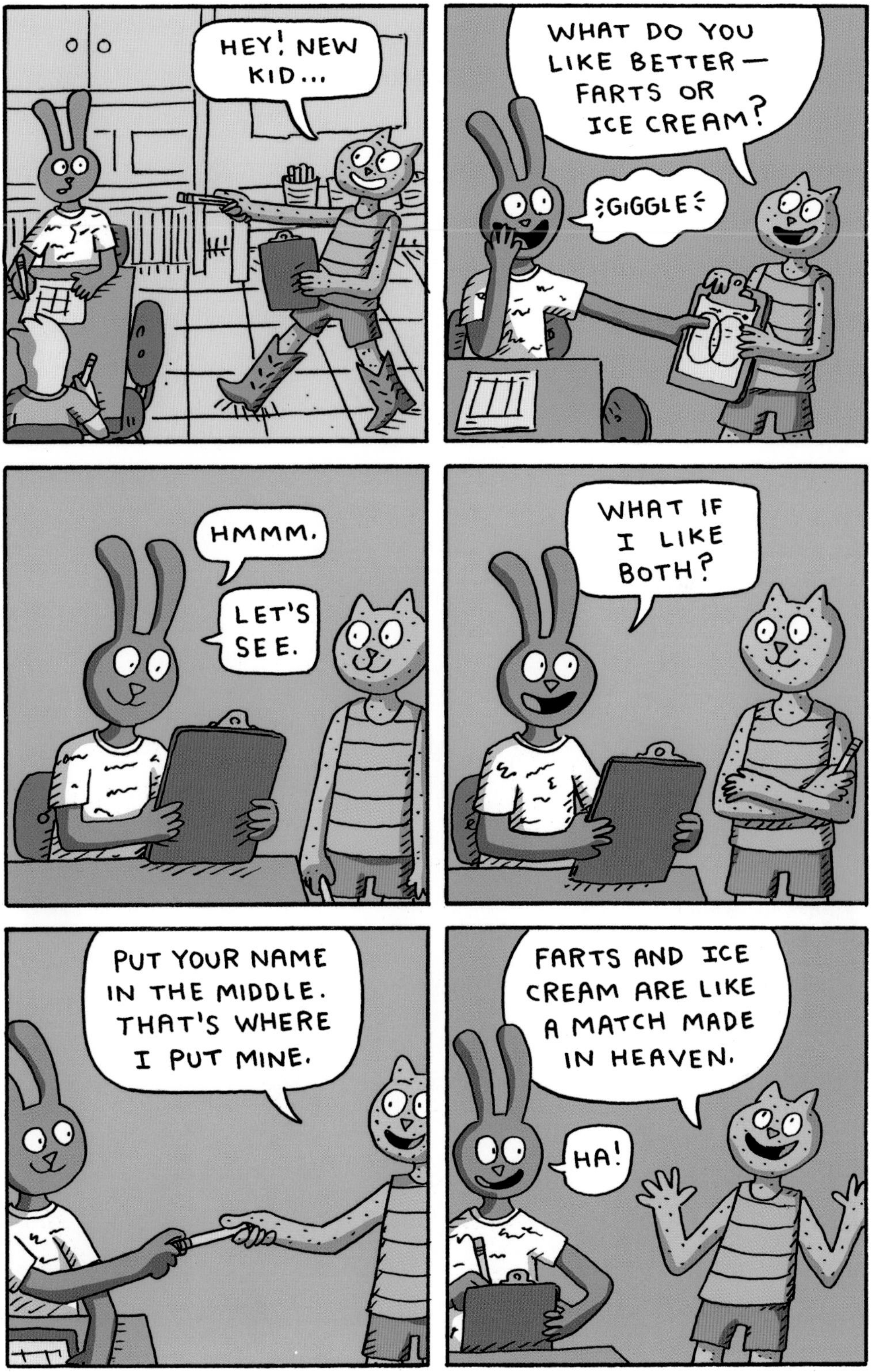
HEY! NEW KID...
WHAT DO YOU LIKE BETTER— FARTS OR ICE CREAM?
GIGGLE
HMMM.
LET'S SEE.
WHAT IF I LIKE BOTH?
PUT YOUR NAME IN THE MIDDLE. THAT'S WHERE I PUT MINE.
FARTS AND ICE CREAM ARE LIKE A MATCH MADE IN HEAVEN.
HA!

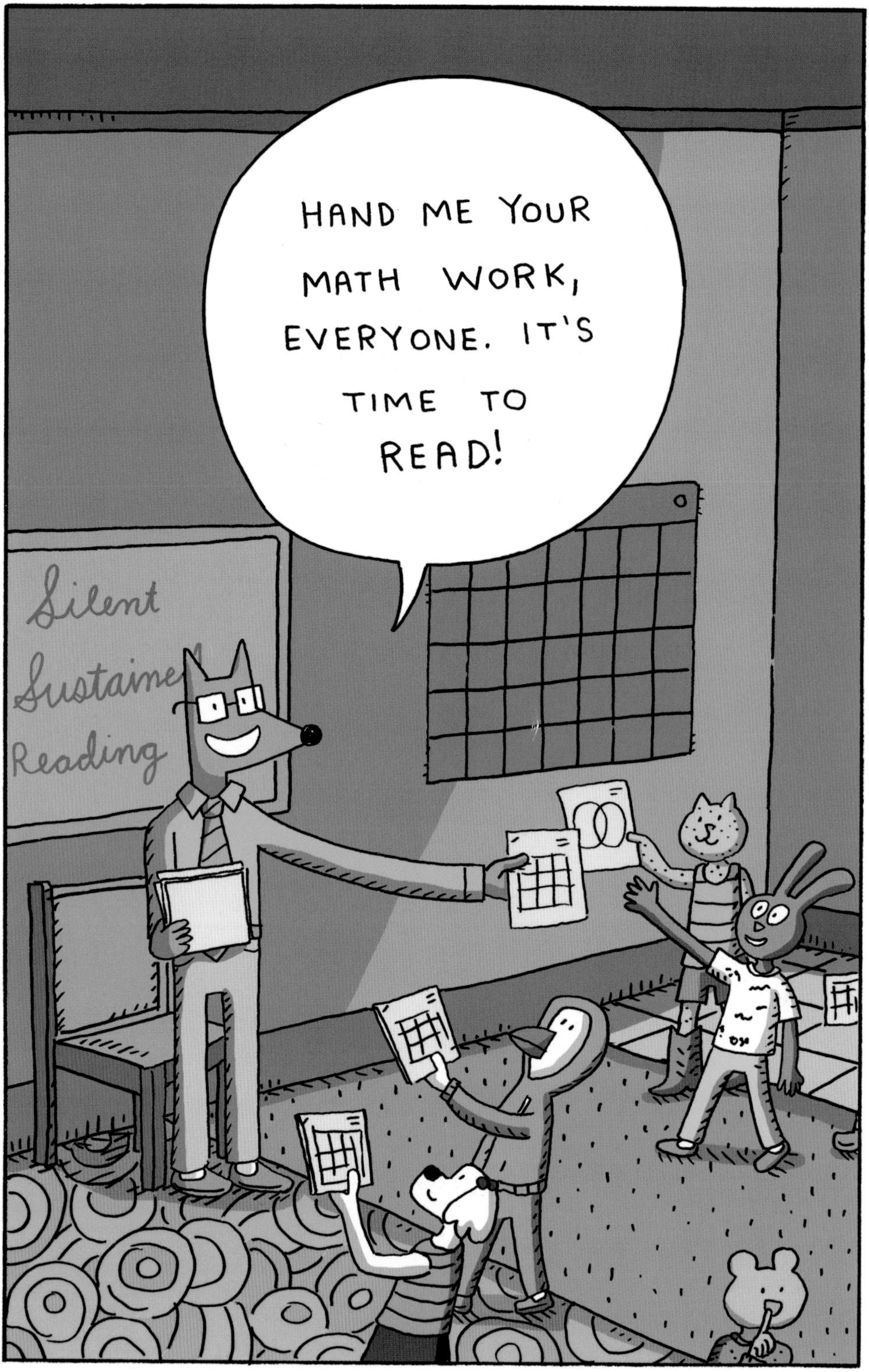
HAND ME YOUR MATH WORK, EVERYONE. IT'S TIME TO READ!
Silent Sustained Reading

CHAPTER SIX
Someone Is Missing

DISCARD
OLD BOOK DONATIONS

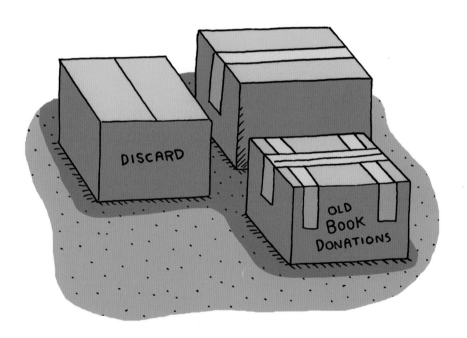

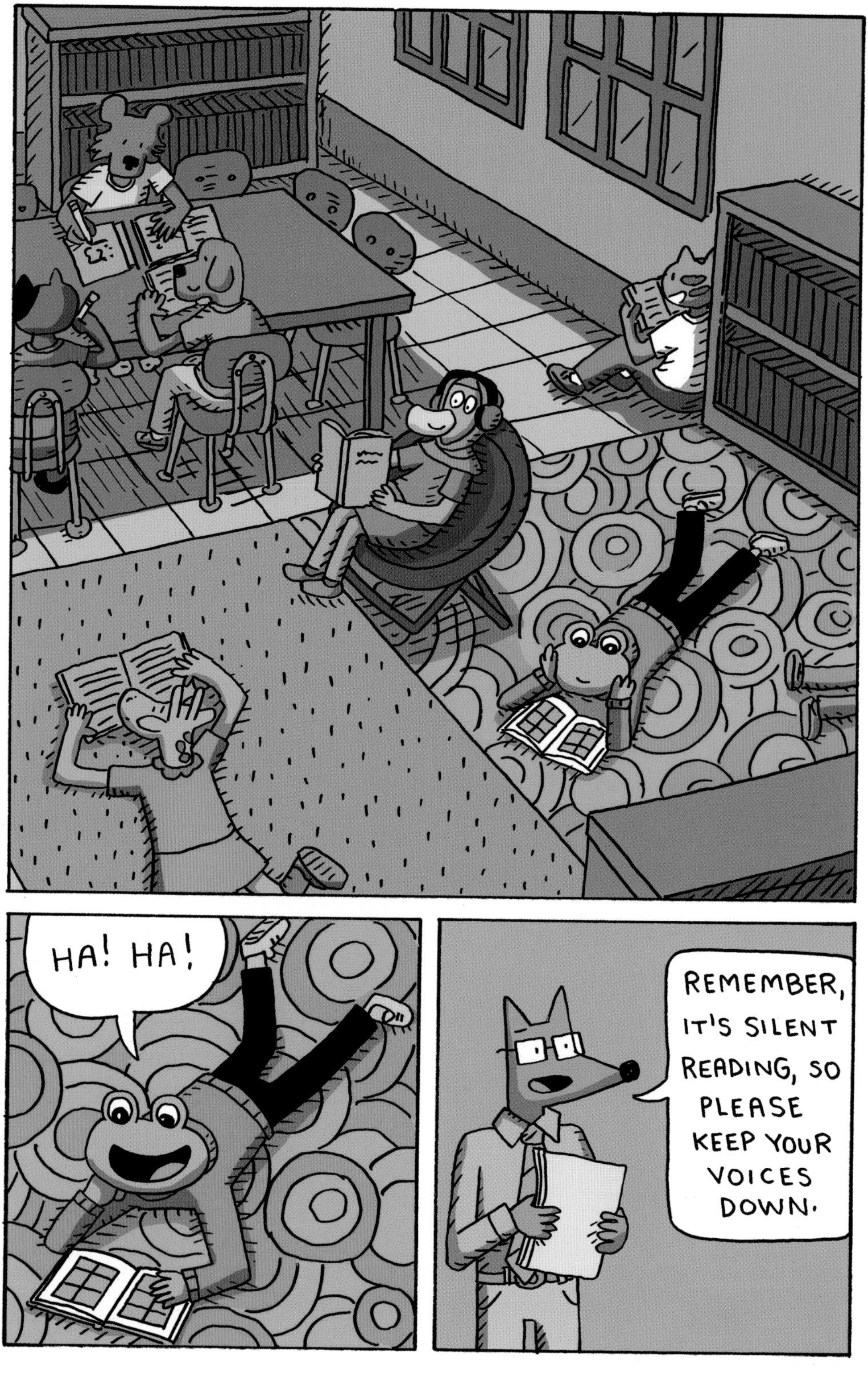
HA! HA!
REMEMBER, IT'S SILENT READING, SO PLEASE KEEP YOUR VOICES DOWN.

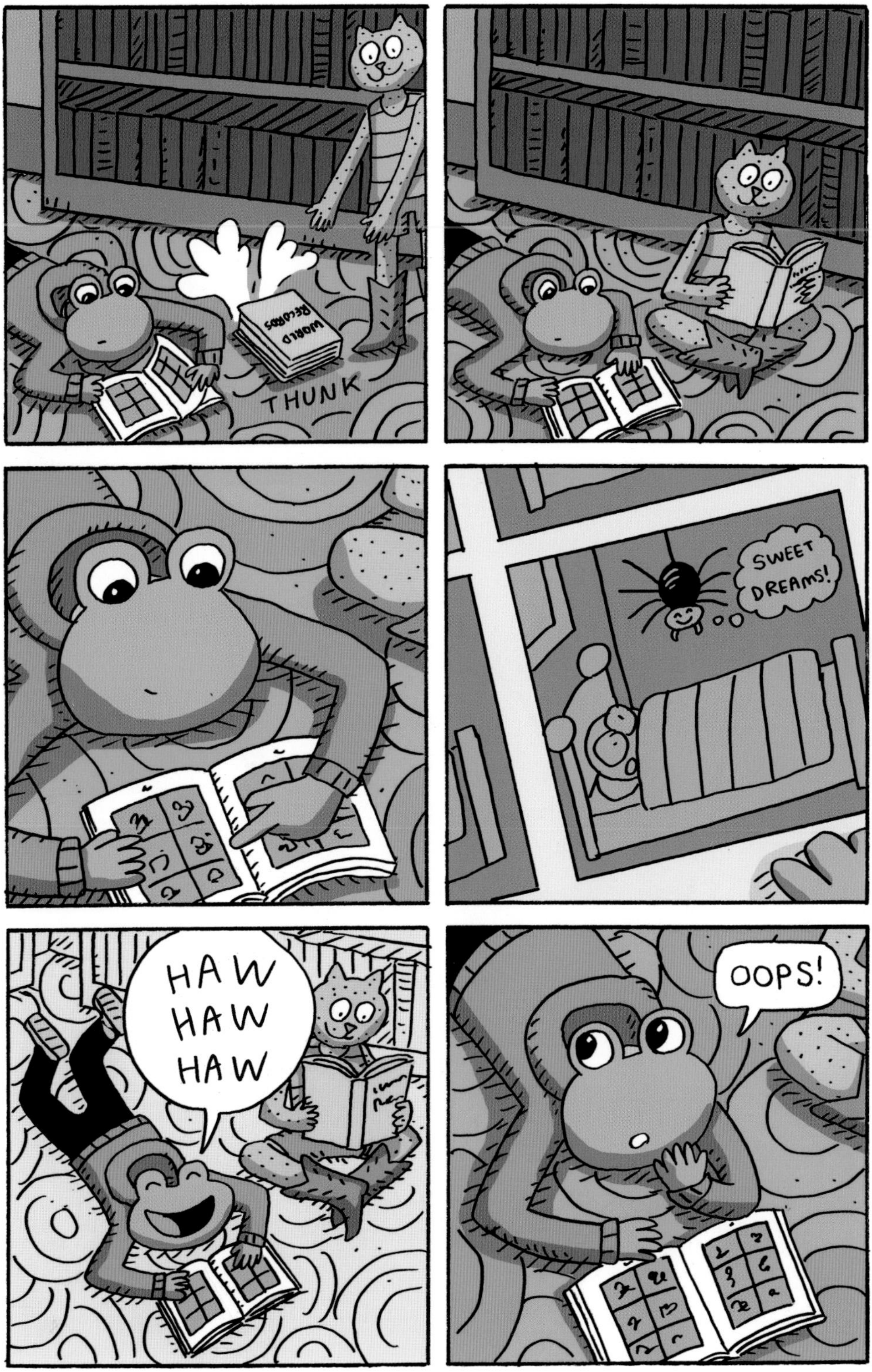
WORLD RECORDS
THUNK
SWEET DREAMS!
HAW
HAW
HAW
OOPS!

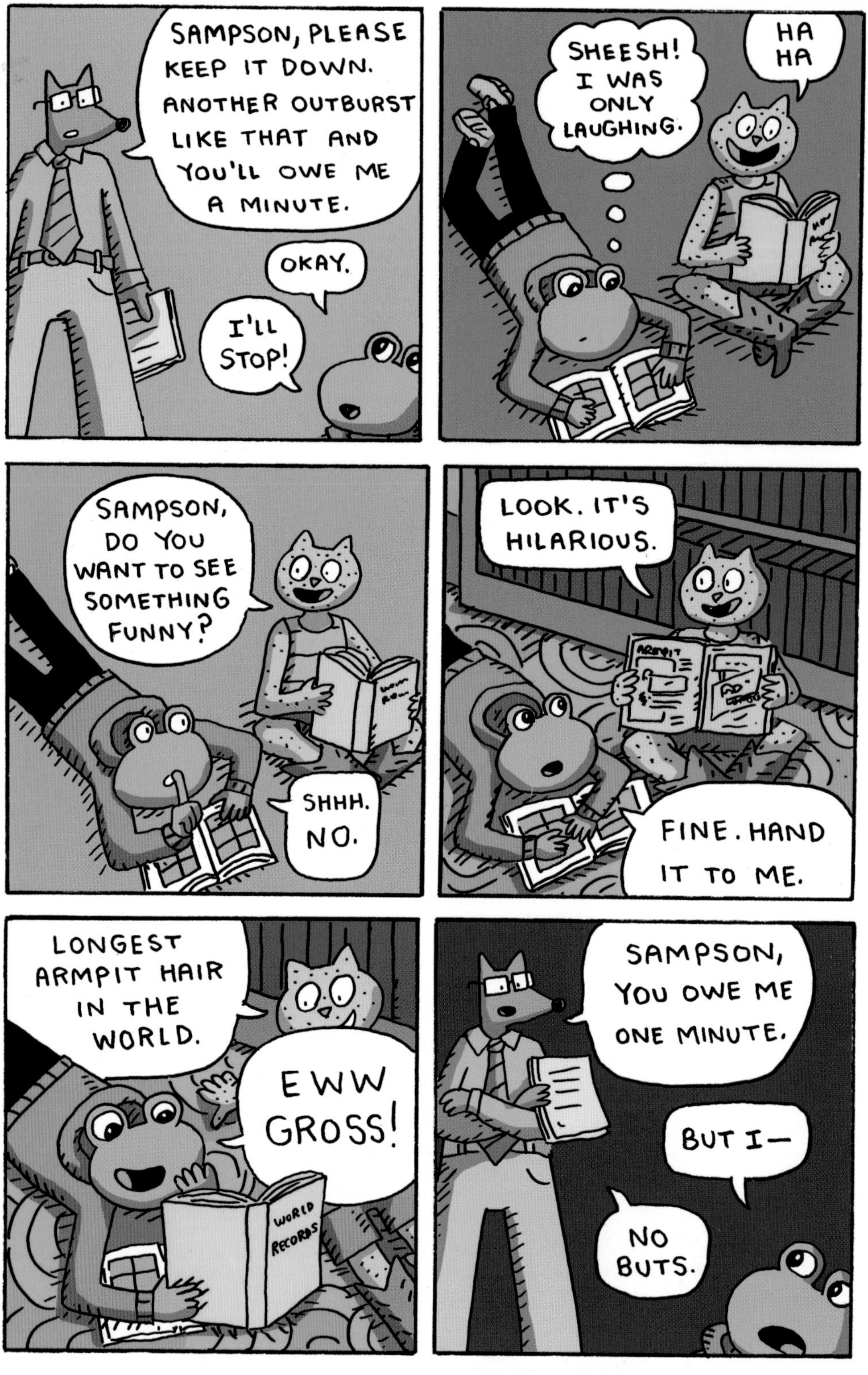
SAMPSON, PLEASE KEEP IT DOWN. ANOTHER OUTBURST LIKE THAT AND YOU'LL OWE ME A MINUTE.
OKAY.
I'LL STOP!
SHEESH! I WAS ONLY LAUGHING.
HA HA
SAMPSON, DO YOU WANT TO SEE SOMETHING FUNNY?
SHHH. NO.
LOOK. IT'S HILARIOUS.
ARMPIT
FINE. HAND IT TO ME.
LONGEST ARMPIT HAIR IN THE WORLD.
EWW GROSS!
WORLD RECORDS
SAMPSON, YOU OWE ME ONE MINUTE.
BUT I—
NO BUTS.

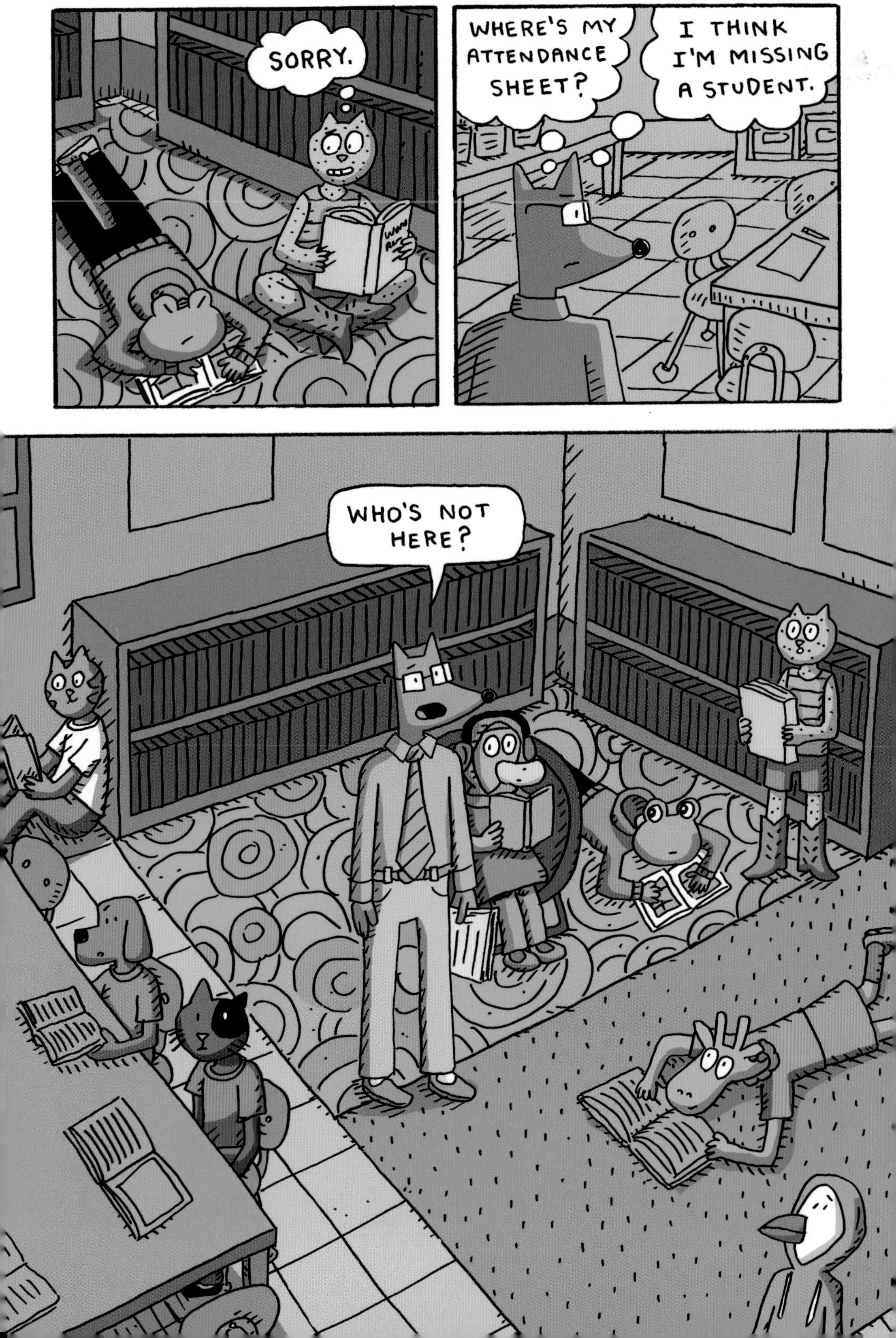
SORRY.
WHERE'S MY ATTENDANCE SHEET?
I THINK I'M MISSING A STUDENT.
WHO'S NOT HERE?

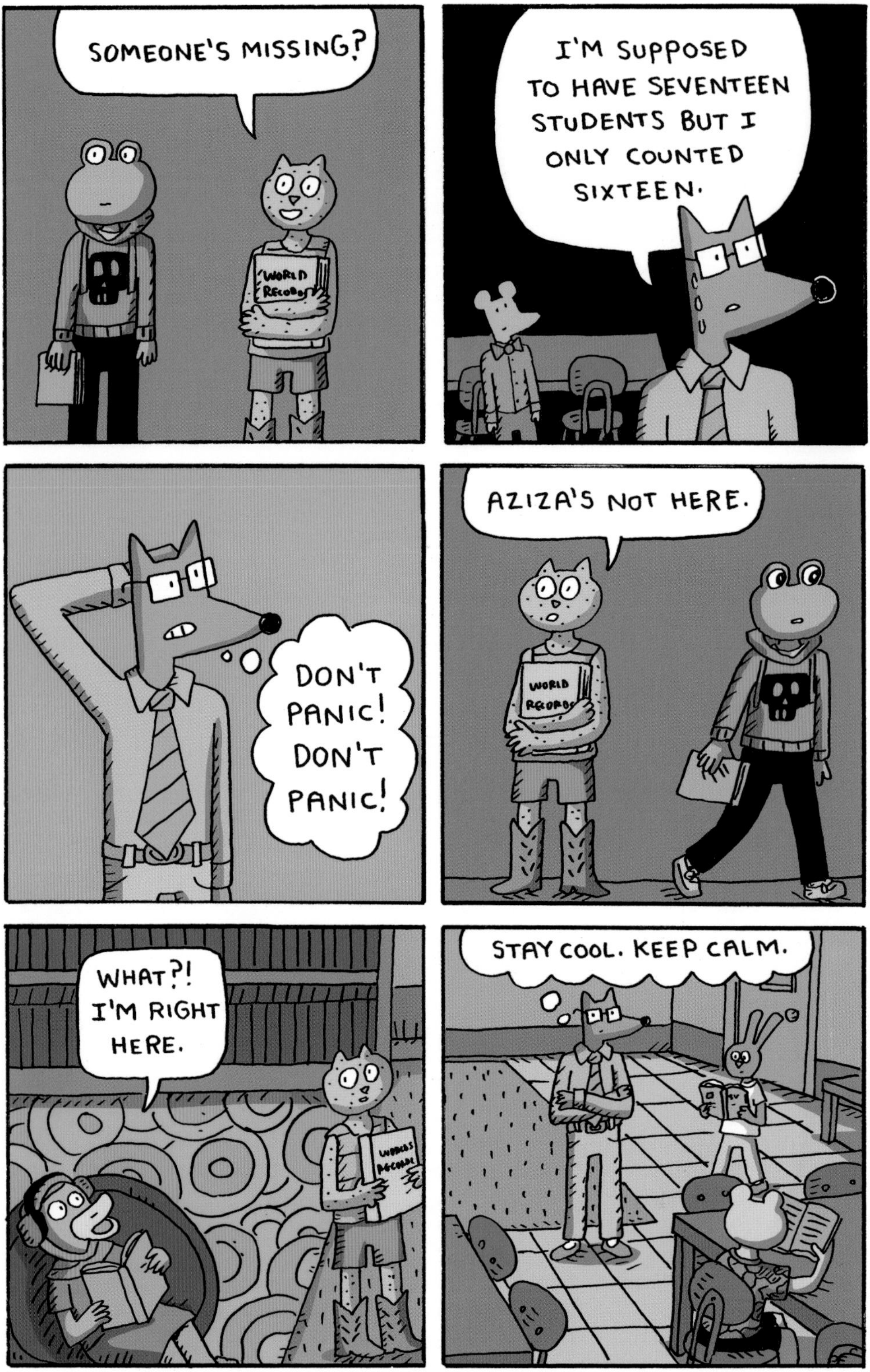
SOMEONE'S MISSING?
WORLD RECORDS
I'M SUPPOSED TO HAVE SEVENTEEN STUDENTS BUT I ONLY COUNTED SIXTEEN.
DON'T PANIC! DON'T PANIC!
AZIZA'S NOT HERE.
WORLD RECORDS
WHAT?! I'M RIGHT HERE.
STAY COOL. KEEP CALM.

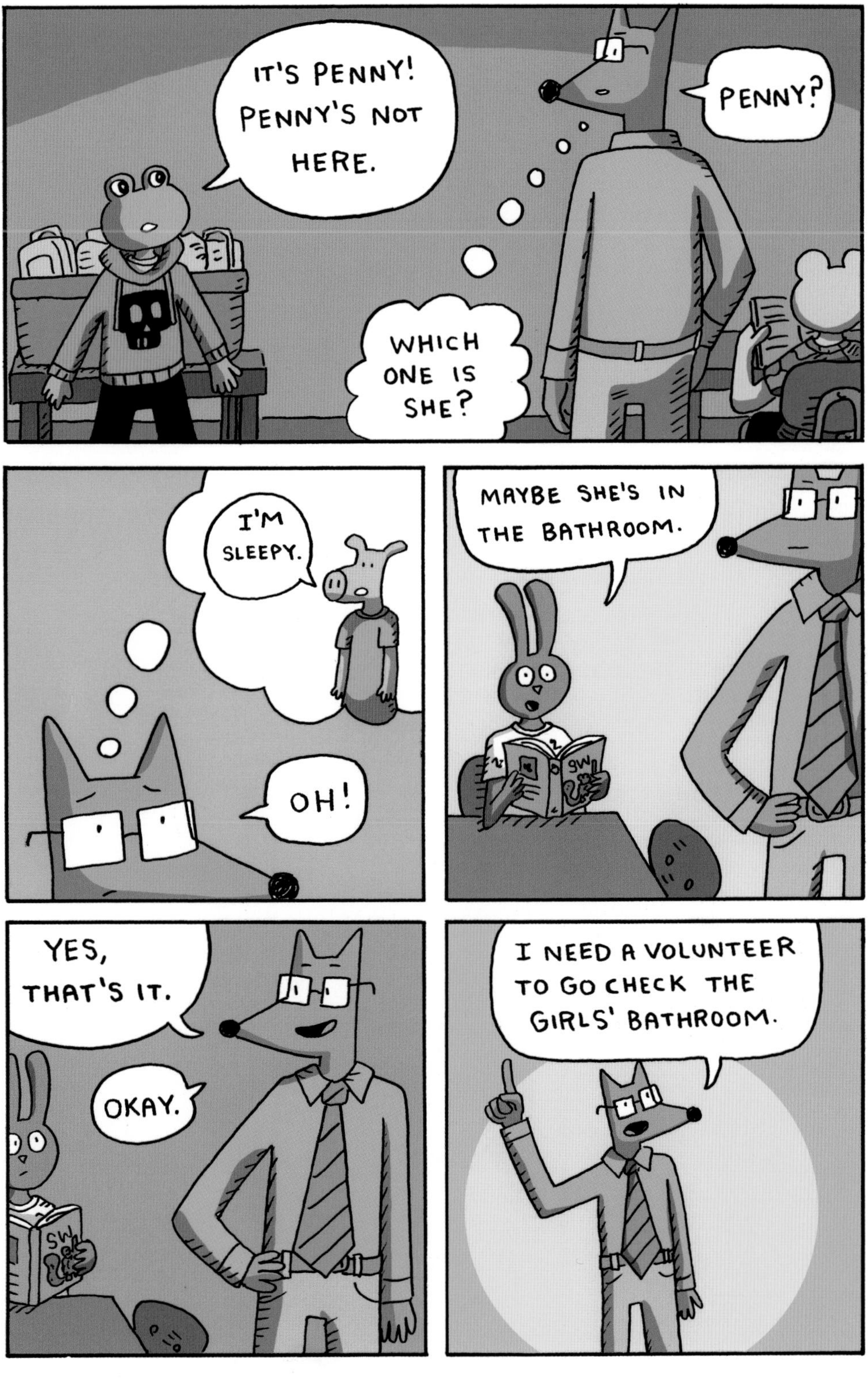
IT'S PENNY! PENNY'S NOT HERE.
PENNY?
WHICH ONE IS SHE?
I'M SLEEPY.
OH!
MAYBE SHE'S IN THE BATHROOM.
YES, THAT'S IT.
OKAY.
I NEED A VOLUNTEER TO GO CHECK THE GIRLS' BATHROOM.

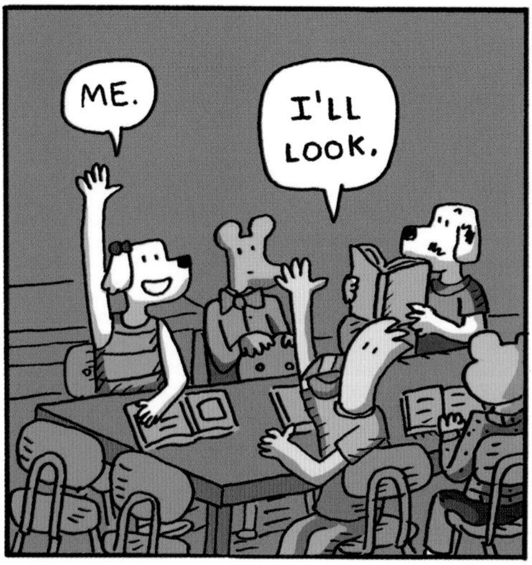
ME.
I'LL LOOK.

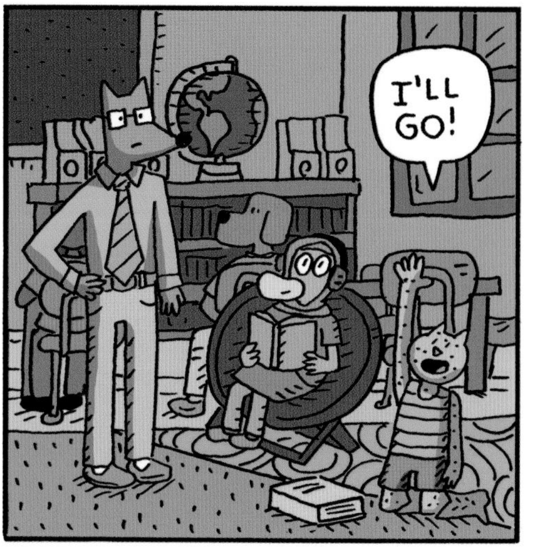
I'LL GO!

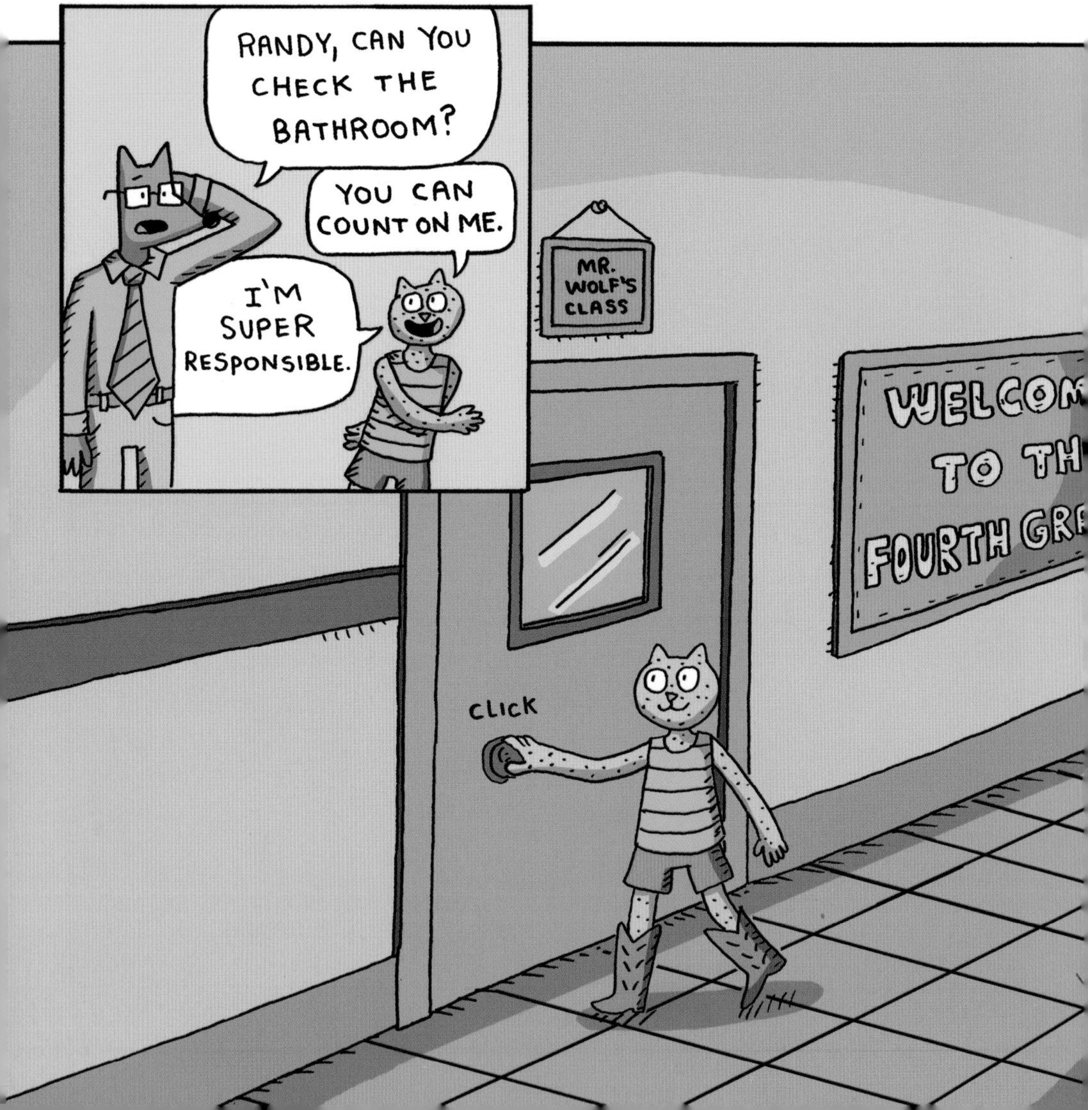
RANDY, CAN YOU CHECK THE BATHROOM?
YOU CAN COUNT ON ME.
I'M SUPER RESPONSIBLE.
MR. WOLF'S CLASS
WELCOM
TO TH
FOURTH GRA
CLICK

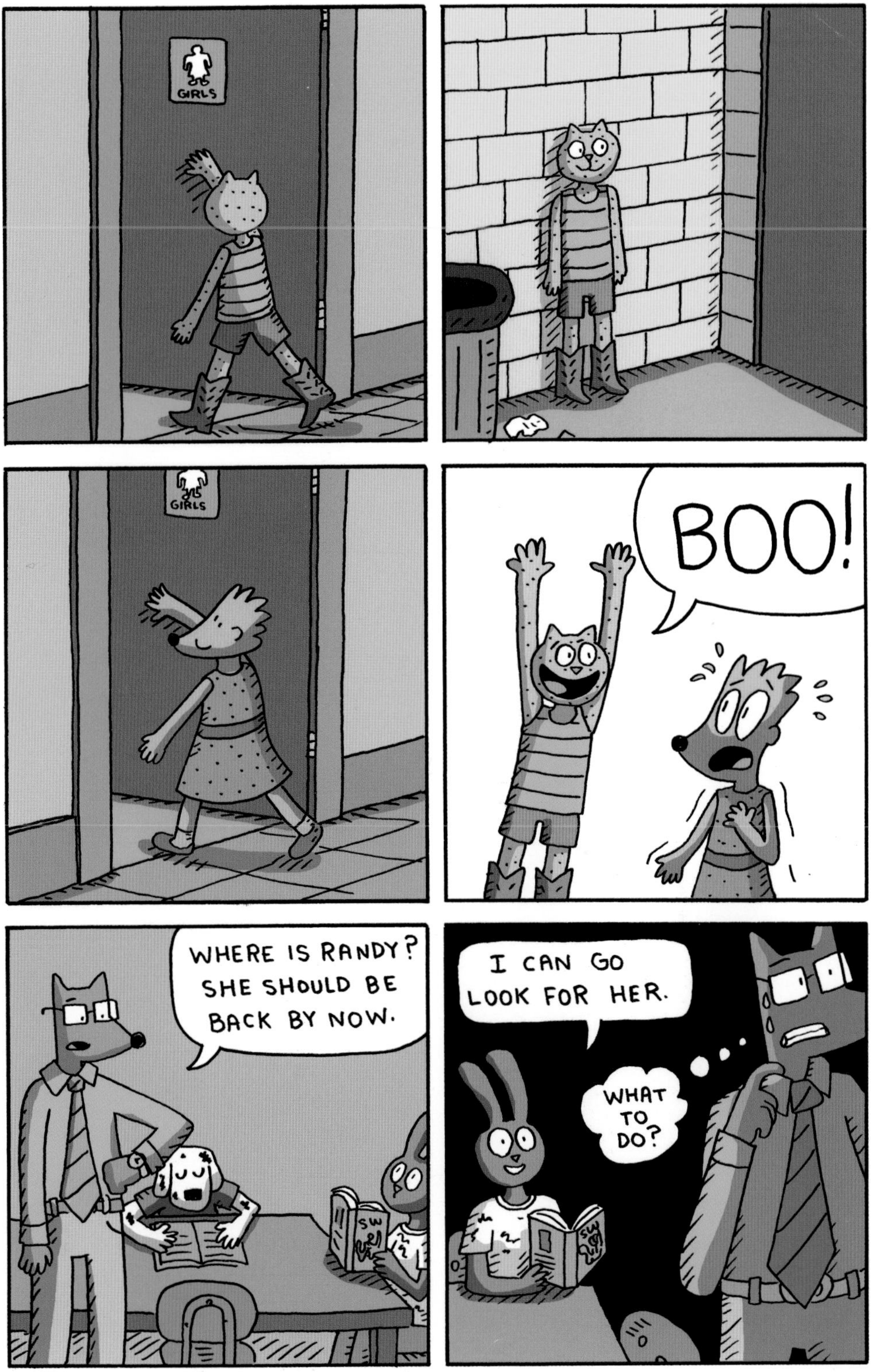
GIRLS
GIRLS
BOO!
WHERE IS RANDY? SHE SHOULD BE BACK BY NOW.
I CAN GO LOOK FOR HER.
WHAT TO DO?

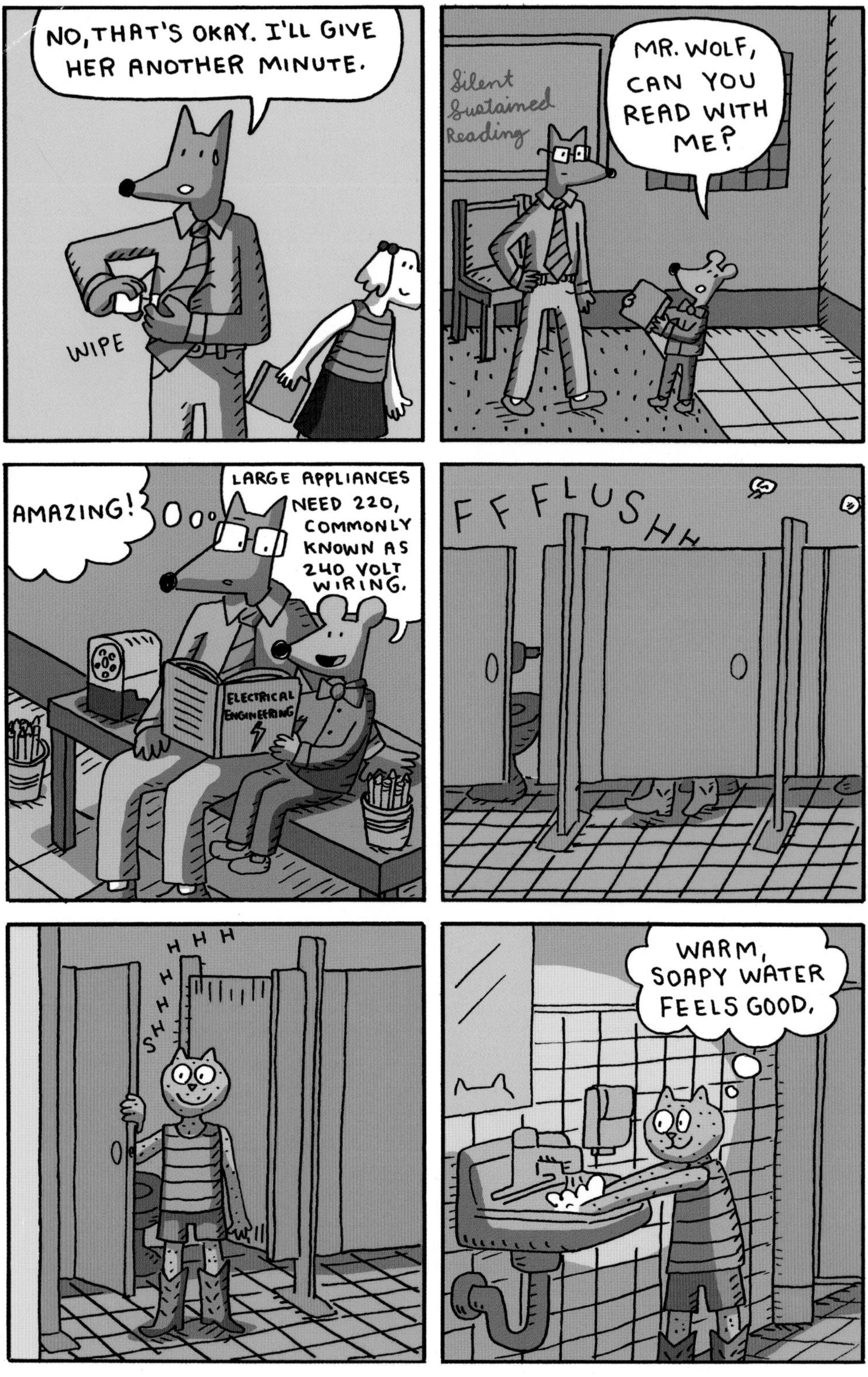
NO, THAT'S OKAY. I'LL GIVE HER ANOTHER MINUTE.
WIPE
Silent Sustained Reading
MR. WOLF, CAN YOU READ WITH ME?
AMAZING!
LARGE APPLIANCES NEED 220, COMMONLY KNOWN AS 240 VOLT WIRING.
ELECTRICAL ENGINEERING
FFFLUSHH
SHHHHH
WARM, SOAPY WATER FEELS GOOD.

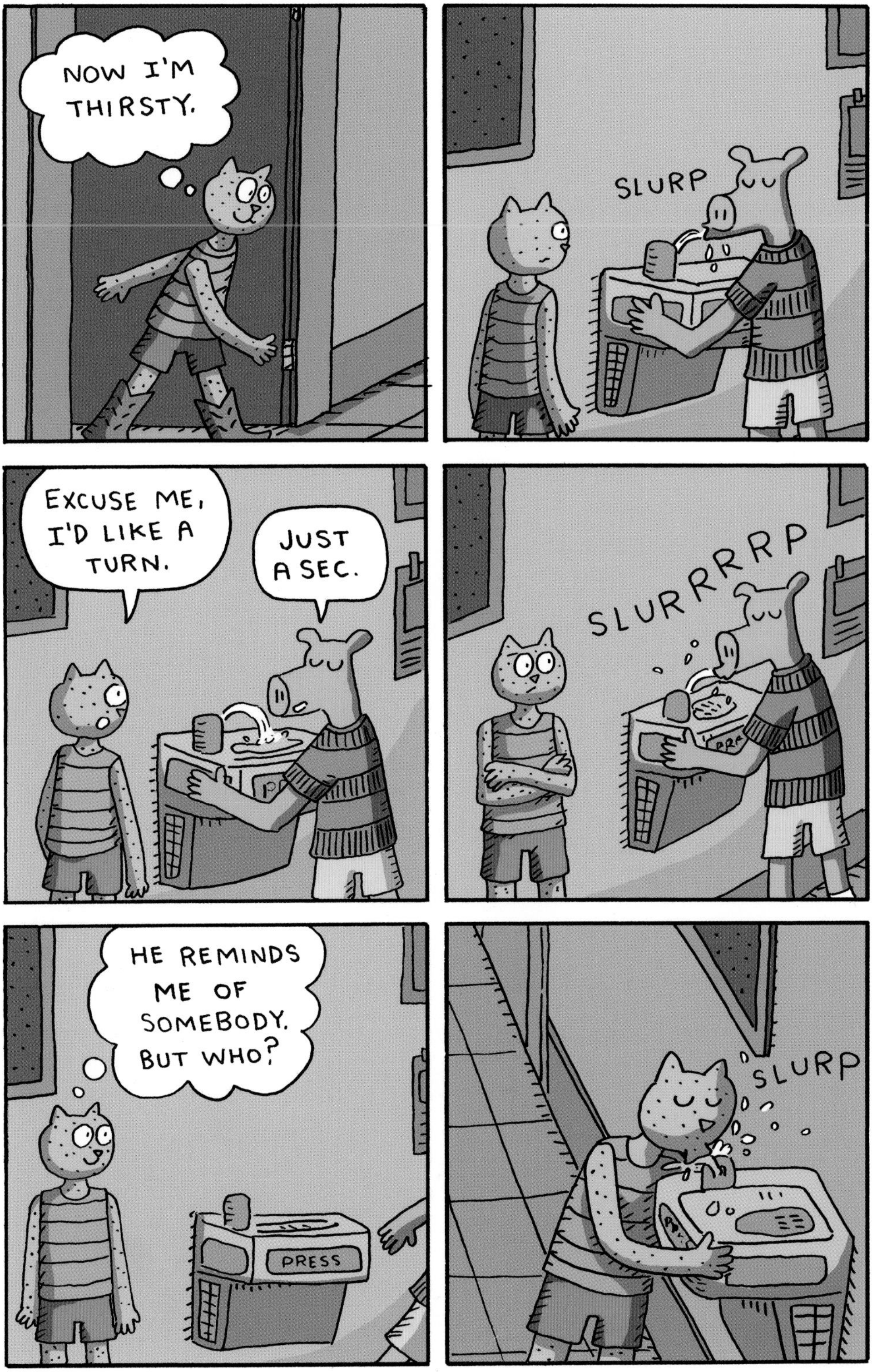
NOW I'M THIRSTY.
SLURP
EXCUSE ME, I'D LIKE A TURN.
JUST A SEC.
SLURRRRP
HE REMINDS ME OF SOMEBODY. BUT WHO?
PRESS
SLURP

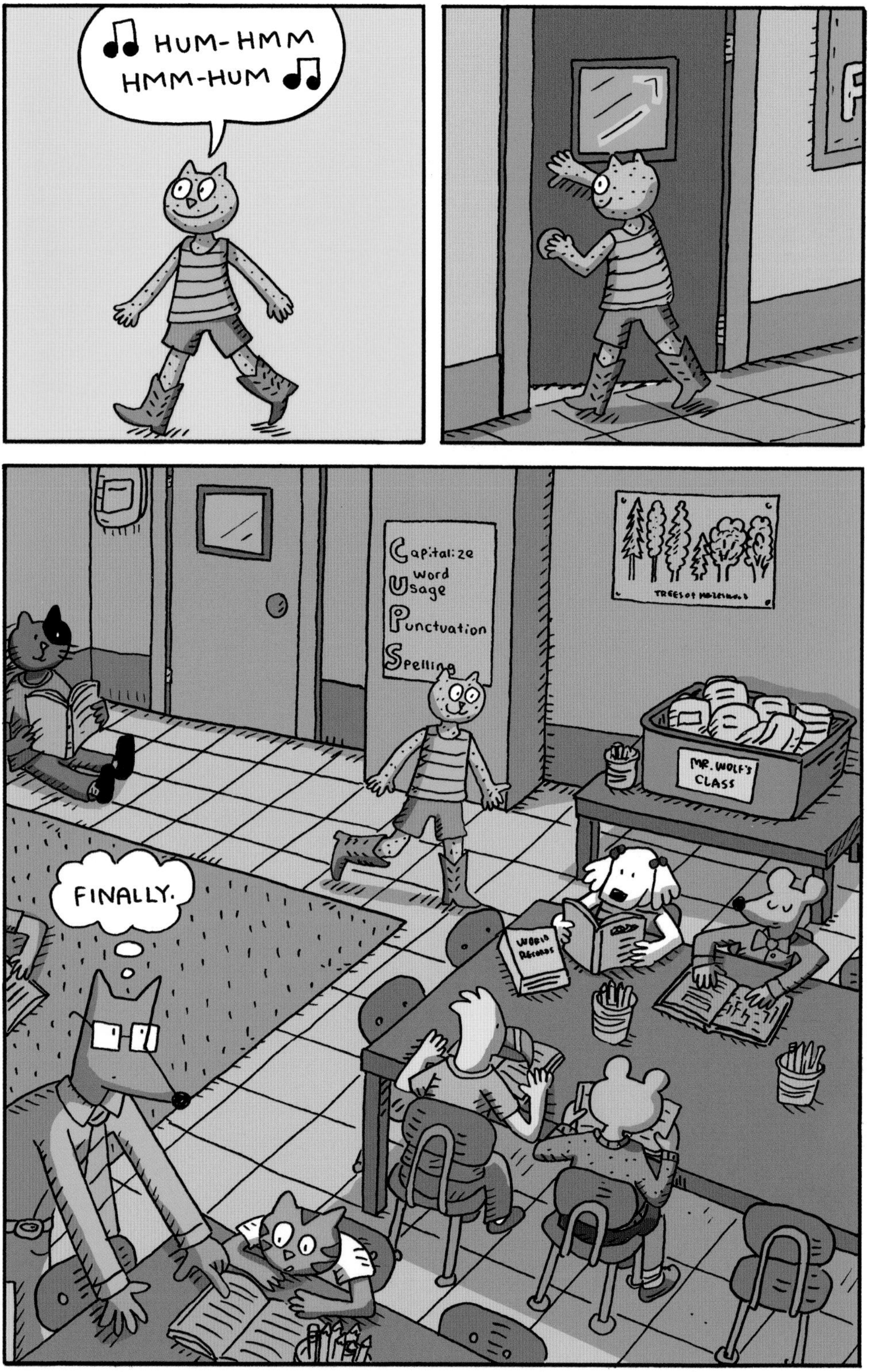
HUM-HMM HMM-HUM
Capitalize
word Usage
Punctuation
Spelling
MR. WOLF'S CLASS
FINALLY.
WORLD RECORDS

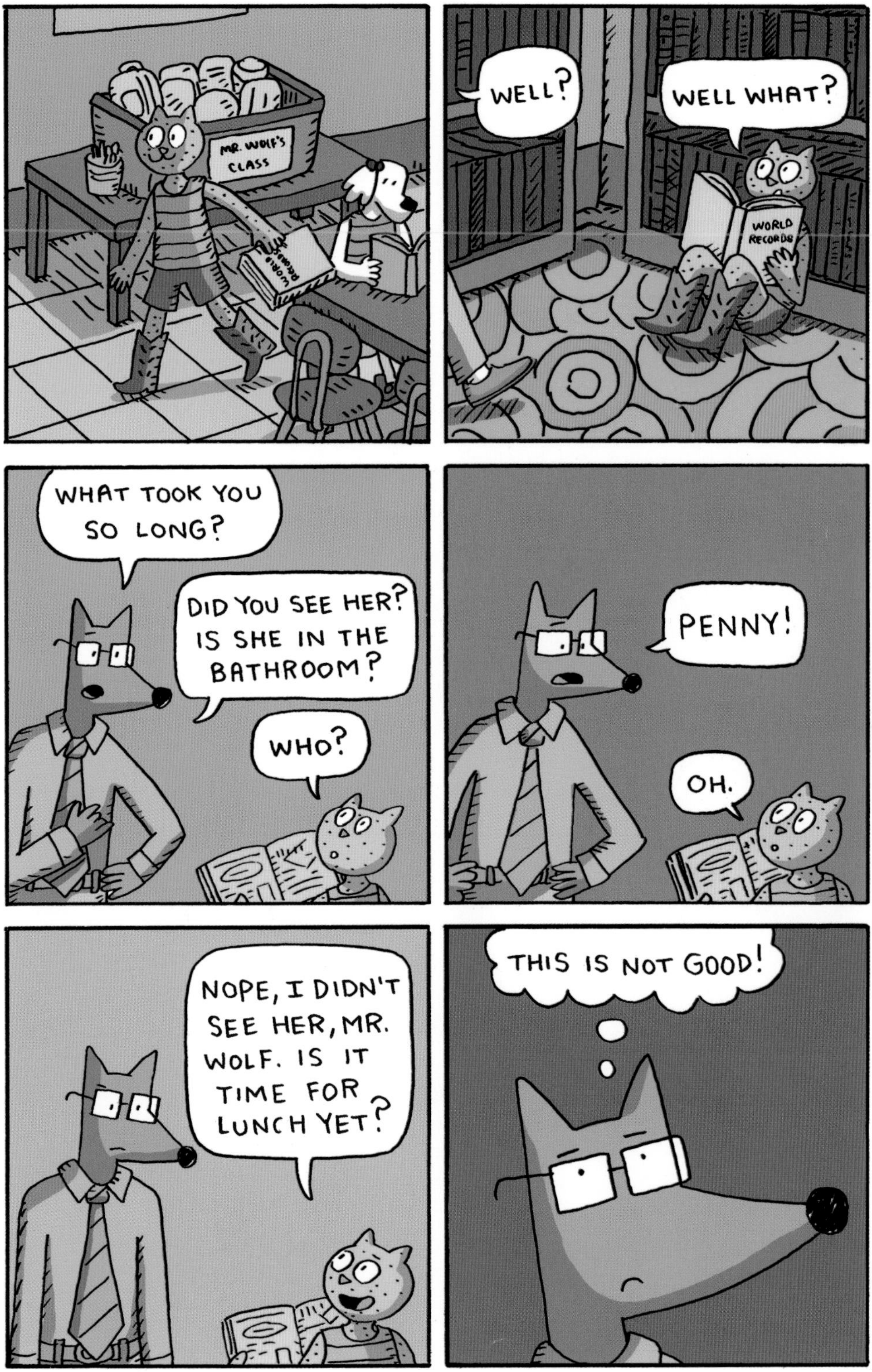
MR. WOLF'S CLASS
WORLD RECORDS
WELL?
WELL WHAT?
WORLD RECORDS
WHAT TOOK YOU SO LONG?
DID YOU SEE HER? IS SHE IN THE BATHROOM?
WHO?
PENNY!
OH.
NOPE, I DIDN'T SEE HER, MR. WOLF. IS IT TIME FOR LUNCH YET?
THIS IS NOT GOOD!

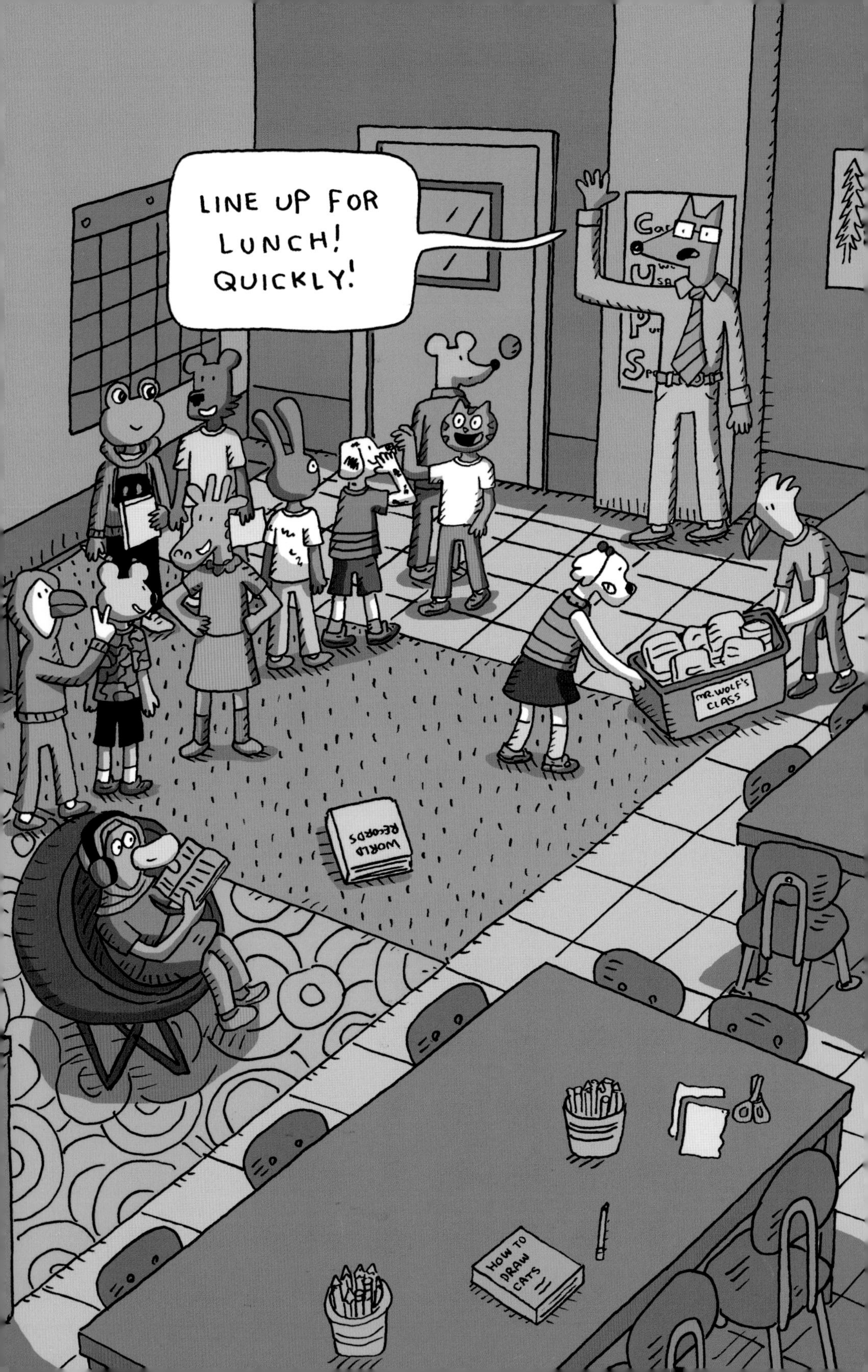
LINE UP FOR LUNCH! QUICKLY!
MR. WOLF'S CLASS
WORLD RECORDS
HOW TO DRAW CATS

CHAPTER SEVEN

Rats!

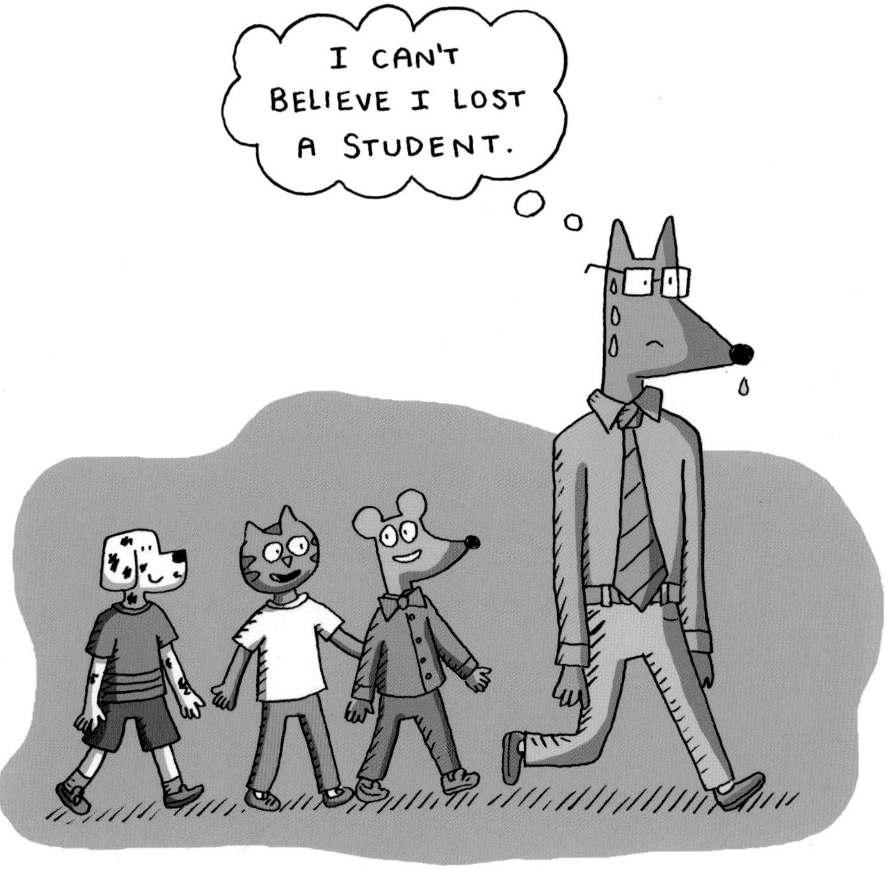
I CAN'T BELIEVE I LOST A STUDENT.

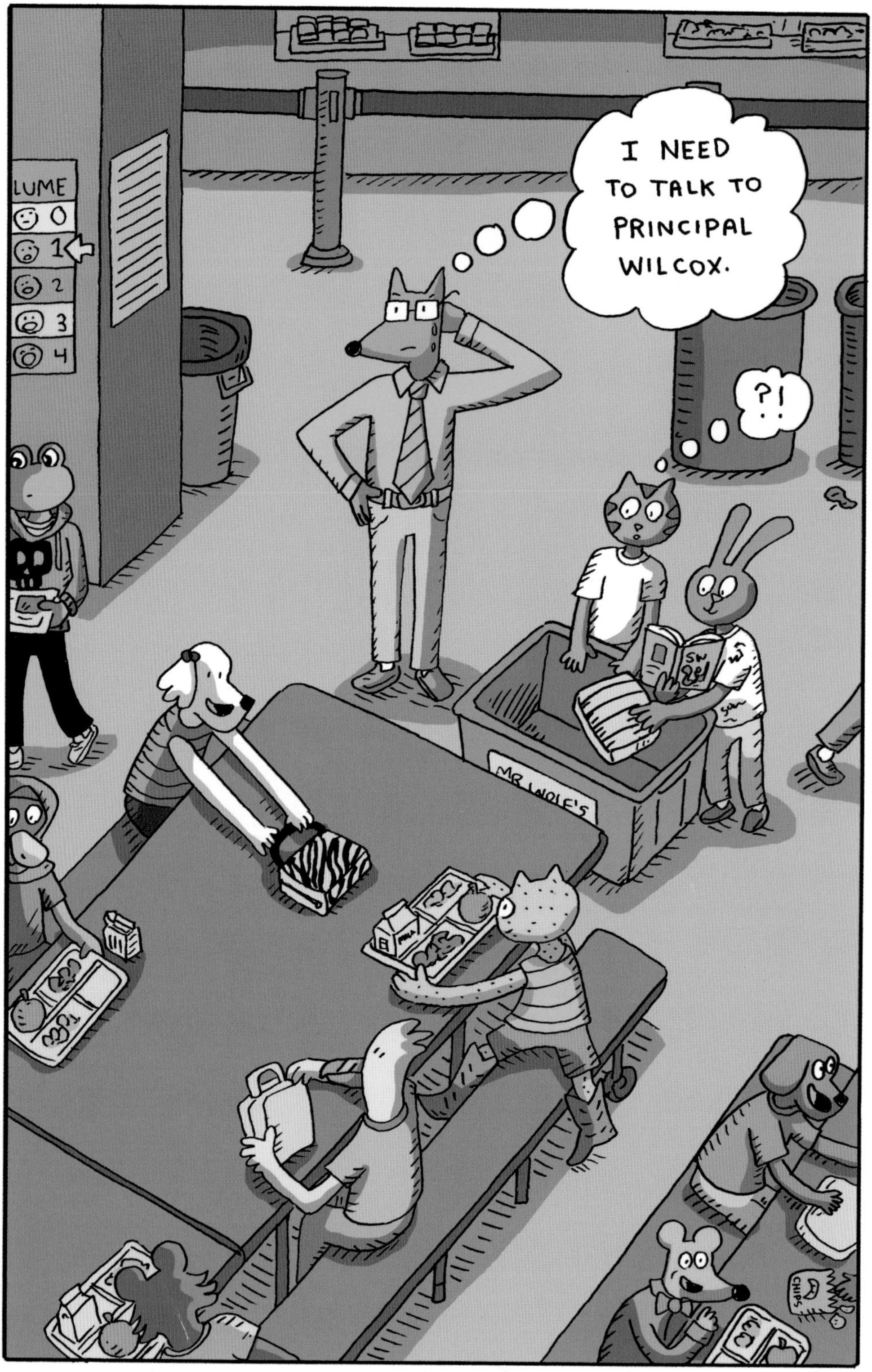
LUME
I NEED TO TALK TO PRINCIPAL WILCOX.
?!
MR WOLF'S
CHIPS

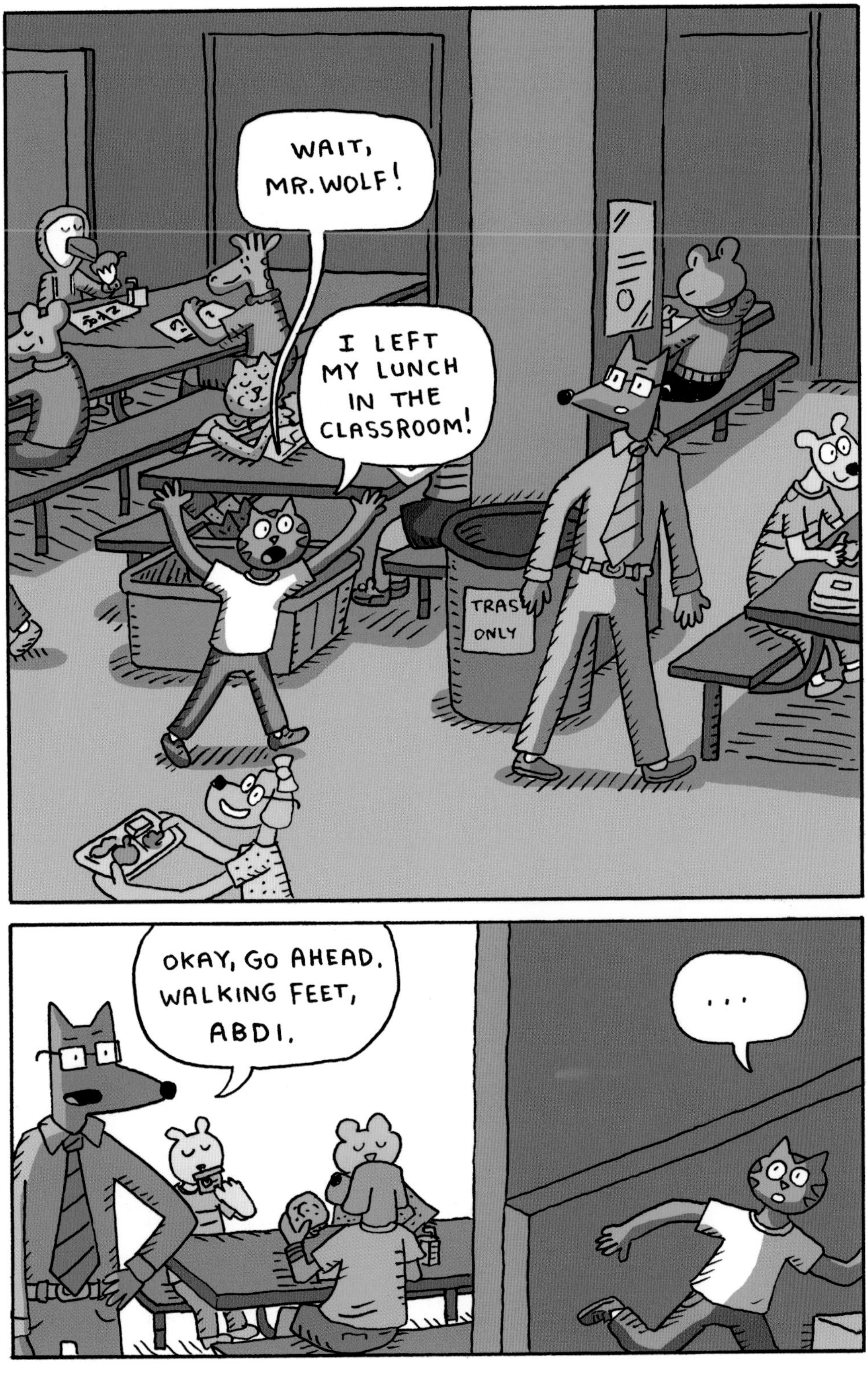
WAIT, MR. WOLF!
I LEFT MY LUNCH IN THE CLASSROOM!
TRAS ONLY
OKAY, GO AHEAD. WALKING FEET, ABDI.
. . .

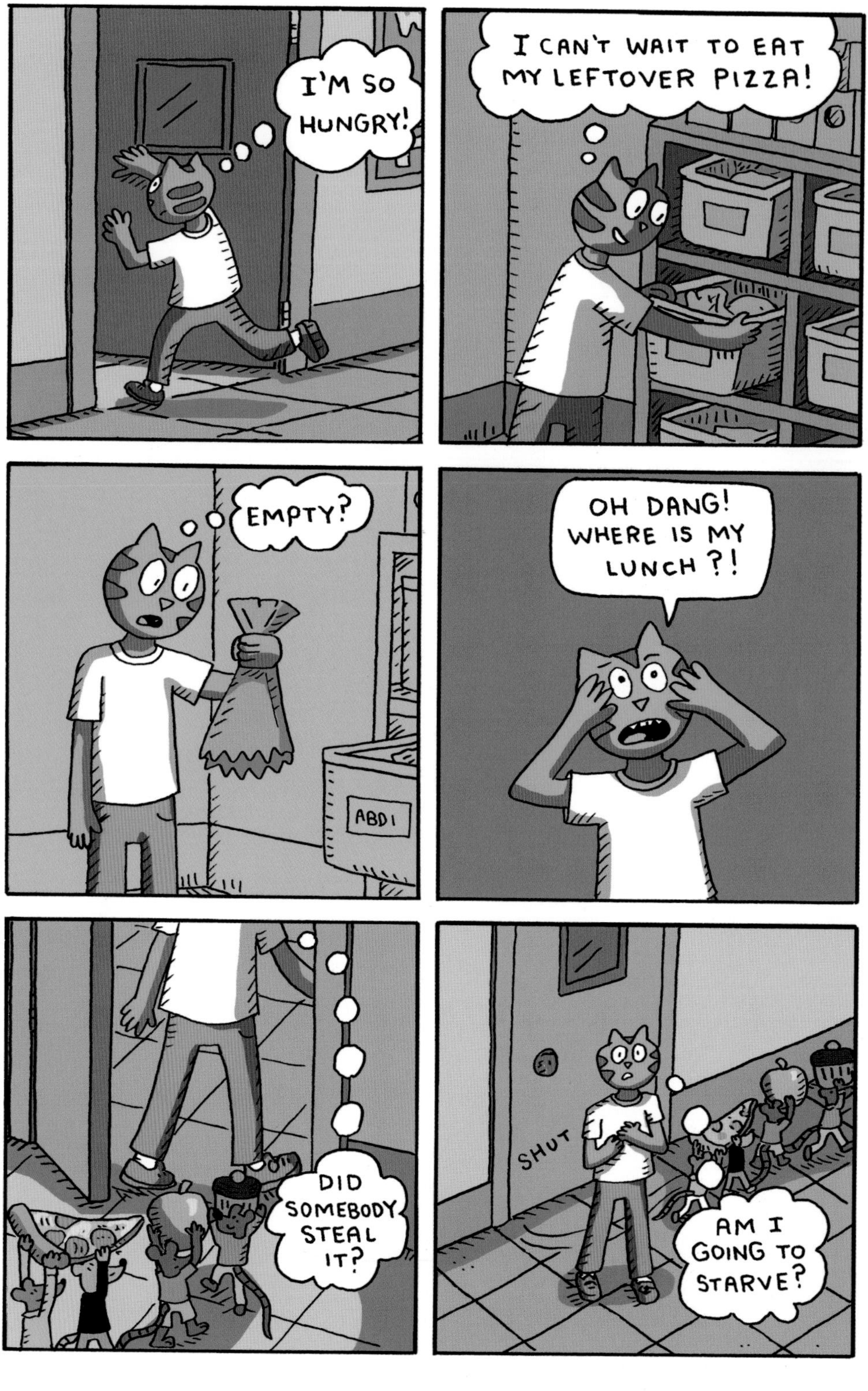
I'M SO HUNGRY!
I CAN'T WAIT TO EAT MY LEFTOVER PIZZA!
EMPTY?
ABDI
OH DANG! WHERE IS MY LUNCH ?!
DID SOMEBODY STEAL IT?
SHUT
AM I GOING TO STARVE?

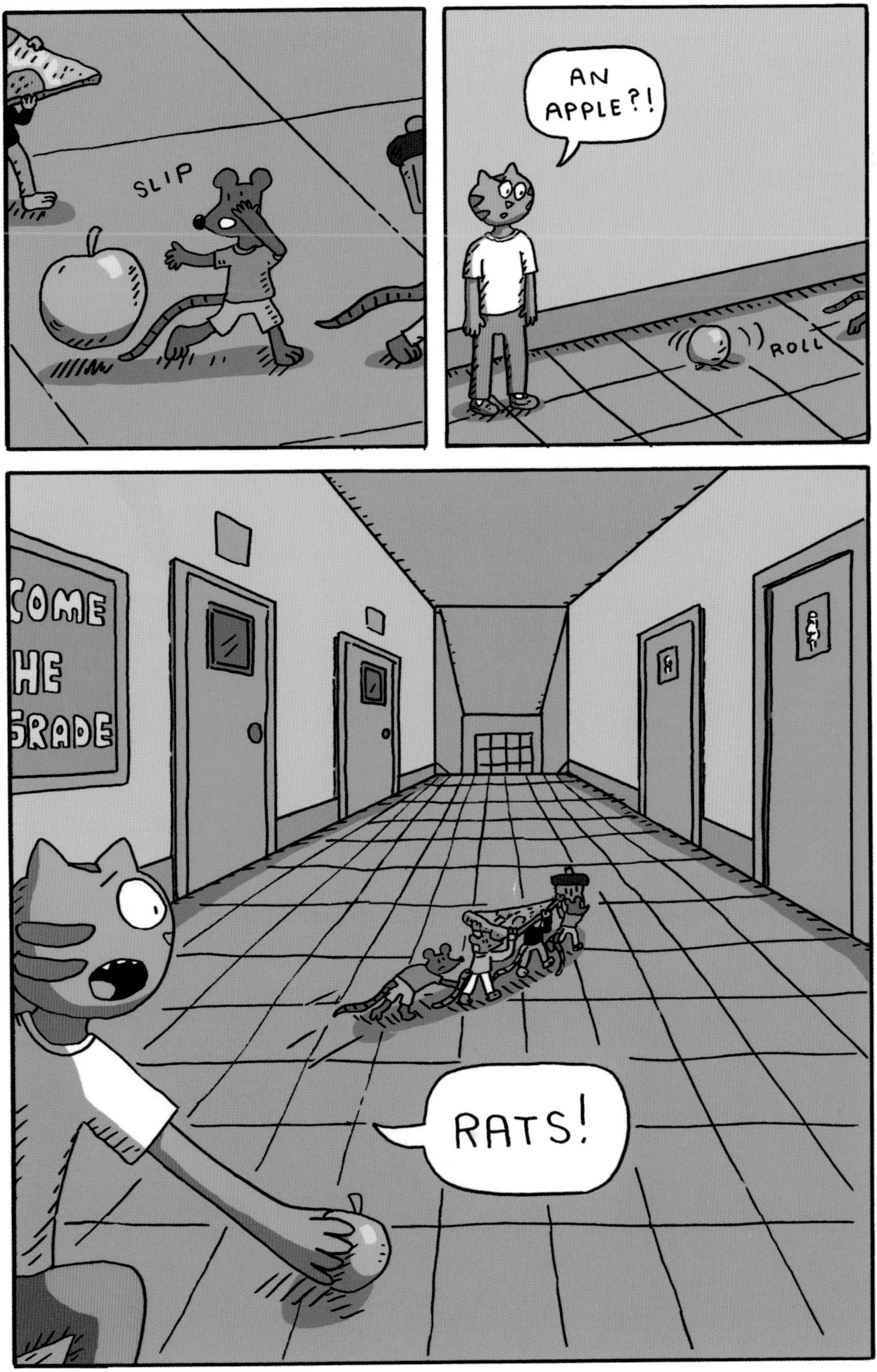
SLIP
AN APPLE?!
ROLL
COME
HE
GRADE
RATS!

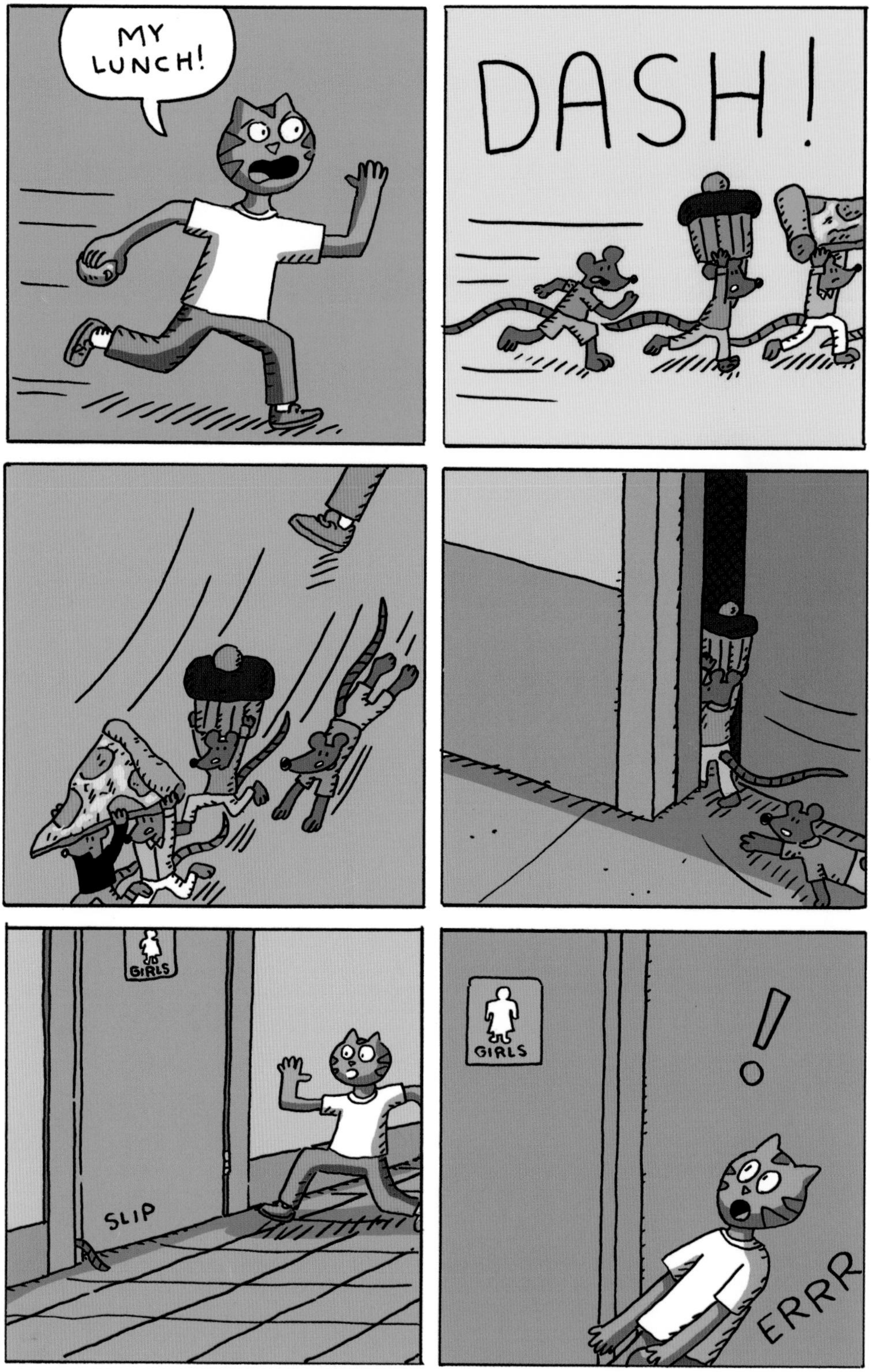
MY LUNCH!
DASH!
GIRLS
SLIP
GIRLS
!
ERRR

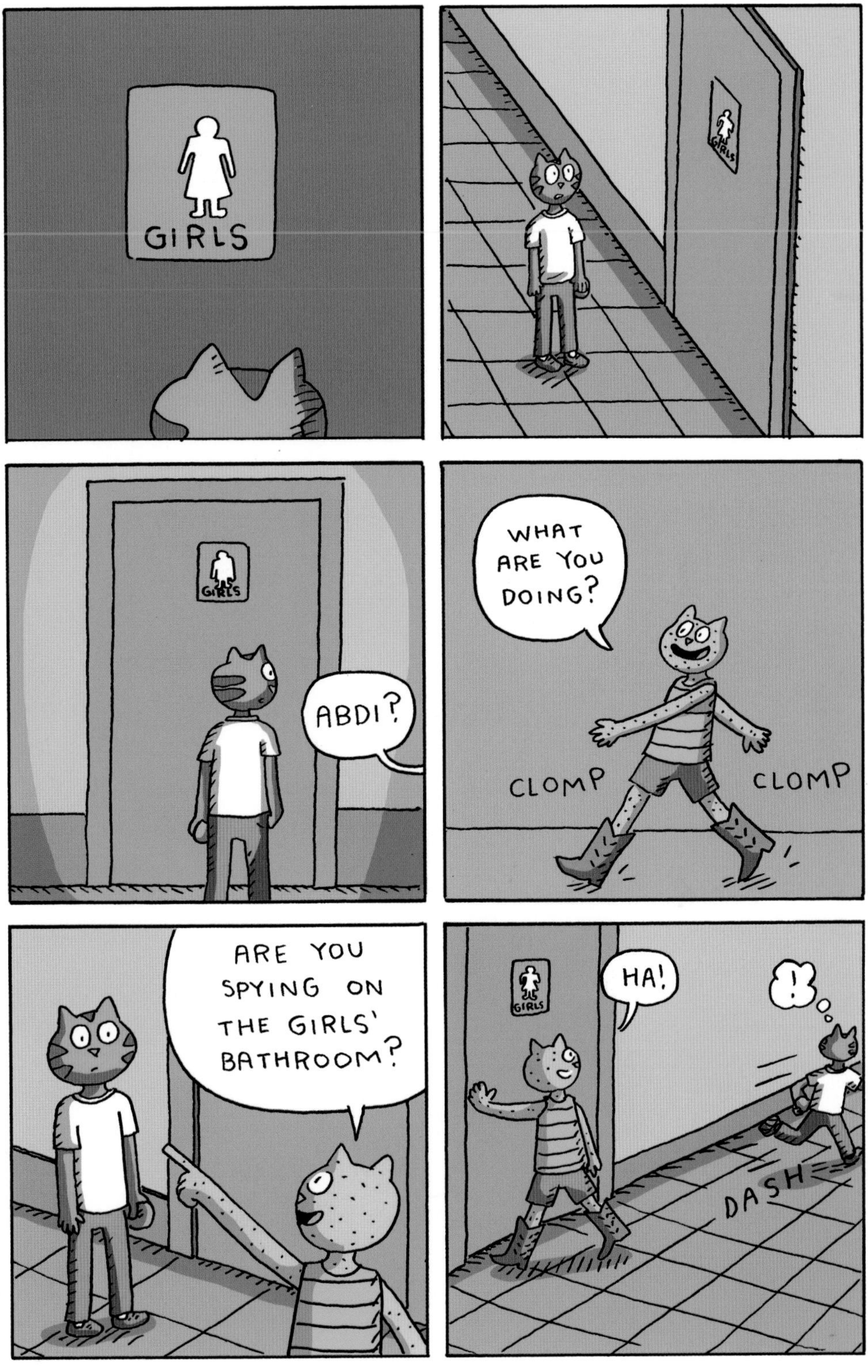
GIRLS
GIRLS
GIRLS
ABDI?
WHAT ARE YOU DOING?
CLOMP
CLOMP
ARE YOU SPYING ON THE GIRLS' BATHROOM?
GIRLS
HA!
!
DASH

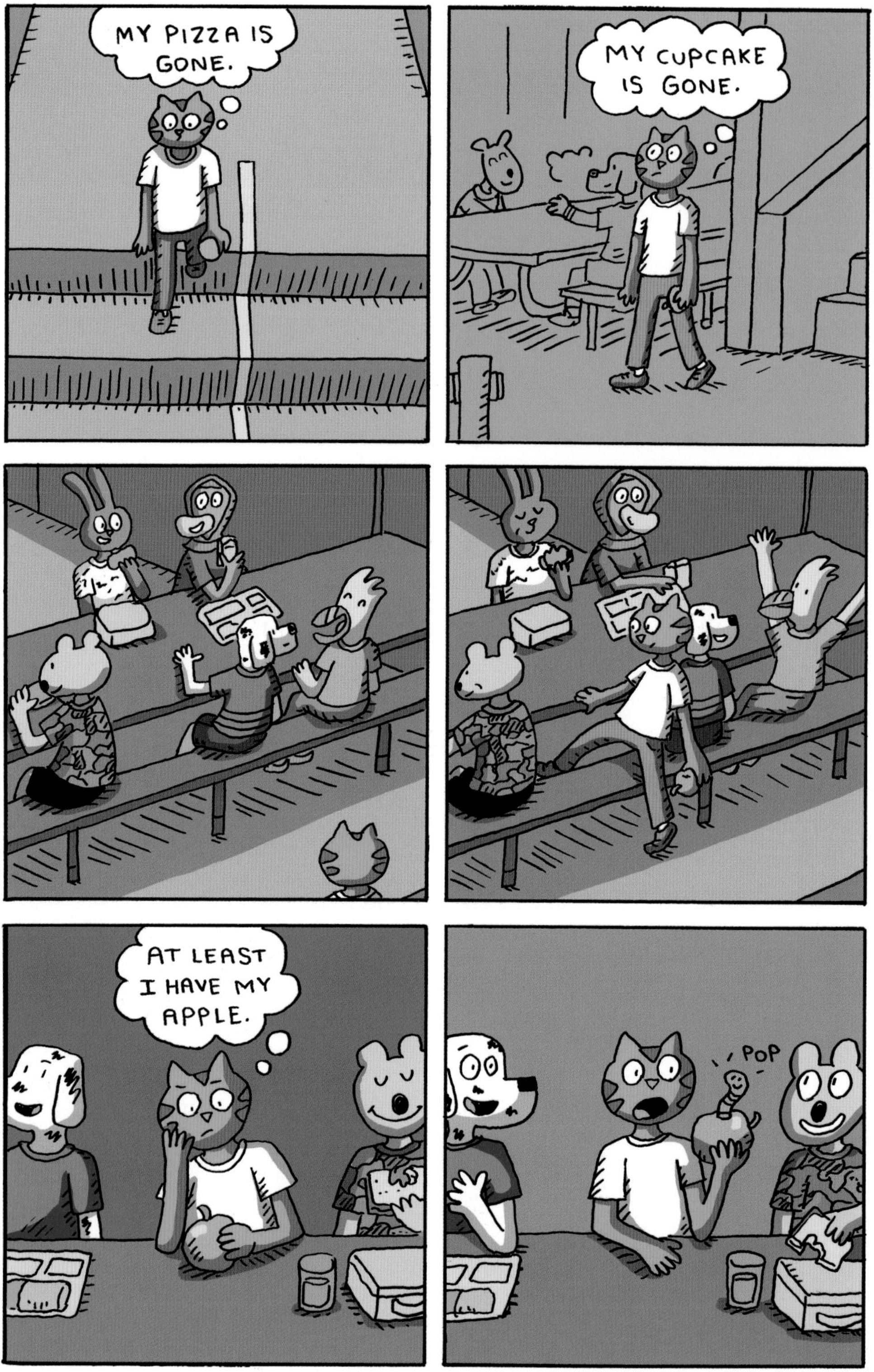
MY PIZZA IS GONE.
MY CUPCAKE IS GONE.
AT LEAST I HAVE MY APPLE.
POP

CHAPTER EIGHT
A Close Call

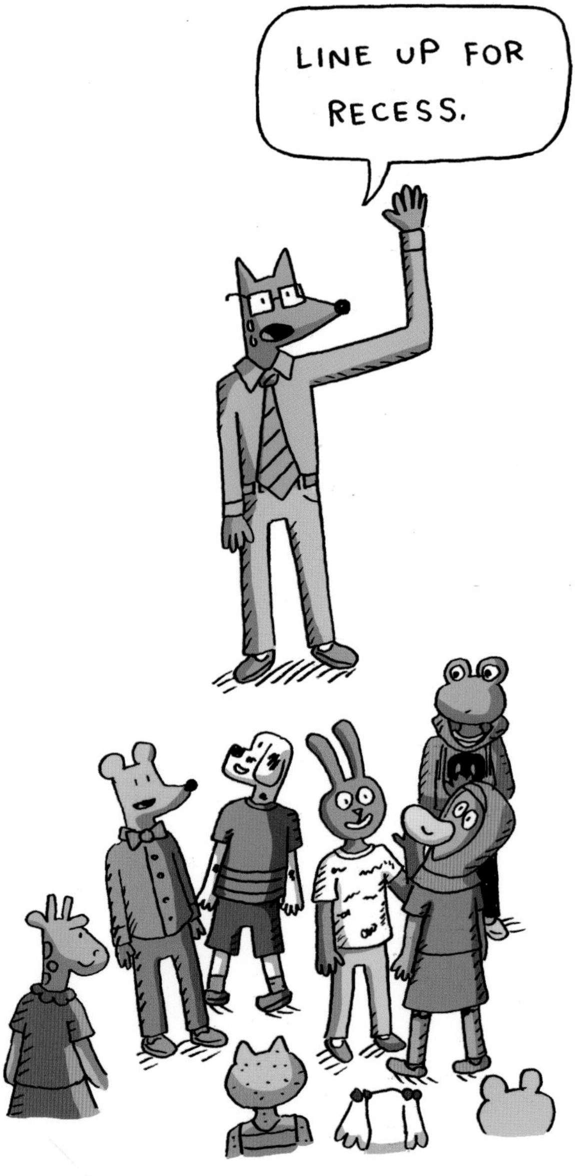
LINE UP FOR RECESS.

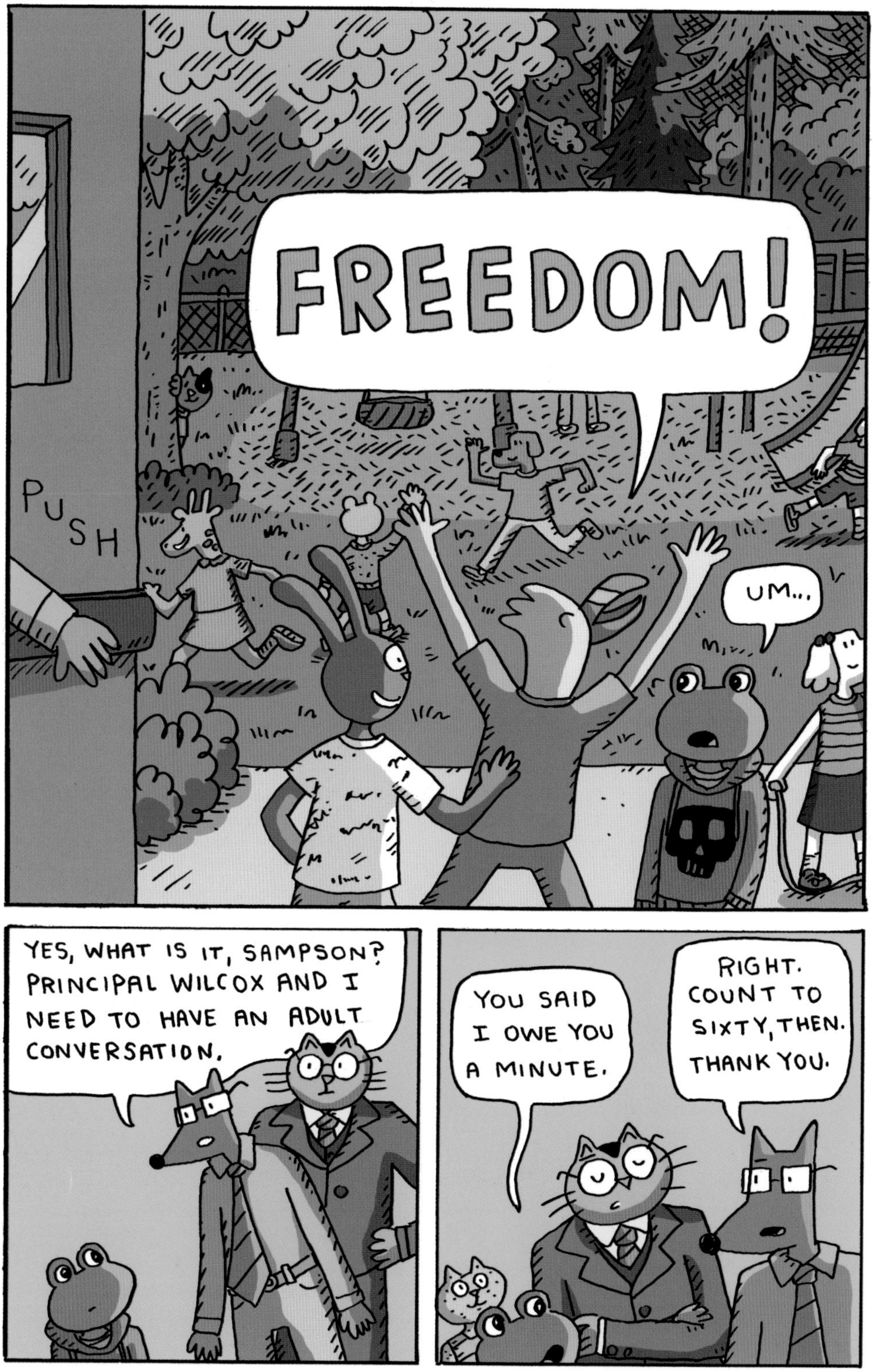
PUSH
FREEDOM!
UM...
YES, WHAT IS IT, SAMPSON? PRINCIPAL WILCOX AND I NEED TO HAVE AN ADULT CONVERSATION.
YOU SAID I OWE YOU A MINUTE.
RIGHT. COUNT TO SIXTY, THEN. THANK YOU.

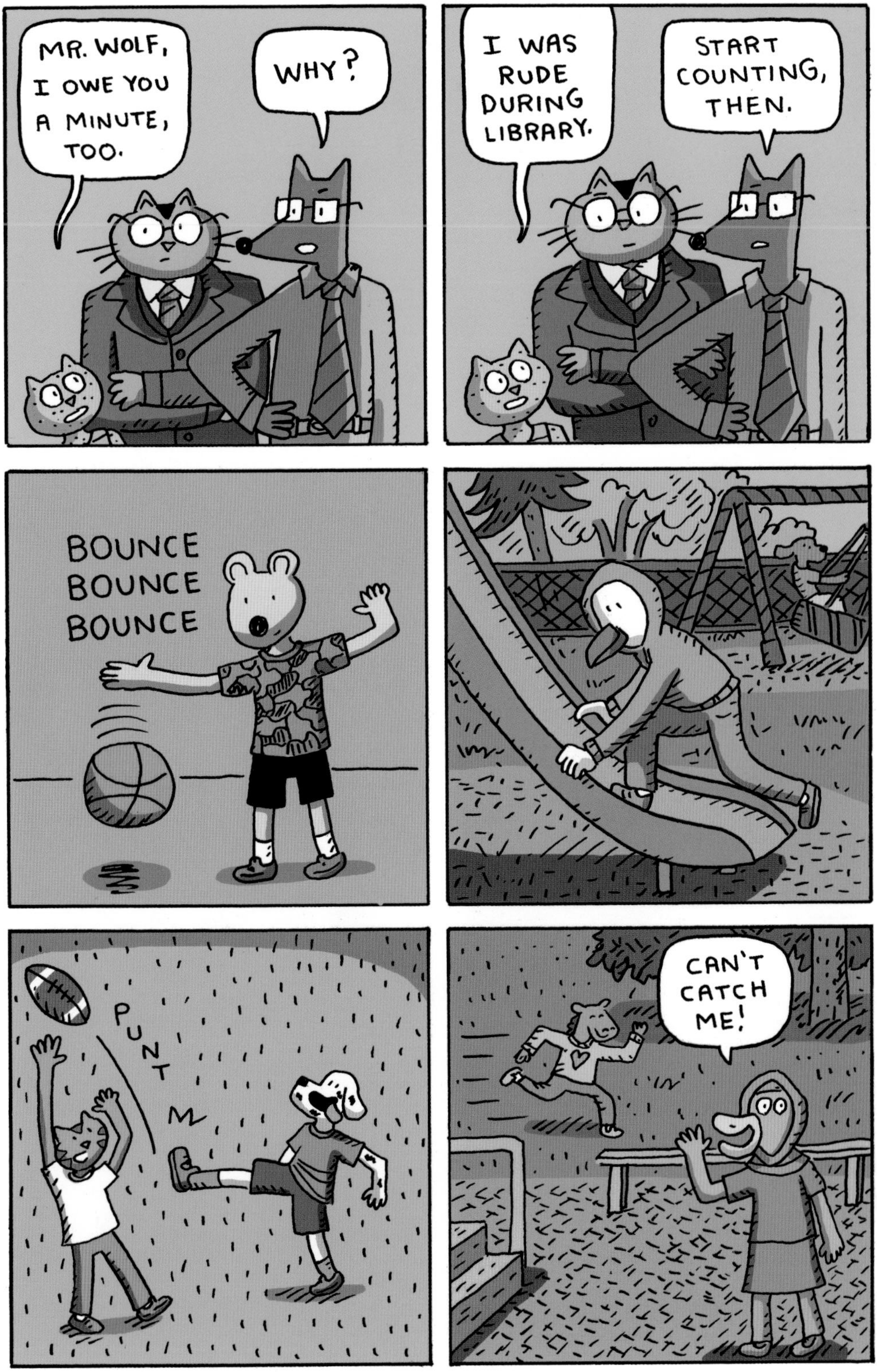
MR. WOLF, I OWE YOU A MINUTE, TOO.
WHY?
I WAS RUDE DURING LIBRARY.
START COUNTING, THEN.
BOUNCE BOUNCE BOUNCE
PUNT
CAN'T CATCH ME!

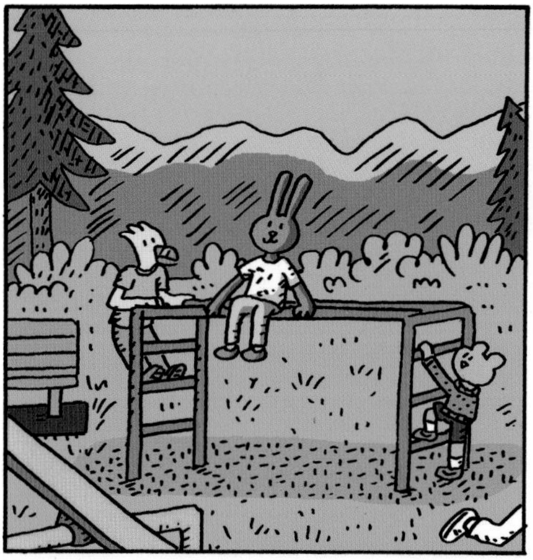

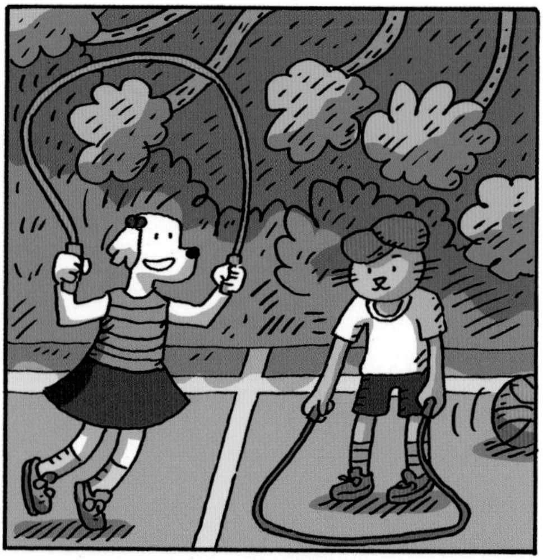

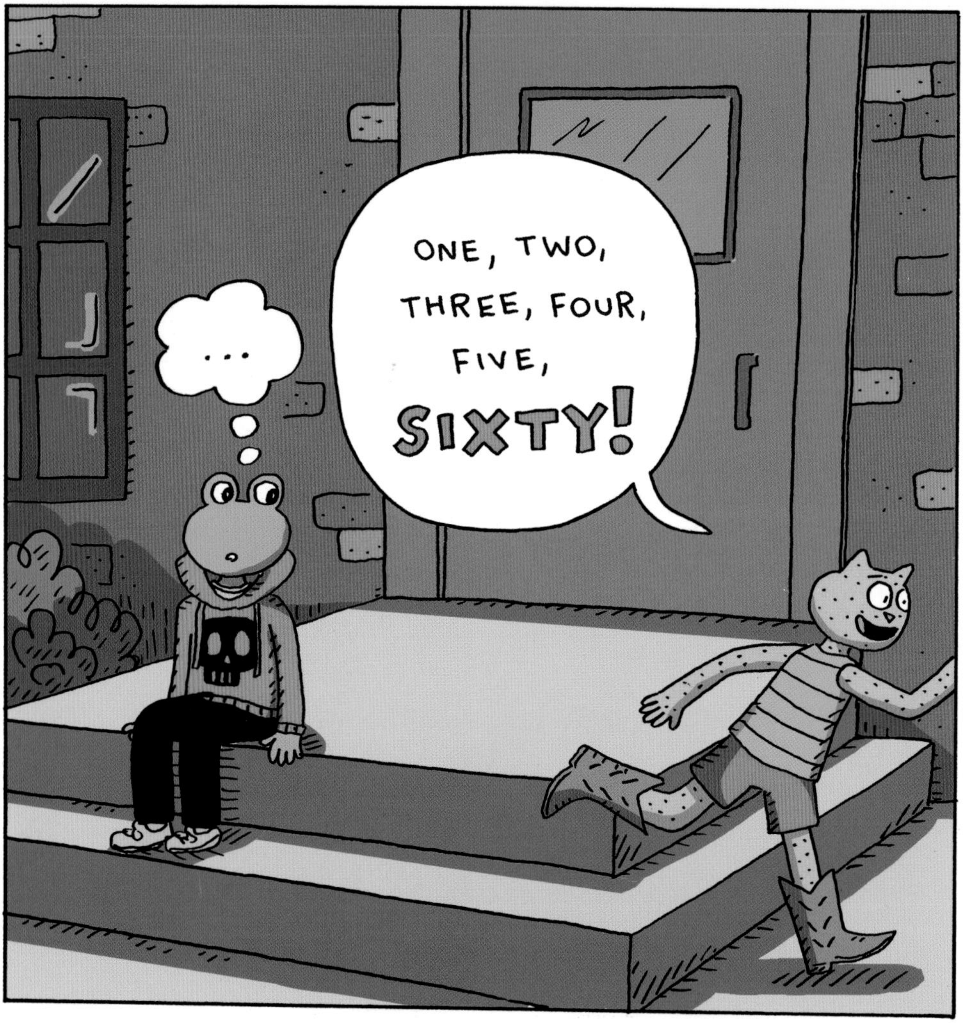
...
ONE, TWO, THREE, FOUR, FIVE, SIXTY!

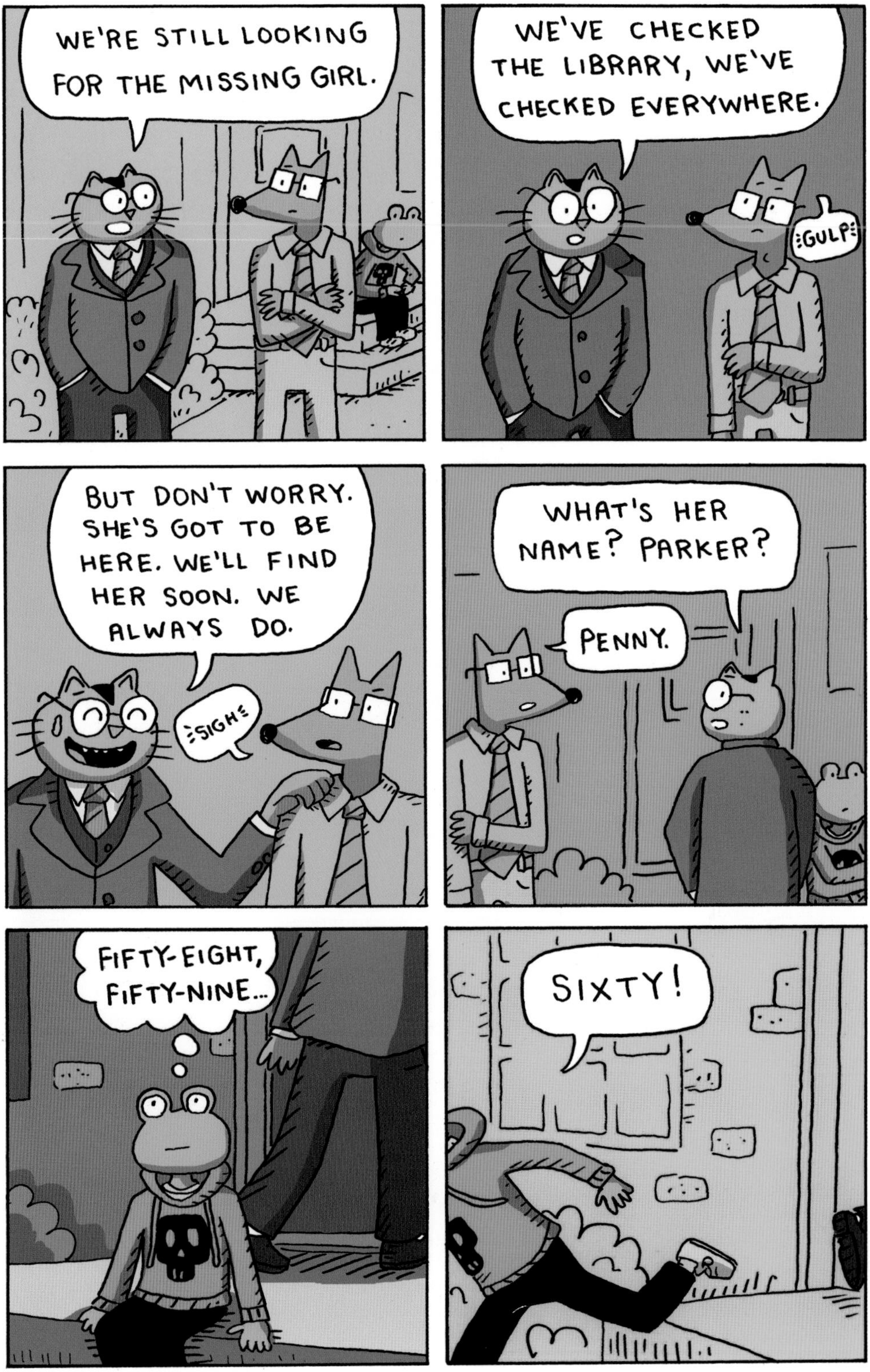
WE'RE STILL LOOKING FOR THE MISSING GIRL.
WE'VE CHECKED THE LIBRARY, WE'VE CHECKED EVERYWHERE.
GULP
BUT DON'T WORRY. SHE'S GOT TO BE HERE. WE'LL FIND HER SOON. WE ALWAYS DO.
SIGH
WHAT'S HER NAME? PARKER?
PENNY.
FIFTY-EIGHT, FIFTY-NINE...
SIXTY!

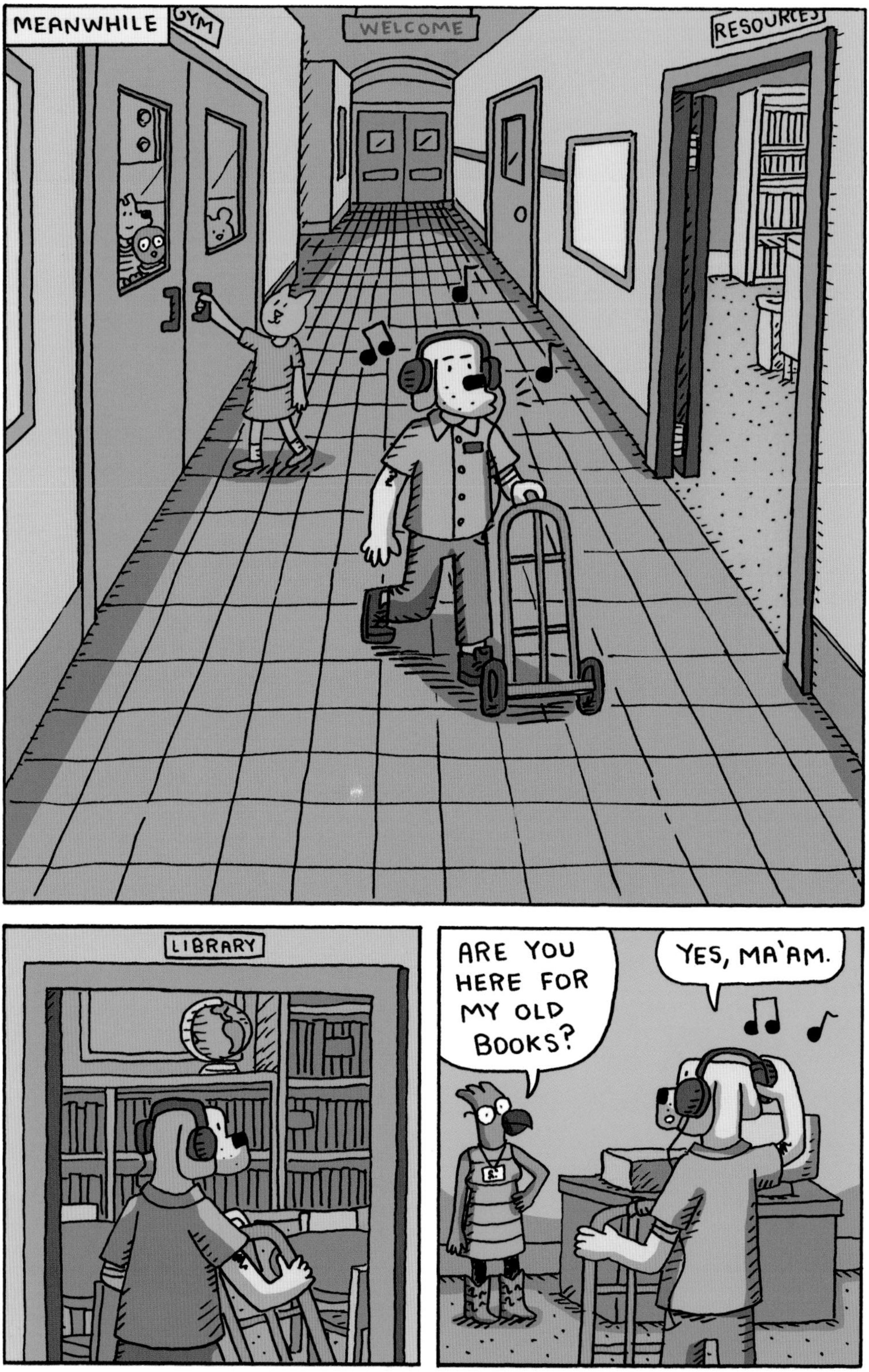
MEANWHILE
GYM
WELCOME
RESOURCES
LIBRARY
ARE YOU HERE FOR MY OLD BOOKS?
YES, MA'AM.

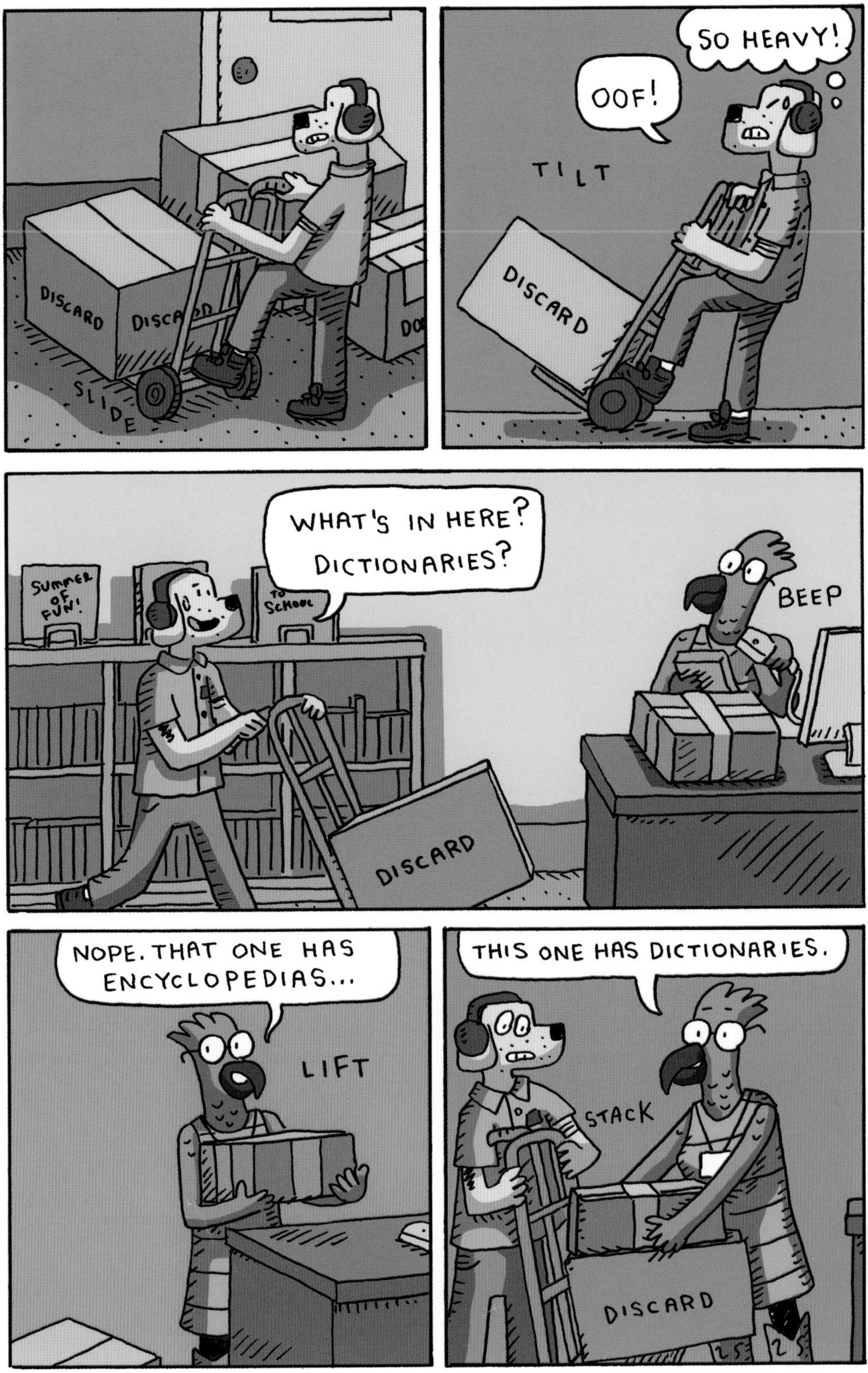

DISCARD
SLIDE
OOF!
SO HEAVY!
TILT
DISCARD
WHAT'S IN HERE? DICTIONARIES?
SUMMER OF FUN!
TO SCHOOL
BEEP
DISCARD
NOPE. THAT ONE HAS ENCYCLOPEDIAS...
LIFT
THIS ONE HAS DICTIONARIES.
STACK
DISCARD

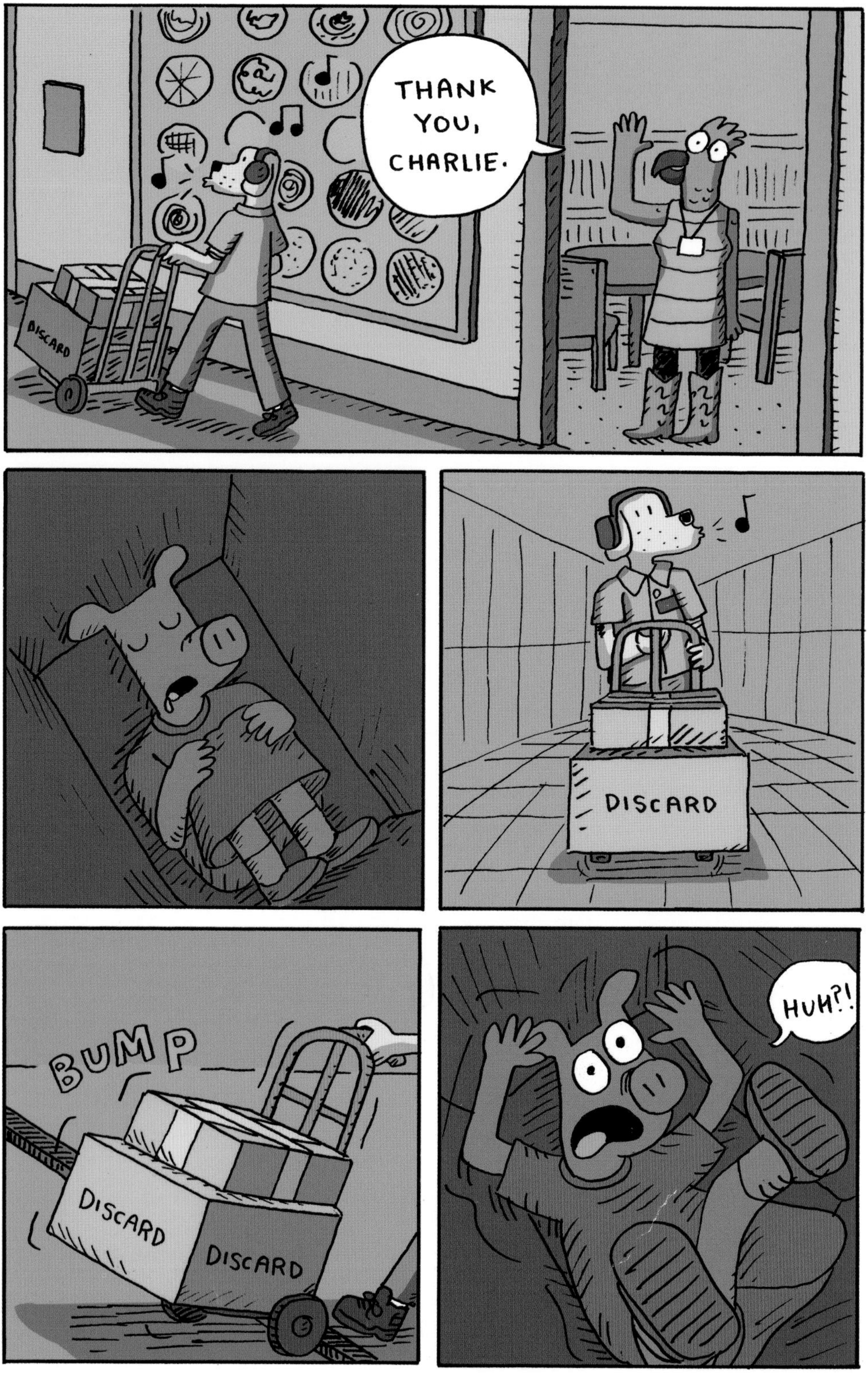
THANK YOU, CHARLIE.
DISCARD
DISCARD
BUMP
DISCARD
DISCARD
HUH?!

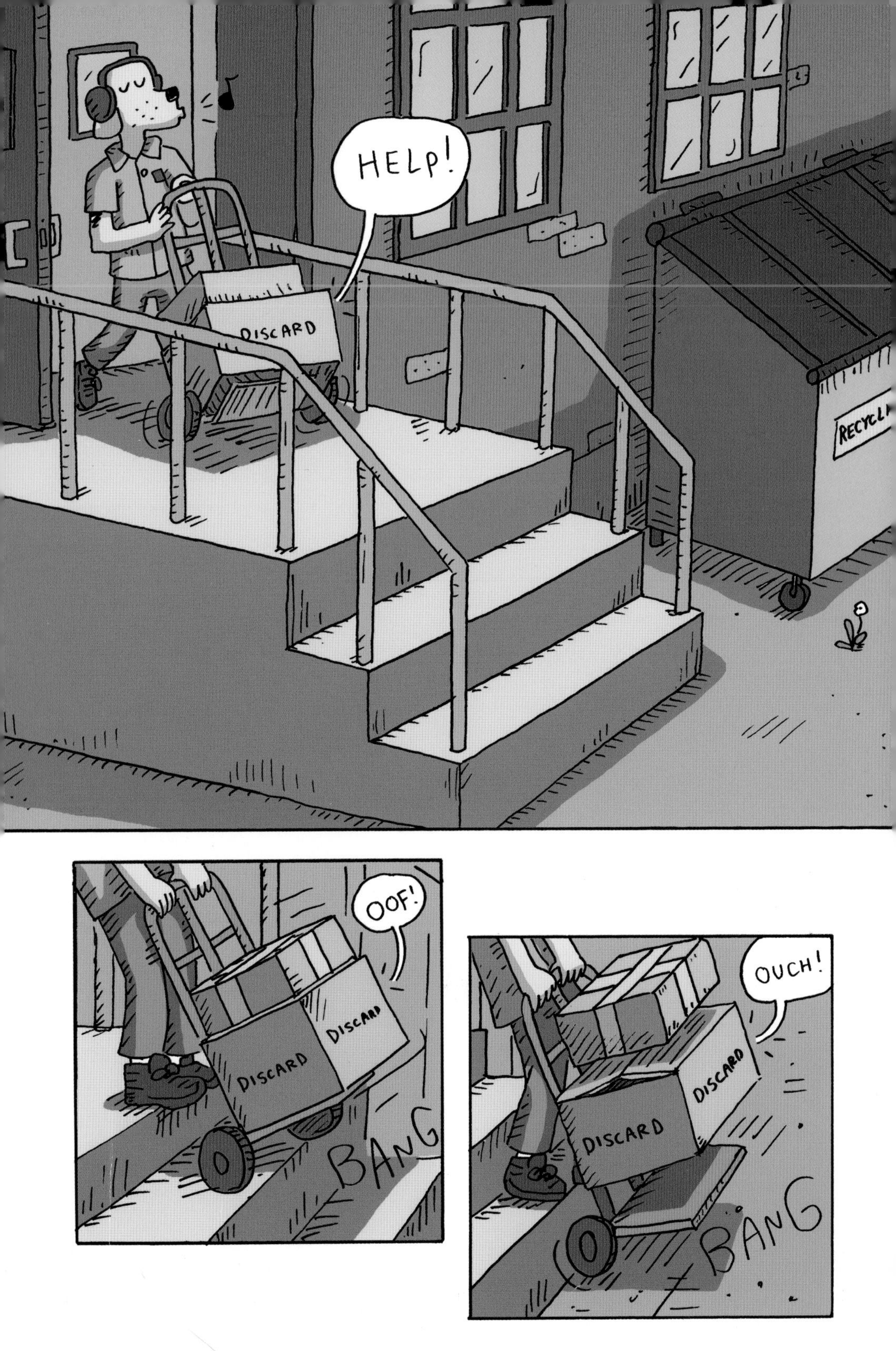
HELP!
DISCARD
OOF!
DISCARD
DISCARD
BANG
OUCH!
DISCARD
DISCARD
BANG

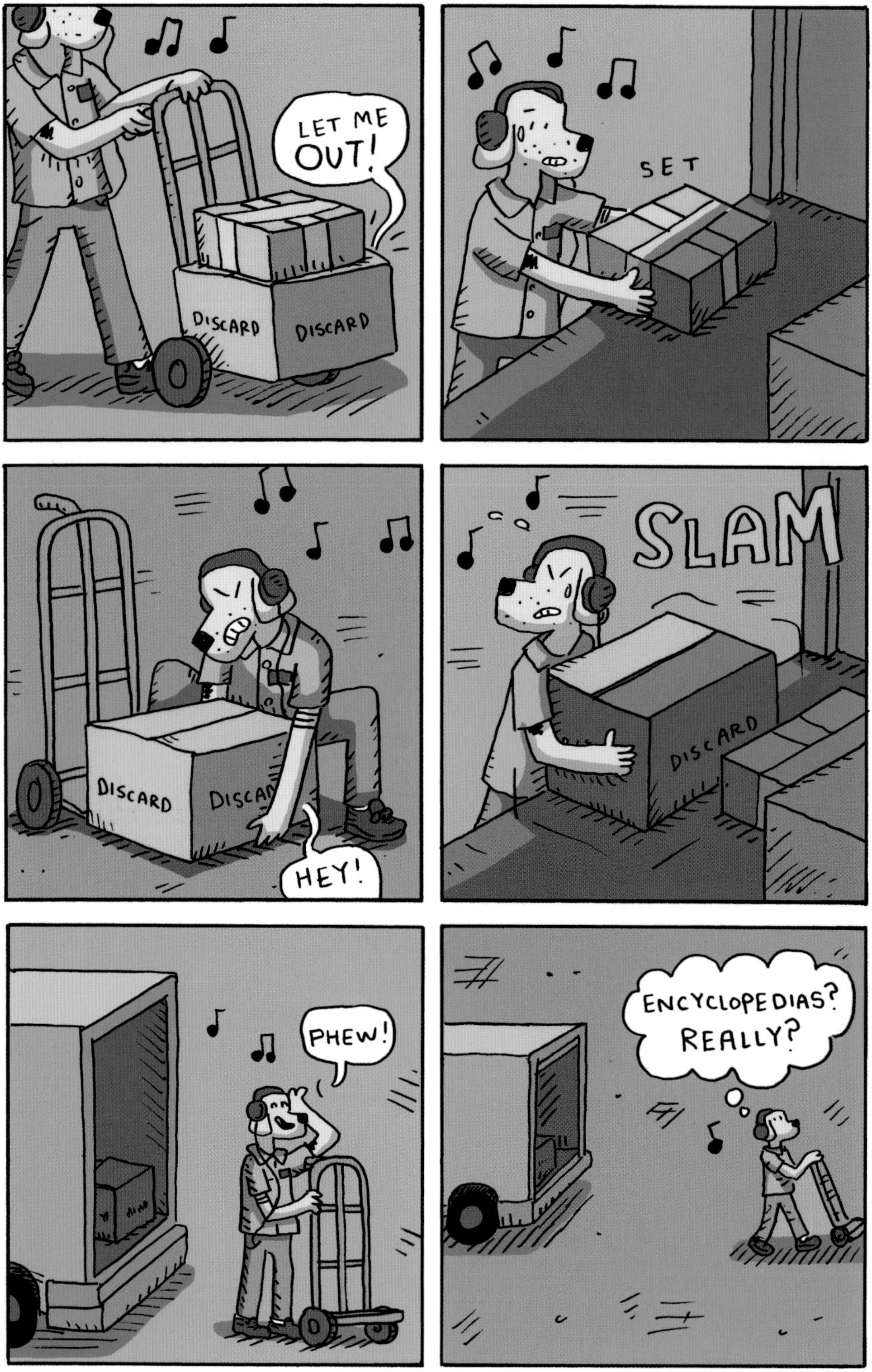
LET ME OUT!
DISCARD
DISCARD
SET
DISCARD
DISCARD
HEY!
SLAM
DISCARD
PHEW!
ENCYCLOPEDIAS? REALLY?

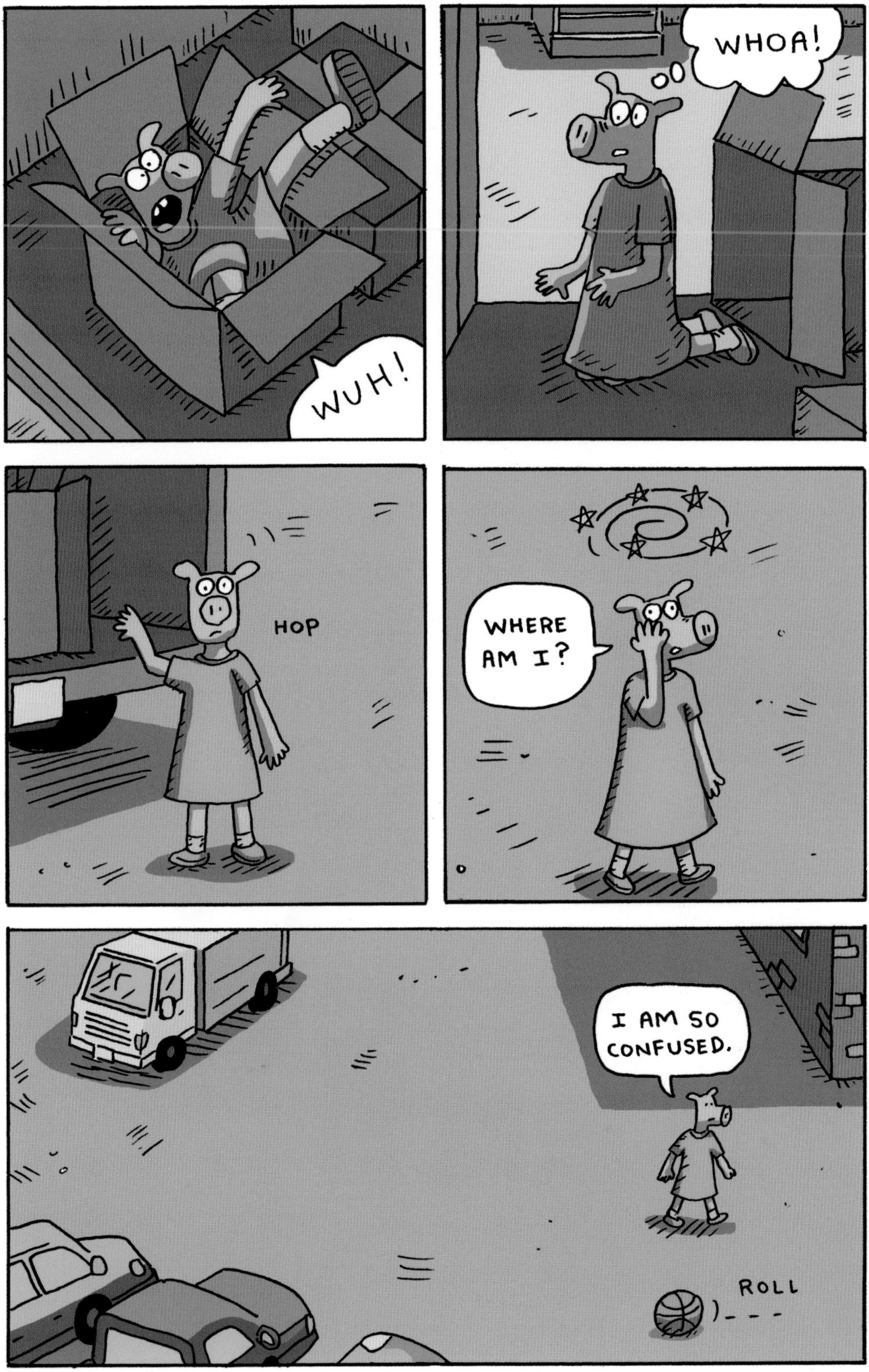
WUH!
WHOA!
HOP
WHERE AM I?
I AM SO CONFUSED.
ROLL

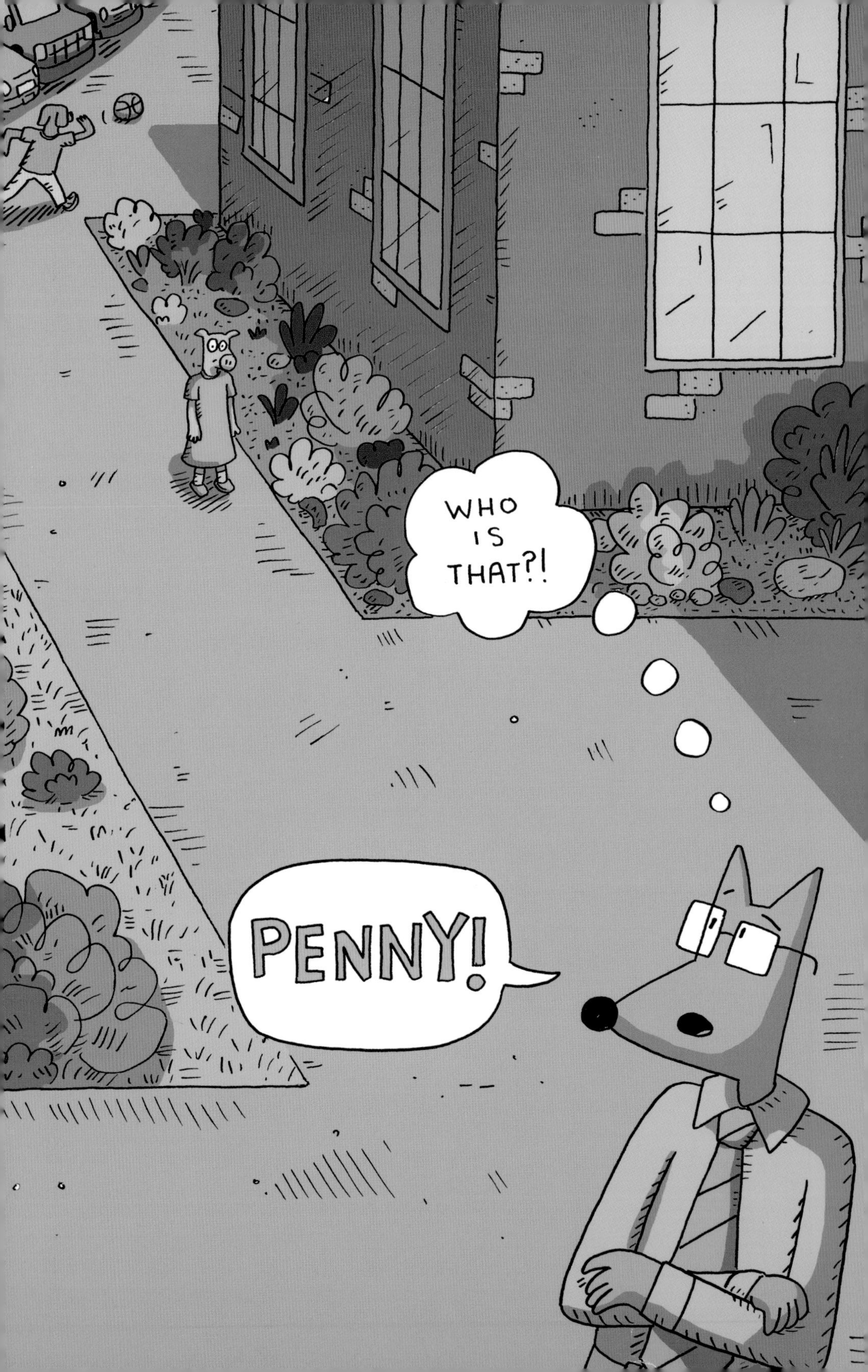
WHO IS THAT?!
PENNY!

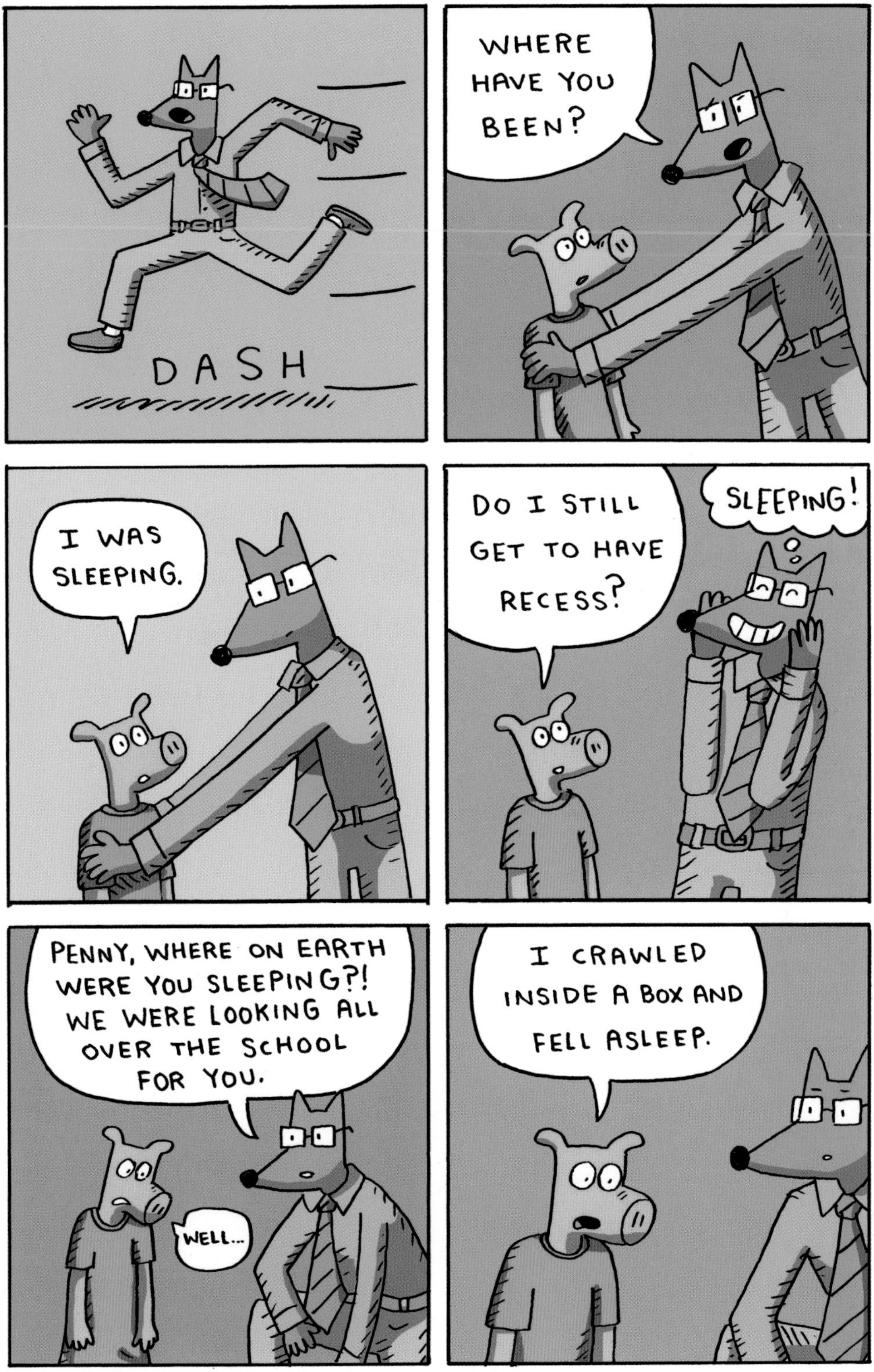
DASH
WHERE HAVE YOU BEEN?
I WAS SLEEPING.
DO I STILL GET TO HAVE RECESS?
SLEEPING!
PENNY, WHERE ON EARTH WERE YOU SLEEPING?! WE WERE LOOKING ALL OVER THE SCHOOL FOR YOU.
WELL...
I CRAWLED INSIDE A BOX AND FELL ASLEEP.

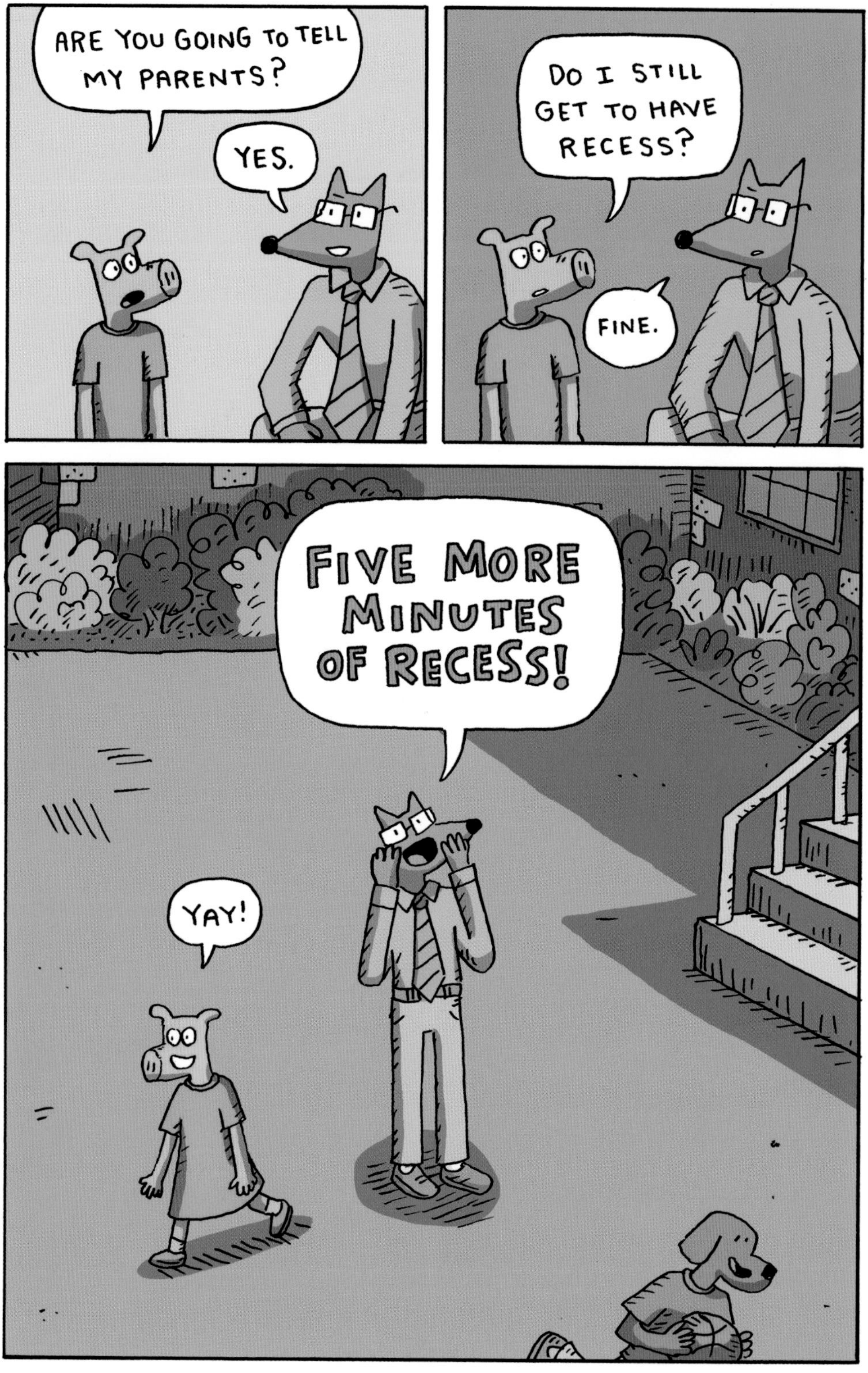
ARE YOU GOING TO TELL MY PARENTS?
YES.
DO I STILL GET TO HAVE RECESS?
FINE.
FIVE MORE MINUTES OF RECESS!
YAY!

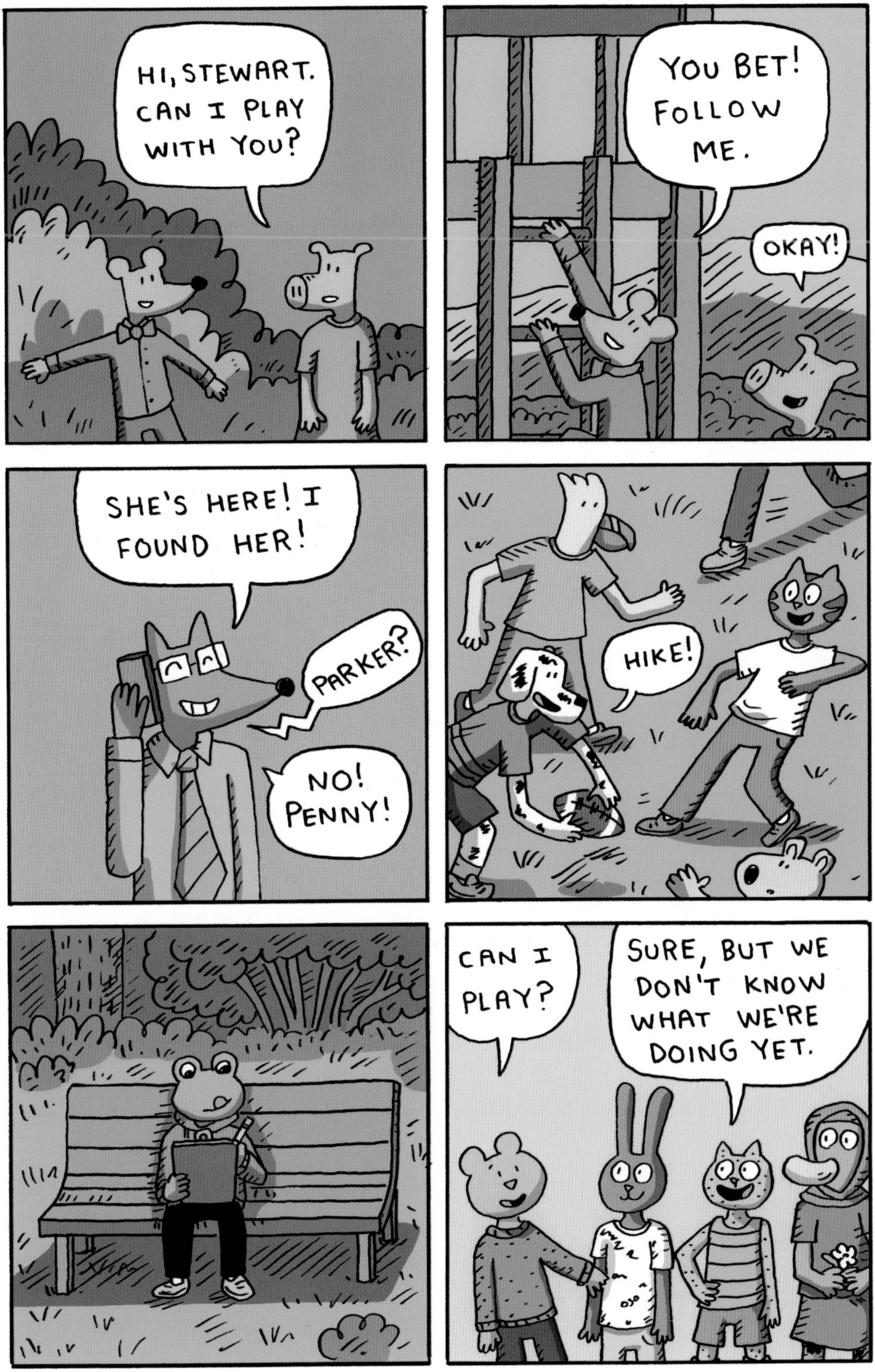
HI, STEWART. CAN I PLAY WITH YOU?
YOU BET! FOLLOW ME.
OKAY!
SHE'S HERE! I FOUND HER!
PARKER?
NO! PENNY!
HIKE!
CAN I PLAY?
SURE, BUT WE DON'T KNOW WHAT WE'RE DOING YET.

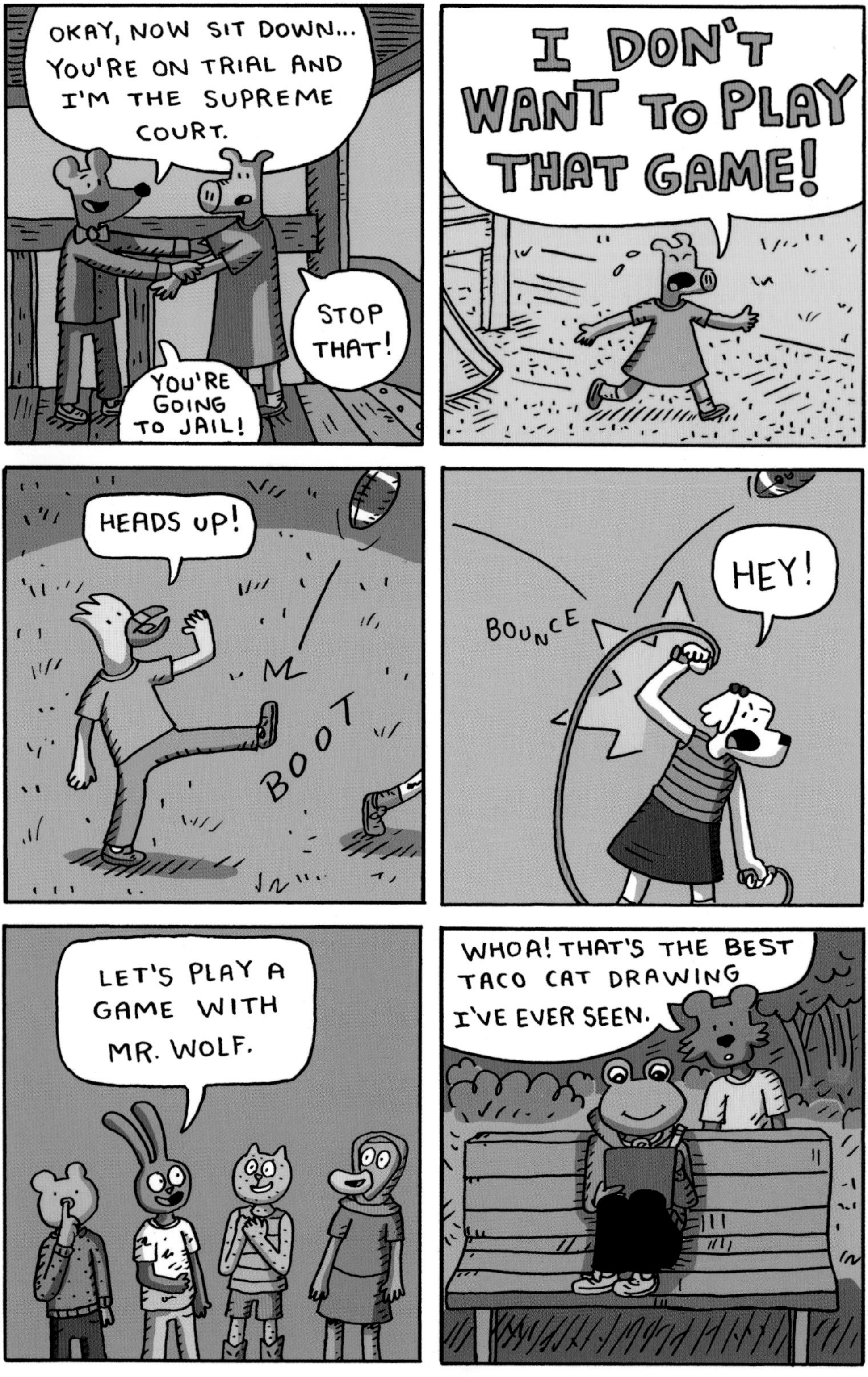
OKAY, NOW SIT DOWN... YOU'RE ON TRIAL AND I'M THE SUPREME COURT.
STOP THAT!
YOU'RE GOING TO JAIL!
I DON'T WANT TO PLAY THAT GAME!
HEADS UP!
BOOT
BOUNCE
HEY!
LET'S PLAY A GAME WITH MR. WOLF.
WHOA! THAT'S THE BEST TACO CAT DRAWING I'VE EVER SEEN.

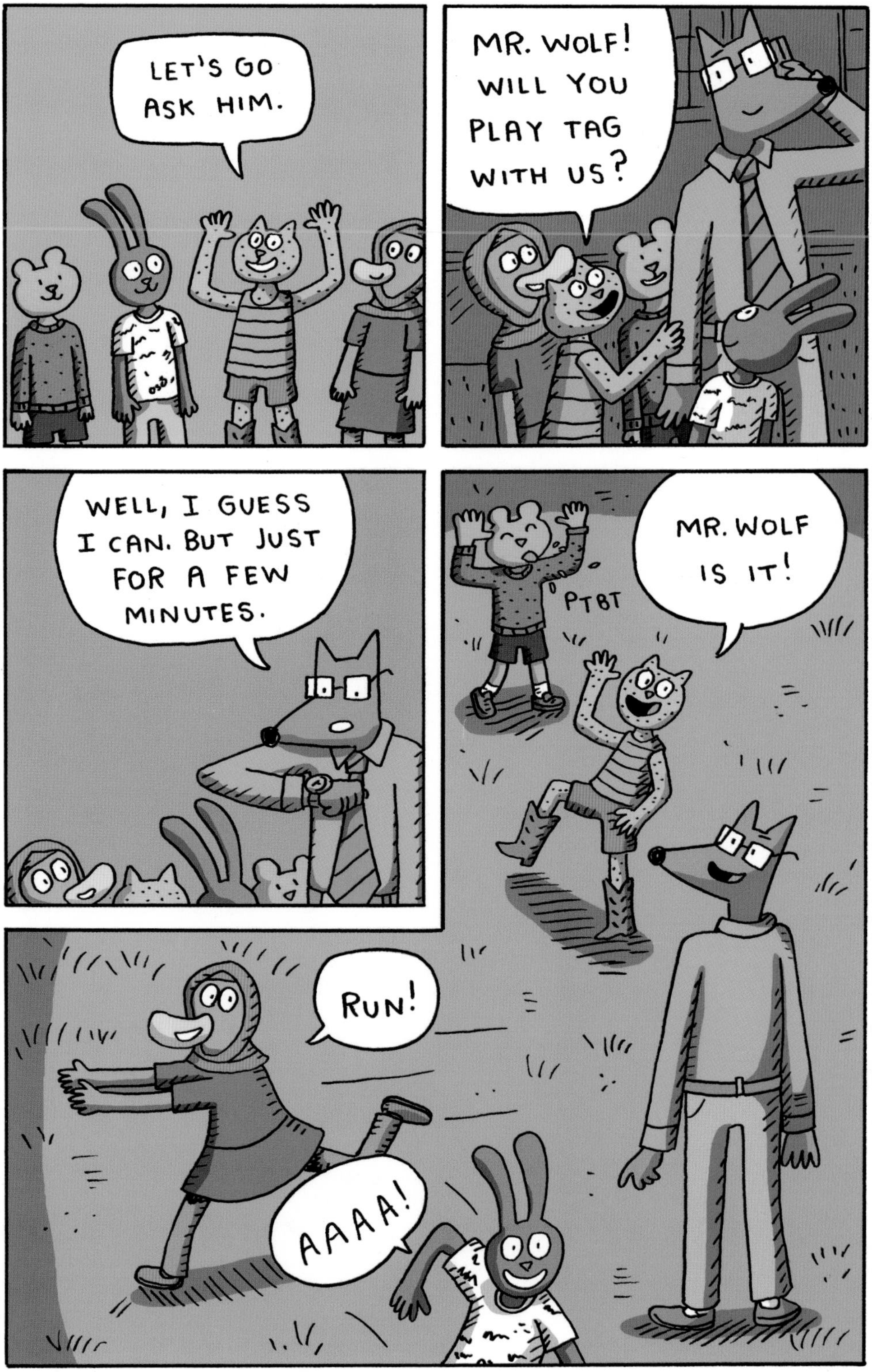
LET'S GO ASK HIM.
MR. WOLF! WILL YOU PLAY TAG WITH US?
WELL, I GUESS I CAN. BUT JUST FOR A FEW MINUTES.
PTBT
MR. WOLF IS IT!
RUN!
AAAA!

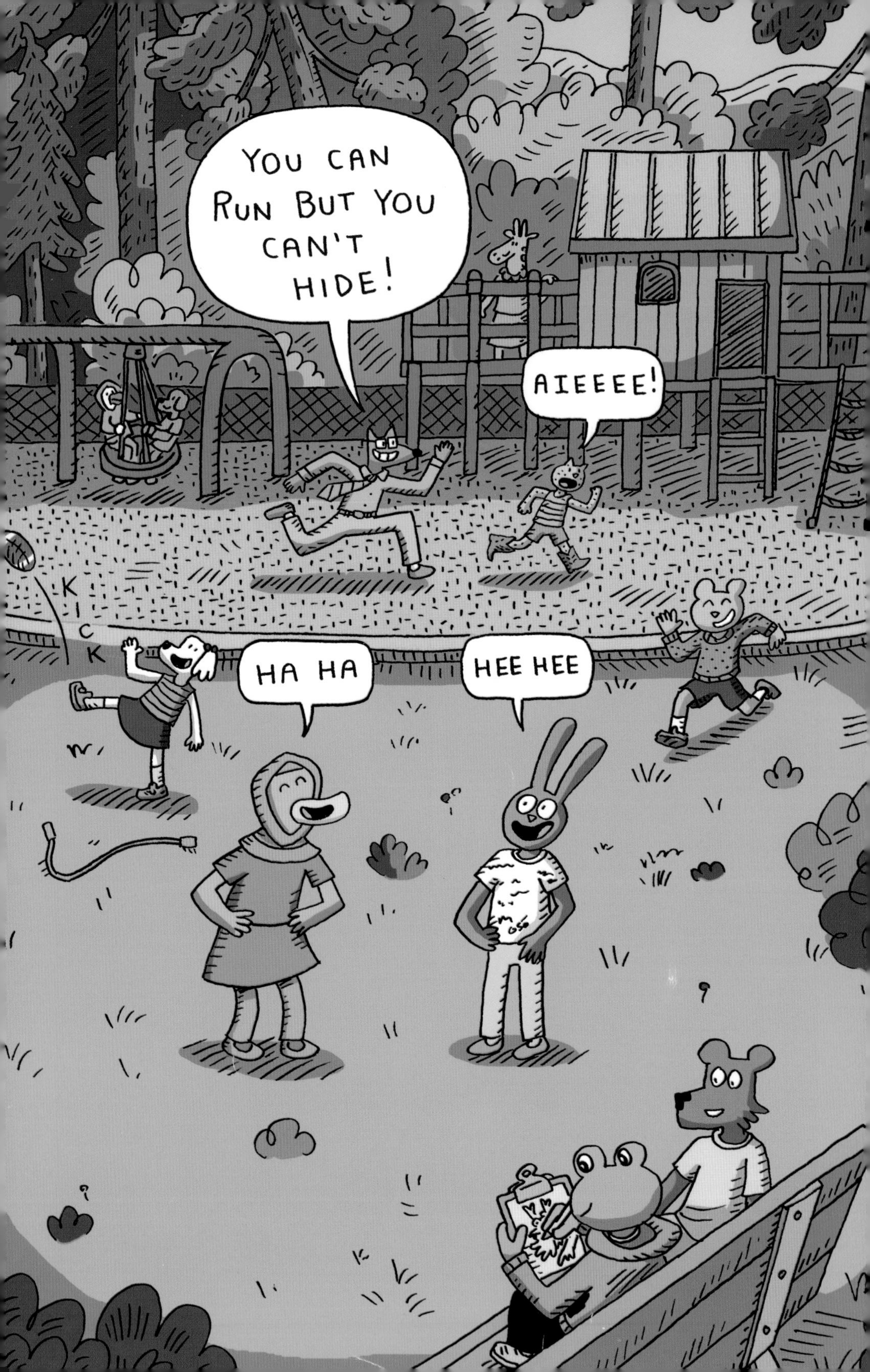
YOU CAN RUN BUT YOU CAN'T HIDE!
AIEEEEE!
KICK
HA HA
HEE HEE

CHAPTER NINE
Show and Scare

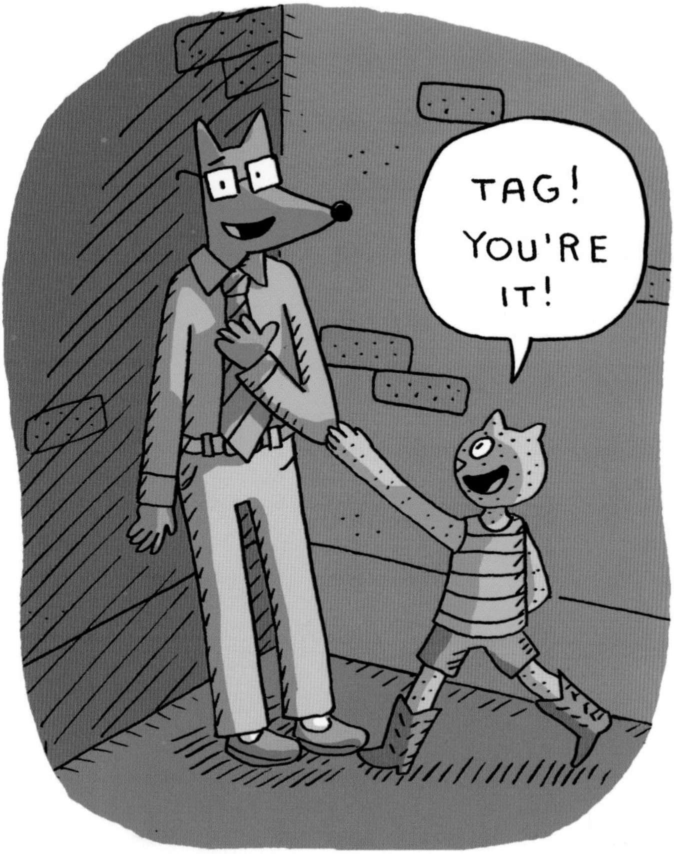
TAG! YOU'RE IT!

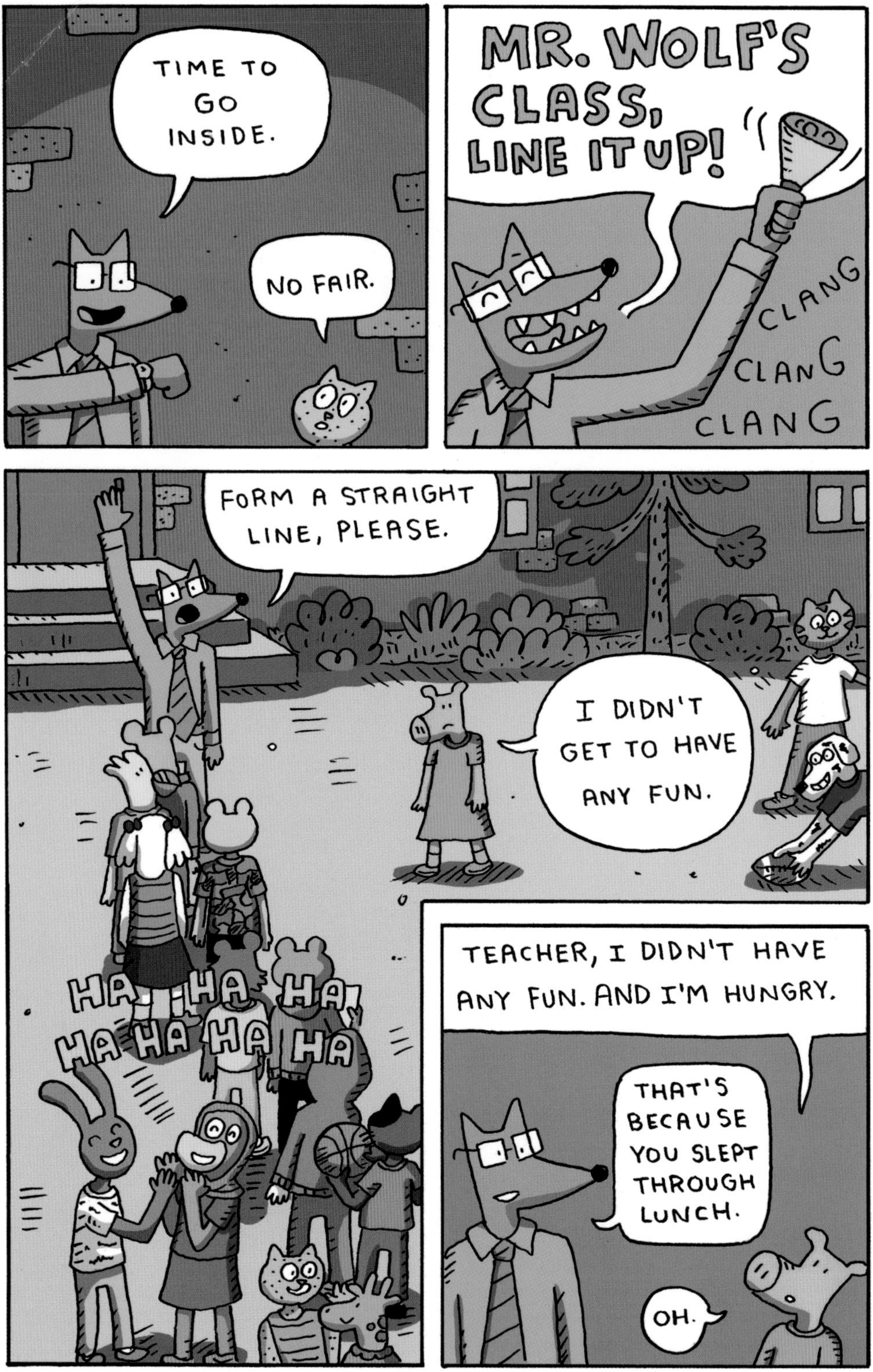
TIME TO GO INSIDE.
NO FAIR.
MR. WOLF'S CLASS, LINE IT UP!
CLANG
CLANG
CLANG
FORM A STRAIGHT LINE, PLEASE.
I DIDN'T GET TO HAVE ANY FUN.
HA HA HA
HA HA HA HA
TEACHER, I DIDN'T HAVE ANY FUN. AND I'M HUNGRY.
THAT'S BECAUSE YOU SLEPT THROUGH LUNCH.
OH.

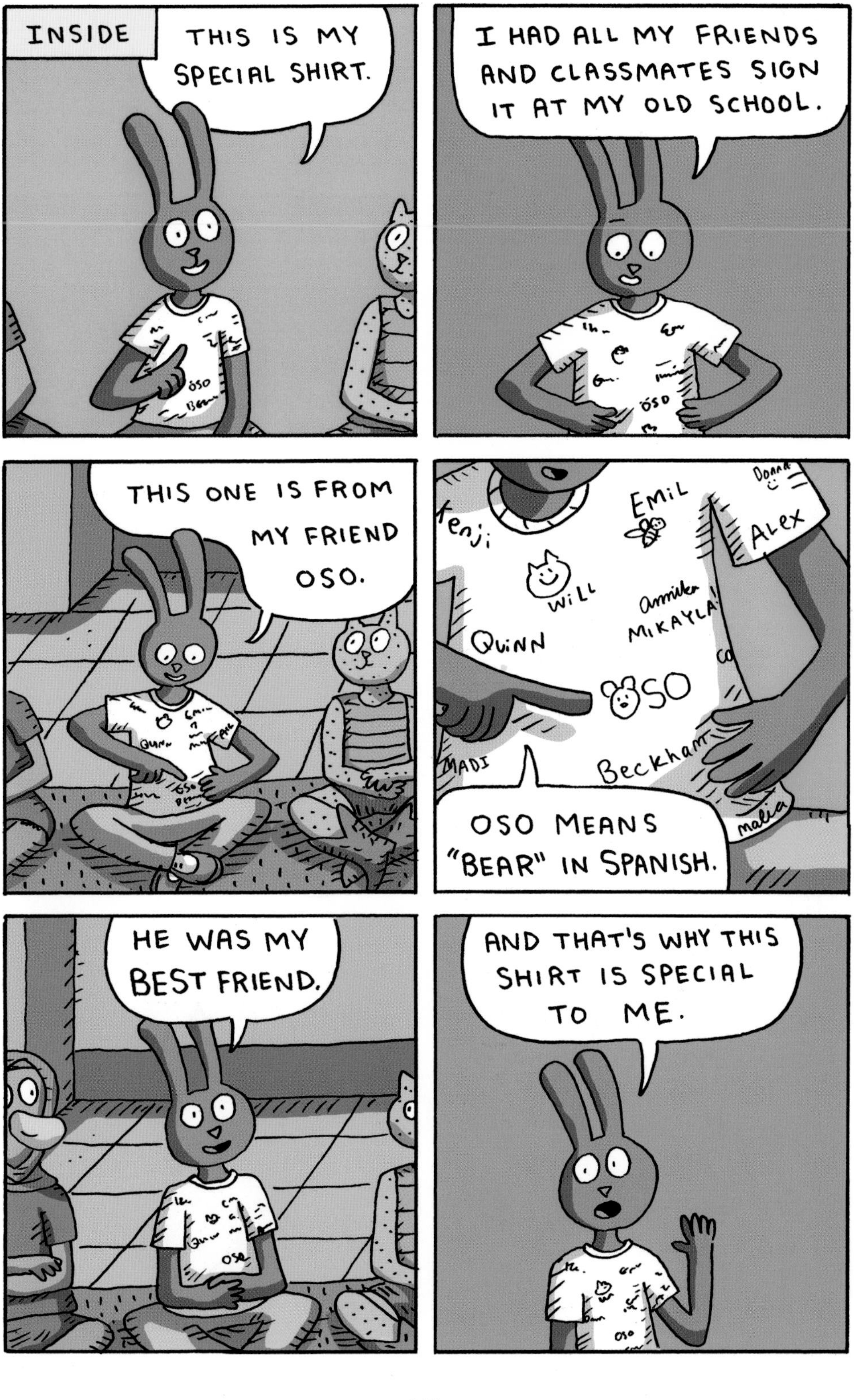
INSIDE
THIS IS MY SPECIAL SHIRT.
I HAD ALL MY FRIENDS AND CLASSMATES SIGN IT AT MY OLD SCHOOL.
THIS ONE IS FROM MY FRIEND OSO.
Kenji
EMIL
Donna
ALEX
WILL
MIKAYLA
QUINN
OSO
MADI
Beckham
malia
OSO MEANS "BEAR" IN SPANISH.
HE WAS MY BEST FRIEND.
AND THAT'S WHY THIS SHIRT IS SPECIAL TO ME.

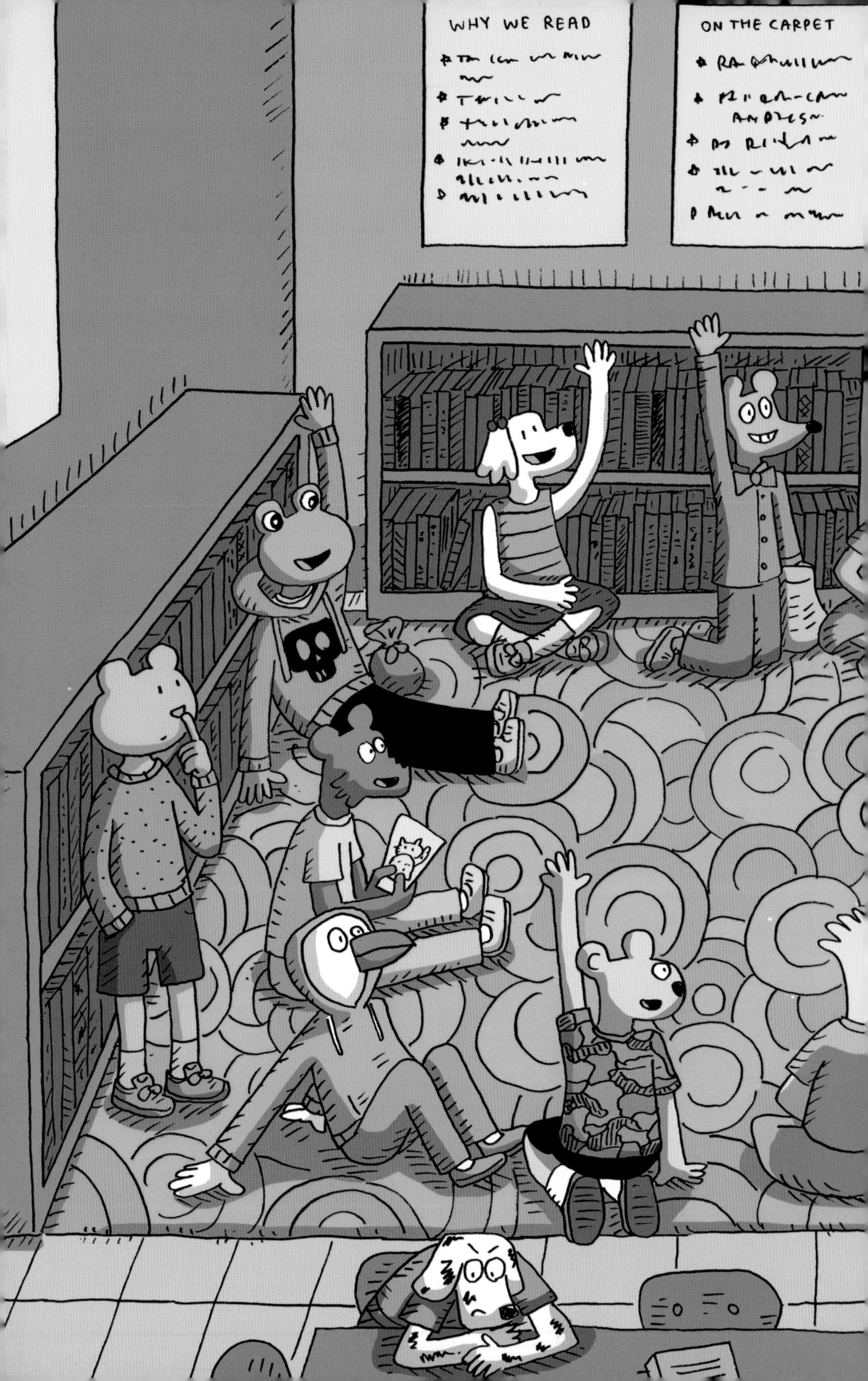
WHY WE READ
ON THE CARPET

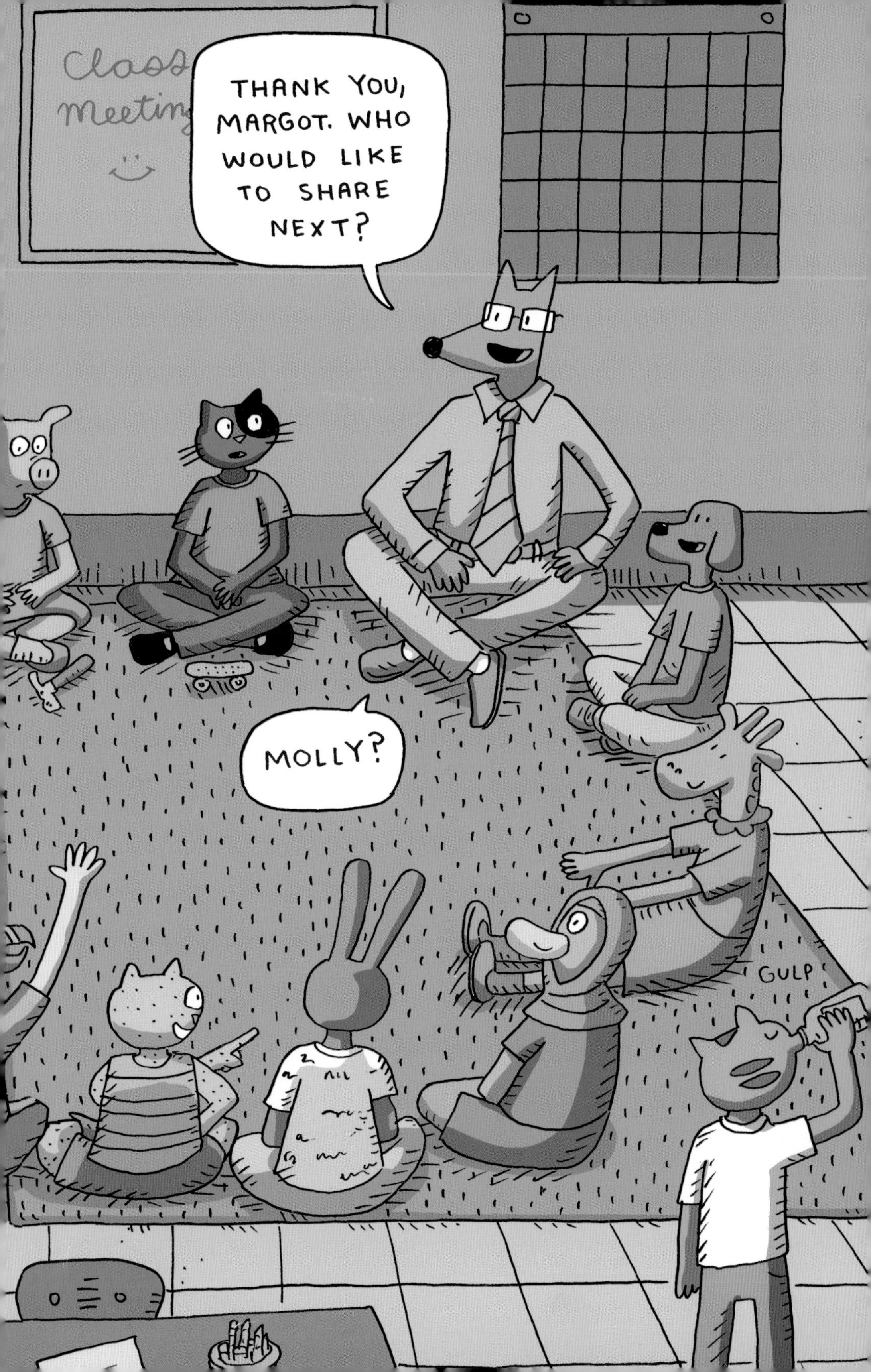
Class Meeting
THANK YOU, MARGOT. WHO WOULD LIKE TO SHARE NEXT?
MOLLY?
GULP

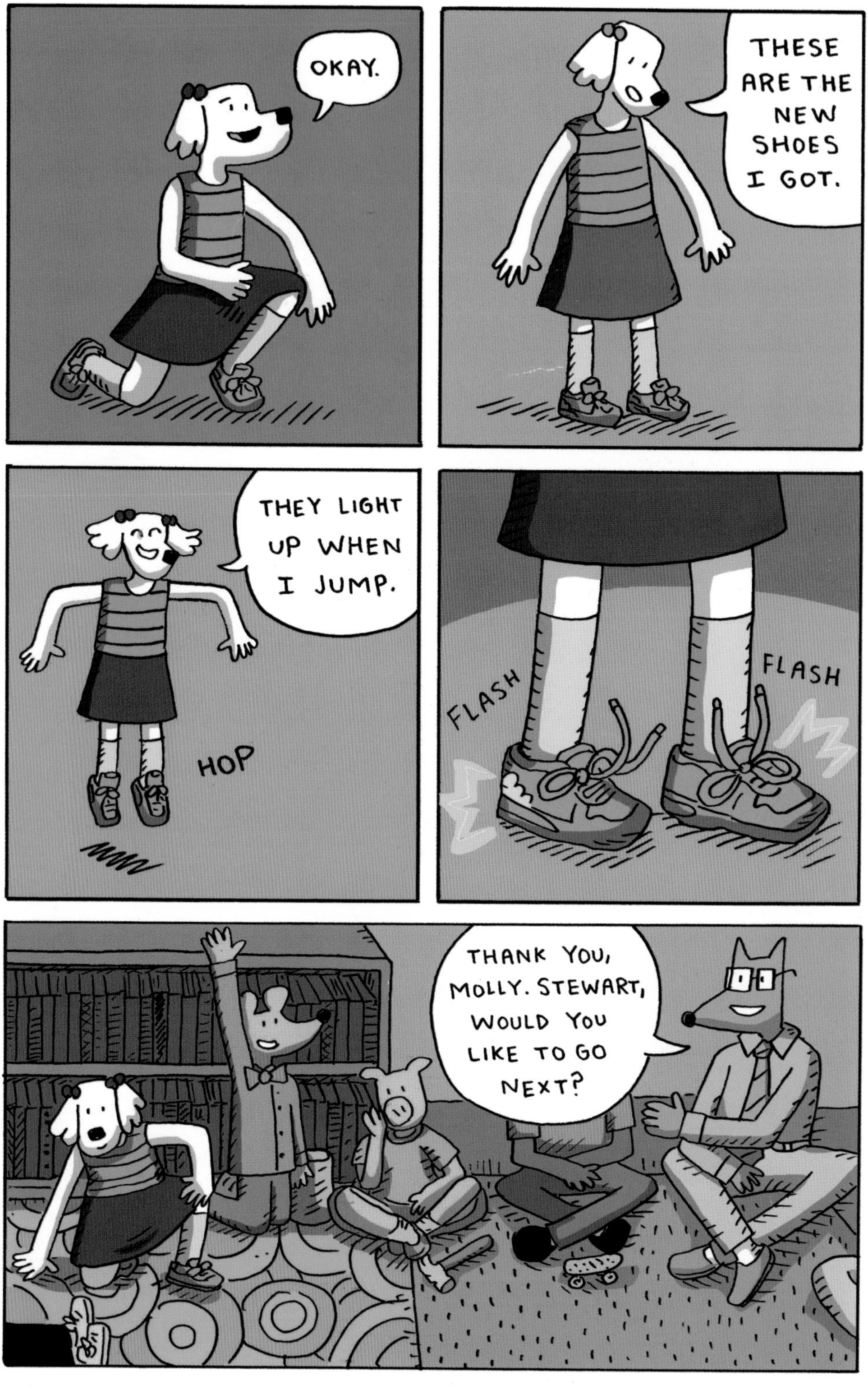
OKAY.
THESE ARE THE NEW SHOES I GOT.
THEY LIGHT UP WHEN I JUMP.
HOP
FLASH
FLASH
THANK YOU, MOLLY. STEWART, WOULD YOU LIKE TO GO NEXT?

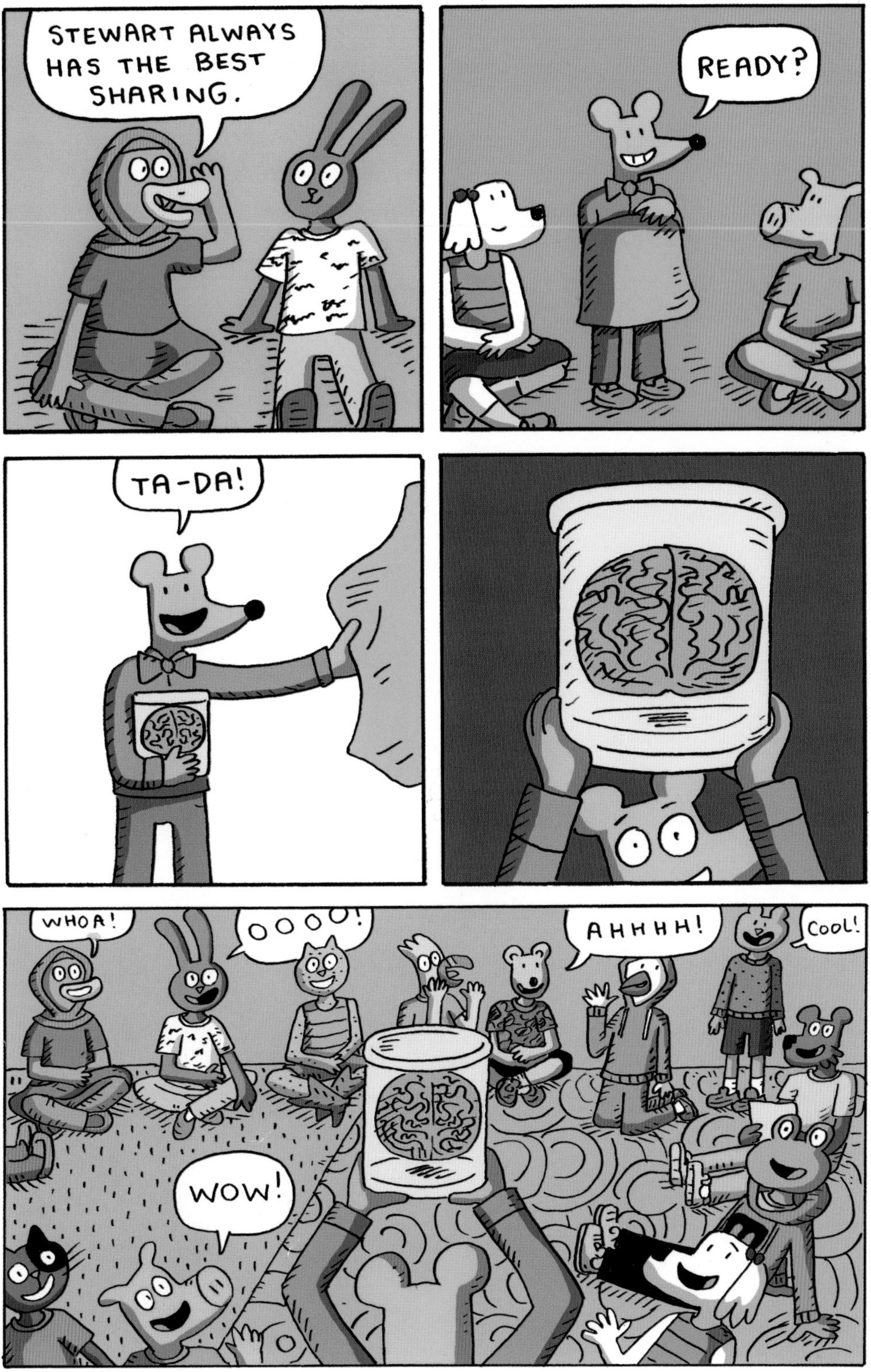
STEWART ALWAYS HAS THE BEST SHARING.
READY?
TA-DA!
WHOA!
OOOO!
AHHHH!
COOL!
WOW!

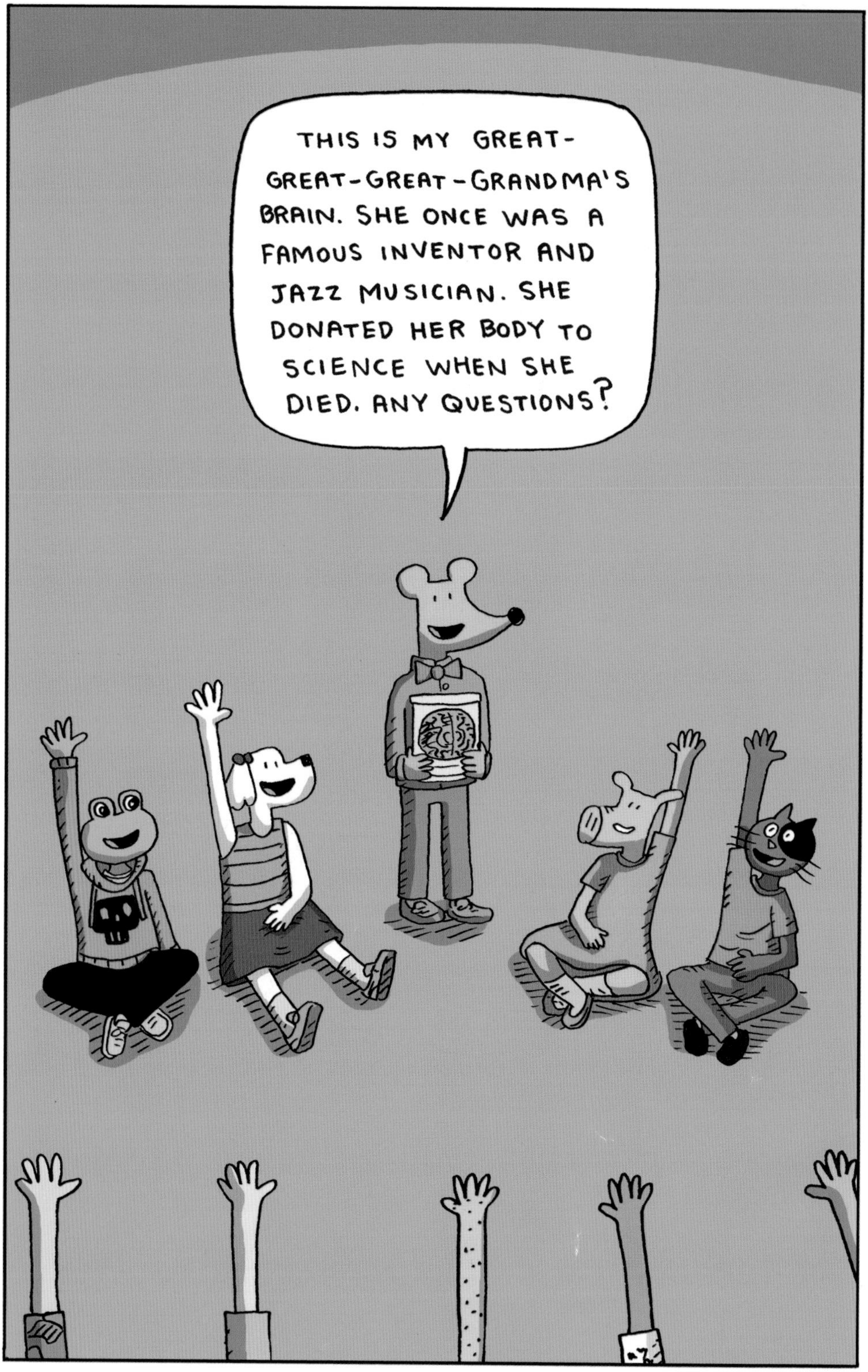
THIS IS MY GREAT-GREAT-GREAT-GRANDMA'S BRAIN. SHE ONCE WAS A FAMOUS INVENTOR AND JAZZ MUSICIAN. SHE DONATED HER BODY TO SCIENCE WHEN SHE DIED. ANY QUESTIONS?

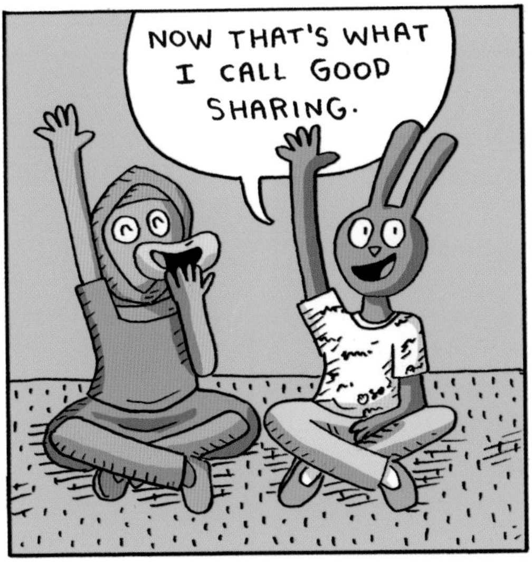
NOW THAT'S WHAT I CALL GOOD SHARING.

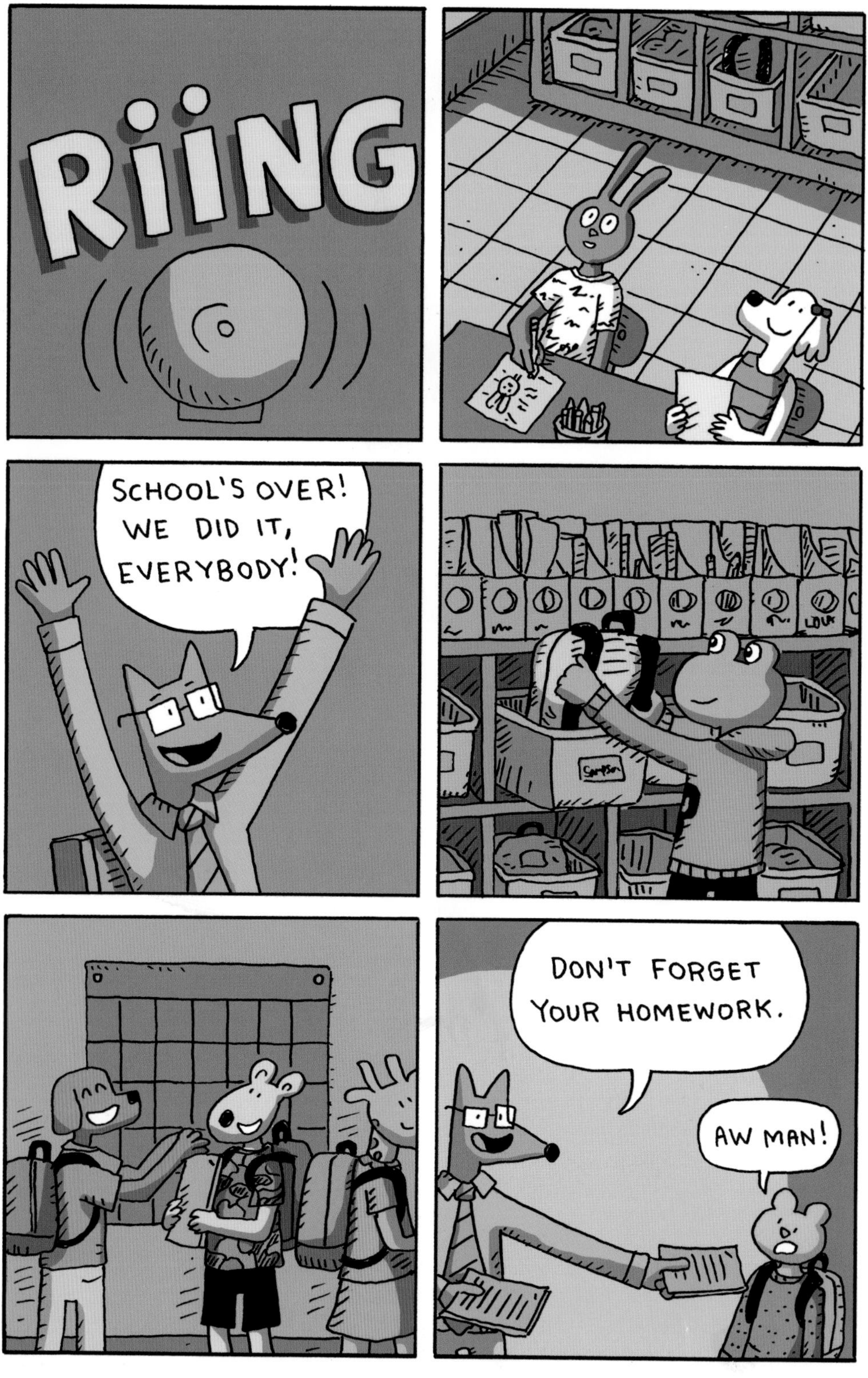
RIING
SCHOOL'S OVER! WE DID IT, EVERYBODY!
DON'T FORGET YOUR HOMEWORK.
AW MAN!

CHAPTER TEN
An Empty Seat

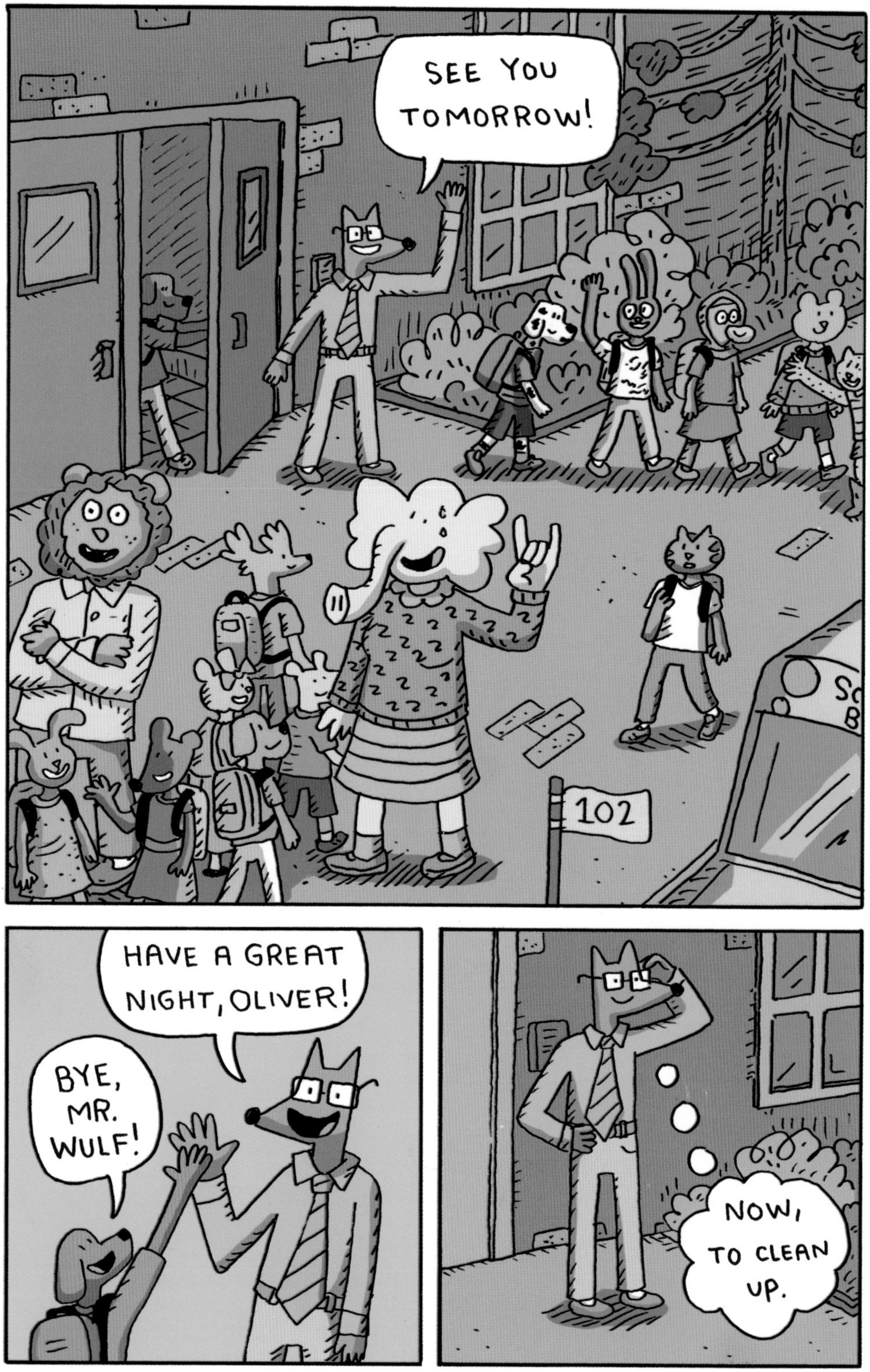
SEE YOU TOMORROW!
102
HAVE A GREAT NIGHT, OLIVER!
BYE, MR. WULF!
NOW, TO CLEAN UP.

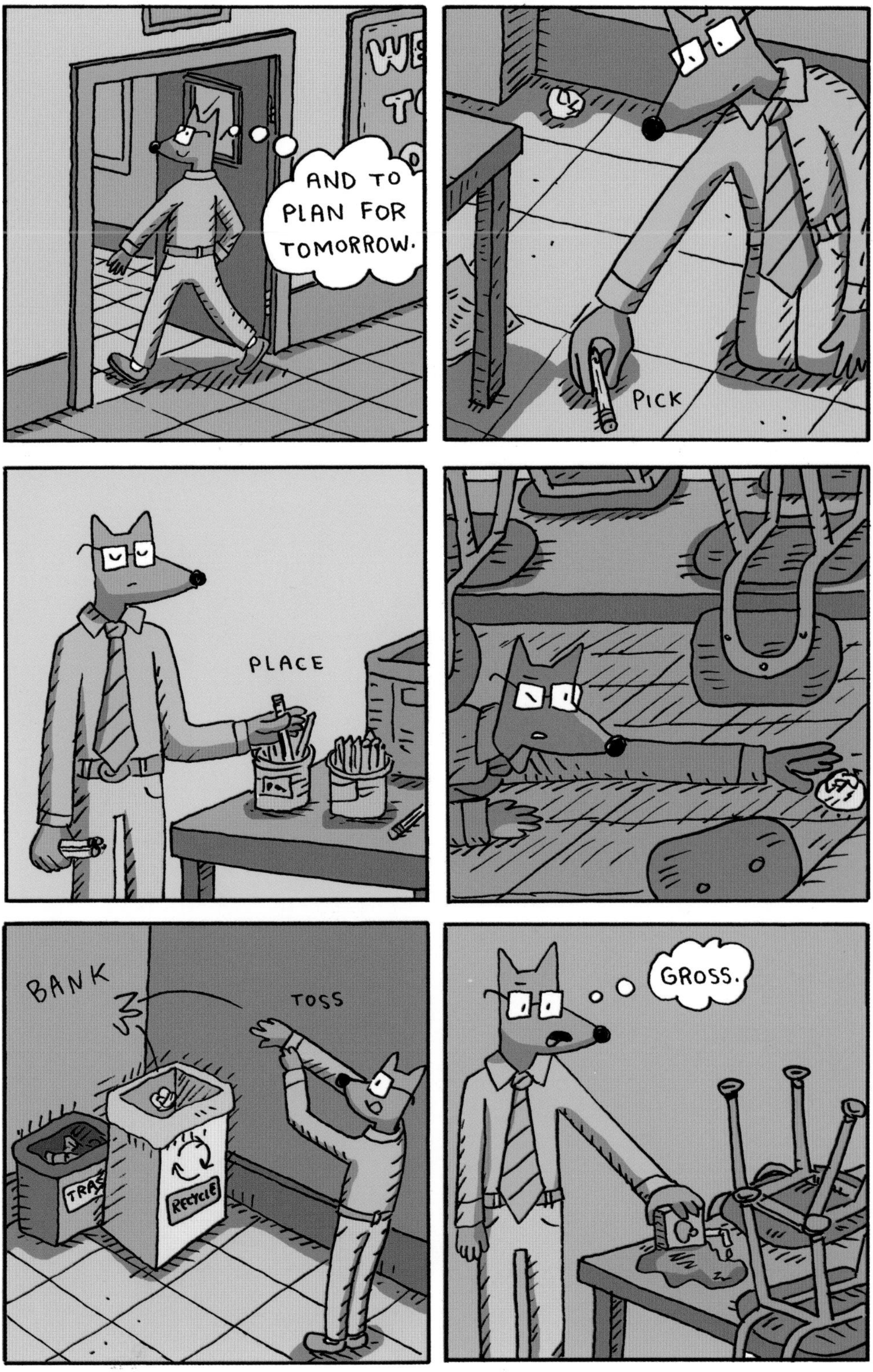
AND TO PLAN FOR TOMORROW.
PICK
PLACE
BANK
TOSS
TRAS
RECYCLE
GROSS.

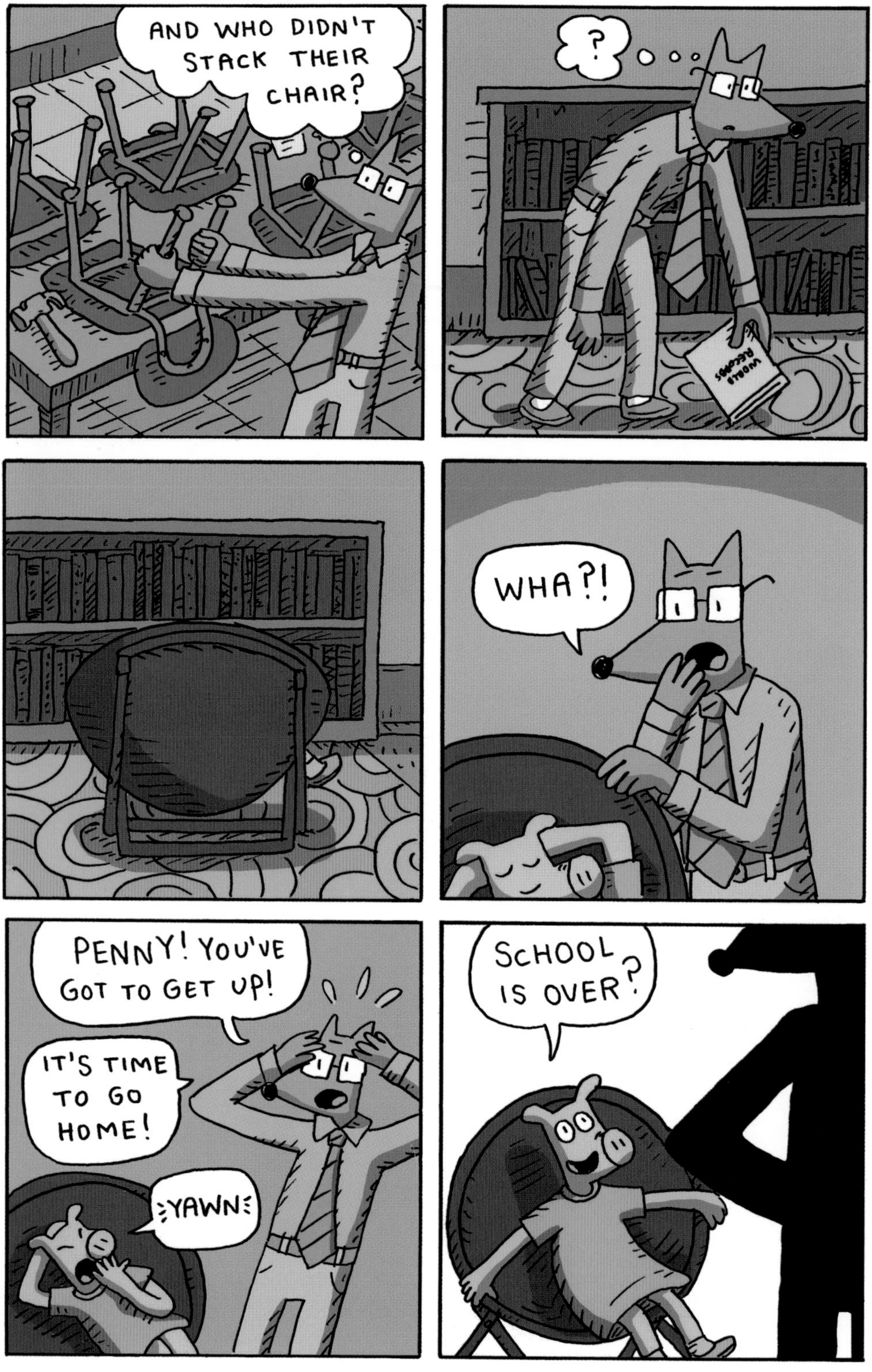
AND WHO DIDN'T STACK THEIR CHAIR?
?
WORLD RECORDS
WHA?!
PENNY! YOU'VE GOT TO GET UP!
IT'S TIME TO GO HOME!
YAWN
SCHOOL IS OVER?

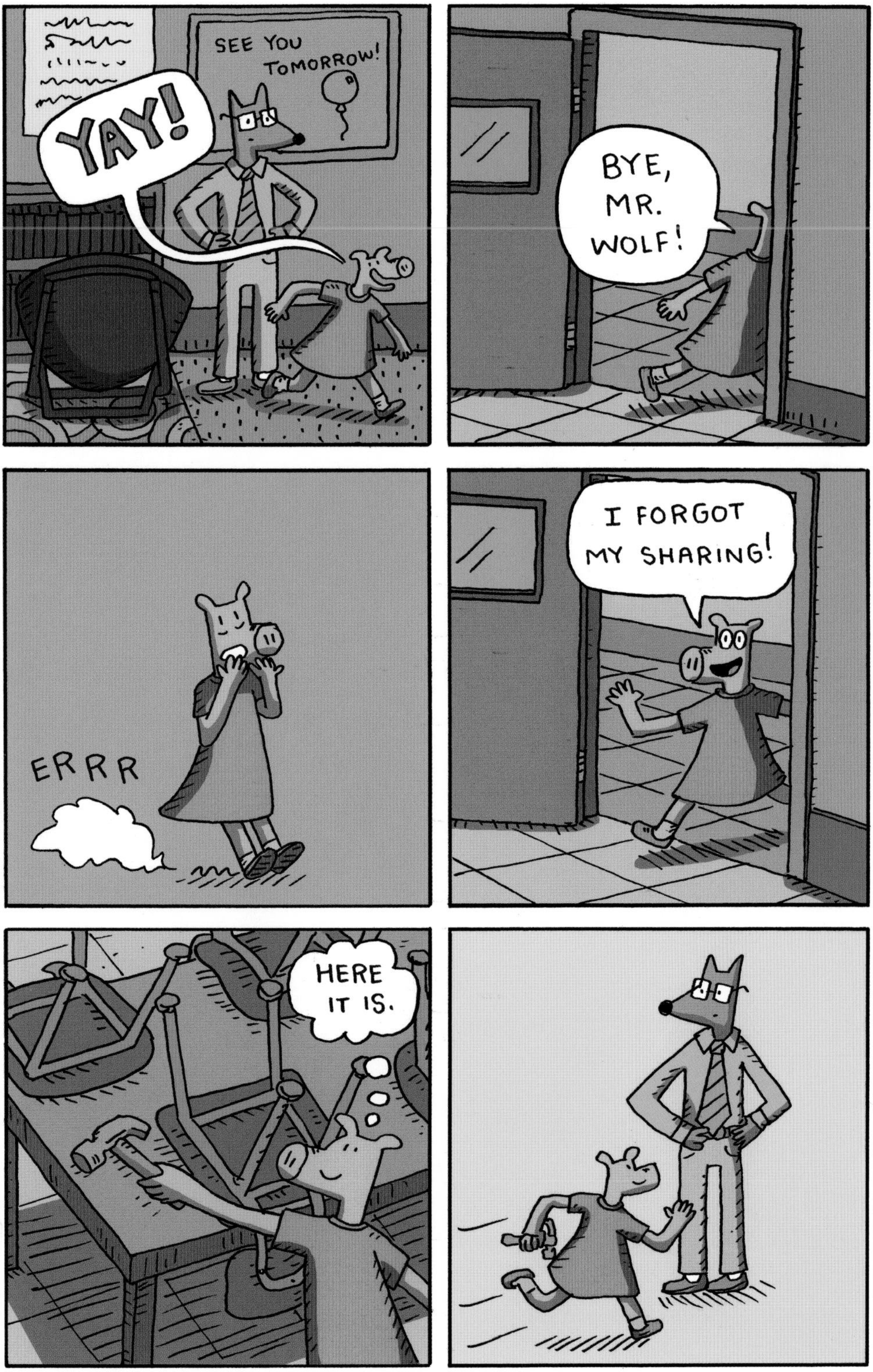
SEE YOU TOMORROW!
YAY!
BYE, MR. WOLF!
ERRR
I FORGOT MY SHARING!
HERE IT IS.

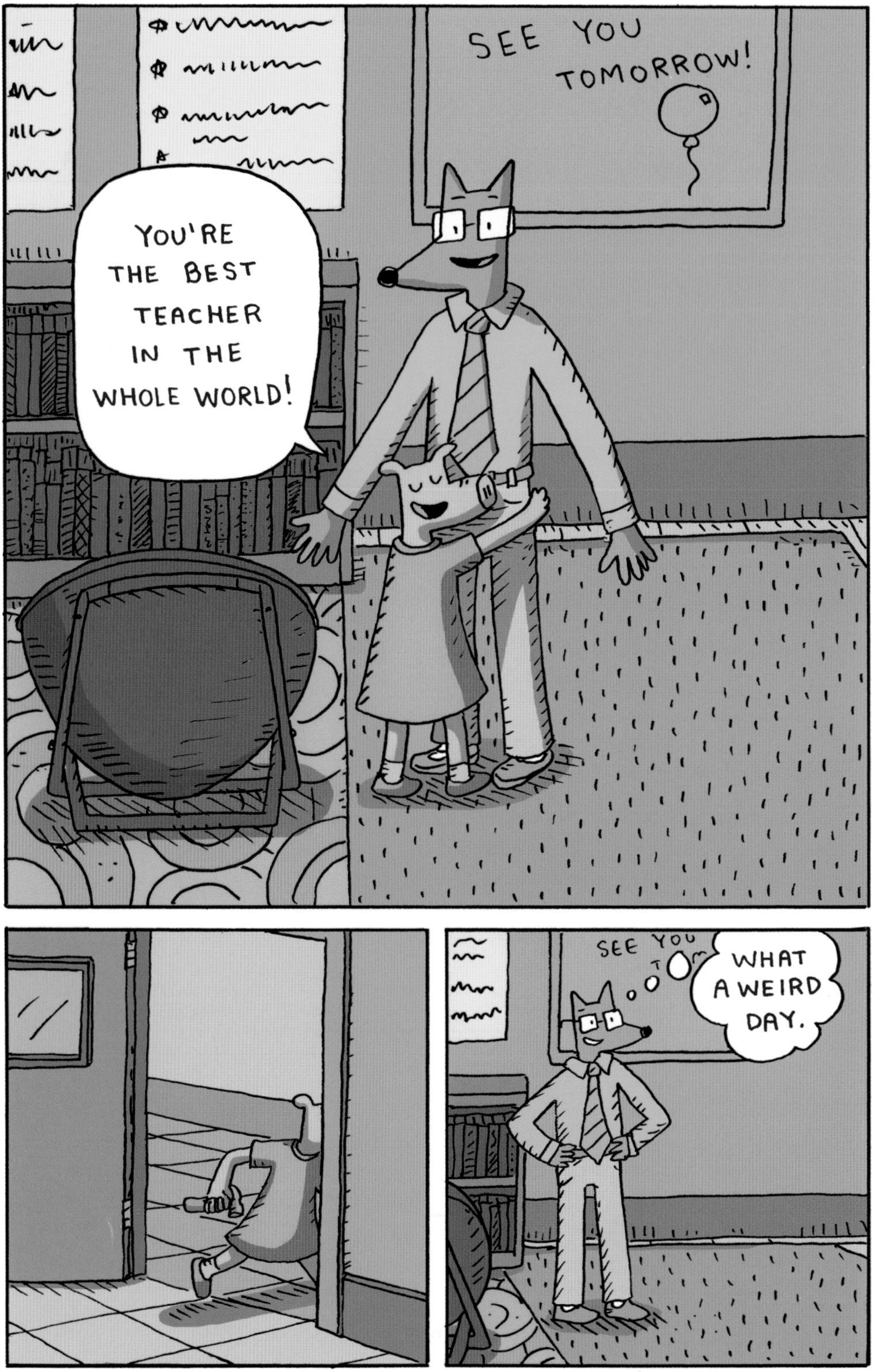
SEE YOU TOMORROW!
YOU'RE THE BEST TEACHER IN THE WHOLE WORLD!
SEE YOU
WHAT A WEIRD DAY.

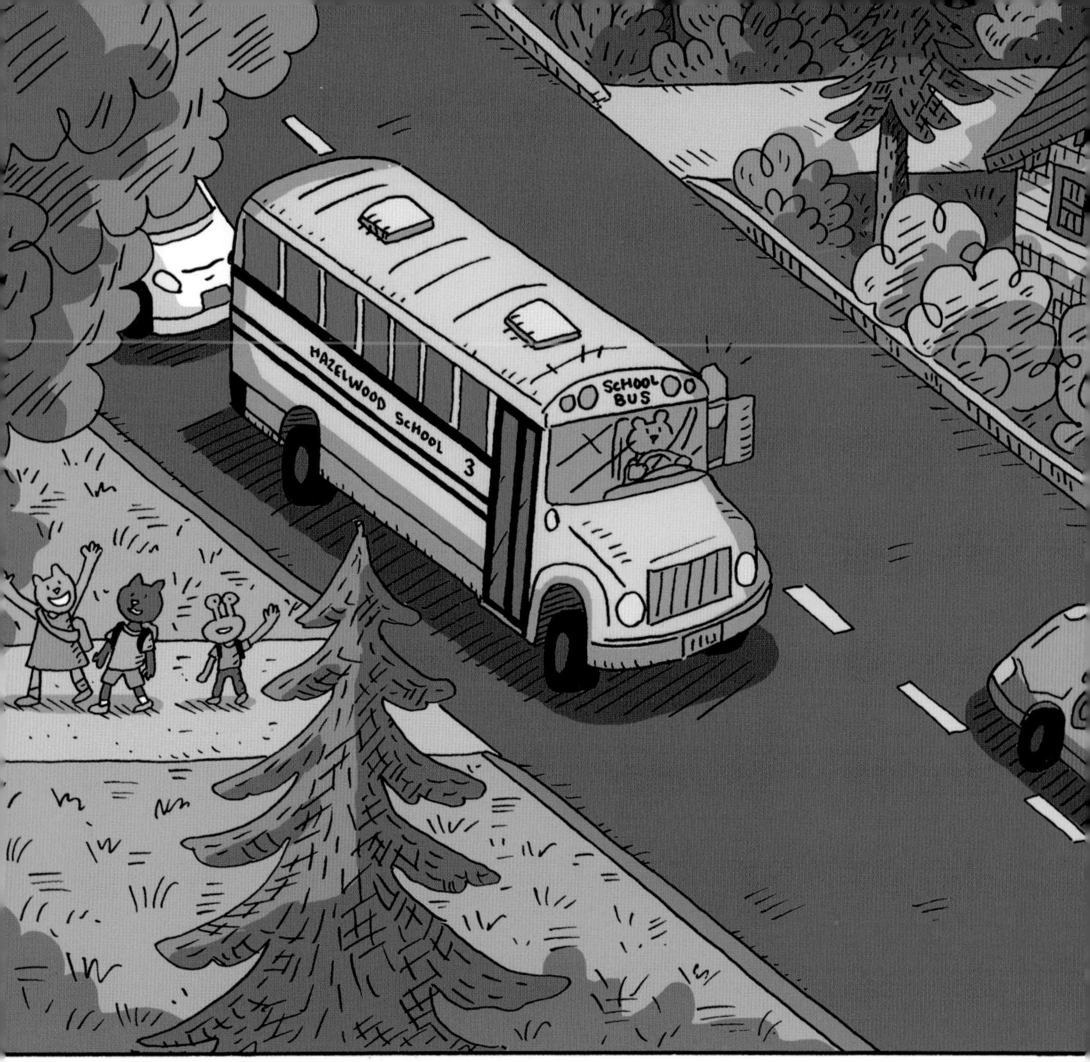
HAZELWOOD SCHOOL 3
SCHOOL BUS
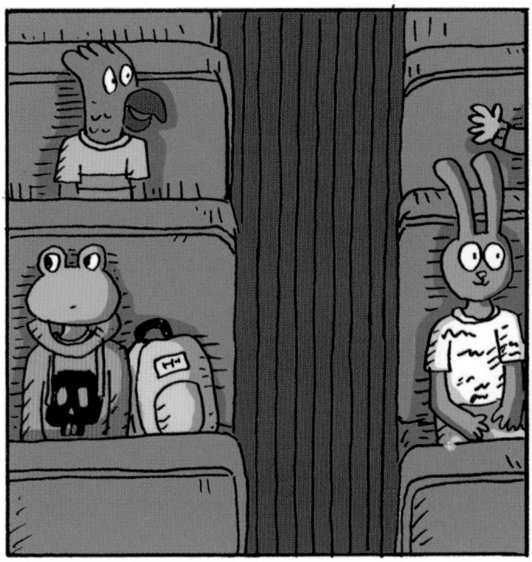
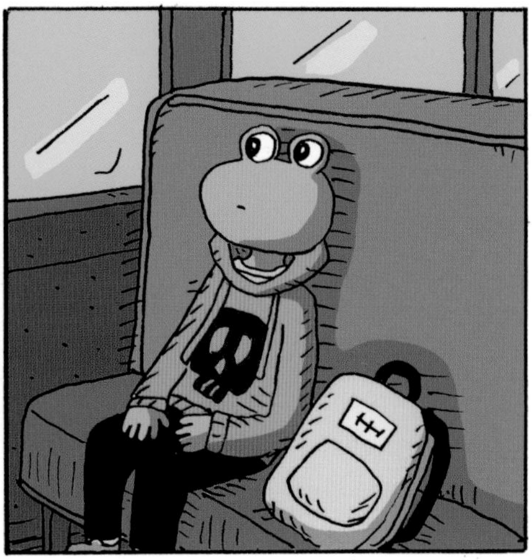

TOSS
HEY!
BOUNCE
OH NO! NOT AGAIN!
!
Can I sit next to you?
Yes
No
(check one)
If you check both that would be really confusing.

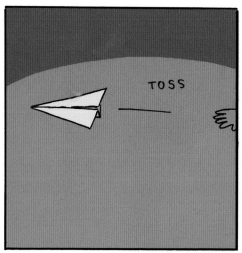

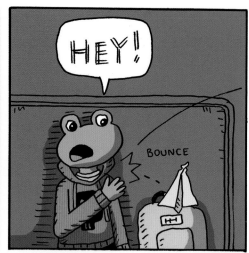

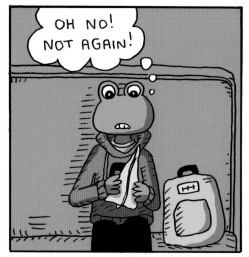

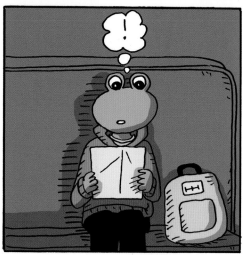

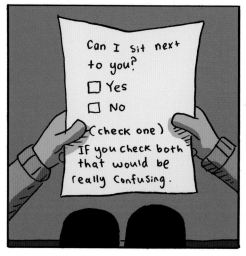

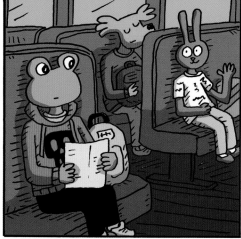

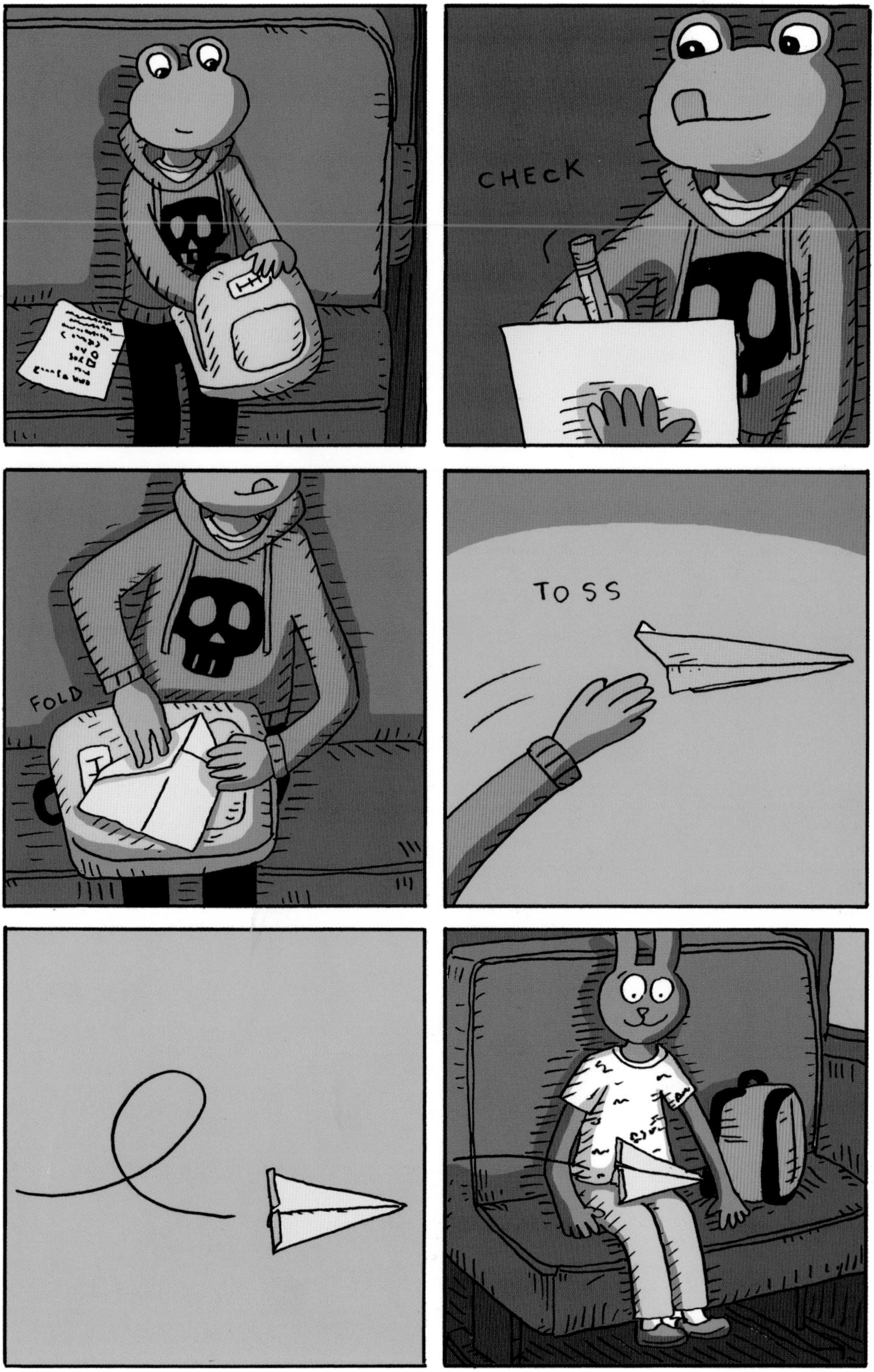
CHECK
FOLD
TOSS

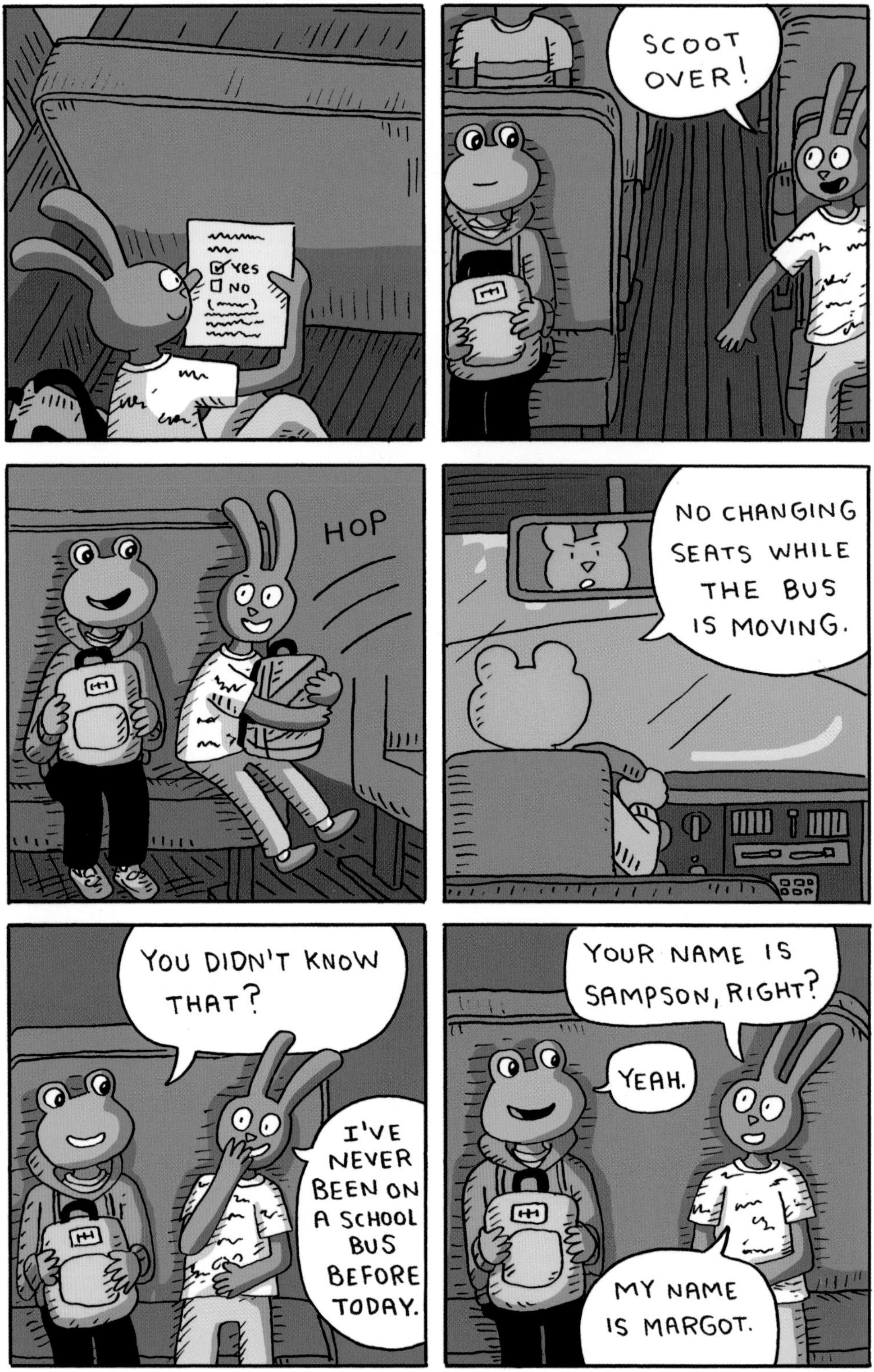
YES
NO
SCOOT OVER!
HOP
NO CHANGING SEATS WHILE THE BUS IS MOVING.
YOU DIDN'T KNOW THAT?
I'VE NEVER BEEN ON A SCHOOL BUS BEFORE TODAY.
YOUR NAME IS SAMPSON, RIGHT?
YEAH.
MY NAME IS MARGOT.

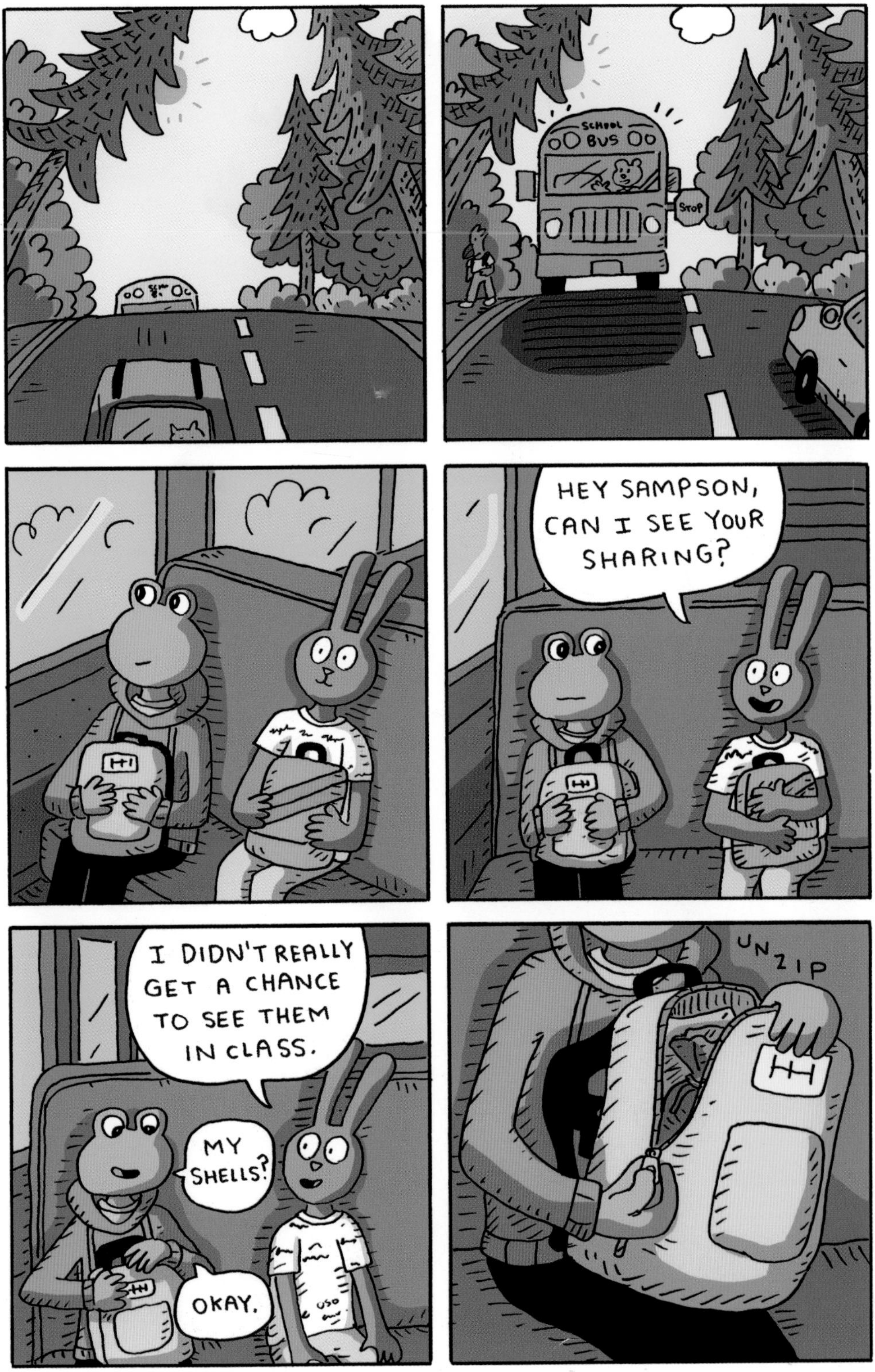
SCHOOL BUS
STOP
HEY SAMPSON, CAN I SEE YOUR SHARING?
I DIDN'T REALLY GET A CHANCE TO SEE THEM IN CLASS.
MY SHELLS?
OKAY.
UNZIP

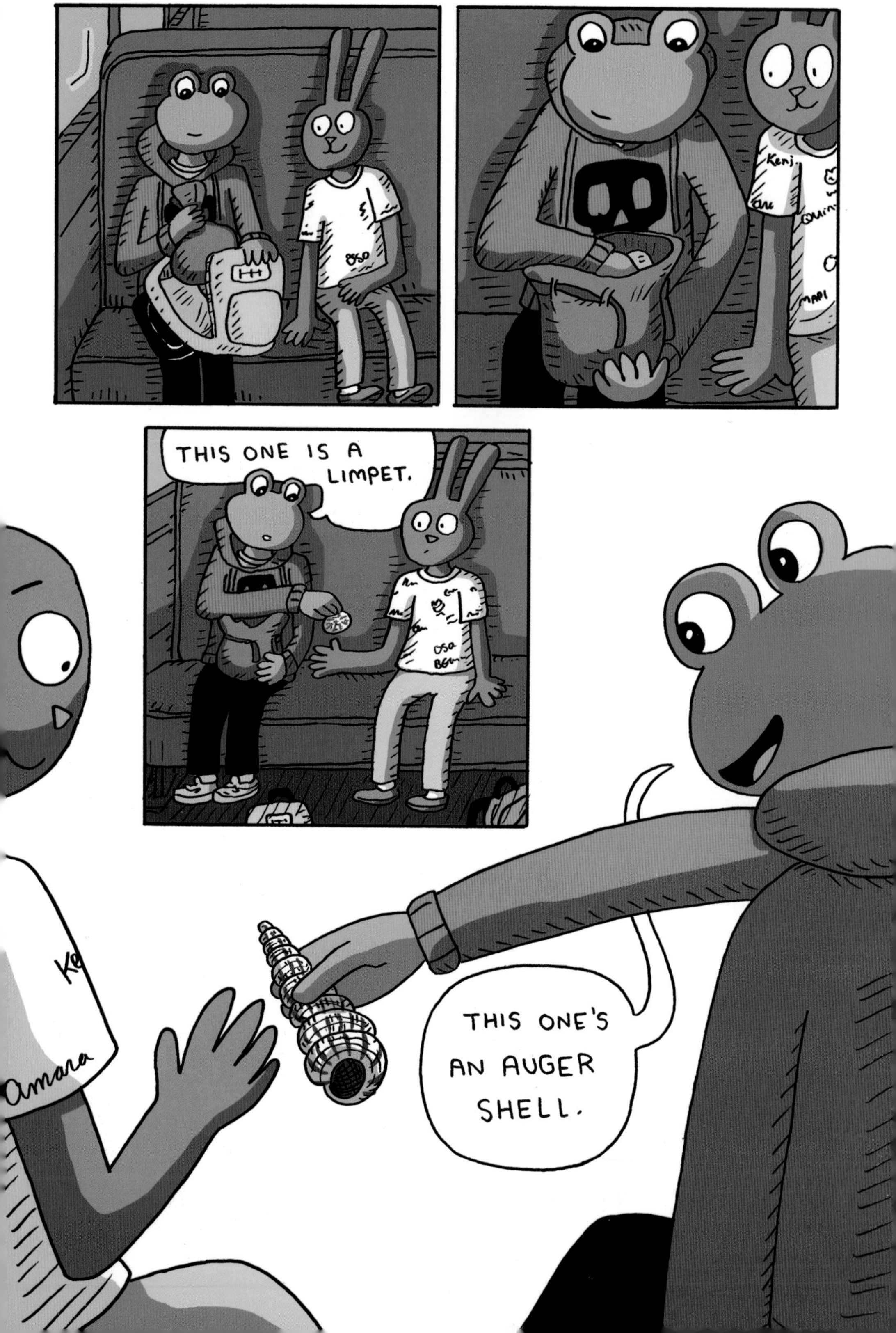
THIS ONE IS A LIMPET.
THIS ONE'S AN AUGER SHELL.

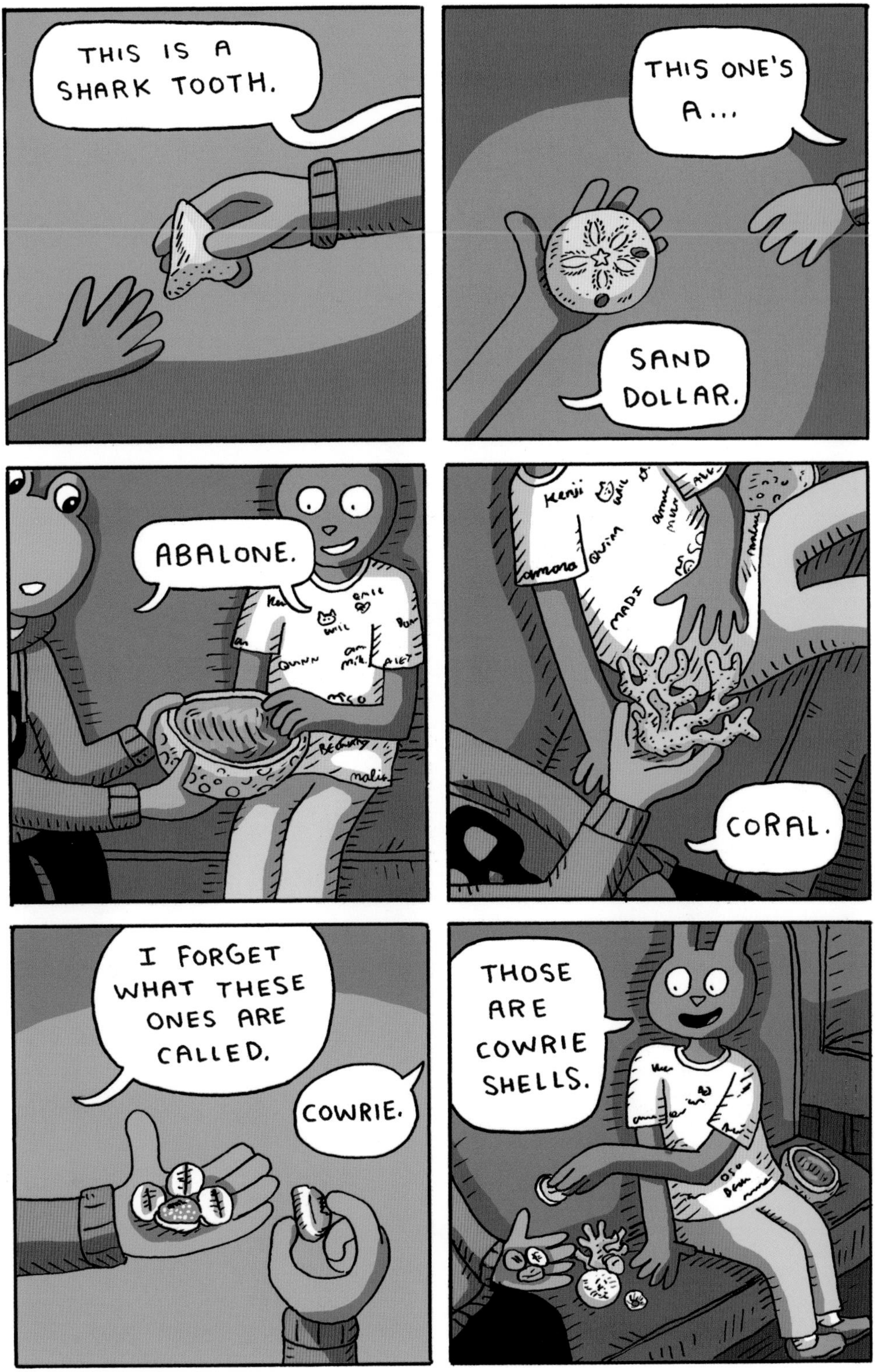
THIS IS A SHARK TOOTH.
THIS ONE'S A...
SAND DOLLAR.
ABALONE.
CORAL.
I FORGET WHAT THESE ONES ARE CALLED.
COWRIE.
THOSE ARE COWRIE SHELLS.

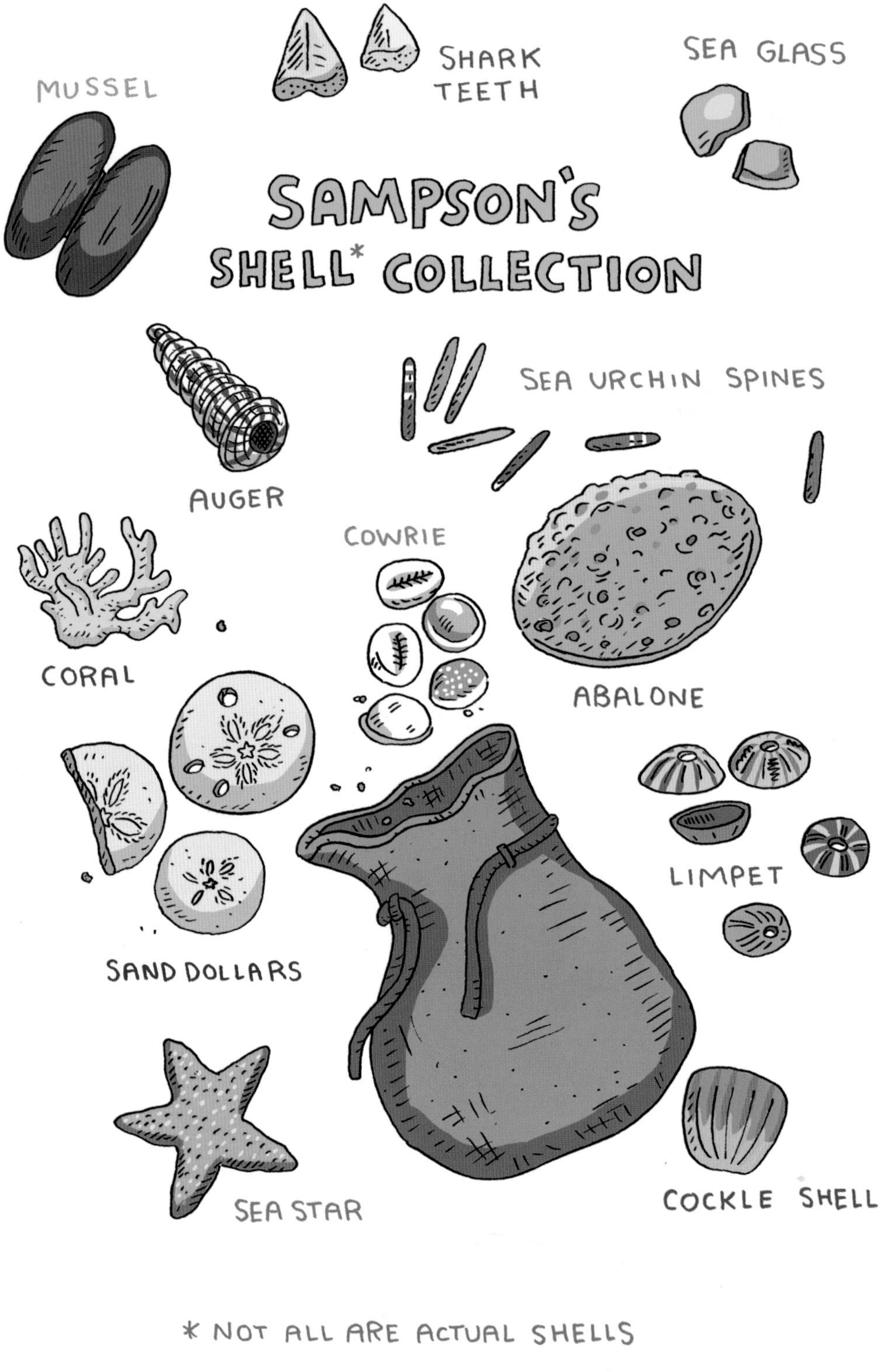
SAMPSON'S
SHELL* COLLECTION
MUSSEL
SHARK TEETH
SEA GLASS
AUGER
SEA URCHIN SPINES
CORAL
COWRIE
ABALONE
SAND DOLLARS
LIMPET
SEA STAR
COCKLE SHELL
* NOT ALL ARE ACTUAL SHELLS

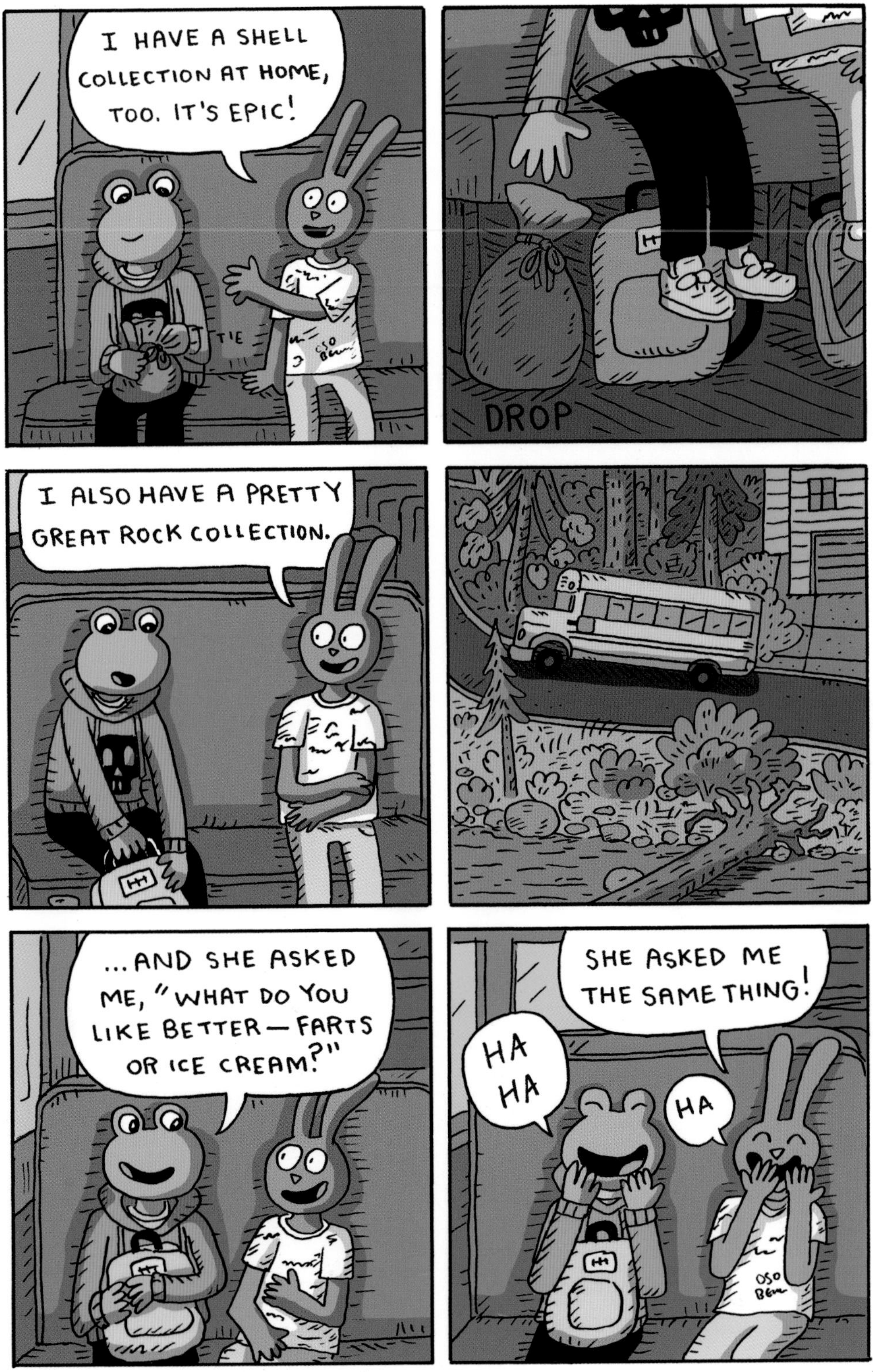
I HAVE A SHELL COLLECTION AT HOME, TOO. IT'S EPIC!
TIE
OSO BEAR
DROP
I ALSO HAVE A PRETTY GREAT ROCK COLLECTION.
...AND SHE ASKED ME, "WHAT DO YOU LIKE BETTER — FARTS OR ICE CREAM?"
SHE ASKED ME THE SAME THING!
HA HA
HA
OSO BEAR

THIS IS MY STOP.

ELWOOD SCHOOL

BYE, SAMPSON.

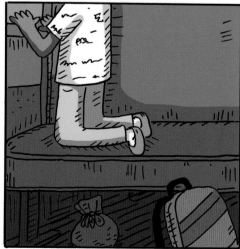

BYE, MARGOT.

CHAPTER ELEVEN

Knock! Knock!

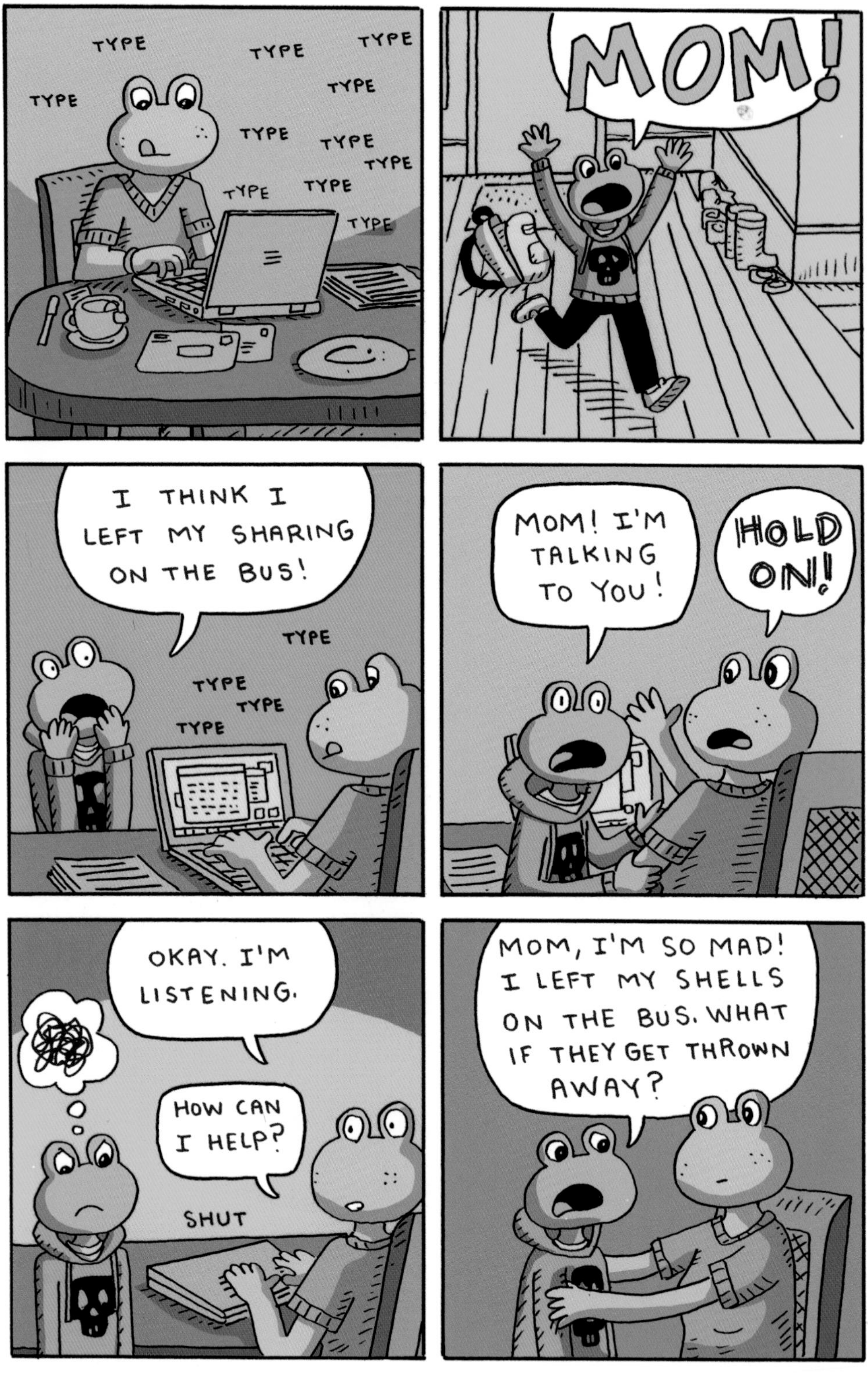
TYPE
TYPE
TYPE
TYPE
TYPE
TYPE
TYPE
TYPE
TYPE
TYPE
TYPE
MOM!
I THINK I LEFT MY SHARING ON THE BUS!
TYPE
TYPE
TYPE
TYPE
MOM! I'M TALKING TO YOU!
HOLD ON!
OKAY. I'M LISTENING.
HOW CAN I HELP?
SHUT
MOM, I'M SO MAD! I LEFT MY SHELLS ON THE BUS. WHAT IF THEY GET THROWN AWAY?

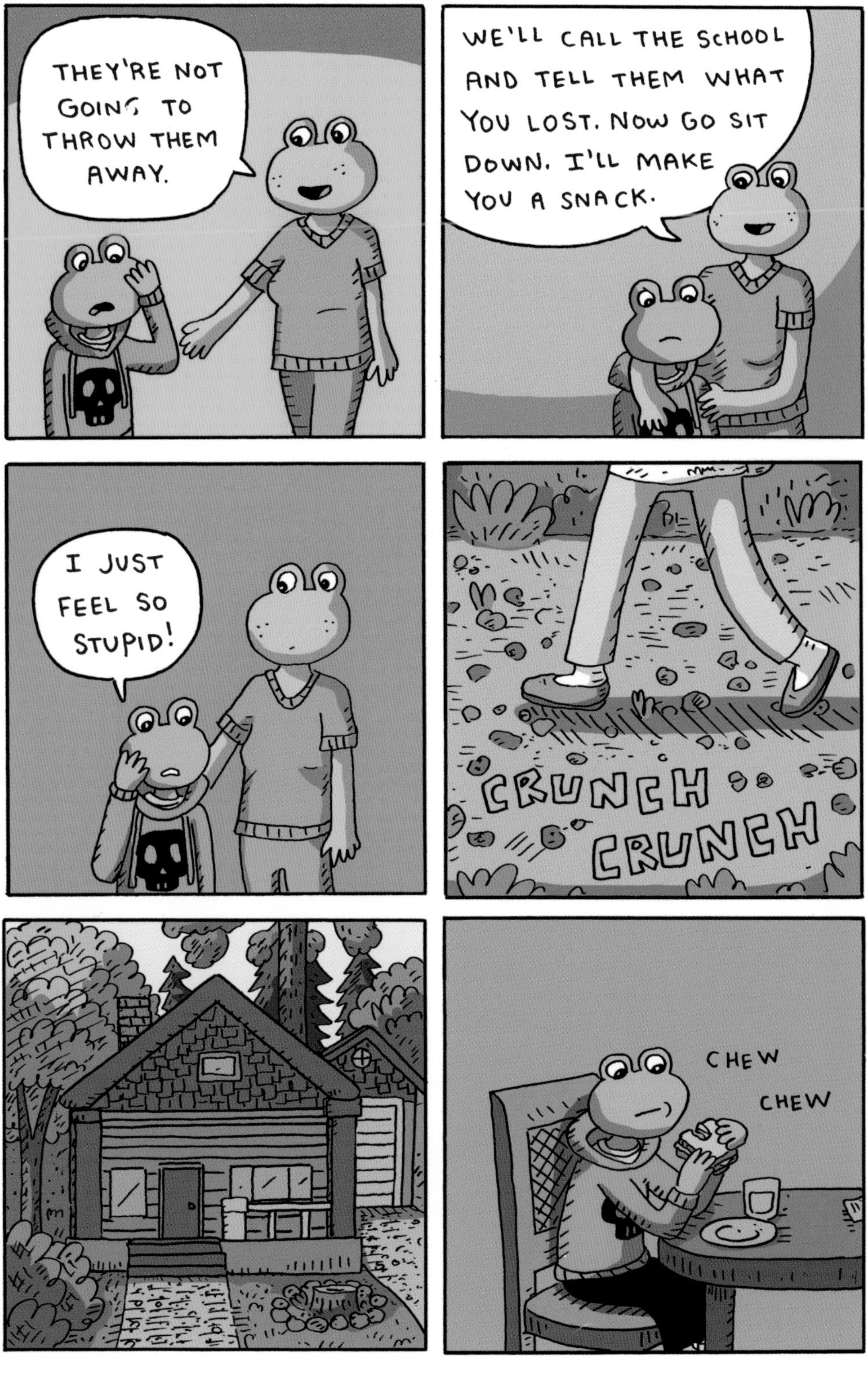
THEY'RE NOT GOING TO THROW THEM AWAY.
WE'LL CALL THE SCHOOL AND TELL THEM WHAT YOU LOST. NOW GO SIT DOWN. I'LL MAKE YOU A SNACK.
I JUST FEEL SO STUPID!
CRUNCH
CRUNCH
CHEW
CHEW

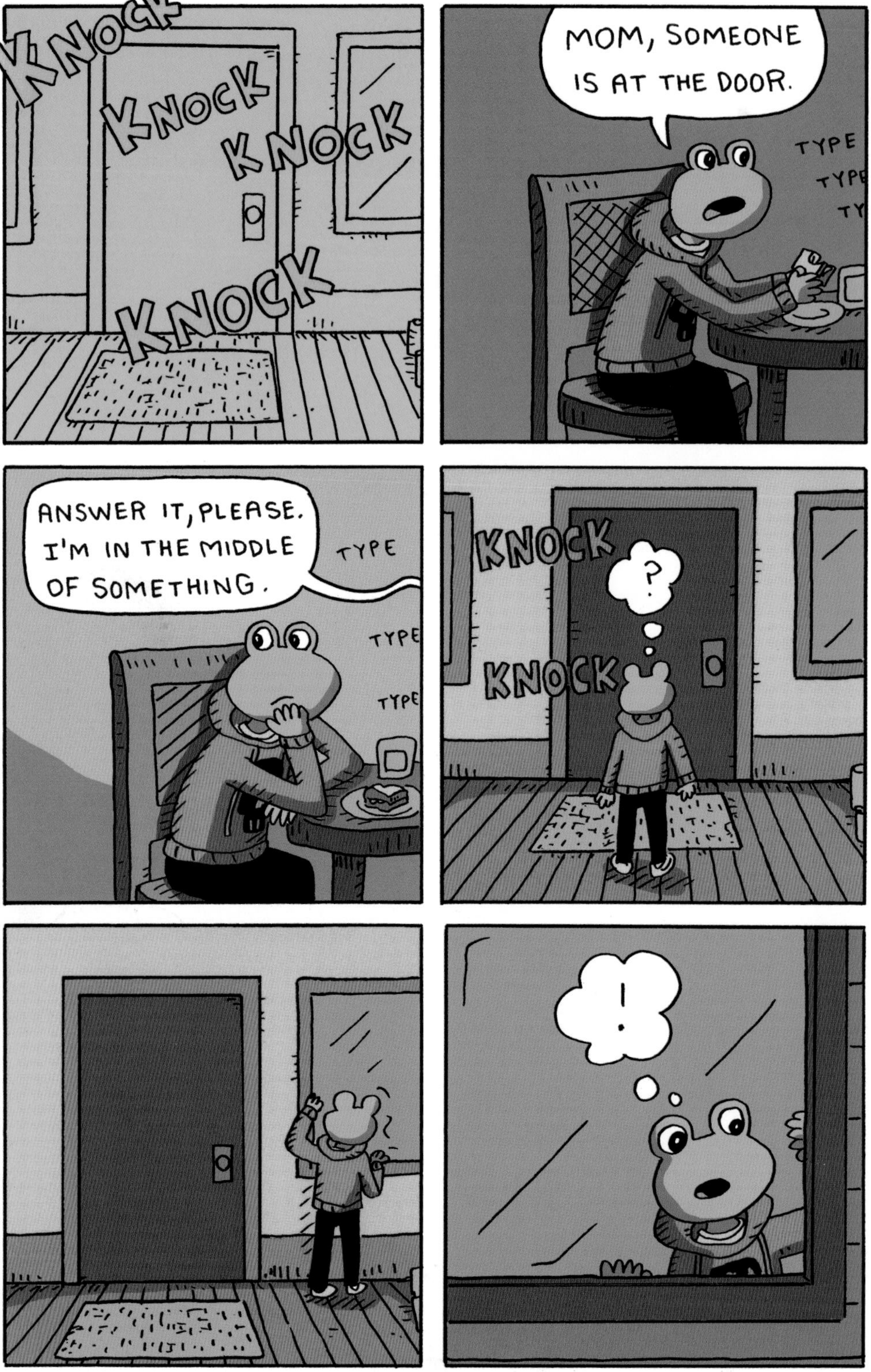
KNOCK
KNOCK
KNOCK
KNOCK
MOM, SOMEONE IS AT THE DOOR.
TYPE
TYPE
ANSWER IT, PLEASE. I'M IN THE MIDDLE OF SOMETHING.
TYPE
TYPE
TYPE
KNOCK
?
KNOCK
!

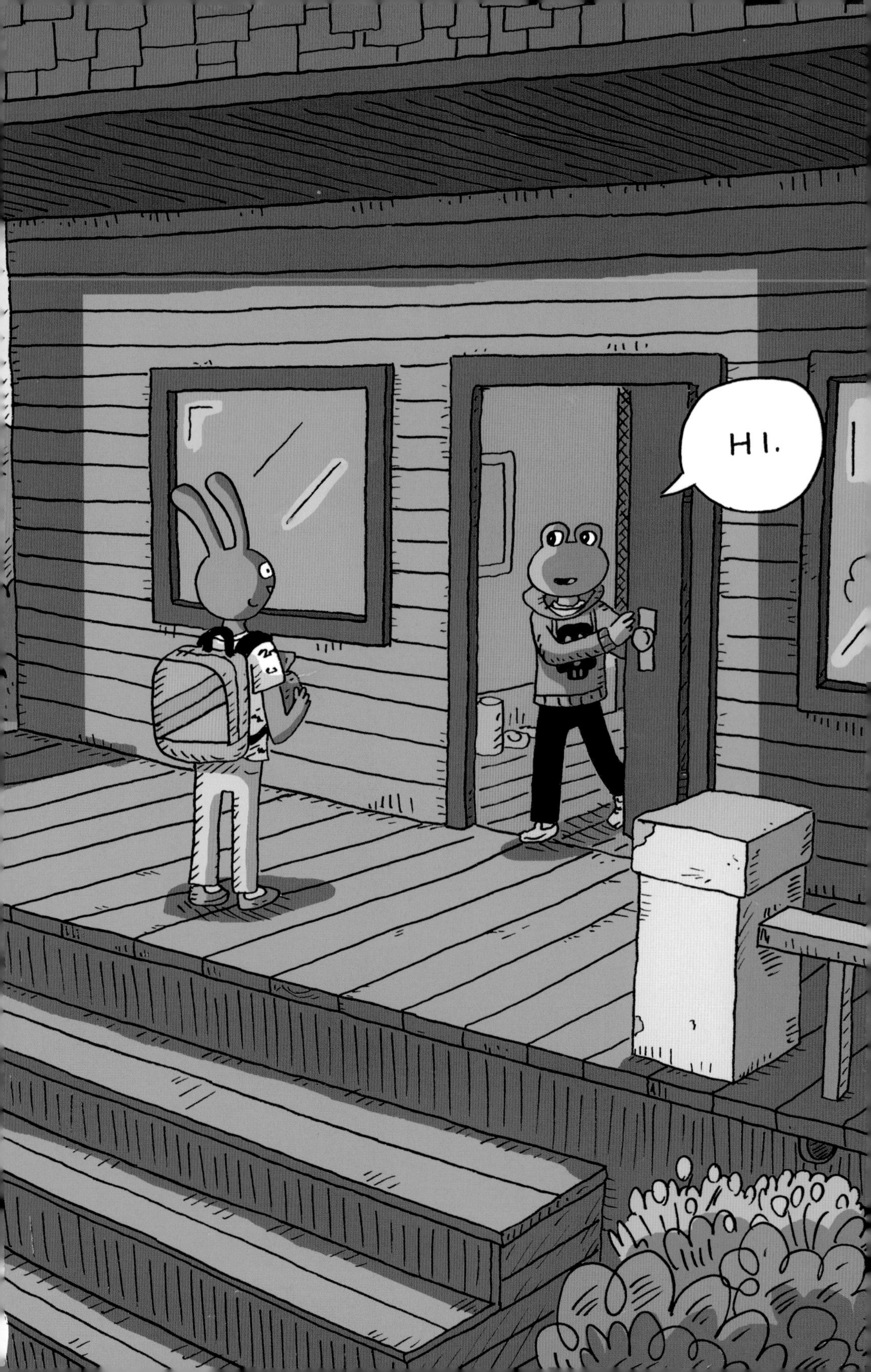
HI.

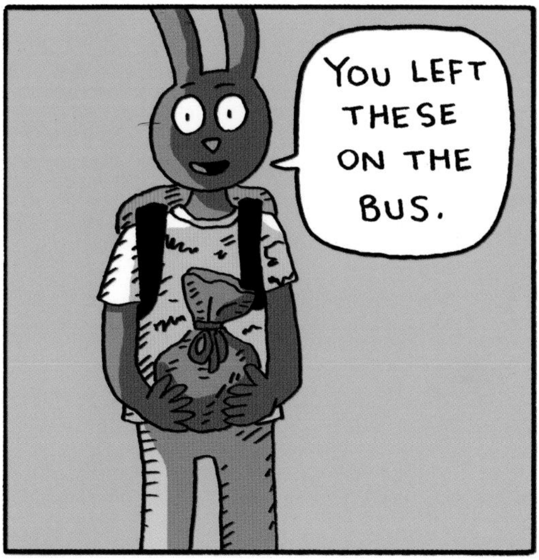
YOU LEFT THESE ON THE BUS.

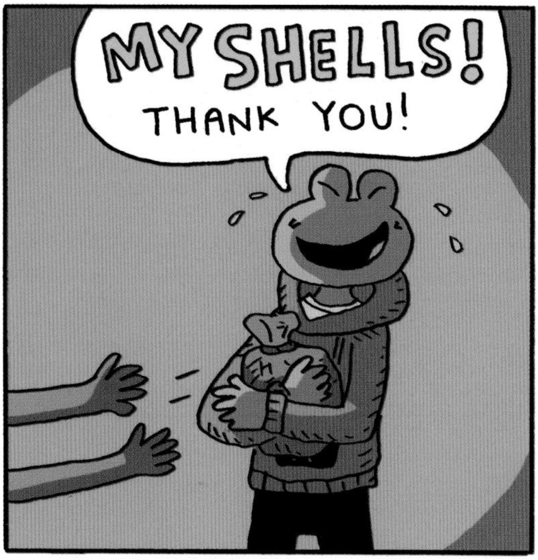
MY SHELLS!
THANK YOU!

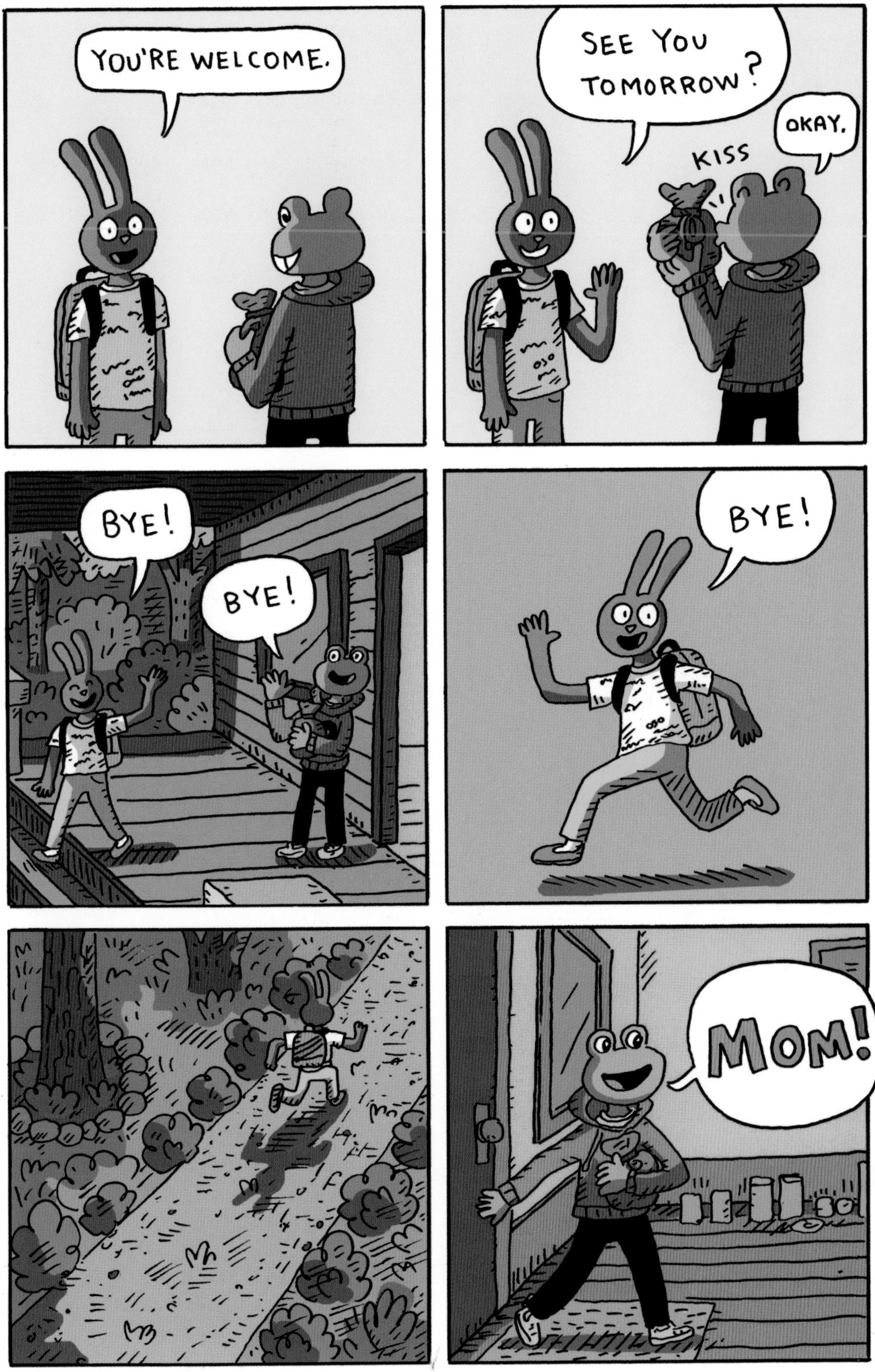
YOU'RE WELCOME.
SEE YOU TOMORROW?
KISS
OKAY.
BYE!
BYE!
BYE!
MOM!

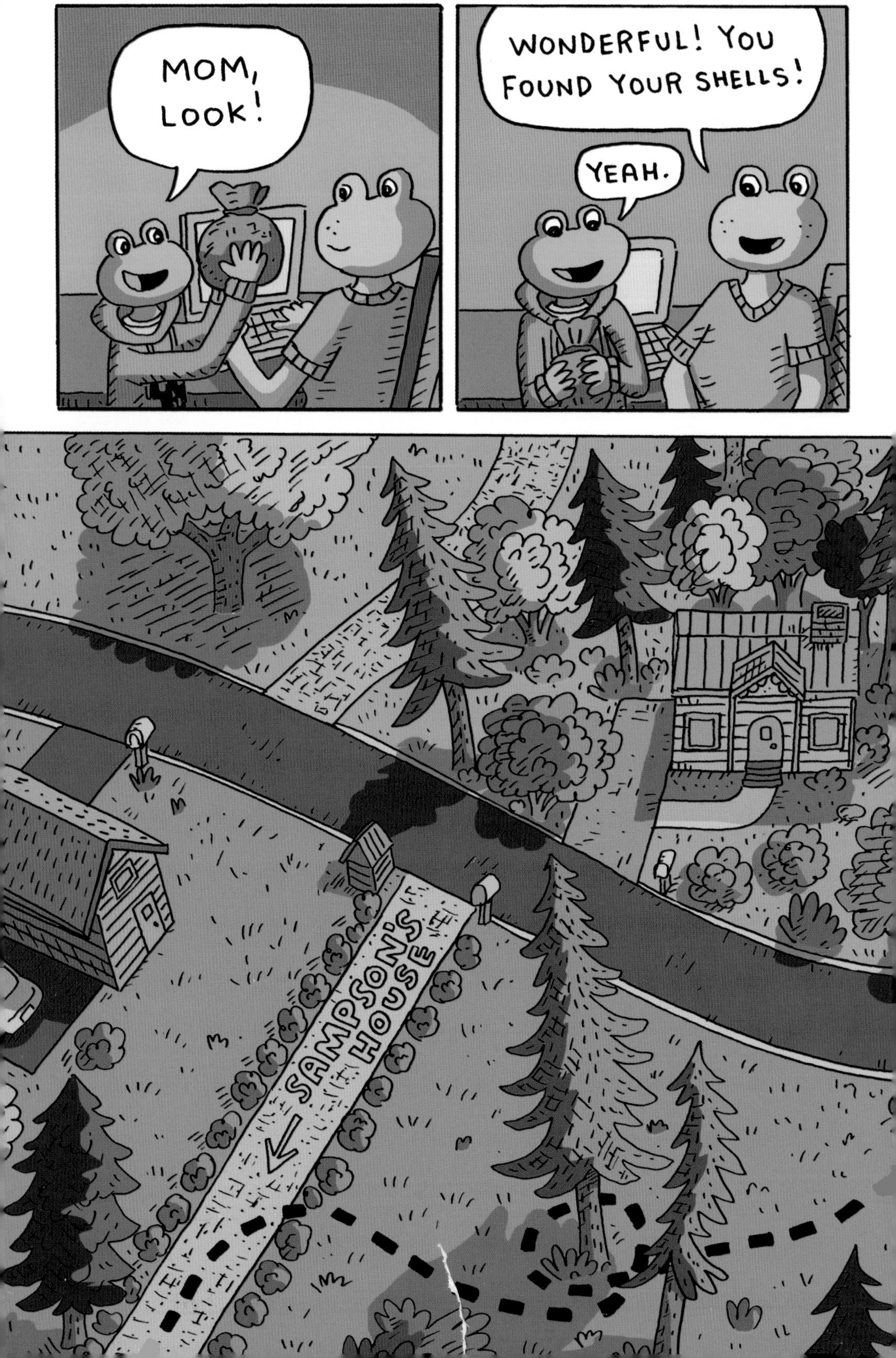
MOM, LOOK!
WONDERFUL! YOU FOUND YOUR SHELLS!
YEAH.
SAMPSON'S HOUSE

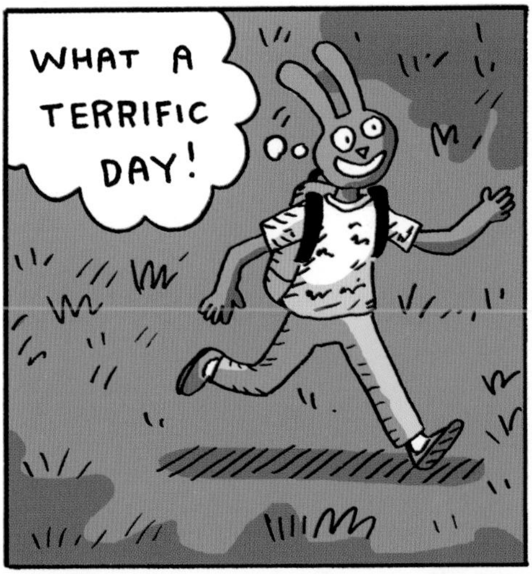
WHAT A TERRIFIC DAY!

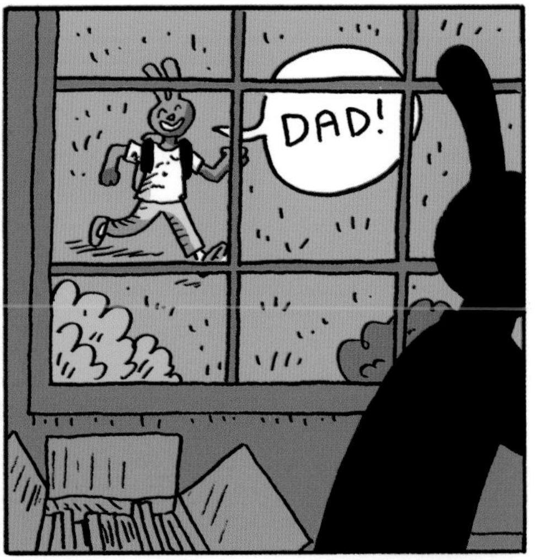
DAD!

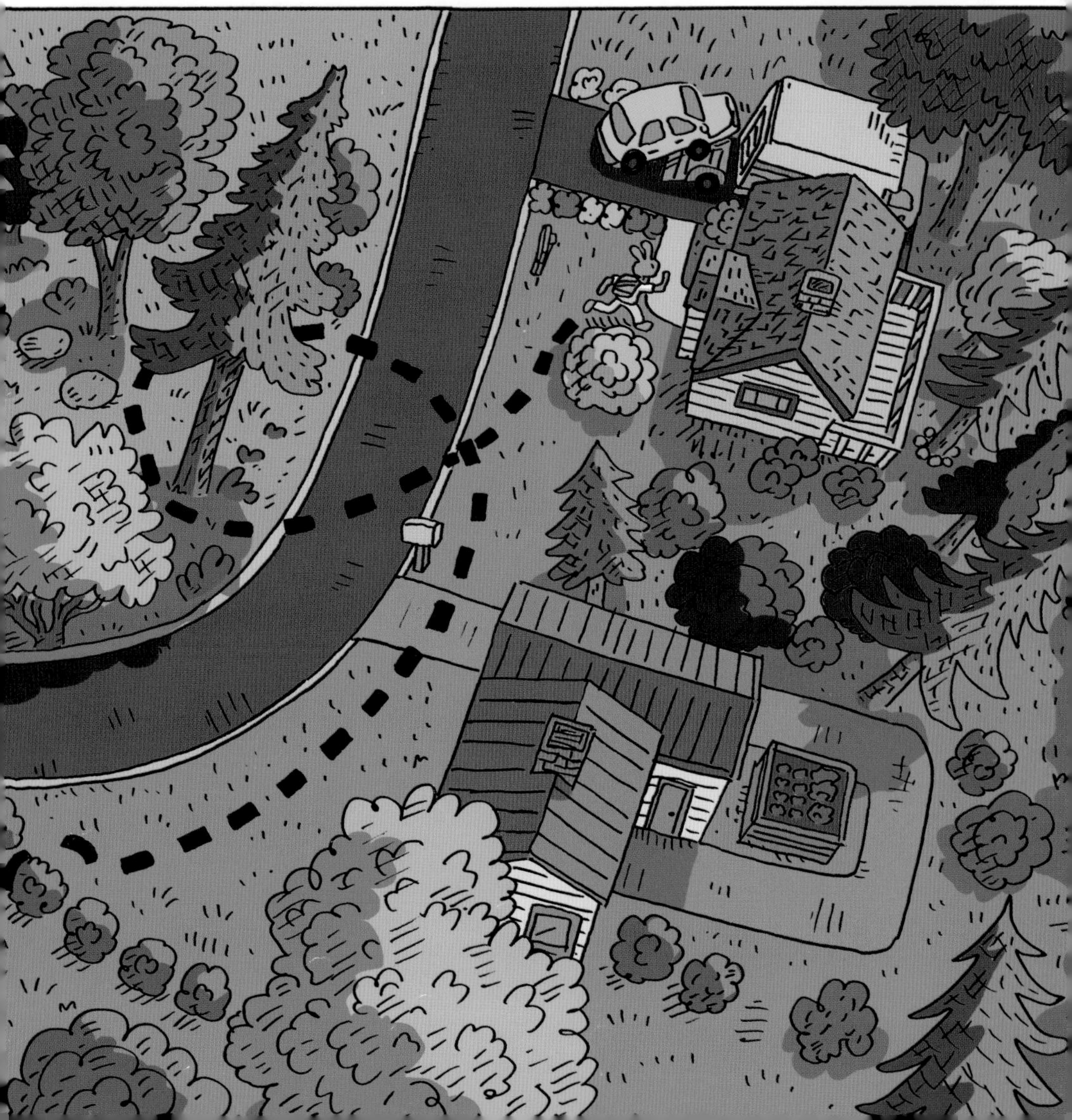

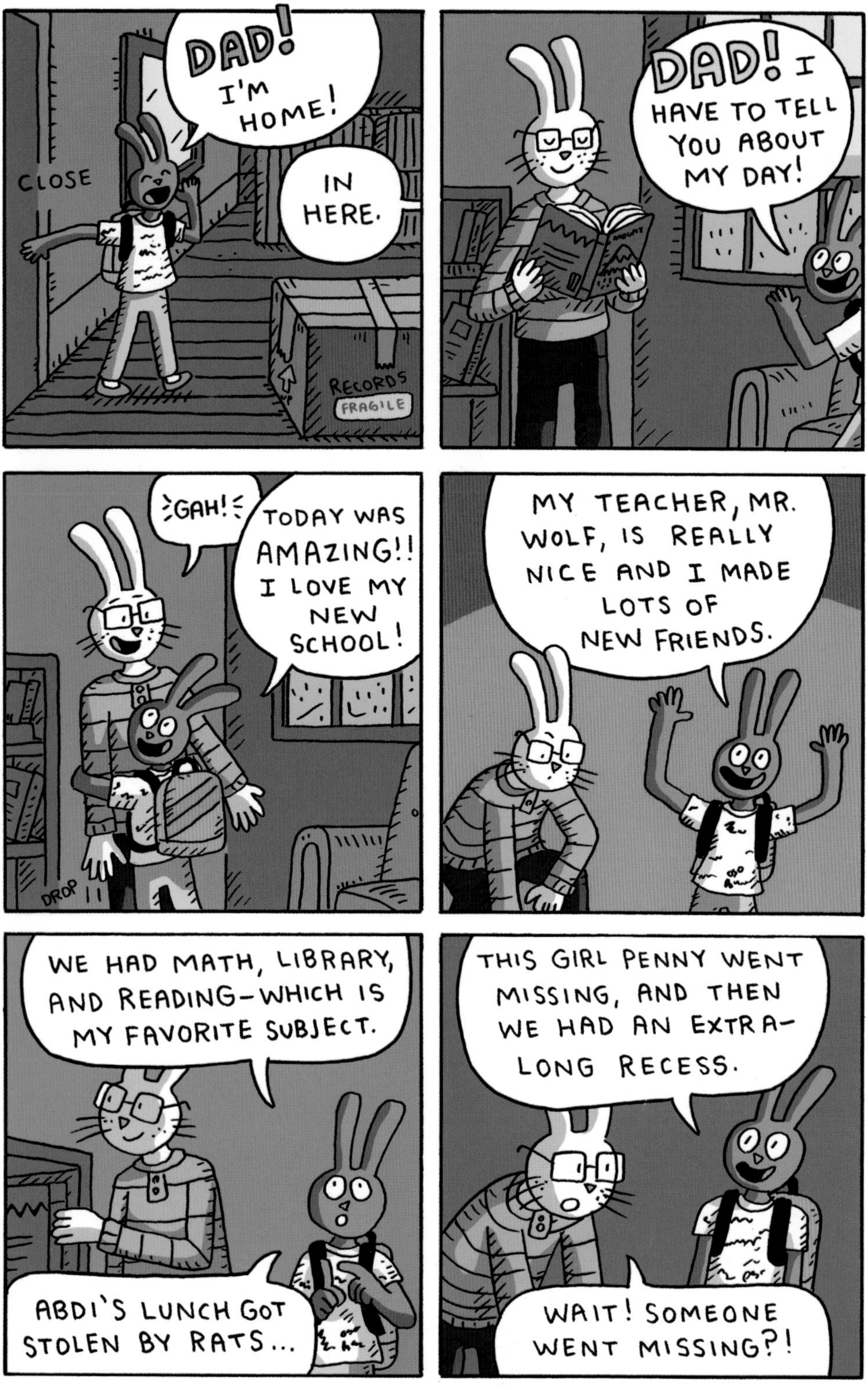
DAD! I'M HOME!
CLOSE
IN HERE.
RECORDS
FRAGILE
DAD! I HAVE TO TELL YOU ABOUT MY DAY!
GAH!
TODAY WAS AMAZING!! I LOVE MY NEW SCHOOL!
DROP
MY TEACHER, MR. WOLF, IS REALLY NICE AND I MADE LOTS OF NEW FRIENDS.
WE HAD MATH, LIBRARY, AND READING—WHICH IS MY FAVORITE SUBJECT.
ABDI'S LUNCH GOT STOLEN BY RATS...
THIS GIRL PENNY WENT MISSING, AND THEN WE HAD AN EXTRA-LONG RECESS.
WAIT! SOMEONE WENT MISSING?!

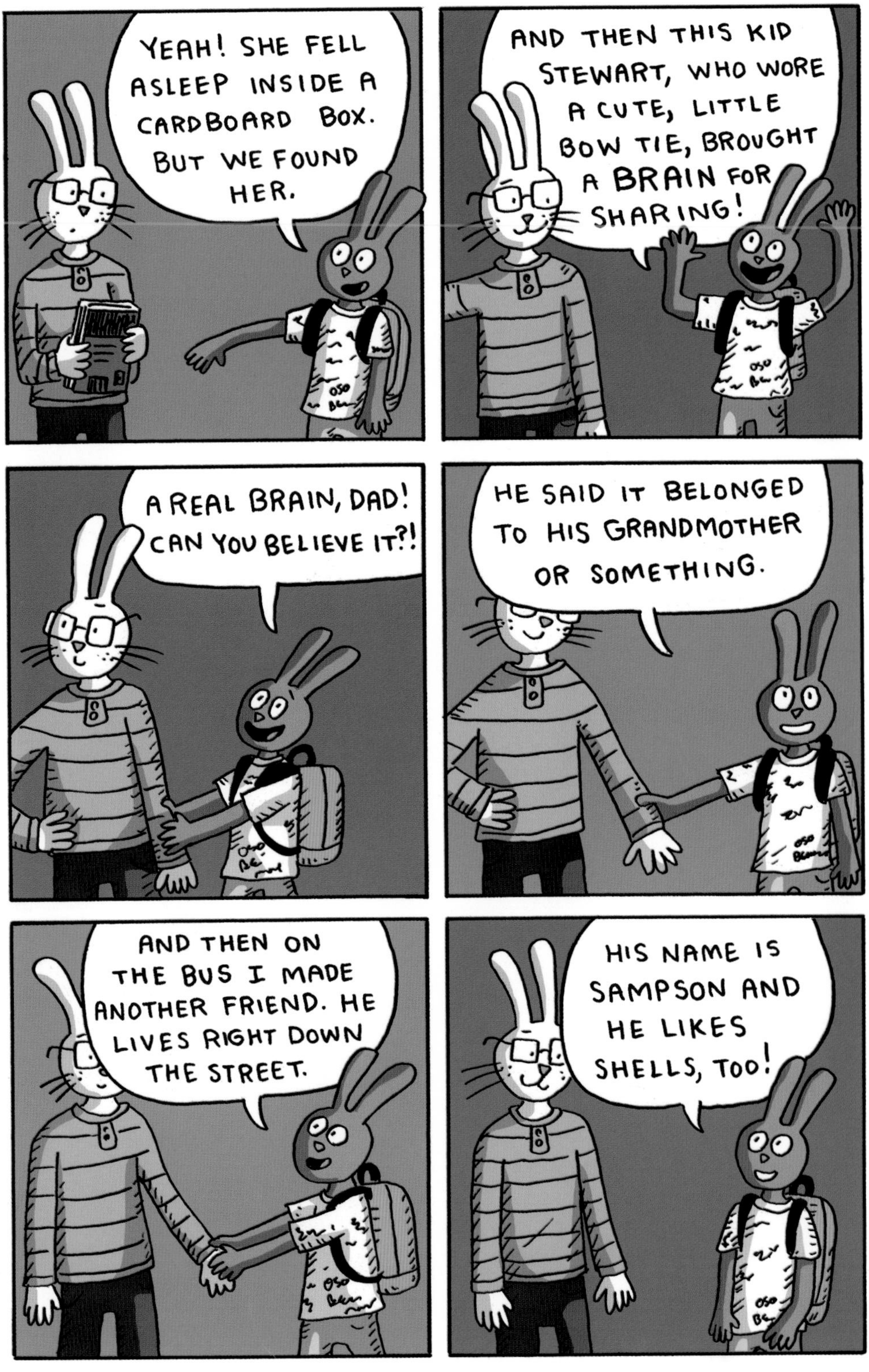
YEAH! SHE FELL ASLEEP INSIDE A CARDBOARD BOX. BUT WE FOUND HER.
AND THEN THIS KID STEWART, WHO WORE A CUTE, LITTLE BOW TIE, BROUGHT A BRAIN FOR SHARING!
A REAL BRAIN, DAD! CAN YOU BELIEVE IT?!
HE SAID IT BELONGED TO HIS GRANDMOTHER OR SOMETHING.
AND THEN ON THE BUS I MADE ANOTHER FRIEND. HE LIVES RIGHT DOWN THE STREET.
HIS NAME IS SAMPSON AND HE LIKES SHELLS, TOO!

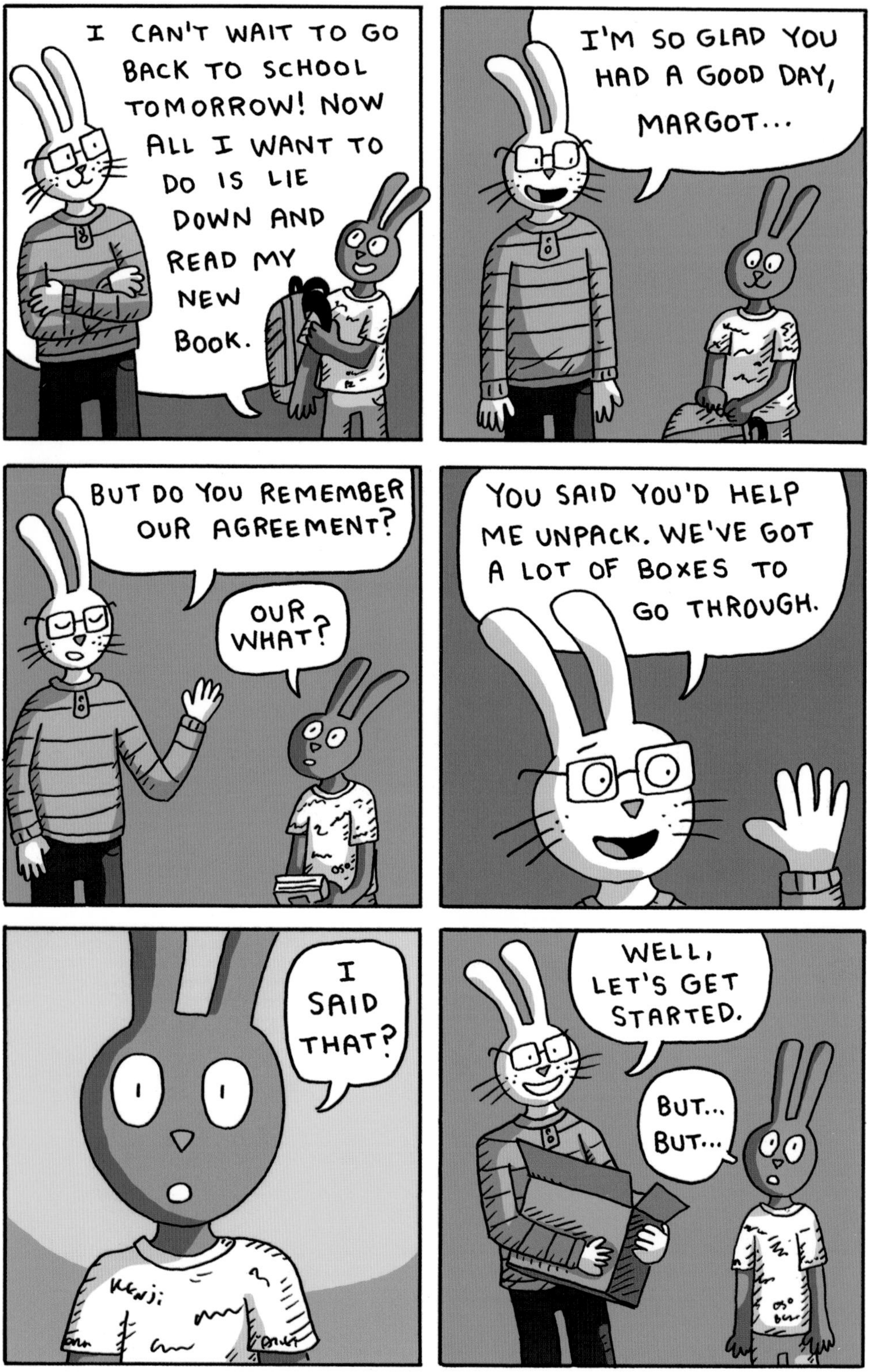
I CAN'T WAIT TO GO BACK TO SCHOOL TOMORROW! NOW ALL I WANT TO DO IS LIE DOWN AND READ MY NEW BOOK.
I'M SO GLAD YOU HAD A GOOD DAY, MARGOT...
BUT DO YOU REMEMBER OUR AGREEMENT?
OUR WHAT?
YOU SAID YOU'D HELP ME UNPACK. WE'VE GOT A LOT OF BOXES TO GO THROUGH.
I SAID THAT?
WELL, LET'S GET STARTED.
BUT... BUT...

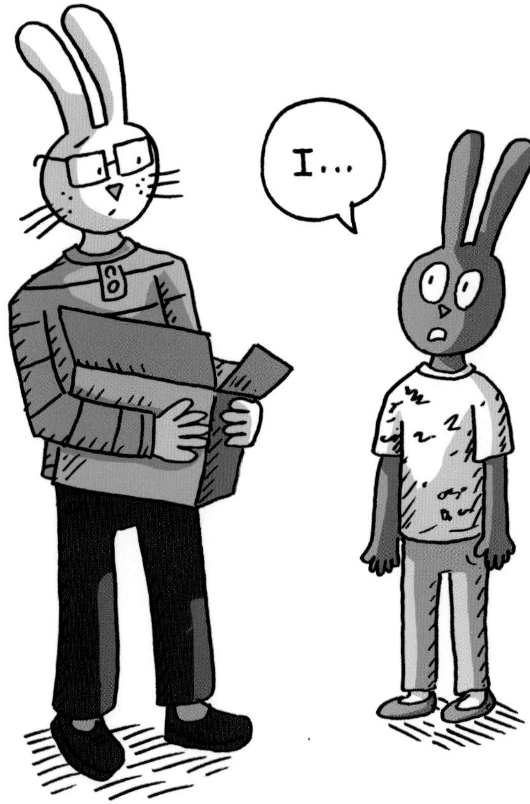
I...

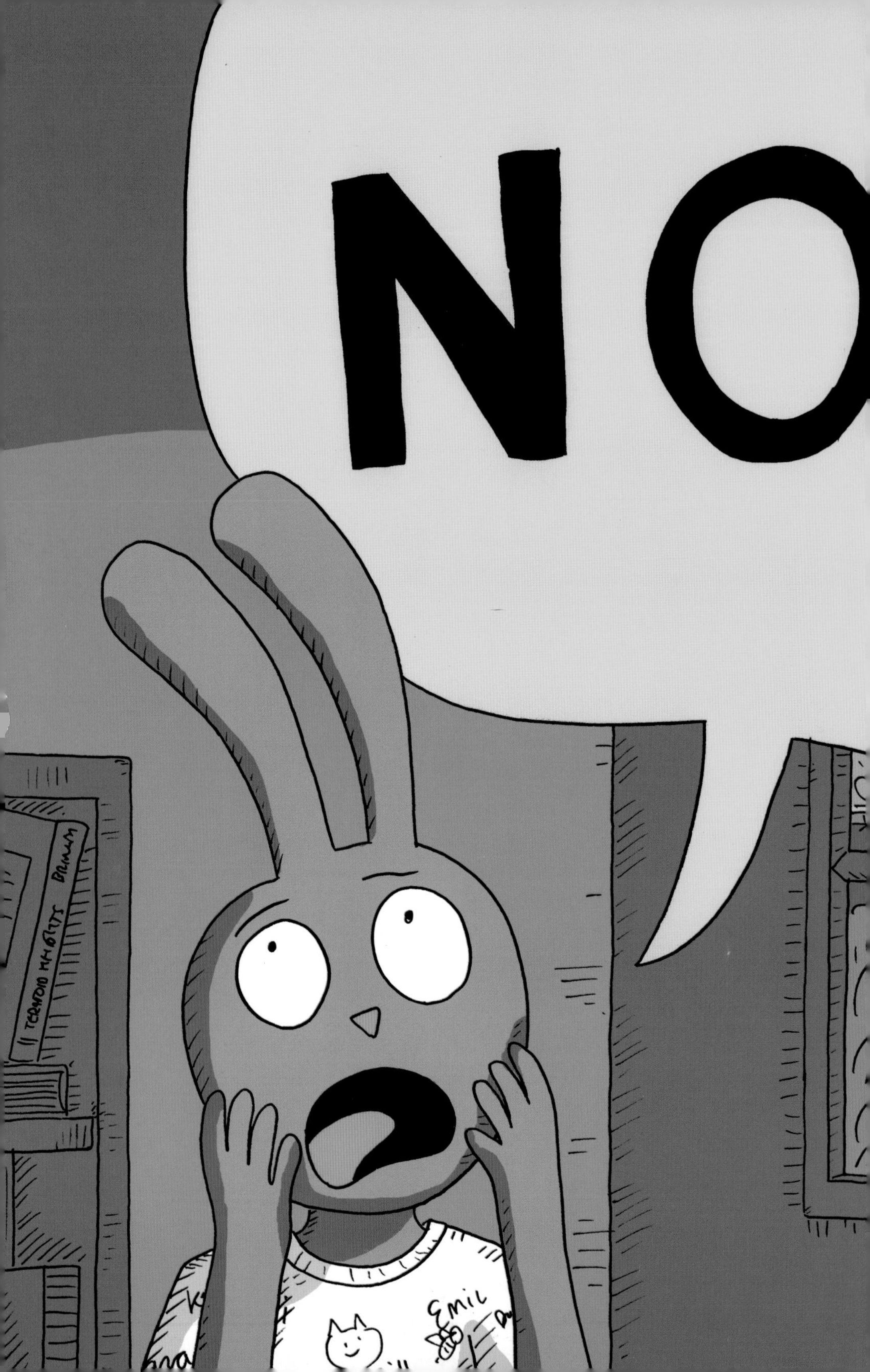
NO

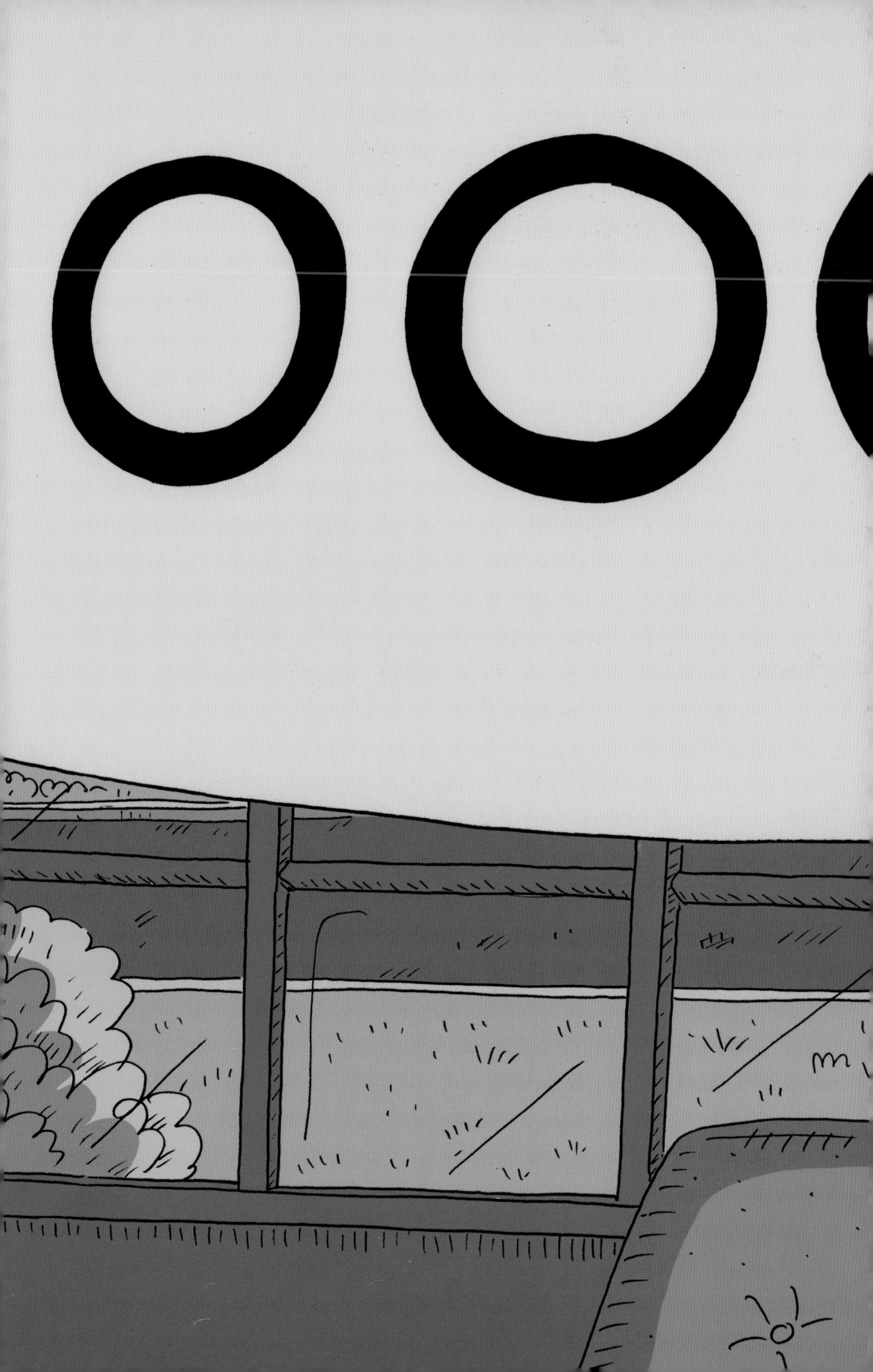
OOO

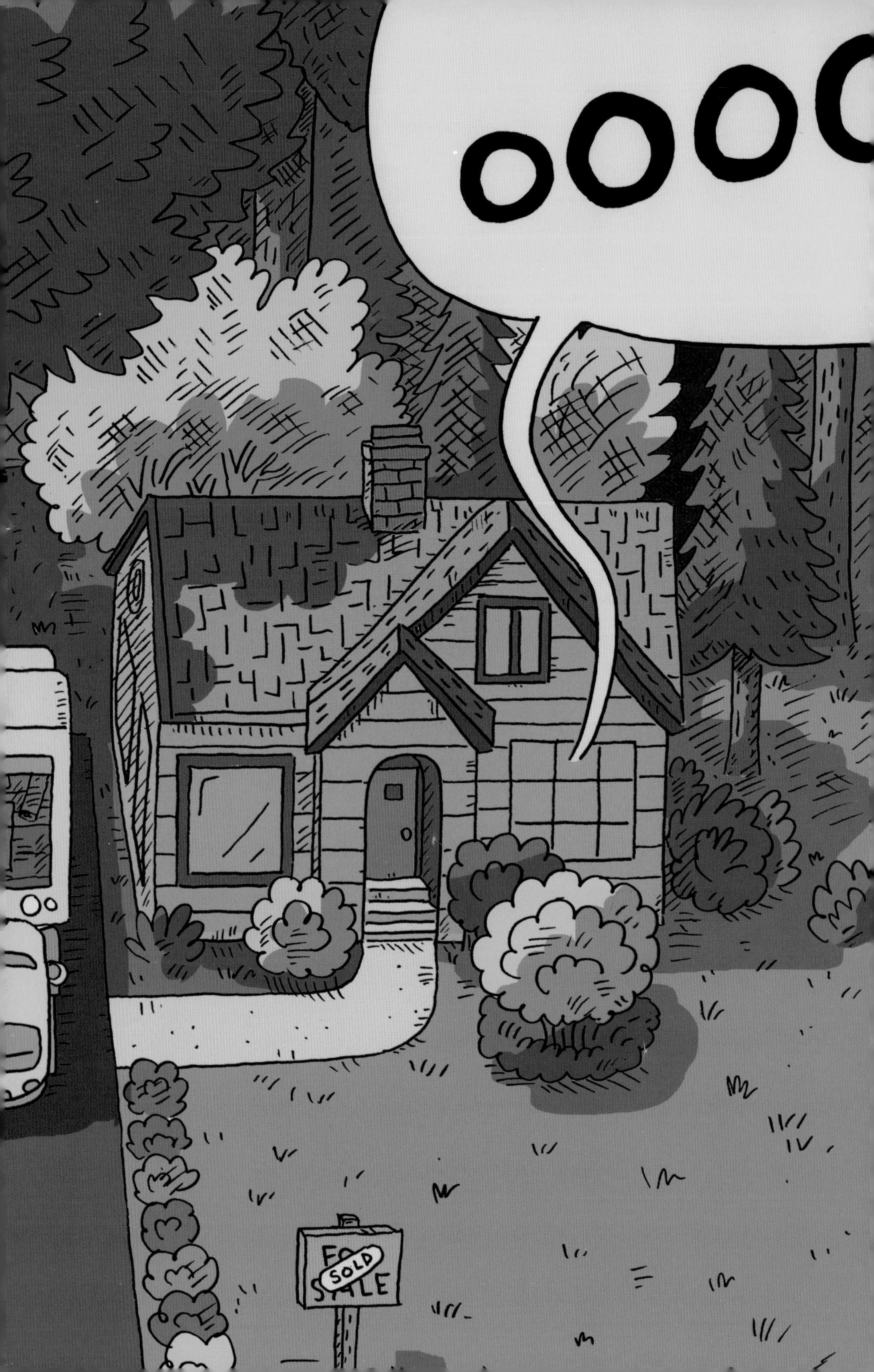
OOOO
FOR SALE
SOLD

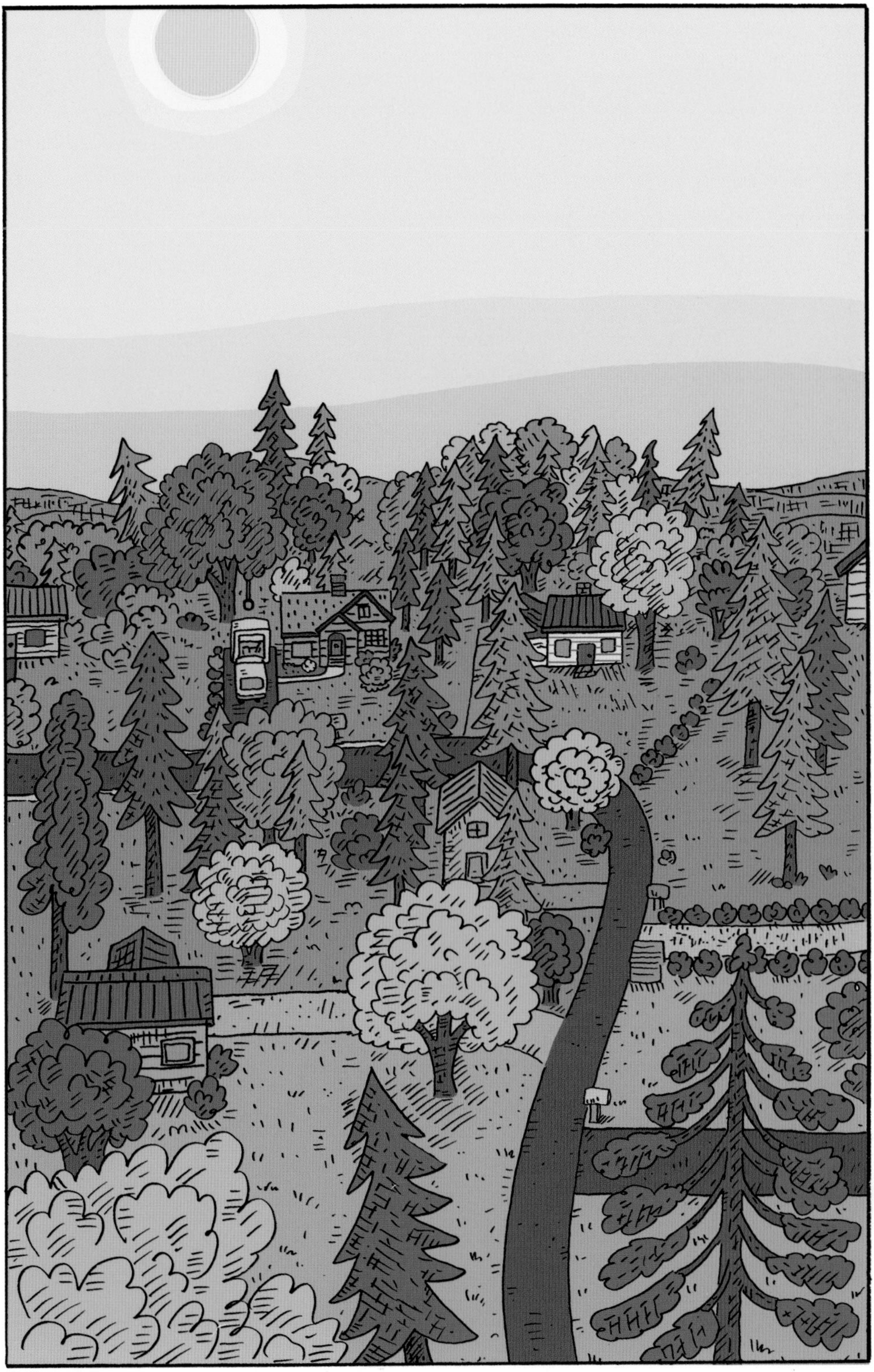

Thank you to . . .

My supportive family: My wife and son, Ariel and Marlen, for putting up with my long hours drawing comics and being the best people I could possibly spend my life with. Mom and Dad, for always encouraging me, sending me to animation school, and spending your golden years fighting climate change. My brother, Jeremy, for being my main artistic influence growing up. My in-laws Lisa and David for all that you do, which is a lot. All my other in-laws, cousins, aunts, and uncles.

My fabulous editor, Cassandra Pelham Fulton, Phil Falco, David Saylor, and everyone at Graphix. Thank you!!!

My agent, Judy Hansen, for looking out and being a boss.

Dylan Williams, Emily Nilsson, and Greg Means, for taking the risk to publish my first book. I love you all. Rest in peace, Dylan. You were a bright light for many.

All of my wonderful students that I've had over the years. I believe the key to a brighter and more peaceful future rests within the hearts, minds, and future actions of our children. I can't wait to see what you all grow up to become. I hope you are happy, healthy, and standing up for justice.

Author photo by Renée Lopez

Aron Nels Steinke is the Eisner Award–winning illustrator and coauthor, with Ariel Cohn, of *The Zoo Box*. After graduating from Vancouver Film School with a specialization in hand-drawn animation, he discovered the magic of making comics and hasn't looked back since. He teaches fifth graders by day and draws comics by night in Portland, Oregon, where he lives with his wife, Ariel, and their Robin Hood–obsessed son, Marlen. In the summer, when he's not hunched over a drawing board, you might find him swimming the frigid rivers of the Cascade Mountains or possibly hugging a tree.

Don't miss the next adventure in Mr. Wolf's class!

MYSTERY CLUB

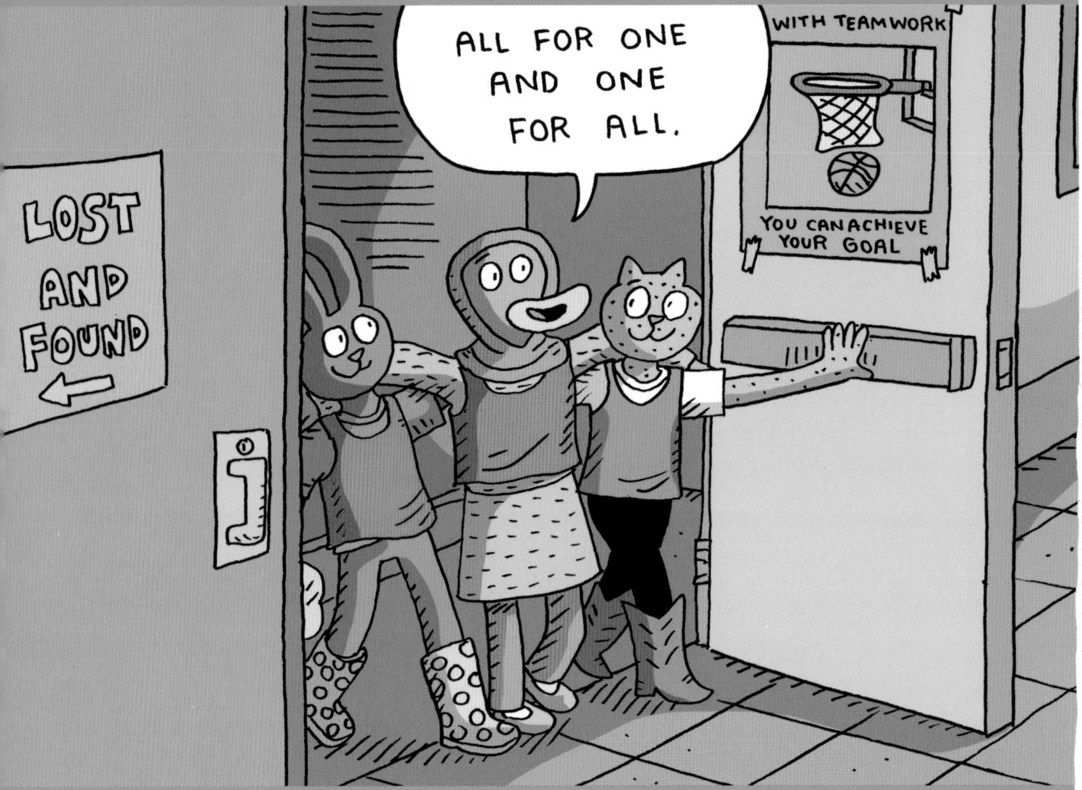

ALL FOR ONE AND ONE FOR ALL.
WITH TEAMWORK
YOU CAN ACHIEVE YOUR GOAL
LOST AND FOUND